The Kings
of
Beacon

To the reader of this book –
This book is my debut novel that
I brought with me on holiday from the
US. I hope you enjoy the read, and
please share with others 😊

The Kings

of

Beacon

Mike Jakubowski

To Rocco, one of the best cats who ever walked this planet.
Rest in peace buddy.

Prologue
15 YEARS AGO

"Cindy, thank you again so much for watching him! We were able to take the carpet out and it's being hauled away tomorrow! I hope he wasn't too much trouble."

"Not at all, he was an angel," Cindy says, letting go of James's hand as Penny picks him up. "I'd love to do it again some time!"

"You'll be the first person I call. Talk soon." Penny opens the car door and buckles James into the car seat as Cindy closes the front door.

"Mommy, why so much stuff in car?"

"Well little man," Penny says, "you and I are going on a little adventure. How does that sound?"

One

The street lights are coming alive as we pass the welcome sign for the town of Beacon, Rhode Island. We had left Vermont late due to Penny needing to thank all of our neighbors for their help over the past year that we lived in our small community. When she asked me if I wanted to join her, I walked away, not before telling her to text me when she was ready to go. I wanted to try and find Andy one more time before leaving, but was unsuccessful. We ended up getting in the car around one in the afternoon, leaving no time to explore our new home upon arrival.

We turn off the main road onto a street with a couple of rundown homes, and ultimately into a gravel parking lot at the end of the street. Penny throws the car in park, sitting in front of what looks like an old motel. Our new apartment building is two floors with open hallways, and set back from the road surrounded by tall trees. The sun is just starting to set, which casts eerie shadows across the front of the building. It's giving off a sorta Bates Motel vibe, but seems to be an upgrade from the cabins Penny tried to sell me on as the 'tiny home experience' we left behind in Vermont.

The Vermont cabin community had been full of a bunch of weird doomsdayers, people Ralph had connections to. But, with Ralph's wife finally leaving him, he could now finally have Penny fully in his life. So that brought us from a tiny remote cabin to what looks like a tinier motel room turned apartment in Rhode Island.

"James, I know it's hard bouncing around all the time," I jump, startled as they are the first words either of us have uttered in the past few hours, "but things are getting good with Ralph now and Beacon is our new home. You'll make new friends, maybe even a nice girlfriend." I've actively tried to avoid meaningful friendships for the past few years. We've lived somewhere new every year since I was in the third grade. After middle school I just stopped putting myself out there. Well, except for earlier this summer with Andy.

I open the car door and stand to stretch, taking in the immediate area. There isn't really much right around the apartment, but the main road we turned off of looked more promising. Penny heads into the leasing office, so I decide to walk around the back of the building. The majority of the yard behind the building is taken up by a swimming pool, which looks like it hasn't been cleaned in a few weeks. I drop into a lounger and pull out my phone, opening Instagram. I open my messages with Andy, reading over the last three weeks of unreturned conversation. The last one, *I'm sorry*, was sent this morning when I couldn't find him in town. I think of sending something to let him know where we ended up, but decide against it.

"There you are." Penny is standing at the edge of the pool fence. "The apartment's ready. We should unpack a bit before it gets too late."

We didn't travel with much, as we typically end up in furnished apartments. It takes only twenty minutes to unload the car and the small trailer we pulled here. Once everything is inside, I bring my bags and boxes into my bedroom. The room has a twin bed, a dresser, and a desk. I start by unpacking my clothes, which fill up two of the four drawers. I stack my books on my desk, along with my laptop, and make the bed.

There's a knock at the front door. I hear Penny open it and some muffled conversation. "James, come out here and meet one of our new neighbors." I pop out of my room and walk over to the kitchen. "James, this is Mrs. Weddle. She lives a few doors down and brought us some homemade cookies. What flavor did you say they were?"

"Coconut chocolate chip! I always keep some cookies in the freezer in case an occasion's sprung on me! I hope you enjoy them. I don't think any of the Beacon High kids live in the building. A few in middle school and some a bit younger than that. There used to be a couple of older kids who lived on the first floor but they moved out when the mother got remarried. Oh, here I am boring you when you are trying to unpack. I'll leave you to it. Please come down and knock if you need anything!"

Once the neighbor is gone, I turn to head back to my bedroom. "James, can you help me unpack the rest of the kitchen?"

"Actually Penny, I'm pretty beat. Want to get some good sleep before school tomorrow. I'll finish whatever's left in the morning."

"For the last time stop calling me P–" I shut the bedroom door and let out a deep sigh, before flopping down on the bed.

I lay down in the dark, staring at the ceiling thinking about school in Vermont and school here. How they will likely be much different. The whole junior class in Vermont was only twenty-seven kids. I hadn't looked too much into Beacon High, but the town already appears much bigger so I assume the school will be as well.

Just one more year to go.

Two

Penny really wanted to drive me to school this morning, and I really did not want her to. It's hard enough being the new kid, but being dropped off by mommy in her beat-up car is not the attention I'm looking for on day one.

"I think it's a couple of miles to the school James. That's too much to walk before school."

"The walk will be good. Give me a chance to see the town a bit since we got in so late last night." She seems like she wants to fight me a bit more but realized she was already running late to her first day of work.

Plugging the school's address into Google Maps tells me it's about a twenty-minute walk door to door, so definitely not miles plural. I start the trek down our road, keeping to the sidewalk once I turn onto the main road. The apartment complex is tucked off what seems to be the main commercial area of Beacon. In a matter of minutes, I pass a McDonald's, a Starbucks, and a strip mall filled with shops and tiny

7

restaurants. There's a park about a half-mile down the road from the apartment, empty on a Monday morning, but looks to provide a good place to escape if needed close by.

I take a left onto the road the school is on. The sidewalks ahead are congested with groups of students walking to school, the road filled with cars with hazard lights flashing conducting drop offs. I pull my hoodie over my head and slide through the masses, trying to keep as inconspicuous as possible. Penny driving me here would have been a nightmare.

When the school comes into view it's massive, bigger than any other school I've ever attended. It stands three stories tall, and spans far both wide in front and back in depth. Ivy creeps up the exterior of the building, and maintenance crews are already at work trimming the shrubbery that lines just below the windows. There is something to be said about the appeal of a school that looks lived in, that hasn't fallen to pressures to be modernized with clean lines and no personality. It's more, for a lack of better word, inviting.

I climb the stairs to the front door, greeted by a row of metal detectors and security guards. I pull my headphones and laptop out of my bag and throw them in a bin, along with my phone, and walk through the detectors. "ID please."

"Excuse me?" I ask the security guard while gathering the items from the bin.

"Your student ID," a voice says behind me. I turn and instantly feel my cheeks flush. My eyes linger a bit too long on the very tall and very attractive guy in line behind me. His biceps barely fit in the sleeves of his polo, his green eyes popping with his dark complexion. He smiles at me, which is not helping the situation one bit.

"Oh...um...I...don't have one," I barely get out, fully aware of fumbling over my words. I turn to face the security guard in an attempt to compose myself. "I'm new to town. Just moved here last night. But my mother said she called ahead to make sure I was all set."

"Got it. You're gonna need to go visit the secretary in the office to get your ID and schedule. Grady, can you help this kid out? Or are you in a rush to go see Coach?"

The guy behind me, Grady, gathers his stuff from his bin on the table. "Not a problem Luis. I'm free first period this semester so I've got some time." He clasps his hand on my shoulder while picking up his bag. "Let's get your shit, new kid." We start walking down the hallway, and it's apparent Grady is popular. Very popular. Everyone either says something to him, or at least waves or smiles in his direction. "So, you've probably gathered my name is Grady. And you are..."

"James," I respond, now noticing eyes moving in the crowd to me. I'm already failing at trying to stay under the radar.

"Nice to meet you, James. Welcome to Beacon High." He shakes hands with a guy standing by a locker. "I'm guessing since you said you moved here last night you don't know much about the school or town." I nod in agreement, with Grady guiding me down a hallway and stopping in front of a door labeled OFFICE. "So, Beacon High is made up of kids from three towns - Beacon, West Beacon, and Beacon Point. This school is in Beacon, and Beacon is kinda where a lot of the businesses are. Normal shit like Chili's and McDonald's and a few too many chain coffee shops. Beacon Point is the beach town area, which is more like touristy but the most fun of the Beacons. West Beacon is where all the rich assholes live, most with egos to match."

"Which Beacon do you live in?" I ask.

Grady opens the office door and gestures to me to walk inside. "West Beacon, of course," he says, winking at me. I slip past him and enter the office. He walks with me up to the main desk and he smiles at the woman sitting behind it. "Good morning, Mary! I missed you over break. How were Theo and Leah this summer?" He reaches in his backpack and pulls out a bag labeled Beacon Donuts, and hands it to her.

Mary grins at Grady, leaning forward. "Grady, you can't play favorites," but she opens the bag and audibly moans. "I'm supposed to say I enjoyed all the day trips and episodes of Bluey and Paw Patrol I watched on repeat. There is nowhere I'd rather be today than in this damn chair." She rolls back and grabs her coffee mug. "So, what is it I can do for you Grady since you are already bribing me?"

"Ahh it's not for me Mary, but for my new friend James here. It's his first day in Beacon and he needs his ID and class schedule."

"Let's see what we have here," Mary starts flipping through a pile of folders on her desk. "Here we are. James Stockton. Looks like you have a first period class...Fiction

Workshop with Mr. Victorino. Did you bring lunch with you today? Normally students load money onto their ID to pay for lunch. It's cheaper that way."

"I didn't. We literally got here last night." I tap my back pocket and realize I forgot my wallet at home. Hopefully I have something leftover in my bag from over the summer. A granola bar or something. I look over and catch Grady staring at me.

"Swing back here before lunch and we can see about loading money on your card. Or you can always use cash or a card in the cafeteria. Here's your schedule. I also included a layout of the campus to help you gather your bearings. I helped draw it up a couple of years ago after new students kept getting lost." It's pretty detailed, which given the size of the school I'm thankful for it. "Anyways, the first period bell is in a few minutes so you should skedaddle. I don't think I would be asking too much of Grady to help you find your first class."

Grady grabs my schedule off the counter and his eyes dart over it. "Not a problem. Looks like it's on the way to the gym. Later Mary!" I wave to Mary as we exit the office. We walk in silence for a bit, winding around a couple of hallways. Grady stops outside a classroom next to a stairwell at the end of the hallway. "You don't talk much, huh?"

I find myself staring at the ground, so I lift my head to meet Grady's gaze. His piercing green eyes are squinting as he stares at me, waiting on an answer. "Sorry. I've moved schools a lot. After a while you kinda just keep to yourself."

Well, that sounded pathetic.

Grady hands my schedule to me. "Well James, that's just not gonna fly here. I'm gonna leave you here for your first class but it looks like we have Life Studies and Gym together. So, if anything, you are stuck with me two times a day." He turns and starts to walk down the hall but stops after a few steps. "Oh, and here," Grady pulls out his wallet and hands me a twenty-dollar bill. "I saw you tap your back pocket and the look on your face, and figured you forgot your wallet. You shouldn't skip lunch on day one." He places the bill in my hand, his fingers grazing mine in the process. "Nice to meet you, James."

Grady is rounding the corner by the time I respond "Great to meet you too."

Three

The rest of the morning is pretty uneventful, breezing through my first three classes. Fiction Workshop dove right in with an impromptu writing prompt, followed by being assigned a three-page short story. Second period was a study hall, followed by Spanish and Chemistry. I had been worried going into the year that my classes up in Vermont may have been a bit behind, given how small the school had been there, but so far that hadn't been the case.

The dread began to seep in for the next item on the schedule...lunch. The first day of every year, bouncing from school to school, always started with the first awkward lunch period. Sometimes I would eat at a table alone, sometimes I would be joined by someone who planned on also eating alone. But, as the years went on, I usually snuck off to other areas of the school. The library, art room, sometimes behind the auditorium stage. Somewhere it wouldn't be noticed how pathetic it looked to be eating alone.

I follow a group in front of me into the cafeteria, and the first thing I notice is the place is massive. Most schools I've been to have served a single option on the daily menu. Nachos on Tuesday, pizza Fridays. This cafeteria has legit stations. Pizza, burgers, a salad bar, sandwiches made to order, you name it. I guess Beacon's budget is a bit larger than what I'm used to.

I step into the pizza line and order a slice of pepperoni and a slice of cheese, grab a Diet Coke, and pay using Grady's twenty-dollar bill. I start to head for the exit just as Grady enters the cafeteria. "James! Don't tell me you were going to go like eat by yourself in the library or something. Come join us." He hooks his arm into mine and turns me around, escorting me over to a table near the center of the room. It's already pretty full, but Grady and I manage to squeeze in at the end of the table. "Guys, this is James. New kid. Don't be dicks to him." Grady heads over to the grill. He flashes a smile at the worker plating the food, leaning forward and says something to make her laugh and blush.

"So, new kid, what's your deal?" The guy sitting across from me says, leaning in.

"My deal? I moved here from Vermont. Just got here last night."

"Where you livin'?"

I want to make something up, something better than our apartment. But what's the point in lying. "Oh, I'm in the apartments off the main road. Near the McDonald's."

The kid laughs. He legit laughs in my face. "Oh man, that trash hole? Good luck with those bed bugs." He laughs and

14

elbows the kid next to him, who just rolls his eyes in response and continues eating his sandwich.

Grady slides in next to me. "Darius, don't act like your ass didn't live there until seventh grade. And the only reason you got out of there is because your mama trapped that dentist by getting pregnant." The rest of the table bursts out laughing. Darius grabs his tray, staring down Grady as he leaves the table. "Don't mind Darius. He's a bit of an asshole who needs to be taken down a peg every once in a while."

"Yeah, but you brutally take him down like no other. And he fucking can't stand it." The words come from a Latino kid with the brightest blue eyes I've ever seen. Jesus, there must be something in the water here. "I'm Davis by the way. Is Grady trying to recruit you for the football team?"

I stifle a laugh, shaking my head. "I don't think so. I've never even thrown a football, let alone play a game of it."

"Understood, understood. Thought I'd ask since the team is down a few players to start the season."

Grady whips his head towards Davis. "What do you mean down a few people?"

"Oh, the king of Beacon hasn't heard? Fucking Trent drove drunk Saturday night and crashed his car into a guardrail. Trent and Jackson are pretty banged up but Freddie and Xander were relatively unscathed. All four, however, have been kicked off the football team. Supposedly Gupta went right to Peters this morning and told him none of them can play this season."

Grady's face goes from shocked, to what only could be described as a streak of anger. "That's the whole kicking unit. Like starters and backups."

"Yeah, well I overheard Peters talking to the rest of the coaching staff about having to get creative finding replacements. So that sounds thrilling. All I know is I'm not giving up my receiving spot to be a fucking kicker. Or worse...a punter."

The bell rings, signaling the end of the lunch period. We all get up and start shuffling towards the exit. "Lunch is usually a bit tamer. Well, maybe not, but Darius usually avoids me. He still thinks I stole his spot on the team."

"You never said what position you play."

Grady smirks. "Quarterback obviously."

Four

I take a seat in the back of the room during Accounting and look up Beacon Football. The first article that pops up is from the Beacon Gazette. Grady's face takes up a chunk of the screen, followed by an article about how he nearly missed setting the state record for passing yards last year. It also brings up the fact that Grady took over as quarterback in his sophomore year, after Darius went down with a shoulder injury. So, not only did Grady kind of steal quarterback from Darius, but just ran away with it.

When I round the corner to the gym, Grady is waiting outside the locker room. "Hope you're ready for a fun gym class. Coach Peters is in the locker room."

"Who's Coach Peters?"

"Football coach. Today's class is his first attempt at 'being creative' to find replacements, like Davis mentioned."

I follow Grady into the locker room, which has about twenty guys already in there. Two men are talking to the side,

17

which I presume are Coach Peters and the gym teacher. "Afternoon gentleman," the man in the blue polo says. "Let's get suited up for class and meet out back on the football field."

Grady and I, along with the rest of the guys, walk out of the school and onto the football field. There are piles of footballs all over the field. Football was not played often in gym class in my other schools, and when it was played it was flag football. But even that stopped in one of my last schools when a couple of juniors collided during class and left the field with concussions.

The man in the blue polo is standing in the middle of the field, along with eight girls. "You are all probably wondering what I'm doing out here and why there's footballs everywhere. I asked Mr. Gibson to let me facilitate today's gym class. For those who don't know me I am Coach Peters, and I coach the varsity football team here at Beacon. This past weekend it appears a few of our football players may have overindulged before one of them crashed their car into a guardrail on Benson Ave. It just so happened that our whole kicking unit was in the car. Between injuries and repercussions from Principal Gupta, all four will no longer be on the team this year."

"What's that got to do with class?" It's a girl I recognize from Fiction Workshop.

"Well Chloe, I'm sure you remember that our football team made it to the state championship last year and lost to East Greenwich. We would like to get back there but obviously can't do that without any kickers on the team. And, on top of that, we are already a bit empty-handed after last year's class graduated.

Today's class activity will be practicing field goals and extra point attempts to see if any of you have some hidden talent."

There is a low murmur, maybe more like a groan, making its way through the class. I have to give it to Coach Peters that this sure is a creative approach to recruiting players. "So," Coach Peters stops pacing around the ten-yard line, "everyone go line up at the fifteen-yard line and one by one come up and attempt an extra point kick. If you make one of the extra points you move on to attempting field goals."

"Hey Coach, what should we be doing?" Three guys are standing off to the side. Judging by their size, probably already football players.

"Go ahead and run some laps on the track. With hustle gentleman, or you'll regret it later in practice. That goes for you too, Grady."

The rest of us have now lined up and I end up next to Chloe. We are about ten people deep in the line, and there's another fifteen or so behind us.

"Peters is usually such a misogynist dick. I cannot believe he is having the girls try out." An awkward silence hangs in the air, and I realize she was talking to me. "I'm now realizing I'm chatting you up like you know me. But you're new, right? I'm Chloe."

"James," I respond. The first guy in line runs up to the tee and kicks the ball. It barely skips forward to the end zone. "This should be a blast."

"It's not like this first public display will make or break your reputation or anything. No pressure." Chloe's lips curl up

19

into a smirk. Up close she is very pretty, the type of pretty where you can tell she doesn't need to put the effort in. The second guy in line hits the goalpost and the ball bounces back into the end zone. "When did you move to town?"

"Last night. We were supposed to get here before the weekend but for some reason my mom changed her mind. Really wanted some time to explore the area and go job hunting before school started."

"Moving the day before school starts? That fucking blows." The fifth person manages to make it through the goalpost, cheering as he runs behind us to the twenty-yard line. "So where were you looking to work? Like, what type of job?"

Number seven kicks the ball like a line drive. The distance wasn't bad but nowhere at the height of the goal post. "Probably something with tips," I say. "Maybe a waiter, or a bartender. Definitely not a coffee shop. Been there, done that. Hated that."

"Don't you need to be eighteen to bartend?"

"Turned eighteen last month. I started school a bit late."

"Well, as we are now besties, I would be more than happy to take you job hunting some day this week. Oh shit, you're up."

I walk up and line myself up with the ball. The class is quiet and I can feel all of their eyes on me. Grady is staring at me from the track, stopping his run to watch with the rest. "Kick the fucking ball!" Chloe yells from the line.

"Jenkins! Language!" Coach Peters screams.

I take a deep breath, run up and kick the ball. It goes through the middle of the uprights. "Holy shit," I say, standing there staring at the ball bouncing on the field. Chloe runs up and high fives me as Coach Peters resets the tee. I walk back to the line, watching Chloe set up to kick. Her kick goes a bit left, but also goes through the uprights.

"Jenkins! New kid! Twenty-yard line!"

Chloe and I proceed with success at the fifteen-, twenty-, and twenty-five-yard lines. Grady jogs over after I line up at the thirty-yard line. "Dude, I thought you said you've never played football before."

"I haven't."

"Yeah, well it looks like you might be now." He heads back over to the track and continues his laps. Do I even want to play football? I look at the group and it's down to four of us - Chloe, myself, and two guys who I overheard say they used to play soccer. Chloe goes first, and her ball again hooks a bit left but makes it through with distance to spare. Caleb, one of the soccer players, goes next and the ball bounces short in the endzone. Bob, the other soccer player, shanks the ball far right.

I line up and, without hesitating, run up and smash the ball. It goes straight down the middle and is good. A whistle blows from the side of the field. "I've seen enough," Coach Peters says. "Jenkins and–"

"--James."

"Jenkins and James are our new kicking team. James seems a bit more accurate so he'll be our kicker. Jenkins will be the punter."

21

"Do we have any choice in this?" Chloe asks.

"Well, yes," Coach replies, "but do you really want to let the school down?"

I guess I'm on the football team now.

Five

The next few days went by in a blur. Chloe and I are immediately thrown into football practice, albeit not nearly as intense as what Grady and the rest of the football team are put through. Our practice always starts with running laps with the rest of the team and joining for some of their conditioning work. When they start running drills is when Chloe and I split off, leaving us with Assistant Coach Tommy to go practice punts and field goals down the hill on Beacon Middle School's field.

Chloe's punt goes easily forty to fifty yards down the field. "Is it weird how randomly fucking good we are at this. Like, honestly, I've never even kicked a football before this. Or a soccer ball. Well, maybe a soccer ball in gym class. What I'm saying is it's fucking stupid."

I look over at Coach Tommy and he shrugs, obviously not as bothered by Chloe's bluntness like Coach Peters is. I kick a ball off the tee, hooking it a bit to the left but in. This one roughly a fifty-yard field goal.

"She's right, you know. You both are weirdly fucking good at kicking footballs." Coach Tommy sets up the tee again a little further back. Chloe and I stifle a laugh as we back up on the field.

The past few days Chloe and I have gotten to know each other a bit better. We started sitting together during Fiction Workshop and Accounting, walking together to classes, and she even tried to get me to sit with her and her friends at lunch. However, Grady insisted I come sit with the football team. He invited Chloe to join, who not so politely declined.

"So did you know Grady before coming to Beacon?"

"No, why?"

She bends down to tie her cleat. "You two just seem to be pretty friendly"

"You and I are pretty friendly, Chloe."

"Right, but not from like your first minute in school." She picks up a ball and punts in downfield. "Grady's a nice guy so I guess it makes sense. He definitely breaks that typical jock quarterback stereotype. Well, except for the fact he's pretty hot." I feel my face flush, so I bend and pretend to tie the lace of my cleats. When I pop back up Chloe's eyes are wide and she looks excited. "James! Are you in–"

"--not here," I interrupt, motioning to Coach Tommy standing a few feet away.

"Coach Tommy, can we finish up by running a few more laps?"

"That's fine Jenkins. Do like four or five laps. That should bring us close to the end of practice."

Chloe and I jog off the field and start looping the track, putting some distance between us and Coach Tommy. She punches my arm. "You ARE into Grady."

I sigh. I truly wanted to fly under the radar at Beacon and it appears no one will be having any of that. "Look, no one knows here and I plan to keep it that way. Part of the reason I'm here at Beacon is because of a relationship I had last year Penny, my mom, found out about. And I'm pretty sure she agreed to move here so she and Ralph could keep a closer eye on me."

"Are you talking Ralph, like Ralph Dursten? Like creepy Virtue Dursten and her even creepier father? Wait, isn't he married? I could have sworn I saw Virtue and her mom at Target like last month."

"Well, he and his wife divorced a couple weeks ago and we almost immediately moved here. I'm pretty sure Ralph did everything he could to push his wife out of the picture."

"Got it. Your mom's a homewrecker...kidding, kinda. Well that whole family is fucking creepy." Chloe kicks a stray football sitting on the track back onto the field. "So, what happened with what's his face you were dating?"

I think back to sitting on the pool lounger, hovering over our DMs. "Andy. He was a friend from school who lived a couple houses down from me. We became more than friends for a short period, until one day when my mom found us making out behind his house. That was only a few weeks ago, and I haven't seen Andy since. Or heard from him."

"I'm sorry James, that's terrible. I hate to break it to you but Grady has had a string of decently serious girlfriends over the years, so you might have to focus your attention elsewhere."

We stop running, leaning against the fence to catch our breath. I'm not used to this much running, my legs feeling like jelly. "I'm not into Grady. You've just assumed that."

"Fuck off. It's not like you don't longingly look at him in the hallway, or on the other side of the football field, or in line in the cafeteria, or–"

"--I get it. Fine. Maybe I'm a little into him. But I've only been here for four days so things can change."

"They might. But the good news is that I think I know exactly where you're going to get a job."

Six

We jump in Chloe's Jeep after practice and race out of the parking lot, heading the opposite direction from the apartment. Soon enough the commercial buildings fade away and what's left is an amazing view of the ocean. We drive over a short bridge filled with pedestrians on the walkways. On the other side of the bridge is what appears to be your typical beachside town. The day is clear and the ocean is just so vast, or maybe it seems that way being the first time ever seeing it.

"I didn't realize the beach was so close to Beacon. Grady had mentioned something about it but he also was talking a lot"

"That sounds about right. This is Beacon Point. My parents moved here in their twenties and I guess it used to be very seasonal, but over time people became full-time locals and now the place is just fucking mobbed during the summer." She pulls into the only parking space open on the main road, in front of a bookstore. "This is where I work, which also happens to be owned by my parents."

"What's with the name? Last I checked your last name isn't Flannery."

"It's been named that forever. They bought the shop from Mrs. Flannery like twenty years ago, pretty much a year after they got here." We get out of the car and Chloe holds the door open. The inside of the bookstore is breathtaking. It is jam-packed with overflowing bookshelves and side tables scattered around with various gift items. It does this all in a way that isn't overwhelming, and more so in a homey feeling.

An attractive older man stands behind the counter and smiles when he gazes our way. "Pumpkin! What do I owe for the pleasure of your presence on your day off?"

"We talked about this," Chloe says, rolling her eyes and grabbing a bag of candy off a table. She opens it and hands me a piece. A chocolate-covered gummy bear. Not sure how I feel about it.

"Right, right. No calling you Pumpkin in front of your friends, or non-friends, or in public. And who is your friend or non-friend you are sharing the merchandise with?" I stop midchew, but ultimately decide that gummy bears and chocolate do make a good combo.

"This is James. I told you about his and my misfortune in gym class being forced into joining the football team."

Mr. Jenkins leans back. "Well, I for one am very excited for the first game tomorrow. My little girl being one of the few girls making a football team in Rhode Island."

"I think it may have been more out of necessity due to shit decisions by Trent and his goons. James, are you looking for something?"

I had, without paying attention, moved away from them and was staring at one of the bookshelves. "No, not really. Well, maybe. Do you have *Breaking the Moon* by chance?"

"That's a fine book and a consistent seller. If you check the bookcase right behind you it should be on the second shelf from the bottom." I crouch down and sure enough it's right where Mr. Jenkins said it would be. I grab a copy and bring it to the counter. "Have you read it before?"

"It's one of my favorites," I say, reaching for my wallet, "but my mom took my copy and threw it in a fire pit a few months ago. Her boyfriend had shared a link to books that should be banned and then caught me reading it."

"Every year that list comes out and sends people into a tizzy, a few new additions to the list tacked on. Little do they know it just drives sales up for titles on the list." He picks up the book and puts it in a bag, handing it to me. I hand some of the leftover money Grady gave me but Mr. Jenkins pushes my hand back. "Let's consider it a payment for dealing with my daughter. And to say fuck it to conforming!"

"Cool Dad," Chloe chirps, "but the reason we are down here is that James needs a job and bad. Do you know if Uncle Sam and Uncle Mitch are hiring?"

"Hmm...they did just have a couple of kids go back to college, so maybe. They were just in here a few minutes ago and were heading over to the restaurant."

29

"Thanks…bye!" Chloe grabs my arm and pulls me towards the exit. I turn to thank him for the book but Chloe pushes me through the door out onto the street.

"So does your whole family work in town or…"

"Uncle Sam and Uncle Mitch aren't technically my uncles. Sam moved here with my mom and dad and they met Mitch here. Uncle Mitch inherited Beacon Donuts," she gestures at the donut shop next to the bookstore, "and Uncle Sam opened Tipsy Mic." The restaurant comes into view. It stands out from the rest of the building, which is painted a beach blue with white trim. Tipsy Mic is painted black with chrome accents on the outside. The sign isn't lit up, but the giant chrome mic is very prominent on the outside of the building. "Now Uncle Mitch runs the kitchen at Tipsy Mic and this guy Derrick manages Beacon Donuts."

Chloe pulls the door handle. It's locked, which elicits a groan from her. She starts pounding on the door, and continues to do so until the door flies open. An attractive man fills the doorway and looks us up and down. "Sorry we don't want any," he says, slamming the door in our faces. I'm about to ask Chloe who that was when the door flies open, the same man standing there with a grin on his face.

"Uncle Mitch you're such a fucking jerk!" She runs up and hugs him, and he picks her up off the ground.

"Shouldn't you be off footballing or something? And who's your shadow over there?"

"Right, so that's why we're here. This is James. He is new to town and is in need of a J-O-B. Is there something you and Uncle Sam can do about this?" Mitch puts her down and eyes me up and down. "Would it help if I told you he, umm, plays for the same team?"

"Chloe!" I yell, looking around me and luckily no one else is in earshot.

"Chloe, do we need to go over the concept of boundaries again? But I won't lie, it does give him a slight upper hand. It was James, right? Do you have any prior serving or bartending experience? Wait, I guess the more important question is, how old are you?"

"Eighteen," I say, "and I have worked at a coffee shop, so that offered some serving experience. But I really need the money and promise I'm a fast learner. I just can't do Friday nights for a while."

"Because of the footballing, as you put it Uncle Mitch."

Mitch disappears into the restaurant, leaving Chloe and I alone on the sidewalk. A car blaring Taylor Swift passes us and honks, Chloe waving in its general direction. "Dana. Her sister goes to Beacon Point Elementary."

Mitch reappears with who I am presuming is Sam. "You're our new guy? Can you start tonight?"

A smile creeps across my face. "Absolutely."

Seven

Chloe took me to Target to get a black t-shirt and slip resistant sneakers, as Tipsy Mic's dress code was a black T and dark jeans. Chloe spotted me the money, knowing I was good for it, given it was for my first night of work.

I find out I'm shadowing Sam for my first shift at Tipsy Mic, who is the bartender for the evening. "We are more pressed for help behind the bar right now with the turnover after summer ended. But we'll place you where we need you. If you can handle bartending, you can definitely handle serving."

Sam walks me through a few basics. How to appropriately pour a beer, what level on a wine glass to fill to for a six- or nine-ounce pour, and what the appropriate amount of liquor is for a typical mixed drink. "These levels can fluctuate a bit if the person is a regular or tips on the higher side," he explains. "You'll eventually get a hang of what goes in popular drinks and what our drink specials are, but for now there are cheat sheets next to the service bar. I printed out copies for you to take home and study."

I look up at the clock and almost three hours have already gone by. The dinner rush seems to be finally winding down. Sam mentioned it was probably against his best interest to start me on a Thursday, which was a popular college drinking night, and that he'd have me out of here no later than eight.

"Samuel, who is that treat behind the bar with you?" I look over and find the voice belongs to a much older man, most likely pushing sixty. He is massive, built how you think an NFL offensive lineman would be. He smiles in my direction, which turns my stomach a bit.

"Henry, stop being a fucking pervert. The kid is barely legal and has no interest in your old crotchety ass. Cosmo per usual, princess?" Henry's face turns red as Sam gets to making his drink. I greet two guys in suits who arrive at the bar and order a couple draft beers. Sam gestures for me to pour them and I do, both clean pours. I catch Henry staring at them when I drop off the pints, looking a bit angry. Jealousy, in this light, was just a tad creepy.

Sam brings me back to the kitchen, where I find Mitch sitting on a stool drinking a beer. The kitchen staff appears to be in cleanup mode. "Mitch can give you a ride home as this is the point of the night where he typically goes off duty. Our late-night menu kicks in at nine and it's just fried food and burgers the rest of the way."

"Babe, did you even look at the specials I put together for the late-night menu tonight?"

Sam sighs. "Yes, and I know the kitchen will really struggle to pull together your cheese curd and mac n' cheese topped burger."

My stomach practically announces itself to the whole kitchen. "That sounds amazing." My lunch was pretty light today, given how Penny barely picked up the essentials at the grocery store. That, and going right from practice to work, left me hours late for a meal.

"At least someone appreciates my culinary excellence. And that is why you get one to go." Mitch hands me a paper bag, which weighs a ton.

"The play here is to sober the college kids up?"

"Bingo."

I find the apartment empty when I get home. There is a note on the counter, next to a box of Kraft mac and cheese.

At Ralph's - see you in the AM. Mom.

Parent of the year right here.

I strip off my uniform and throw it in the corner of my bedroom. I'm going to need to pick up some extra shirts once my training is done. I feel my phone vibrate in my pocket. It's a text from an unknown number.

UNKNOWN: Hey I'm having people over after the game tomorrow - you should join

UNKNOWN: It will be good whether we win or loose

UNKNOWN: Lose*

UNKNOWN: But we're gonna win

UNKNOWN. Oh shit. This is Grady hahahahaha

Where did Grady get my number from? Oh. Chloe.

JAMES: Sure

GRADY: Awesome.

Eight

"WELCOME BACK TO BEACON COLTS FOOTBALL! We have a great game for you folks tonight. Our Colts, runners-up in the State Championship last season, are taking on the Hendricken Hawks to start out the year. This should be an interesting season for the Colts, who lost their whole kicking unit right before the school year began due to...I am now being told this was on the do not discuss list. So...here are your Colts starters!"

The crowd goes absolutely wild when Grady's name is called first, but continues throughout the whole team. Even when my name is called people are screaming, although no one has a clue who I am. Chloe is announced last and the girls in the stands go crazy.

Grady goes to the fifty-yard line and shakes the Hawks captain's hand. The other team wins the coin toss and defers to the second half. Grady shuffles off the field and the special teams unit heads out to receive the kickoff. The whistle blows and the ball is in the air.

The game feels like it is moving at a ridiculous speed. Grady moves the offense down the field with such precision but also finds a way to just eat up the clock. Suddenly the crowd is going nuts and I realize that I missed Grady throw a touchdown pass to Rob, one of the tight ends.

"Stockton, you're up! Let's see what that leg is made of in real time." I jog out onto the field with Chloe and the rest of the special teams.

"I'm not asking a lot of you here Chloe, but don't fuck up the hold." She discreetly gives me the finger and we wait for the snap.

"Ready?" I nod, and the ball is snapped. The defense is closing in as the ball hits Chloe's hands.

Time seems to slow. I feel, and I think also hear, my heart beating like crazy in my chest. My foot connects with the football and I stand back and watch it go through the middle of the uprights.

"THE EXTRA POINT IS GOOD! BEACON GOES UP 7-0!"

We steamroll the Hawks the rest of the game. The Hawks turnover the ball four times, and in the end, we beat them 49-7. I hit all five field goals and all but one of my extra-point attempts. I had originally expected the locker room to be out of control but it turns out we are all just beat. We shower up quickly and head out of the school. Grady and I, along with Rob and Davis, are headed towards the parking lot. I notice, at the edge of the parking lot, two parents are still hanging around.

"Grady! You played so well sweetie. And so did the rest of you!" These must be Grady's parents. They are decked out head to toe in Beacon gear, with his dad's face painted in blue and white. "Are you boys still headed over to our house?"

"Yup. Did you guys order the pizzas?" His mom nods. Grady turns to me. "It's tradition after the first game that we go back, play Madden, and get pizzas from Gino's. Hope you're good with pepperoni or buffalo chicken."

"And you must be the kicking phenom Grady's been talking about. And, well, what we just saw. You sure you've never seen a football field before?"

"Yes Mr. Tomlinson Very sure."

"Oh please, call me Mark. None of that mister bullshit."

"Dad, reel it back. You're acting thirsty."

His mom smiles at me. "And you can call me Julie, and nothing to do with thirst. Were your parents at the game James?"

I don't realize I'm frowning until I see the look on Julie's face. "Oh, it's just my mom and no, she didn't come to the game." When I had told Penny I had made the football team, and that I also got a job, she seemed more concerned I wouldn't have enough spare time to hang out with Ralph and help out at his little collective, The Wishing Well. I had heard enough about Ralph's little group to know it leaned more cultish than anything else. When I told her about the game, she told me she already had plans to attend a meeting at Ralph's house.

"That's too bad. Maybe the next one," Julie offers. "Alright, we are going to pick up the pizzas and will see you boys back at the house."

As Julie and Mark walk away Grady leans in closer to me. "Sorry about that. They can be a bit intense."

"Are you kidding me? It's great. I deal with the complete opposite. I've had either Kraft mac and cheese or instant ramen every night this week. Alone."

Grady shakes his head, face filled with disappointment. He hangs an arm around my shoulder. "Well let's get you some of the best pizza ever. Wait, no. The best that Beacon offers!"

"That's even debatable," Rob says.

Nine

Seeing Grady's house really puts into perspective how small the apartment is. The house appears to span the same length as the apartment complex, but is three-stories tall. The outside of the house is lit up by spotlights, with a fountain outside in the middle of a large parking area.

"This is your fucking house?"

Davis bursts out laughing. "Dude, I said the same thing the first time I came here. I had met Mark and Julie multiple times before coming here and they just don't seem like the type of people who would own a legit mansion."

"Mom's a lawyer and Dad's a cardiologist. He also helps out with the Nursing program at Rhode Island College. But they legit can't stand most of our neighbors. All of them are very West Beacon, where we just live in West Beacon."

We make our way through the house, ending with Grady bringing us to his finished basement. Mounted on the wall is quite possibly the largest TV I have ever seen. Shelves line both sides of it, filled with video games and movies. Grady bends down under the TV, pulls a handle on the wall, and a long piece of the wall swings open to reveal the game consoles.

"Wow you are rich rich," I blurt out, immediately regretting it.

"Yes, yes he is," Rob responds, "but he's too nice to shove it in anyone's face. Just like Mark and Julie."

"Well, except our house. And the fact that they do a walk around the neighborhood in their gameday war paint to make the neighbors uncomfortable."

"Don't any of their kids go to school with us?"

Grady laughs. "Not a single one besides me. I think most of them go to a boarding school in Portsmouth. My parents never even asked me. They said they did just fine at public high schools." Grady heads over to the fridge and grabs four beers, passing one to each of us before flopping on the couch.

I freeze. "Aren't your parents coming back soon with the pizza?"

"It's fine," Grady says, "they don't mind as long as we don't leave the house and don't get out of control. My dad usually drives everyone home at the end of the night."

The thought of going back to the apartment after drinking is terrifying, but the idea of being able to relax for a bit also sounds pretty good. I take a swig of my beer right when Mark and Julie walk down the stairs with the pizza.

"Alright guys, one pepperoni and one buffalo chicken. And some Crumbl cookies for dessert. Holler if you need anything."

I place my beer down on the coffee table, careful to use a coaster because I can't imagine what the furniture in this place costs. "Are you not joining us?" Grady's eyebrow arches at the question, and I can tell by the way it catches Mark and Julie off guard that this hadn't been asked before.

"Oh, it's fine. We'll have our food upstairs."

"Go grab it, Mom. We haven't started playing Madden yet."

The six of us crowd around the coffee table, plowing through the pizzas. Mark and Julie share a bottle of wine while the four of us enjoy our beers. Mark lets me try the wine, a first for me, and it's not half bad. The other guys made a face when they were offered the same. Mark gets in on the rotation of Madden, eventually taking my spot. It becomes quite clear that Grady isn't the only one using the PlayStation in the house. Mark and I switch seats at some point, so now I'm sitting next to Julie.

"So, you really just moved here on Sunday?"

"Yeah. We were up in Vermont last year, and have bounced around almost every year before that."

She sighs. "That must be really tough. My father was in the military so I had a similar situation, always moving to wherever he was stationed. I think that's why most of my friends I still have today are the ones I made in college. It was

43

the longest I was ever in one place." She breaks a cookie in half and offers the second half to me, which I gladly accept. "But I have to say I'm surprised you're here. It's nothing against you, but those three are thick as thieves and Friday nights have always been the three of them for as far back as I can remember."

I chuckle. "I was surprised too, but Grady has been so nice to me since school began. He was the first person I met walking into school."

"So, tell me about you. Your family. What brought you here to Beacon?"

I tell Julie how Penny has been a single mom for practically my whole life, how she had always called a new place home but within the first year got the itch to move somewhere new. Then she met Ralph and had fallen in love with him, playing the slow game until Ralph and his wife went their separate ways. How she immediately moved the two of them here into the apartment, where she hasn't stayed a single night since Sunday.

"I don't want to discourage you, but Ralph and his daughter are…a bit odd."

"Believe me Mrs. Tomlinson…Julie, I am more than aware. Both from personal experience and what I've already heard around town."

She fills her wine glass back up. "He and his little group once in a while pop up and cause trouble around town. A few weeks ago, his daughter gathered people to picket outside this restaurant in Beacon Point because the two owners are gay and

44

held a speed dating event for LGBT individuals. Which was ingenious on their behalf because I don't recall ever seeing a speed dating event that wasn't catered to straight people specifically."

"Julie and I met at a speed dating event in college." Mark adds, looking away from the screen. "She kept pushing the next person out of their seat so she could keep talking to me."

"Yeah, I think you may have that confused. I distinctly remember talking to multiple people and then you chasing me down in the parking lot begging me to go on a date with you."

"My story sounds better," he says, focusing back on the game.

"Was the restaurant Tipsy Mic?" I ask.

"It was! How do you already know about that place?"

"His girlfriend got him a job there," Davis says, passing me another beer.

"Not my girlfriend. But she knows the owners."

"Sam and Mitch are good people. I bet you'll enjoy working there."

Eventually Julie and Mark head upstairs, telling us we have a deadline of midnight for a shuttle home. The night continues on with more Madden and more beers. By the time 11:30 rolls around, Davis and Rob have started cleaning up the empty bottles and pizza boxes. I realize I may have drunk a bit more than I intended to, and now the panic is setting in.

"You good?" Grady asks, grabbing the last slice of pizza out of the box.

"Yeah. Well, no. I think I'm just worried about getting home and my mom being there and seeing I'm a bit drunk.

"Just stay here," Grady says, "my parents won't care."

"You sure?"

"Of course."

The four of us finish cleaning up the basement and carry everything upstairs. Grady tells Julie that I'm staying over. She says it's fine but I think I catch a glimpse of surprise on her face. Mark leaves to drop off Davis and Rob, and Grady and I head up the stairs to the second floor. Grady leads me to a room at the end of the hall, which opens into a massive bedroom easily five times the size of mine. He heads over to a dresser on the other side of the room, strips down to his underwear, and starts rummaging through the drawers.

My eyes linger a little too long on the lines and curves of his muscular body that I think he catches me staring when he turns around. "You want something to change into?" He throws a tank and some running shorts at me. I change quickly, feeling self-conscious being half naked in a room with someone who looks like Grady.

"We can sleep head to toe. The bed's big enough." And he's right, and anything would be big enough in comparison to the twin bed I sleep in. Grady throws me a pillow as we both lay down in the bed, his head at the headboard and mine at the foot of the bed. I am becoming very aware of how close I am to

Grady in his bed, so I turn to face away from him. "Night James."

I hope he can't hear how fast my heart is racing. "Night Grady."

I wake up early, the clock by the bed reading 5:30. I feel a weight on me, and when I look Grady's arm is over my legs and his leg has swung over my midsection. I immediately become aware of his touch, and am standing at full attention. I slowly slide out from under him, quietly lifting myself off the bed. I slip out of Grady's clothes and pull mine back on, and head out of the bedroom. The house seems quiet, so I tiptoe down the stairs and start to head for the front door.

"Morning James," Mark calls from the kitchen counter. He is sitting there in pajama pants and a Beacon Football t-shirt, taking a sip of his coffee. "You need a lift home? I was about to head over to the hospital."

"You don't look dressed for work," I say, gesturing to his outfit.

"That's because I change when I get there. I don't like to bring work home with me. And they have a laundry service at the hospital so why not take full advantage of it." He gets up and takes two travel mugs out of the cupboard, making two coffees. He passes me one and heads toward the door. "Let's get this show on the road."

Ten

The weeks fly by leading up to Halloween. Beacon Football is undefeated and Chloe and I continue our success as the team's kicking unit. One day, in the middle of October, Coach Tommy called me into the coach's office to tell me I was on pace to break the single season point record for Rhode Island high school football. College scouts were visiting in a few weeks and I was suddenly on their radar, along with Grady and a couple of the other players.

I was also settling in at Tipsy Mic, working a steady schedule of shifts split between the bar and serving tables. Sam and Mitch have been great, and I use them as my sounding board about Grady and my feelings. Chloe got some of it, but I felt I could get more practical advice from Mitch and Sam.

One night I arrive home exhausted from a particularly busy shift to find Penny home on a rare weekend evening. "Oh, you still work at that place? Ralph and Virtue told me about the owners. Are you sure you want to work there? Isn't there anywhere else in Beacon? Don't want them to be a bad influence on you, like that Andy kid." I just stare at her, then continue on to my bedroom and shut the door. Convenient of her to pretend to parent on one of a handful of times she's been here the past month.

Not that I had been there all that much. Football and work keep me pretty busy, and Julie had given me an open invitation to join them for dinner any night of the week. I'm pretty sure Grady had told them about my eating habits with Penny not really being around. So now most days after practice, when not working, I go to Grady's house. It was becoming a problem, having all of this solo time with Grady. I often hung out for hours after dinner, doing homework or watching TV or playing Madden, and it was only adding to the fire how I felt about him.

It could be my imagination, but as time passed by, it seemed like he was sitting closer to me. Laying on the bed next to me, even making sure the house was stocked with Diet Cokes specifically for me. He even scolded Julie once for buying Diet Pepsi instead.

"It's fine Grady. Julie, thank you," I said.

"No more Diet Pepsi," Grady said, shaking his head at Julie. Which elicited a laugh from her.

School was a bubbling frenzy the last week of October. Halloween was on a Friday, which happened to coincide with Beacon Football having a bye week. Davis was throwing a party at his house, which I learn happens every year. I was told it was

50

always a wild event that every adult turned a blind eye to. I was starting to see how that stereotype exists that athletes get away with anything and rule the school. The school and town rallied around Beacon Football, especially amidst a season like we were having.

At the end of Monday's practice Coach gathers the team into the gymnasium for an impromptu meeting. When I walk in, I notice some of the teachers are there as well as some parents, including Julie and Mark. We take our seats in the bleachers and Coach Peters takes center stage. "Boys, we want to tell you how proud of you we all are. You are kicking the ever-living shit out of every team you face, and Beacon has never been undefeated at this point of the season. So, the school, the parents, the community...they wanted to show you how much they appreciate what you're doing. Saturday we are leaving for New York City for an overnight trip, and Sunday heading to MetLife to see the Giants play the Cowboys."

The room erupts. I've never been to a major city, let alone New York. I think of all the places to eat, shows to see, museums to go to. "Settle down," Coach Peters says, and we eventually do. "Use Saturday to explore the city, get some better food than what's here in Beacon. Your guidance counselor has set up tours at NYU, Columbia, and Pace. If you are interested in any of those colleges please stop by and see Guidance Counselor Dotson to get on a list. We will leave at eight sharp Saturday morning to get to the city by lunchtime. I say this because we all know about a certain event Friday night that often gets out of hand. If you miss the bus, you miss the trip."

51

"One more thing. The trip will be chaperoned by your coaching staff, along with Grady's and Chloe's parents. Do not make this harder on them than it needs to be. Dismissed!"

The rest of the week crawls by, but finally I'm at Grady's house getting ready for Davis's party. I look in the mirror and we just look ridiculous. "Where did your parents even get these clothes from?"

Grady turns to face the mirror, checks himself out. "I think Amazon, maybe Goodwill? I know for a fact my pants and your shirt came from Dad's personal collection."

"Oh, that's embarrassing," I say, as we head out the door.

Part of the agreement between Davis and his parents for letting him have the party as is and unsupervised was that the parents pick the costume theme, and that they get pictures of group costumes. There is supposedly a scrapbook that haunts Davis and the rest of the class that has evidence of every year's costumes. This year the theme was musical acts from the 90s to early 2000s, covering the music that was popular with all the parents when they were our age. Mark and Julie begged Grady and I, along with Davis, Rob, and Cody, to let them put our costumes together. We had agreed, only to our dismay, when we were dressed to match some embarrassing music video from the boy band Justin Timberlake used to be in. "Maybe a picture of this can convince them to do a reunion tour!" Julie exclaimed, taking a photo of the five of us before driving us to the party.

It feels like half the school is at the party, and drinks start flowing quickly. Kegs and mixed drinks are set up on the back patio, with the pool not a danger for anyone being already closed for the season. I'm talking with Rob when Chloe walks in, wearing the tiniest lime green shirt and ridiculously shiny pants. "Have you ever heard of the Spice Girls? Because I guess I'm a Scary Spice per my mom. And also, where the fuck is Grady? He's getting a slap because Julie put these awful outfits together. Supposedly our parents got drunk one night a few weeks ago and came up with this terrible idea."

I gesture towards Grady, who is talking with this girl Shannon that Chloe hangs out with. She's also one of the football cheerleaders. Chloe marches up to him, jabbing her finger into his chest and flailing her arms wildly. He laughs at her as she stomps off over to the keg. "These outfits are kinda cute," Dana says as she saddles up next to me. "I feel like we haven't had a lot of time together since you came to Beacon. But you do steal a lot of my best friend's time."

"Oh, it's not like that."

She laughs. "I know, Chloe said the same. Just giving you a hard time. I'm supposedly playing wingwoman for her tonight."

"Is that so? Does she have her eyes on anyone?"

"Ha! She does still tell me things she doesn't tell you. It's Rob. She's been into him for years but he's been with Heather Richardson since freshman year. That is until last week when Heather dumped him." Now that Dana mentions it, Rob had seemed a bit down last weekend. At least until the news of the

53

New York trip was announced. "Did Chloe tell you I'm going with you guys to New York tomorrow? Since she's the only girl on the team she technically has space in her room."

"She didn't but that's great. Maybe I can be your wingman this weekend for someone on the football team."

Dana bursts out laughing, keeling over. "OMG James no. I'm not becoming part of that incestual dating pool. One of the reasons I stopped cheerleading was that they just made their rounds with the football team and I didn't want to be associated. It's much more fun drinking in the stands watching Chloe fucking kick ass and embarrass other teams. Girl power and all, yada yadda."

Eventually Dana and I go our separate ways and I mingle throughout the party. I tend to get chattier the more I drink, so I introduce myself to a few of the more attractive juniors. Who, in turn, say hi and continue to ignore me. I guess I'm not interesting enough without cleavage pouring out of a costume.

It is fun trying to decipher what some of the costumes are, some more obvious than others. There is a group of girls that have dressed as different versions of Britney Spears throughout her early career.

I swing back to the patio to refill my beer when I notice Grady is still talking to Shannon. She has moved in closer and her hand is on him, fingers massaging into his side. I feel jealousy burning through me, that Grady hasn't talked to me the whole party and that he is still talking to her. He turns as I stand there, and as his eyes catch mine the smile disappears from his face. I need to get out of here. I turn and walk through the house and right out the front door.

I'm two houses down when I hear "James, wait up!" I turn and Chloe is jogging towards me, holding her chest so nothing pops out. "What's up? Were you just going to leave without telling me?"

I stop and turn to face her. "Sorry. I just had...I needed to get out of there."

"Does this have to do with Shannon shamelessly fondling Grady?" I nod, and I can feel tears welling in my eyes. "Oh James," Chloe closes the gap and hugs me in the middle of the street. "I know nothing I say will make it better. Let's go back to my house, binge eat candy, and watch scary movies."

The credits from *It Follows* are scrolling on the TV in Chloe's bedroom. "What a creepy fucking movie," she says, grabbing the remote and going back to Netflix's home screen.

"Can I ask you something?" I say, staring up at the ceiling.

Chloe lays down on the bed and grabs my face, turning it so it faces her. "Shoot."

"Did you and Grady ever–"

"--oh god no! James, why would you think that?"

"I dunno. You two are friendly but also kinda get weird around each other sometimes."

"First of all, no. I would never. But it has nothing to do with him as a person, he is fine in both personality and in his looks. He will make someone very happy someday. But I grew up with Grady almost like a brother. Our parents are best friends and we are both an only child, so we are practically siblings the way we were raised. Holidays? Together. Birthdays? Together. Nights the parents went through six bottles of wine? Together, although trying to avoid the parents. They always came up with the stupidest ideas on wine nights."

"Do you think I have any chance?"

Chloe's face scrunches up, and there is an extended silence. "Here's what I know. Grady has dated many different girls in our grade and some juniors that seemed serious, but none lasted particularly long. Like a semester tops. But with me he would never talk about girls, not that I said we couldn't but we just never did. He is one of the nicest people I know, and he stands out when compared to the other football players. Some of them are just so gross."

My phone vibrates on the bed and Grady's name pops up. I sigh, swiping the screen.

GRADY: Where are you
GRADY: About to call for ride home
JAMES: I'm at Chloes
JAMES: No need for a ride
GRADY: Oh
GRADY: OK
GRADY: But you left your stuff for NYC at my house
JAMES: Can you bring it tomorrow
GRADY: Yeah. Sure

GRADY: Sorry

I put the phone down and show Chloe the messages.
"James, I know you are going to read into that message more
than you probably should. You can keep your hopes up, as long
as it doesn't crush you if he doesn't reciprocate."

He already has.

Eleven

Chloe and I leave her house around seven so I can stop and change out of my Halloween costume, and also grab some much-needed coffee and donuts. Mitch and Sam are in Beacon Donuts when we stop for breakfast. Sam takes one look at me and just laughs. Mitch holds his phone up and takes a photo. "I'm going to need a copy of that," Chloe says as she collects our breakfast, "and we're not paying for these. Thanks Uncle Mitch!"

When we pull up to the apartment complex Chloe snorts. "Okay, you were right. This definitely used to be a beach motel. I'm pretty sure there is a picture of Sam and my parents sitting on that balcony from when they first came to Beacon."

I unlock the apartment door and Penny is sleeping on the couch. I hold a finger up to my lips and we sneak through the kitchen and slip into my bedroom. Chloe looks around, taking in the room. She leans in and whispers "love what you've done with the place."

I change into a pair of jeans and a light sweater, and it dawns on me I never told Penny about this weekend. The school never reached out to her because I'm eighteen and don't need her permission. I grab a piece of paper from my desk and write her a note:

Left for a school trip to NYC with the team. Be back late Sunday.

I drop it on the counter as we quietly exit the apartment. Chloe jumps as Mrs. Weddle pops up at the top of the stairs. "Good morning, James. And our other football star Miss Jenkins! Are we sneaking around this morning?"

"No Mrs. Weddle. We have a team trip to New York City and just needed to stop home quick to change."

"Naughty boy out all night," she says, leaning in and winking at Chloe. "I promise to keep your secret." Mrs. Weddle shuffles to her apartment and disappears behind the door. We jog down the stairs and jump in Chloe's Jeep.

"She fucking scared the shit out of me. And how the hell does she know my name?"

"I am now coming to the conclusion that my neighbor might be a bit of a gossip. I'm sure by the time we're back the whole building will know about my new girlfriend."

Chloe rolls her eyes. "No offense, but barf."

We arrive at the school about ten minutes before the bus leaves. When we walk up, Julie and Mark are standing at the door taking a headcount. "James! We missed you last night,"

Julie says, leaning in and giving me a big hug. "I hope it had nothing to do with why Grady was a bit pissy this morning."

"Julie, stop making assumptions and gossiping." Mark leans in and also gives me a hug. "I already put your bag under the bus so you are good to get on." He swipes the Beacon Donuts bag out of Chloe's hand, reaching in and ripping off a piece of her strawberry frosted. He salutes her with it after passing the bag back.

"Thanks Mark," I say, giving him a slight smile. Despite my irritation with Grady at the moment, it was near impossible act the same towards Mark and Julie.

Chloe and I enter the bus, her walking in front of me. Three rows from the back Grady's sitting in a seat by himself. He smiles at me and waves but as Chloe takes her seat, I plop down next to her. Three hours is a long time to be trapped in potentially awkward conversation. The bus engine comes to life and the chaperones climb on the bus.

"Hi Pumpkin!" Mr. Jenkins says, waving at Chloe. This causes a ripple of laughter throughout the bus. "Alright, we have a three-hour bus ride ahead of us. You were all warned to pee before getting on this bus. We are only making one stop midway. This is your last warning to go use that porta potty if you need to pee." No one moves, so the chaperones take their seats and the bus starts out of the parking lot.

"I love you and all but I'm putting my headphones in. Need to zone out and catch up on my murder podcast." Chloe sticks her earbuds in and leans against the window. I steal a quick glance to the back of the bus, and notice Dana took the

61

empty seat next to Grady. Who is, in fact, still staring in my direction.

I pull my headphones over my ears and find my sleepytime playlist, turning it on in hopes of getting a nap in before the city.

And quite a nap I had. I slept right through the rest stop and woke up as people were standing to exit the bus. "I have to say, that was pretty impressive. You were fucking out cold." Chloe says as she puts her headphones away. We stand and join the line, eventually making it off the bus.

Mark and Julie step back and face the entire group. Mark whistles and everyone goes quiet. "Here is the plan. This is going to be a very hands-off day for you today. I am hoping you don't betray this trust we are bestowing upon you. You have some minimal rules to abide by. Do not leave Manhattan. Do not go off on your own, try to stay in groups of at least 3 or 4. Do not get in a stranger's car unless it's an Uber, Lyft, or taxi. But try to use the subway as much as possible. Do not go into bars and do not drink alcohol. And be back to the hotel no later than nine for final headcount. We are handing each of you an envelope which contains a hundred dollars to use on lunch, dinner, and transportation. Anything you spend outside of that is your responsibility. Oh, and do not under any circumstances do something to get yourselves arrested. Are we clear?" A grumble of agreements flows through the team. "Okay. We will take care of getting the bags to your rooms, and will have your room keys when you come back to the hotel. Now go have fun."

Twelve

The team immediately separates out into cliques, and eventually it's just Grady, Davis, Rob, Dana, Chloe, and I. "NYC crew? Where to first? Should we make a list of things we wanna do?" Rob pulls out his phone and opens the Notes app, starting a new checklist. He passes the phone around in a circle, and I'm the last to get it. The list has Central Park, Empire State Building, The Met, Rockefeller Center, Chelsea Market, Good Cupcakes, Food. I hand the phone back to Rob. "You don't want to add anything?"

"I don't know much about the city so I'll follow the group's lead."

"I'm assuming no one signed up for a college tour," Grady asks, which the group's silence amounts to a no. "Okay, so plugging these things in and they are all relatively close to each other. Well, except for Chelsea Market. Should we take the subway down there and then walk back up after?"

The subway was...interesting. Outside of a bus I've never taken public transportation, and was taken aback by just how many people there were. Yes, the city in general has people everywhere, but there was something different about being squished against strangers underground that hit different.

When we get to Chelsea Market, it takes my breath away. The sheer variety of food options is overwhelming but amazing at the same time. A store dedicated to hot sauces, which Rob and Davis immediately run to. A store full of vintage goods which peaks Chloe and Dana's attention. That leaves Grady alone with me for the first time since the party.

"Do you want to check out the bakeshop?" he asks, pointing over to a case full of croissants.

"Sure," I respond, heading into the bakery. The smell inside makes me salivate almost instantly. "Holy fuck. Look at those croissants." I've only ever had bland, probably day-old plain croissants. The case has so many flavors - pistachio cream, pumpkin cream, Nutella, peanut butter chocolate. I can literally feel the envelope of money in my pocket begging to be opened.

"What are you going to get?" Grady looks at me while I stare into the case.

"Oh, I probably won't."

"Why not? This is literally what the allowance they gave us was meant for."

When I was handed that envelope of money it was like being given a full night's tips. Which was great, since I was missing three shifts coming on this trip. Sam and Mitch didn't give me any issue about it, especially when they found out

Grady and I were sharing a room. That, of course, was a whole other bundle of awkwardness that would be unpacked later.

"I'm not very hungry," I say abruptly, turning and heading out the door. There's a bookstore next to the bake shop, so I peruse the display of books on clearance outside. Minutes later Grady pops out of the bake shop, large bag in hand.

"I didn't know what you wanted so I bought one of each of those croissants. You can have one if you tell me what's up."

"It's nothing." I pick up a book and pretend to read the back of it.

"James." I feel his hand on my back. I turn and Grady is frowning, shoulders slumped. "Tell me."

I put the book down. "Going on this trip was very exciting. But it's also very costly. Not in the sense that I had to pay to come. I realize the school and PTA and parents paid for it, and I probably benefited more than others. But I'm also missing three work shifts being here, which is kinda a lot of money."

"It's only one weekend. You deserve to have fun."

"What I deserve and what I need are two different things. I need to go to college next year. While I deserve to have parents who will pay my way, I need to save as much money as possible to make it happen. It's different for you. You have parents who will pay for you to go anywhere you want to go. Hell, you'll probably get a scholarship for football. I have one parent that I can't stand, who I'm pretty sure can't stand me, and all I want to do is put as much distance between her and I as I can. Which. Costs. Money."

We fall into a silence, which despite our scene hasn't even tracked on the radar of anyone around us. "James, can we sit?" He gestures to a bench outside the bake shop. I sit down, catching sight of Davis in the hot sauce store fanning his face after putting a chip in his mouth. A pistachio croissant appears in front of my face. My stomach rumbles and I accept defeat, taking it from Grady. "I'm sorry. It's going to sound elitist for me to say this but I wasn't considering all that. College costs, needing to work to make it an option and having spending money. I've received an allowance since I was ten that has gradually gotten bigger throughout the years, and I just didn't put two and two together. Even on that first day of school when I gave you twenty bucks. It didn't mean anything to me, but it probably turned your day around. But I could see how it may have been embarrassing to rely on a stranger for lunch money."

I take a bite of the croissant and it's probably one of the best things I've ever tasted. I pass it to Grady. "You need to try this," he takes a bite and his eyes practically roll back in his head. I can see his inner struggle until he slowly passes it back to me.

"Just, please promise me in the future that you will call me out for being an asshole and not just avoid me. I'm not sure what Mom and Dad would do if you stopped coming around. All Mom talks about is wanting to start a book club with you based on your book recommendations. I can't even remember the last time I picked up a book that wasn't for school."

"It's not hard, you know. To pick up a book and read. There are literally thousands of them right in front of us."

"Can you recommend some to me?"

We leave the bookstore with a variety of books from Blake Crouch, Karen McManus, and Grady Hendrix. I kept him away from some of my favorite LGBT authors, not wanting to push something that may not be there.

"And I'm sorry for whatever caused you to leave the party last night. If it was something I did, please know it was unintentional. I just got caught up in conversation and lost track of time, and realized you were gone."

"Don't worry about it." The other four have gathered outside the bookstore. They all are carrying an obscene number of bags, Davis and Rob's faces are still flush from their hot sauce tastings.

"Nothing for you James?" Dana asked, noticing my empty hand.

"Well Grady literally bought the whole bakeshop so I felt like I could just steal some of his." Grady smirks in my direction. "So, where to next?"

We walk Central Park, where I am told it is a tourist must to get a hot dog from a cart. I insist I only will do it if everyone else does and they do, despite Dana's initial hesitation. "I'm part-time vegetarian and while I do occasionally eat meat, hot dogs concern me." In the end she ate half of it, discreetly throwing the other half away when she thought we weren't looking.

We decide that the Empire State Building is a bit overrated. It was originally recommended by Rob, who ended up staying as far away from the edge as possible. When we approach the Met we stare at the building, and hesitate entering. "Does anyone actually care enough about art?" Dana asks, and we all laugh. We wander Manhattan and find a Dave and Buster's, which we go into and split off into pairs. Grady's impressed by my skee ball abilities. Chloe and Rob get into a very heated game of air hockey. And Dana and Davis realize that not only are they equally matched at beer pong, but should be a team going forward at parties.

I have spent about a third of what was in the envelope, which was only possible with Grady picking up some of the costs throughout the day. He bought the croissants, and we used his game card at Dave and Buster's. We bicker amongst each other on what we're getting for dinner, before collapsing into a booth ripping at the seams at some hole in the wall burger place. The menu consisted of exactly six burger options, with the choice of fries or tots.

We end up ordering one of each and sharing all of the burgers, creating our own little tasting menu. I sit back once I've finished eating, taking in the moment. I feel like we entered this day as two groups but now we have merged into one. Something way more than I ever expected to happen coming to Beacon.

"So, we have about an hour and a half to kill before we have to go to the hotel. Was there anything else left on the list?" Rob pulls out his phone. "Right. One more thing."

I make a disclaimer that I have only ever been ice skating once in my life. And it quickly became very clear I was the least experienced of the group. Grady, Davis, and Rob had actually become friends due to a youth hockey league they played in as kids. Dana had taken ice skating lessons, which just so happened to finish right before youth hockey practice started. And when Chloe would follow her and Grady's parents to youth hockey, she demanded that she also take ice skating lessons.

The one time I had skated was on a lake in Minnesota when I was a kid. And it showed. It took me approximately four seconds on the ice until I fell right on my face. Chloe burst out laughing, leaning against the rink wall. Grady offered his hand and I took it, him pulling me up. "Break anything?" He looks me over. "I think you're fine. Until you get the hang of things you will link arms with one of us. Start with me and we will do a few loops around the rink."

As soon as I was confirmed fine, the others took off. Rob was chasing Davis around the rink, trying to knock him over. Dana and Chloe were leisurely looping around, occasionally adding a little spin to see what tricks they still remembered. I, not begrudgingly, hung onto Grady's arm and selfishly didn't let go as we skated around.

By the time we reach the hotel it's 8:58. Mark, Julie, and Chloe's parents are sitting at the bar drinking martinis. They notice us and wave us over. "Cutting it close!" Mr. Jenkins says, pointing at his watch. "It looks like you kids had fun. Glad you took advantage of the day. The rest of the team was back here around seven with bags of McDonald's and headed up to their rooms."

Julie reaches into her purse and pulls out three envelopes. "Room key time. Grady and James are in 1109, Rob and Davis in 1117, and the ladies are in 1105. Go get some rest. We are meeting in the lobby for breakfast at nine. We want to be on the road no later than 10:30 in case there is traffic."

When we reach the eleventh floor, Chloe turns to me and Grady. "We should exchange one room key, just in case one of us oversleeps we can wake up the others?"

"What about Rob and Davis?"

Dana leans in. "Rob brought running gear for tomorrow. Like he's legit excited to go for a run in the city. On his day off from practice while on a trip. What a monster."

We say our good nights and head off into our own rooms, letting the door shut behind us.

Thirteen

We have spent the last two hours in the room watching college football, UCLA now playing USC. Grady intensely watches the quarterback, trying to predict each play. I look up from my phone when the field goal unit comes on and say "I bet you they are going to kick the ball here." I'm suddenly smacked in the face with a pillow.

"Have you not been enjoying my play-by-play predictions?"

"No Tony Romo, I have not." That gets a chuckle out of Grady.

The game is about to hit halftime. "Do you know what I could go for?"

"What?" I say, turning to face him.

"McDonald's. Ever since Chloe's dad brought it up, I can't stop thinking about some nuggies and fries."

"Let's go to McDonald's." I type McDonald's into Maps. "The one in Times Square is literally a six-minute walk from here."

"What if my parents are down in the lobby still? Or we get caught sneaking out?"

After putting on my shoes I rest my hand on his shoulder. "You are the golden boy. Nothing is going to happen."

There wasn't much to worry about. Not only were all of our chaperones out of the lobby, but the lobby bar and outside seating were packed. It allowed us an easy way to exit the building undetected.

Out on the street the city was loud and active. It was hard to not be amazed by it, being used to quiet small towns my whole life. We start walking towards the center of Times Square, dodging people on the sidewalk. A man to my left is using empty coffee cans and chopsticks as drums, to a tune that's familiar but I can't place it. The whole place just seems so alive.

Soon enough we are at McDonald's, and there is quite the line. "Shit," Grady says. "Look at that line. We don't have to wait."

"Grady, where else do we have to be? Laying in the room watching TV? You want McDonald's, we are getting you McDonald's."

Shockingly the line moves pretty fast. It split in two when we entered, one for using the self-order kiosks and the other for ordering at the counter. The kiosk line is about half the length so we head that way. In a few minutes we are ordering at the kiosk. Grady gets a ten-piece nugget meal with a root beer. "You want anything?"

"Just a Diet Coke."

"Do we need to have a chat again?" Grady's face is stern.

"Grady, could it be possible I'm just not that hungry? And, if I end up getting hungry, there are like sixteen croissants left in the room."

"Fair," he says, paying with his credit card. We head up to the counter and wait for our order to be called. "It's so crazy that with everything to eat in the city all these people still just want McDonald's, myself included."

"It's a comfort food," I say. "Growing up McDonald's was like the treat my mom got for me. I'm pretty sure when I was little the majority of my toys were Happy Meal toys."

"That's so sad," a thirty-something girl says standing across from us. "Sorry, didn't mean to eavesdrop, but even Happy Meal toys took a nosedive after the 90s."

Our number's called, so Grady grabs the food and we head outside. We spot an open bench and take a seat. Grady starts eating while I people watch. Suddenly, the billboard in front of me turns to a movie preview and I almost immediately recognize it must be for the *Breaking the Moon* movie. Oh no, the casting is all wrong. Will I still see it? Yes. Will I likely be happy? Likely no.

"Okay, your face just went through something. What were you just watching? What is *Breaking the Moon*?"

"Oh, it's my favorite book. And I think I just didn't agree with some of the casting choices."

"I don't remember you grabbing me that one earlier today."

"Umm...I didn't think it would be something you would like."

"Okay. For one, rude. Second, I would be willing to give it a shot if the book is literally your favorite book in the world."

"Noted."

Grady finishes his meal and throws the bag in the bin across from us. "Since we're already out, did you want to walk around a bit?"

"No longer scared to get caught?"

"Ehh," Grady says, "damage is already done."

We walk for a bit down the road, heading further from the hotel but still in Times Square. We stop in front of a screen that's playing the second half of the USC-UCLA game. UCLA must have scored to start the half because they were losing when we left.

"Can I ask you something?" Grady says.

"Sure."

"Are you into Chloe?"

I pause, considering this question. Is he into Chloe? Because that is going to crash hard for him given Chloe's brotherly opinion of him. Or is he being protective of her? "Absolutely not. We are just friends."

"Why not?"

"Why am I not into Chloe?"

"Yes. I am asking you why you aren't into her."

I'm suddenly feeling very warm. This conversation has escalated quickly into something I don't think I'm ready to talk about.

"James."

"I...umm...I'm just not. She's not my type."

"Then what is your type."

It feels like the city has slowed down, gone suspiciously quiet. All I can hear is my panicked heart beating in my chest.

"Look at me," Grady says.

I look up at him and he is staring intensely at me. "I...Grady..."

And in a flash Grady moves forward and his lips crash into mine. His arms wrap around my back and he pulls me into him. I feel my body unclench. I push forward into him, wrapping my arm around his waist, my other hand moving up and running through his hair. His hand is moving up and down my back until he pushes me against a telephone pole, my head making a clunking noise.

He pulls away from me. "Are you alright?"

I just stare at him. "I'm not sure how to answer that."

He grabs my hand and starts running down the street.

The journey back to the hotel is a blur, mainly because we sprinted through Times Square, through the lobby, and impatiently rode the elevator. When our room door shuts our hands are all over each other. Clothes flying in all directions. Falling onto the bed. Ripping Grady's boxer briefs off.

Fumbling under the sheets while UCLA scores two more touchdowns. Smiles ear to ear, disappearing into each other. Two bodies intertwined fueled by months of wanting and need. It was every single thing I have wanted and hoped it would be.

Eventually we become tired and lay back. He turns to me, without saying anything, and wraps his arms around me. It's perfect.

Fourteen

Sunlight is starting to peek through the blinds as I roll over, and smack right into Grady. Oh shit. That actually happened. Grady opens his eyes and smiles at me. "I see that panicked look on your face. You don't need to panic."

"Grady..." I start and trail off, staring at him as he looks at me.

"I kissed you, remember? In the middle of Times Square. We weren't drinking so you can't spin this. I kissed you because I wanted to, and had wanted to for some time. I also did those other things to you because I wanted to." I blush, and my body reacts to the memories of last night. Grady's eyes widen, and then he disappears under the covers. I pull the covers over my head and start what can only be described as a sexually charged wrestling match. Which is really hot and isn't helping. All I know is I'm glad this happened after two months of football conditioning, when I'm at my peak physically.

"Oh my god!" We stop moving, our eyes locking under the covers as we hear our room door click shut. "Oh my god oh my god it happened! Oh my god it actually fucking happened!"

I pop my head out from under the sheets to find Chloe standing by the door, her eyes moving from me, to the clothes strewn about everywhere, to the fact that Grady's bed remains untouched. "Chloe, umm...can we have a moment?"

"Yes of course, of course. I'll jump into the bathroom so you can gather yourselves. Although you should know we are supposed to be downstairs for breakfast in like five minutes."

"Okay, well Grady and I are going to need the bathroom to shower, which won't work if you're in there. Can you please, oh I don't know, wait in the hall?"

Grady finally sticks his head out from under the covers. "Hey Chloe."

"Holy shit I still can't believe you manifested this into existence. Shit. I can't go out into the hall. Davis is out there. He was waiting for me, or us, to go down to breakfast."

"Okay," I say, "Chloe, you are going to go sit on the other bed and face the wall while we run into the bathroom. I don't know what to tell you about Davis other than don't let him in this room."

"Got it." Chloe goes to the bed and sits facing the wall. We each grab a pair of underwear and run to the bathroom. "Oh hey!" Chloe calls out. "Is any of this contaminated or can I help you clean up?"

We anticipated showering together would be more efficient, but between needing to shift for water usage and getting handsy in between, it would have been faster to shower separately. We both emerge from the bathroom in our underwear, where Chloe has laid out our jerseys and jeans for the game. "Personally, I don't want either of you. But I do somehow see this as super hot."

I throw the jersey over my head, scowling at Chloe. "While I know you are very excited for me, or both of us, this literally just happened like last night. We need time to process it, what it is, where we go from here. Then we can circle back and have the talk with you."

"Ugh you are no fun," she says, zipping up my bag.

"Did you think that was just some one-time fling?" Grady says, hurt on this face.

"No no no, I did not say that. We literally just woke up and now we have a Chloe in the mix. I think it's just you and I need to have a conversation about last night to make sure we are completely on the same page. With whatever we decide. Wait, when did the tables turn and I'm now the rational one?"

"Probably because you got dick last night."

"CHLOE!" We both yell, only to be greeted with a smile.

"We should head down to breakfast, seeing how you two made us late."

On the way down to breakfast Davis won't stop yammering about how we are going to be in trouble for being late to breakfast. But, when we get down there, half the team is still missing. I spot Julie and she waves at me, and then I suddenly feel awkward. From last night to now I had totally forgotten they were our chaperones, and the things their son and I did last night–"

"Get it together Jamie," Grady says, clasping a hand on my shoulder.

"Get what together?" Davis asks, looking over at the breakfast buffet.

"Yes *Jamie*, get what together?" Chloe says, stifling a laugh.

"Fuck off all of you. And my name is not Jamie, it's James." I walk towards Mark and Julie, leaving Davis confused with a cackling Grady and Chloe, who is catching her breath while leaning on a table.

"You four are late, but still earlier than most of the team. Hence why I told you all nine when I meant nine-thirty," Julie stands up, grabbing her plate. "And I see fresh bacon has been put out."

The four of us drop our stuff on a table a safe distance away from the others. In line I am reaching for pancakes when I feel Grady's hip bump into mine. I give him side eye, grab some pancakes and bacon, and head back to the table. Chloe and Davis are already well into their plates. Grady shuffles in shortly after. Chloe's eyes keep shifting back and forth between Grady and I, and a silence has blanketed the table.

"Okay, why is everyone acting so fucking weird?" Davis drops his fork on his plate and he's staring at the two of us. "Grady warning you to get your shit together, the table being quiet. What the fuck did I miss? Did you all hang out last night and left Rob and I out?"

"Davis, I can guarantee you that Dana and I watched three episodes of Love Island and passed out."

"Okay, then what's your excuse?" His fork is back in his hand and pointed in our direction.

"Davis, what are you even talking about?" I turn to look if they refilled the hash browns when Chloe gasps. "What?"

"Oh nothing."

Davis laughs. "Ah ha! You were up to something last night. James has a giant hickey on his neck!"

"Jesus Christ," I say, shooting daggers in Grady's direction. Grady averting my gaze while stifling a laugh.

Davis immediately switches from laughing to a look of shock. "Oh. Oh! Ohhh! It all makes sense now. I can't believe I didn't see it before!"

Grady leans forward. "Whatever great revelation you have, can we keep it at a much lower volume? Seeing how two sets of the table's parents are sitting twenty feet away from us."

Davis shoots a quick look over to the chaperones, and leans in closer to us. "Are you two, like…doing it?"

Chloe bursts out laughing. "I'm so sorry. The way Davis asked that just hit me funny. Fucking Davis."

I look at Grady and he just shrugs. "Okay fine there is something going on here. That is very new. Very new like last night Davis. So, let's keep this within this circle."

Chloe leans in. "Coming in with the truth bomb. James has been crushing on Grady since the first day of school." She makes an exploding noise with her hands up in the air.

"Chloe! That is a you and me need to know item!"

81

Grady is grinning ear to ear. "Wait. Was it when I was your knight in shining armor from the moment you stepped in Beacon High?"

I put my head down on the table.

"In all honesty guys I am happy for you. It does throw our dynamic off a bit so it will take getting used to. And I'm used to being Grady's favorite so I'm going to hate that. But man James, you have been hanging around a lot. You are one thirsty dog."

"Uhh," I start, pointing to Grady. "If anyone is thirsty, it's this kid. Inviting me to the lunch table, practically recruiting me for the team, inviting me to Friday night hangs. Do I need to keep going?"

"Guys, here come Dana and Rob. Let's table this for now and we can talk about it later. Although James, we need to do something about that hickey."

About ten minutes later Chloe has finished touching up my neck to cover the welt Grady left there, and we are now loading on the bus to head to the stadium. This time, however, I choose the open seat next to Grady.

The game ends up being a blowout win by the Giants, beating the Cowboys 35-6. The bus ride home is quiet, everyone exhausted from the overnight. I scroll through my Instagram feed, seeing the photos everyone took over the past day. No one else but us posted photos outside the game. Us skating, us with our burgers, at Dave and Buster's. Everyone just looks so happy.

Fifteen

The two weeks after the New York trip were brutal. Our final game of the regular season was that Friday, which we clobbered Portsmouth 63-10. This only fired up Coach Peters more the following week, going into our semifinals game on Saturday. It seemed like the whole town came out for it the way the stands were filled. And we did not disappoint, knocking out Cumberland 47-13.

I had successfully avoided going to Ralph's for over two months, but that luck came to an end the Sunday before the championship game. Sam and Mitch had closed Tipsy Mic for a few days to get some repairs done in the kitchen and update the restaurant layout a bit. When Penny caught wind of this, she told me I had no excuse not to come to dinner.

JAMES: Texting you just in case I get kidnapped or murdered by crazy Ralph
GRADY: Maybe we should have a codeword

GRADY: Like a bat-signal for trouble

GRADY: Like serious trouble tho. Not like help I need a waffle

JAMES: It's settled. Codeword is WAFFLE

GRADY: Now I'm hungry

GRADY: Good luck

I find myself sitting down for dinner at five in Ralph's house, Virtue is sitting across from me, with Penny and Ralph at the heads of the table. Ralph's house is barely in Beacon, sitting far off the road on the edge of Beacon Woods. Behind his house I could see some structures inside the trees but couldn't make out what they were. There was also a large barn at the back of the property, which Penny had told me was where Ralph held his services and meetings.

I look around the inside of the house as I sit at the table. Every single thing is dated. Not in the, 'I'm trying to go for the antique look' or just being thrifty, but more so it just gave off a creepy vibe. I catch Ralph's eye and immediately look down at my empty plate.

"It's so nice of you to join us for dinner tonight, James. Since you are our guest, would you like to say grace?"

"I think I'll leave that to one of you."

Ralph's face falls flat. "Very well. We ask those above us to bless the food we are about to eat. Bless this woman who hath came into our lives and pulled us from darkness. Bless the children that bring us joy at this table, that they do not fall to the impure pressures of today's society. And grace us with health as long as we follow your doctrine."

Penny and Virtue then stand up, take Ralph's plate and make him a full spread. They then do the same for my plate, and end with their own.

That was fucking weird.

Ralph shoves a huge chunk of chicken into his mouth, taking his time chewing while staring at me. "So, James, Penny tells me you are on Beacon's football team. Do you find that rewarding?"

"I don't know if rewarding is the right word, but it's something I'm good at. And I've made some really good friends as a result." Virtue coughs and her lip snarls up. "I'm sorry, Virtue, did you have something to add?"

"I wouldn't say you've made good friends, as you put it. There is nothing good about those people."

"I have heard much of the same James," Ralph says, patting Virtue's hand. "I've heard about the parties and the alcohol and the women that hang around the football team. Not what I would consider to be good traits."

"Is that true James? Are these the types of people you have been hanging around with?"

I look at Penny, with what I can only imagine is a look of disgust. "Well Penny, you might have a better idea if you had bothered to come to a single game this season."

"You will know a boy's place and not speak to your mother in that manner at this table!" Ralph roars, slapping the table. The plates shake, food splattering across the tablecloth.

"And isn't part of religion seeing the good in people? Or is this something you just pick and choose to apply as you like."

"Son, you will shut your mouth if you know what's good for you. And, if you bothered to actually be here with your mother as she starts her journey in Wishing Well, you would know what you are talking about. Instead of sitting at my dinner table talking out the side of your mouth."

"Well, it's a two-way street. She doesn't come to what's important to me and I don't come here with her. I'd say we're even."

The room goes quiet for an extended moment, nothing but the scrapes of forks and knives on plates. I can feel Virtue's eyes on me, but I choose to ignore her.

"And I think we should talk about your course of employment. Your mother tells me you are working down at that restaurant run by those disgusting men. They bring such disgrace to this town."

I pause, collecting my thoughts so I'm not flying fully off the handle. "I heard that Virtue had protested outside an event there. I think it was a speed dating event for the LGBT community?"

"That is correct," Ralph says, his jaw clenching.

"Right. So, Virtue, why were you protesting this?"

Virtue looks over to Ralph. "Well, they are spreading a disease amongst the community. Holding an event like that can be impressionable on children."

I laugh. "Right. The event that was held during the hours where only adults are allowed inside, is impressionable on the children who don't even know what's going on. Got it."

"I've had enough. Penny, you need to control your child before he is brought into this house again. Both you and he have disgraced this dinner table. Bring him home and we will discuss this matter when you return."

"Gladly," I say, pushing my chair back hard enough that it scratches the floor. I can hear Penny pleading with Ralph as I walk out the door.

I'm leaning on the car when Penny walks up. "How dare you act like that to a man who has done so much for us. You have brought disappointment to this family."

"If anything, Penny, you've brought disappointment to this family. That man is a psychopath."

I barely register her hand before it slaps me across the face. "I am your mother and you will show me, Ralph, and Virtue more respect. Otherwise, we will have to talk about consequences."

"You do realize I'm eighteen, don't you? You can pretend to hold some power over me, but I can hang out with whoever I choose, work wherever I want, and make my own decisions. So maybe you need to think about the consequences your actions have on our relationship."

The whole car ride back is silent, outside the hum of the car's engine. I feel my pocket vibrate but do not dare pull out my phone for Penny to see. When the car rolls in the apartment parking lot there are no words exchanged between us. I just get out and the car pulls out of the parking lot. I tap my phone awake.

GRADY: Wanna come over if you're still alive?

Sixteen

Coach Peters is standing in the middle of the Cranston Stadium locker room, all of us huddled around him. We are fully dressed and ready for game time, only fifteen minutes until kickoff. Five until we need to be on the field. My leg is bobbing up and down uncontrollably. I don't think I've ever been this nervous.

"Team, we've been here before. Well, most of you. We came up a bit short last year, which I know was devastating. But I know this and you know this. We are a better team than we were last year. Grady has been lighting up defenses with some baffling side arm passes. Cody and Quentin have formed into one of the best backfield duos the state has ever seen. Benji and Jeremy have more sacks combined than any team has had in the past ten years in Rhode Island. And I think we all can be forever thankful for open tryouts in gym class this year. Chloe has the highest punting average in the state and James is the state's leading scorer with a near perfect field goal percentage on the season. What I'm trying to say is that we have all the pieces.

Let's make sure they fit together and let's go out there and bring that championship trophy home to Beacon tonight! On three!"

"One two three COLTS!" The room erupts as players jump up and down heading out of the locker room.

"Are you as nervous as I am?" Chloe asks as we head down the tunnel to the field.

"I just keep worrying that the final play will come down to me." The noise of the crowd is pulsating through the tunnel.

"You've been in that position before and done just fine. I'm more worried we will win the coin flip and I'll have to punt to start the game. I don't want to fuck up the first play."

"I'm sure you'll put the ball down on like the five-yard line. And..." We walk out onto the field and the view is breathtaking. The stands are completely full, family and friends jumping up and down screaming, holding signs and wearing blue and white. Literally breathtaking.

"Holy shit that's a lot of people." Chloe says.

"AND HERE ARE YOUR BEACON HIGH COLTS, LED BY CAPTAINS GRADY TOMLINSON, DAVIS ANDERSON, AND JEREMY FRASIER!" The crowd somehow gets louder as the team fully exits the locker room and lines up on the sideline in front of them. "AND NOW PLEASE STAND FOR THE NATIONAL ANTHEM, WHICH WILL BE SUNG BY BEACON HIGH'S A CAPELLA GROUP THE PITCHERS."

The flag is flying above our fan section so we turn and face them. The Pitchers begin singing and I feel hands grab both of mine, the team linked together while the anthem is sung. I scan the crowd, knowing that Penny and the whack jobs won't show but just to make sure. Earlier I had thought I would be disappointed if she didn't show, but at this point she would be more of a liability if anything.

The Pitchers finish and the crowd again erupts in applause. "Go Grady and James!" Sitting in the first row pretty much on top of us are Mark and Julie, holding up a big sign with both of our names and pictures on it. I feel myself tear up a bit but I fight it back. At least someone came out to support me. I wave to them before turning around to face the field again. Grady, Davis, and Jeremy are at midfield with three of the East Greenwich players and one of the officials.

"East Greenwich, you will be calling the coin toss. Heads or tails?" One of the East Greenwich players leans in and says something to the referee. "The call is for tails." He flips the coin in the air and it lands in front of Jeremy. "The coin is heads. Beacon wins the coin toss."

"We would like to defer," Grady says.

"Fucking Grady," Chloe murmurs. She leans her head left and right and I hear a loud crack.

"You got this." I give her arm a quick squeeze. I take a seat on the bench with most of the offense as Chloe and the Special Teams players head to the field. Grady flops down on the bench next to me

"I can tell you're nervous," he says, throwing an arm across my shoulder and leaning in close. "You're one of the best players I've played with on this team over the past four years. And I'm not saying that because I'm biased or anything." He smiles at me, briefly distracting me.

"JENKINS LINES UP FOR THE KICKOFF. AND. HERE. WE. GO!" The ball leaves Chloe's foot, flying towards the end zone. "JENKINS DOING WHAT SHE DOES BEST, A FAIR CATCH BY EAST GREENWICH AT THE TWO-YARD LINE." The bench is jumping up and down, yelling as Chloe runs off the field to join us on the sideline.

"Great job Jenkins!" Coach Peters yells, clapping as he paces the sideline.

The crowd goes quiet as the offense and defense line up. The ball hits the East Greenwich quarterback's hands and he drops back, scanning the field. Benji comes flying on his right and slams him to the ground. "IT'S A SAFETY! A SAFETY! HAVE WE EVER SEEN A SAFETY SCORED IN A CHAMPIONSHIP GAME?!?!" The crowd behind us has reached deafening volume.

In the next possession, Grady manages to move the ball down the field pretty efficiently despite East Greenwich's strong defense. The ball ends up on the twenty-five-yard line for fourth down, and Coach is standing in front of me. "You're up Stockton."

I slowly jog onto the field and I take in the view of the crowd and the end zone. Oddly, my nerves seem to have subsided a bit. Chloe is waiting, kneeling on the ground. I backup and take my stance, and everything seems to slow down. The ball is snapped, Chloe grabbing it and placing it down. I breathe out, run up, and smash the ever-loving hell out of the ball. Right between the middle of the uprights. The crowd is jumping up and down. "AND WE HAVE OUR FIRST

OFFENSIVE SCORE OF THE GAME OFF OF STOCKTON'S FOOT! FIVE NOTHING COLTS!" Chloe high fives me as I trot off the field, Mark and Julie's sign catching my eye before I take a seat on the bench.

The rest of the half goes by in a blur, involving two more successful field goal attempts and two extra points by me. We head into the locker room up 25-10.

"Good work team. Everything is clicking so far. I'd like to give a special shoutout to Titus for scoring the first ever safety in a Rhode Island State Championship!" Benji does a little bow to us. "And to Stockton, for scoring eleven points in the first half. He needs two more points to take the state record for points in a season! It's up to you Grady to get him that record!

"Got it Coach!" Coach pulls in Grady and the receivers and they start working out plays for the second half.

Chloe plops down next to me. "So, per usual, I heard some asshole in the stands for East Greenwich make a comment about a girl on the team in the second quarter." Chloe rolls her eyes as she readjusts her cleat.

"Just jealous they don't have the best punter in the state on their team."

"Damn right," she says, "and probably hated it even more when I responded by putting the ball on the three-yard line. Their punter hasn't even put the ball inside the twenty once tonight."

I grab my phone out of my locker. Coach doesn't allow us normally to have phones in the locker room on game days, but thought we might need a distraction with nerves running high.

JULIE: AWESOME FIELD GOAL
MARK: YOU TWO ARE KILLING IT!
JULIE: GO GET THAT RECORD!

After finding out about how close I was to the record I wanted to keep it quiet, to not bring attention to myself. Then the school put it in their newsletter that goes out to both students and parents. And obviously Julie reads the newsletter, and the local paper which also picked up the story of all the state records Beacon was challenging this season. Touchdowns by a quarterback (both for season and career), team rushing yards, total team sacks, and how close I was for total points for a season. The total points record was one of the longer standing records for football in the state. I had even brought it up to Penny after the newsletter, knowing she doesn't read them, and it didn't even phase her. She mentioned something about a fundraiser Ralph was hosting in response. That should have been the indicator early on she wouldn't be attending any of the remaining games.

The group disperses, with Coach and Grady taking seats on either side of me. "Two minutes left until we are due back on the field. We have a fifteen-point lead going into the second half. Keep the game tight. Don't try anything flashy and just stay focused. We are up by multiple scores and I know, in my heart, you have the ability to hold. We've got the ball to start the half so keep the momentum up. On three."

"One two three COLTS!"

Seventeen

Except it didn't go that way.

On the second play of the half Cody fumbles the ball and East Greenwich returns it for a touchdown. With the ball back, we're only able to move it to our own thirty-yard line. The ball's mishandled on the fourth down snap and Chloe has to scramble to get the kick off, the ball only going twenty-five yards.

East Greenwich's running back, on the first play, torches our defense for a fifty-five-yard touchdown run. They go for the two-point conversion and get it. After some defensive back and forth, we are now tied 25-25 with three minutes left in the third quarter.

"Obviously things haven't been going great out there this half," Grady said on the sideline, "but you heard Coach at halftime. We can win this game. We will win this game. They've been loading up the left side of the line knowing Cody prefers to run that direction. Coach...what if we put both Cody and

Quentin in the backfield and lean left but have Quentin run right?"

"Grady, please focus on your own play and not coaching the game. But that is a pretty good idea. Fine. Let's try that after having Cody run one play."

It works. Cody's run on first-down goes three yards, but Quentin runs for twenty-six on Grady's play. Grady connects with Devon for a thirteen-yard reception and then Adam for another fourteen yards.

Cody and Quentin are stuffed on the next two downs and Grady's pass on third down to Petey just misses his fingertips. It's fourth down on the twenty-yard line. "Chip shot Stockton. You could hit this in your sleep."

Chloe and I run out on the field, with Chloe crouching in position. "Don't get in your head. You've got this."

It's a short kick. A short kick to take the lead. A short kick to claim the state record. Coach said there were going to be scouts from colleges at the game today. While the line got set, I found myself scanning the sidelines to see if I could pick any of them out of the crowd. Focus. The ball could be snapped at any second.

The snap is on target, with a clean hold before my foot connects with the football. The ball starts hooking left as it heads to the goal post. The ball hit the left upright....

"AND IT'S GOOD! BEACON TAKES THE LEAD AND KICKER JAMES STOCKTON BREAKS THE STATE RECORD FOR MOST POINTS IN A SEASON!"

I'm staring at the scoreboard in disbelief, 28-25 at the end of the third, when I am lifted off the ground. Petey and Kyle are carrying me to the sidelines as the team jumps around me. Mark and Julie are screaming their heads off in the stands. I'm let down as we get to the benches and Grady runs up and hugs me. "Proud of you," he whispers in my ear.

"Congrats Stockton! The team effort on that drive was exactly what I was talking about at halftime. Maybe we should let Tomlinson give pep talks more often! But we have one quarter to go and we have just a three-point lead. Let's play smart out there. They have been favoring the right side of the field on passing plays, so let's make sure to cover the receivers well lining up on that side. Their running back has been limping a bit so I expect them to throw the ball a bit more this quarter."

Coach was right. East Greenwich struggled out of the gate with our defense covering the right side of the field tighter. But their defense also stepped it up, sacking Grady twice and holding us to two three-and-outs.

Grady slumps down next to me on the bench. Four minutes left in the game and we were still up by three. "I'm exhausted. I hit the ground hard on that last sack and can still feel it down my left leg."

"Well," I whisper, "if you can manage to make it through the game, I'll make sure to massage it later for you."

"Absolutely not," he said, "that shit is going to hurt.

The East Greenwich side of the stands are screaming. East Greenwich's quarterback faked out our defense and ran the ball for 39 yards to the sixteen-yard line.

"Shit," Chloe says. Soon after, they're in the end zone for a touchdown, leaving us down 32-28 with only three minutes to go and one timeout left.

"Huddle up offense," Coach says. I look around and it's not just Grady, but the whole team looks spent. Davis is trying to massage out his leg and I notice Rob's arm is bleeding. "I don't have anything different to say now than what I've already said here today. This is likely the last drive of the game, the last drive ever for most of you. No matter the outcome, I want to say how proud I am of this team. I know I put a lot of pressure on you this season, but you have taken it in stride and have exceeded all of my expectations. Just go out there and do what you do best."

Things are clicking. Cody for an eight-yard run. Davis with an eleven-yard catch. Rob and Devon with back-to-back receptions of twelve and seventeen yards. Thirty-two seconds left on the clock on the twenty-seven-yard line with the ball in Grady's hands. He doesn't see the defender on his right as he scans the field. Grady hits the ground and the ball comes out. Luckily Davis jumps on top of it for the recovery.

When Coach calls timeout there are thirteen seconds left on the clock. As the team makes it back to the bench, Grady is whispering in Coach's ear. Coach's eyes go big as Grady is talking to him, but he nods in agreement.

"I know that play was ugly. I didn't see their defensive end until I was heading to the ground. Team, we have one play left. I have Coach's permission to run a play a few of us have been working on outside of practice."

Shit. The play. THE play.

Over the past couple of weeks Grady had been watching a lot of game footage on YouTube, specifically around various trick plays to throw off defenses. The types of plays that work in a one-shot scenario.

Grady's obsession turned into Davis, Grady, and I trying out a couple of options until finally settling on the only one we successfully pulled off on the first try. The basics were that I line up in the backfield with Cody and Davis behind Grady. Kyle would snap the ball directly to Davis, who would run a few feet before flipping the ball back to me. Cody would swing by me and fake taking the ball, and start running up the field. By this point, Grady should be running full speed towards the end zone waiting for my pass. My passing abilities were really the one thing that needed work, given up until about four weeks ago I have never thrown a football. But the ultimate hope was that Grady would catch the ball for the go-ahead score, adding to Grady's already stellar highlight reel.

Grady finishes explaining how the play works. "Wait. You want the kicker, who hadn't even stepped on a football field until two months ago, to throw his first pass on the final play...of the championship game? Are you fucking insane?"

"Correct Darius. That's the plan, and I may be fucking insane." Coach nods towards Grady. "But I trust Grady that they have indeed practiced this, and that he is comfortable enough passing the reins over. In the final play of his high school football career. Now get out there and win this game!"

I look back to the stands and lock eyes with Mark. *The play?!* He mouths. Mark had watched us run the play many times, often providing some insight on fine tuning it. I nod, and turn to run onto the field. I line up to the left behind Grady, with Davis in the middle and Cody to the right. Grady looks at me, asking if I'm ready. I nod, and he calls for the ball.

Grady is in motion as Davis runs to the left, who turns and lobs the ball in my hands. I shift to the right by Cody, taking note that Grady is beyond the first line of defenders. I see a flash of green to my right. I crouch down just as one of the East Greenwich defenders reaches out, causing them to fall to my left. I run further out to the right, look downfield, and launch the ball in Grady's direction before getting slammed into the ground. I look up and see the ball shaky in the air, with what appears to be an impossibly long hang time. The crowd has gone utterly silent, watching the ball sail through the air. Watching the ball land right in Grady's arms as he crosses into the end zone.

"Oh! My! God! The Colts did it! What a comeback! To win on a touchdown pass from kicker James Stockton to quarterback Grady Tomlinson! What. An. Ending! The Colts win! I don't believe it!

Eighteen

If dinner at Ralph's before the championship game was tense, it was nothing compared to the blowout over Thanksgiving and Christmas.

I tell Penny Thanksgiving morning that I planned on splitting the day between Ralph's and Grady's house.

"Absolutely not. Thanksgiving is for family, which we will be celebrating at Ralph's."

"Ralph and Virtue aren't family. Maybe more so for you, but they're practically strangers to me."

"Whose fault is that?" She snaps, her look a mix of anger and disappointment.

Penny leaves to go to Ralph's around nine to help make the meal. At eleven I felt my phone buzz.

PENNY: Ralph said you either come only here or don't come at all.
PENNY: But he expects you here for noon.

JAMES: I already told Grady's parents I was coming. I guess I'm going there

PENNY: Hope you are happy with your choices.

I was. Grady must have clued Julie in on what was going on this morning, because when I walked through the door she rushed over and gave me a big hug.

"You are always welcome here," she says quietly enough that only I could hear.

I have been subjected to Penny's cooking, or lack thereof, over the years. Being at Mark and Julie's was truly eye opening. The turkey wasn't dry. Mashed potatoes that didn't come from flakes in a box. An actual homemade apple pie in lieu of some bland grocery store pie. The meal was probably one of the best I ever had in my life.

And I had equally loved that it was just the four of us. While Mark and Julie still didn't know about Grady and I, it painted the picture of what could be. After dinner we lazily shuffled to the couch, catching the four o'clock football game. Well, we intended to catch the four o'clock game. Mark passed out in his recliner almost instantly. Julie, after scrolling on her phone for a bit, quickly followed. Grady, the third to fall, fell asleep with his head leaning on my shoulder. I fought sleep as long as I could, trying to take in the moment.

After a few busy weeks of school, we arrive at Christmas. I was struggling to figure out what to get Grady for a present, or how much to spend. Grady has a habit of just buying pretty much anything he wants.

On the last day of school Grady and I plan on heading to his house for a bit. His parents were going out to do some last-minute Christmas shopping, which gave us some time by ourselves. A light rain started to fall on the ride over, which caused Grady to start cursing when his wipers left streaks over about half his windshield.

"I'm shocked you haven't replaced those yet."

"I keep forgetting to ask Dad. He knows what type to get. I went into Walmart and just stared at the aisle of them, got frustrated, and left."

That was the moment I found the perfect gift for Grady.

Later that night Mark offers to give me a ride home, as Julie had given him a last-minute shopping list for Christmas dinner.

"Mark, would you mind if we stopped by Walmart on the way home? I want to pick up something for Grady for Christmas."

"Not a problem. What did you have in mind?"

"It's going to sound stupid, but new wipers for his truck."

"He still hasn't replaced those? That kid..."

In Walmart, Mark immediately finds the right wipers. I made a quick pass of the candy aisle, picking some of Grady's favorites. It didn't seem like much, but I hope it was the thought that counts. When Mark puts the car in park at the apartment, he looks over at me. "I know you probably have something going on with your mom and Ralph, but Julie and I wanted to let you know you are of course invited over for Christmas Eve. Even if it's for a little while."

I smile, grabbing my bag off the floor. "Sounds great. It gives me an actual excuse to escape from Ralph's."

"I'll let Julie know we can expect you at some point. She's going to be thrilled."

Back in the apartment I quickly wrap Grady's gift, which looks like a toddler wrapped it. I suddenly realize I have nothing for Mark and Julie. So, against my best judgment, I go for a walk to brave the night before Christmas Eve crowds at the Trader Joe's and Target down the street. I select some fancy cheeses for Julie, and hit up the candy aisle for a second time tonight as Mark loves candy as much as Grady does. I even manage to grab the last two cheap Christmas baskets Target has to dump everything in.

On Christmas Eve, Penny and I go to Ralph's around two in the afternoon. When we arrive, the house is full of other families. "I didn't realize Ralph has such a large family."

"They aren't family." Penny replies, "They are some of the higher-ranking officials in Wishing Well."

Great. I'm spending Christmas Eve with a bunch of cultists. The conversation around the table ranges from misguided LGBT youth to the benefits of homeschooling children, to who from the table should run for public office to right the ship in this town. All of it troubling and not what I would consider appropriate holiday discussion topics. I try to catch the eye of some of the younger people at the table, but they all just stare off with blank expressions on their faces. Like zombies. I need to get out of this house.

Once dinner finishes, I notice many of the other guests start heading out the back door and walking towards the woods. The woods are oddly lit up. Penny passes by me carrying a pile of dirty dishes. "What's in the woods?"

She places the plates next to the sink. "Some cabins Ralph had built for Wishing Well."

"Wait. Are all of those people staying the night out there? On Christmas?"

"Oh yes. Ralph says they all come for the holiday every year. They have a big Christmas breakfast in the morning and discuss blessings of the past year and what they wish for next year."

"That sounds kinda...creepy."

Penny's face frowns. "These are good people. Maybe if you hung around here more you would know them a bit better. I made sure to set up one of the cabins out there for you and I tonight, to be in the center of it all."

"Yeah, that is not something I have any interest in doing. I'm going to head back to the apartment for the night."

Ralph suddenly appears in the kitchen doorway. "This is a tradition here in this house and with the members of Wishing Well. It brings our unit closer together, spending the entirety of the winter break conducting workshops and prepping for the new year ahead."

"Ralph, I'm going to have to pass on all of that. If that's your cup of tea by all means. It's just not for me."

"Son, I'm not sure you have much of a choice in the matter." Is that a threat? I pull out my phone to text Grady quickly.

JAMES: Any chance you could come get me from Ralph's? Things are heading south here
GRADY: Leaving now. Is this a WAFFLE situation?
JAMES: Not yet but could be. I'm going to head down the road a bit

"Ralph, I hate to break it to you but I have all the choice here. And I am choosing to leave this house." I start to head towards the door and he grabs my arm. I rip my arm out of his grasp. "Do not fucking touch me again." He goes for me but I'm already out the door, running down the driveway.

Grady is flying up the road when I am about a quarter of a mile away from Ralph's. I jump in the truck and Grady pulls a quick U-turn and we are barreling down the road.

"You good?" He links the fingers of his open hand with mine.

"Now I am."

We make a quick pit stop at the apartment so I can grab some essentials, and also the gifts. When Grady parks the truck at his house, I feel my pocket vibrate.

PENNY: You can be such a disappointment. And selfish.

Gonna leave that one on read.

Mark and Julie are waiting by the door. "Tell us what happened." As we settle into the living room I recount the weirdness of the other attendees, Ralph's fight to not let me leave, and show them Penny's last text.

"Oh James. I'm so sorry about all that. What a terrible start to winter break and the holiday." Julie pats my hand. "I'm glad you came here."

"I'm really sorry about crashing."

"Nonsense!" Mark yells from the kitchen. "It felt weird not having you here. Almost too quiet."

Mark brings in two large bowls of popcorn, plopping one with Grady and I and the other between him and Julie. "It's our family tradition to watch *Elf* on Christmas Eve. Oh, and *Die Hard*."

I laugh. "You are one of those families who think *Die Hard* is a Christmas movie."

Grady's eyes widen. "You don't?!?"

Before *Elf* starts, there is a heated debate on *Die Hard* as a Christmas movie. I end up conceding just to appease everyone.

As *Elf* wraps up and Mark searches for *Die Hard*, Grady leans in and whispers in Julie's ear.

"Shall we do gifts before the next movie?" She grabs the two remaining presents under the tree and hands them to me.

"We always do our gifts after dinner on Christmas Eve so we've already exchanged."

I reach into my bag and pull out my three gifts and pass them out. "Oh James, you didn't need to get us anything!"

"You have to put up with me all the time so it's the least I could do."

Julie opens hers first and smiles as she lifts each cheese out of the basket. "Ooo a delice! My favorite. Thank you so much James." Mark has already started eating some of the 100 Grands in his basket, mumbling something indecipherable.

Grady laughs as he opens the wipers. "How is it you're able to figure out what wipers my truck needs and I can't?"

"Anyone can Google it to figure it out. But I also had Mark's help at the store." He, like Mark, starts immediately digging into his candy.

"Go on James. It's your turn," Julie says, nudging the gifts at my feet. Grady picks one up and drops it on my lap. "Since you're opening Grady's first, I'll run and put the cheese in the fridge. And get more wine!" I tear into the wrapping to find a limited-edition copy of *Breaking the Moon*.

"There's a note inside," Grady says, flipping the cover open for me:

James - Even when hope is at its lowest, let your greatest power shine through. The ability to be resilient and beat all odds.

Signed by the author.

"Grady, how did you…"

"After you told me what your favorite book was, I did some research and found the author's website. He offered up the option to add a personal message inside the book if you provided some details about who the book is for."

My mouth gapes open. "This isn't some canned response?"

"if it is, we'll never know." Grady says with a smile.

"Our turn!" Julie yells, returning from the kitchen and pushing the last gift towards me. I tear the paper open to reveal a giant shadow box in Beacon colors. Inside the box are a football, a newspaper article, and a picture of Grady hugging me after breaking the state record. The article was one I had been interviewed for after the championship, and the plaque under the football states it's the ball that broke the state record.

"Mark...Julie...this is amazing. I don't know what to say." I feel tears well up in my eyes.

"We just wanted to let you know how proud we are of you. What you did this year was extraordinary. And, not to be downers, but we know how you aren't appreciated as much as you should be at home."

Mark must notice the mood shifting in the room, so he cuts it off by starting *Die Hard*. As the movie starts and the lights dim, Grady discreetly squeezes my hand.

We sleep in separate rooms that night, not wanting to push our limits. But Grady does sneak in for a bit and we climb under the covers.

I climb down the stairs to find a full breakfast spread in the kitchen. "Good morning," I say, sliding into a chair at the table.

"Merry Christmas James!" Julie put a cup of coffee in front of me. "Please feel free to help yourself. Christmas in this house involves an elaborate brunch, followed by doing a lot of nothing, and then having an early dinner of Chinese food. How does that sound?"

"Sounds perfect."

We eat in silence for a bit, before Julie clears her throat. "Who wants to ask him?"

"Ask me what?" I reach for a couple more pieces of bacon.

Mark drops his fork. "I am more than happy to take the credit. We asked Grady if you wanted to join us in going to our cabin in Maine for the remainder of winter break, even before what happened at Ralph's. And I think, given the circumstances, might do you some good. And maybe Grady won't be as bored this year."

Grady rolls his eyes. "Dad I'm only bored because you guys never change things up. Movies? Same. Meals? Same. Board games made in like 1985? Obviously the same."

Julie playfully slaps Grady's hand. "You're really selling it to James, geez Grady. I promise it's not that bad. So, what do you think? Would you like to come with us?"

"I would love to," I start, pulling out my phone, "but I would need to see if I could get out of my work shifts." Only a month ago this would have sent me into a panic thinking about money, but Julie's right. I do need to get out of here, even if it's only for a week.

"Ahh well I may already have that covered just in case you said yes. I had Chloe go down and ask Sam and Mitch just in case, and they seemed thrilled." Of course they seemed thrilled. When I had told them about Grady, they almost led a parade through Tipsy Mic in celebration, swooning over his photo.

"Well then yes, I would love to."

Nineteen

Julie and Mark said we would leave around ten in the morning, and would swing by the apartment so I could quickly pack for the trip. We had all agreed it would be best that I didn't stay at the apartment the night before. Luckily, I had managed to do some laundry right before going to Ralph's on Christmas Eve.

Grady asked if I wanted him to come and help but I told him I better go in alone in case Penny was home. And of course she was.

"Where have you been?" She grunts, following me into my bedroom as I grab my duffle bag out of the closet.

"Why do you even care? I thought I was a disappointment? Oh, and since you didn't bother to text, Merry Christmas I guess."

"Communication goes both ways, James."

"And given your actions it should have been you reaching out to me."

"Why are you packing a bag?"

I throw three pairs of jeans into the bag and turn my head towards her. "Grady's parents invited me to spend a week in their cabin in Maine. Since I don't have a lot going on this week, I took them up on their offer."

Penny snorts. "The hell you are. You're supposed to be helping Ralph at Wishing Well this week. He needs everyone on deck for the turn of the year."

"Do you even listen to yourself? How weird you sound? Turn of the year? It's New Year's. And you never mentioned that, and I certainly would never have agreed to it."

"I'm not giving you a choice James. You will respect my decisions. I am your mother."

I laugh, throwing my underwear into the bag and zipping it shut. "And I remind you I'm eighteen and legally an adult. I really don't have to listen to you unless I want to." Penny tries to block the door but I just bump into her as I pass through the doorway.

Any anxiety I had about spending a week in the middle of nowhere with Grady, with no escape, has been squashed.

"Is there even supervision for you up there? What are you even going to be doing? If I find out you are drinking and doing drugs–"

"Jesus Penny. I already told you it's Grady and his parents. We will be doing satanic rituals around a lake while blowing lines of coke."

"What have I said about calling me Penny? And I don't even know these people." My phone vibrates in my pocket.

GRADY: You okay?
GRADY: Guessing your mom was home
JAMES: Be out in a second
GRADY: Do you need my mom to talk to her
JAMES: Nooooooooooooooo

"If you had bothered to come to even one of my football games you would have met them. You may have even sat with Mark and Julie."

"You call them by their first names too?"

I open the door, turning in the threshold. "Well with them it's a term of endearment and they asked me to. When it comes to you it's just a lack of respect." I'm halfway down the stairs when I hear footsteps behind me. "Are you following me?"

"No, I am on my way to Ralph's to explain it will only be me this week."

When we get to the bottom of the stairs Mark and Julie are standing at the open trunk. "Hey Penny, how's it going?" Julie walks up to us. "We wanted to make sure you had emergency contact info and our location. Here's the phone number for the cabin. I think cell service was a bit spotty the last time we were up there."

"How long's the trip?"

"A little over five hours? Maybe six with rest stops?"

"James, call me when you get there. Stay out of trouble." Penny looks at Julie and Mark at the word trouble, and gets in her car and takes off.

"Was she…"

"Insinuating that you," I point at Julie, "are going to be the cause of the trouble? Yes, she was. The teachings of Ralph are deep within her. I also may have joked about satanic rituals around the lake."

Mark spits out his coffee. "Wow, I mean we're going to the middle of nowhere. Of course we are going to get into a bit of trouble. Probably not satanic rituals, but we'll play it by ear."

After about four hours in the car, Mark and Julie pull off the highway and into a strip mall with a Shaw's grocery store. I haven't seen a Shaw's since Penny and I left Vermont. She cuts the engine and turns around to us. "First of all, super impressed with our bladders and not using any rest stops. But when we get inside there will be a cleanup in aisle four if I don't find a bathroom."

"Gross Mom," Grady says. Besides some idle chit chat from Mark and Julie the ride had been pretty quiet. Grady had been playing his Switch almost nonstop, with his only break being to grab a backup charger. I had been reading most of the time, so I didn't mind.

"And second, we are stopping here for groceries because the options get a little scarce from here to the cabin. We packed a cooler with some ice for anything frozen we get. I'm giving you two a list to work from so we can make this stop quick. Feel free to grab whatever snacks you guys want for the week."

"I'm starvingggg," Grady moans, taking the list. "You mentioned lunch when we got in the car and that was like four hours ago. All I've had since then is a granola bar. I don't even care what it is, as long as it's not Burger King." Grady loves him some fast food but hates Burger King. Never told me why, but I kinda agree.

"We can grab something after we shop, but again. Clean up. Aisle four." Julie is off sprinting for the inside of the store.

"I guess I'm in charge of our list," Mark says, stretching outside the car. "I'm going to get some Bud Light and some IPAs for the cabin. For Julie and I of course," he says, turning with a smirk on his face.

Man does it feel good to stand up. It feels pretty warm out for December, so I throw my hoodie in the car before we start walking for the entrance. "What's on our list?"

"Looks like we are in charge of frozen stuff, dairy, and the bakery. Oh, and snacks." The list looks enormous, and its only half. It now strikes me that it must have seemed odd that Penny didn't offer to give Julie or Mark anything for bringing me on the trip. And they would never take anything from me. I'll have to figure out something to give them as a thank you for bringing me along.

We hit the cookie and cracker aisle first and Grady starts piling stuff in. "Anything in particular you want?"

"Well," I say, reaching for the top shelf, "I've always been partial to Better Cheddars." I grab a box and place it in the cart.

"Are those pretty much Cheez-Its or Cheese Nips, or like Cheddar Goldfish?"

"Such disrespect to Better Cheddars. So much disrespect. We're getting another box because I don't want you eating all of them once you taste how much better they are than that crap list you just churned out."

"You care about the most random shit." We make our way down the cereal and candy aisle and grab a few staples like Fruity Pebbles and Twizzlers. Grady grabs four giant bags of peanut butter M&Ms.

"You think I like peanut butter M&Ms...Dad LOVES them." We've now made it to the dairy section, and Julie has a lengthy list of different cheeses, yogurts, and dips, amongst other things.

"You two still haven't hit the freezer section?" Julie is crossing into an aisle. Mark is standing on the back of the cart, zooming past her. He narrowly misses a display of Pop-Tarts.

"You know you got it good with them, right?" I ask Grady, who is staring at the shredded cheese.

"Huh? Oh yeah, I guess. Sorry, I was trying to figure out what cheese makes the difference so there has to be both a four-cheese blend and a five-cheese blend."

"Now who cares about, how'd you put it? Random shit?"

We ended up getting Wendy's. Julie eliminated Taco Bell due to the amount of time left in the trip, and being outnumbered three to one in the car. I notice Mark's eyebrow arch when, with everything Grady and I ordered, I end up getting a Diet Coke. "I just like the taste better," I explain. He still seems skeptical.

Now that we have abandoned the highway, the roads have narrowed and we drive into smaller and smaller towns. Julie was right to stop when we did. There's hardly anything other than trees or the occasional house or gas station that would be picture perfect settings for a horror movie. It was getting to be later in the afternoon and the sun was beginning to set, which made it seem even more remote.

Julie pulls down a dirt road and, at the top of the hill, are a set of two cabins. Smoke was billowing out of the chimney of the cabin on the right, and Julie pulls the SUV in front of the left one. The cabin is a lot bigger than I expected it to be. It's one-story, but looks enormous from the front and seems to extend back a bit. The porch has a chair and table set on either side of the front door.

I jump out of the car and join Mark at the trunk, grabbing about half the grocery bags. "James, don't kill yourself. We can make multiple trips."

"But who wants to make extra trips?" Julie enters the cabin and leaves the door open. I sidestep through the door, barely clearing the doorway with the bags and gasp. The cabin is amazing. It definitely gives the vibe of a cabin, but like the nicest version of it all. Plus, what I'm assuming is, an at least 75"

TV on the wall in the living room. A giant fireplace takes up almost the whole wall diagonal from the TV, two large couches taking up the rest of the room. I have a feeling it's where a lot of the time is spent at the cabin.

The kitchen is to the left and Julie is already busy unpacking groceries. This kitchen, in this cabin in the middle of nowhere, is better than any kitchen anywhere I've lived. It might even be better than the one they have back in Rhode Island. I drop my bags on the kitchen island near the fridge. "Julie, this place is amazing."

"Oh James, thank you! My grandparents built this one and the one next door, and left one to me and one to my brother when they died. We each use them a few times a year, but always make sure we both come up here between Christmas and New Year's." So it's more than just the four of us here this week.

"Are you expecting us to empty the whole car?" Grady appears at the front door, dropping what appears to be the rest of the groceries. He heads back out to the car and Mark is talking to another guy. It's Julie's brother. I mean, it has to be. They look almost identical.

"Hey James, come over here. This is Kevin, Julie's brother. He and Grady's cousin Danny are up here for the week with us."

"It's nice to meet you Kevin," I say, Kevin's handshake practically crushing my hand.

"Likewise. Danny is around here somewhere, probably wandering the woods. You'll meet him later at dinner. Grilling over at our cabin."

"James. Bags." Grady says from the car. "Hey Uncle Kev." Kevin waves to Grady as I head back to the car once Kevin and Mark start talking again. "Half of me was rescuing you from getting lost in Uncle Kev's stories, but also I seem to be the only one unloading the car." He passes me three large duffle bags, one of them being mine. "Usually I stay in the bedroom up in the loft, but we'll be staying in the basement. I told Mom it would be better for noise level, with video games and movies and stuff."

"Are there like, uh, big spiders in the basement? We're in the middle of nowhere."

Grady rolls his eyes. "I will protect you from the very scary spiders. But there shouldn't be any because they spray the outside of the house every year to keep stuff out. And what are you imagining this basement is going to look like where we would be staying down there?"

Grady brings his parents' bags down the hall into a bedroom on the back side of the cabin. When Grady returns, he gestures to what I thought was a door to a closet. I open the door, and it instead is a narrow stairwell that cuts to the right after a few steps. And my perception of a basement in a cabin in the woods was very, very wrong.

The main room is probably about two-thirds the size of the first floor. It has another giant flat screen TV on the wall, matching the one from the upstairs. But one wall is lined with

125

vintage arcade machines. Mortal Kombat II, Ms. Pac Man, House of the Dead, X-Men, and some pinball machines. And, immediately to the right of the stairs, is a small bar. That appears to be fully stocked.

"Holy shit Grady. This is awesome."

"I've never brought any of my friends up here because I knew they would talk, and then there would be pressure to throw huge parties up here. And that is a headache I don't want to deal with from Mom and Dad."

"You've never brought anyone here, ever? Do you think it looks weird that all of a sudden you asked to bring me?"

Grady laughs. "Honestly, I had considered asking them. It was actually Mom and Dad that brought it up. They asked me if I wanted to bring you for the week. You practically spend more time at my house than yours. I think they have known for a while the situation between you and your mom and Ralph isn't the best, and thought it would be good to get away. I mean, could you imagine the shit you'd be doing with them if you were home from school and had nothing to do all week?"

"Well I really appreciate it."

"The rest of the tour is pretty quick. See those three doors on the back wall? The one on the left is the bathroom, the one in the middle is a storage closet with a hatch to the backyard, and the one on the right is the extra bedroom." We walk over and Grady opens the bedroom door. There are two beds on opposite walls, each with a nightstand, and a dresser near the door. There are two small windows higher on the wall covered with curtains.

"So which bed is yours? Just so I know where to put my bags." I say, and Grady backs me up into one of the dressers and presses against me.

"Doesn't matter. We'll only be using one." He points to the doorknob, which has a lock.

"Well now I know why you invited me up for the week." I kiss him and wrap my arms around his waist. He leans in to kiss my neck. "We should help them settle in," I say, "so we don't make them suspicious on day one."

"Fine," Grady says, making an adjustment before leaving the room. I do the same.

Twenty

Around six we head over to Kevin's cabin. From the front yard I can see Kevin is on the back deck manning the grill.

"So," I say, leaning in closer to Grady, "what's the deal with your aunt? Are they not together or does she just not make the trip up here?"

"It's complicated. They divorced when I was like five, but they randomly get back together here and there. She's been remarried and divorced a few times after Uncle Kevin too. I think the last time she was around she was actually still married. She's also had problems with alcohol for, well, forever. And Kevin was given full custody of Danny."

"Guys, I know you think you are being quiet back there but you actually are doing the Morris Whisper and should cut it before we get to the deck."

I go to ask but Grady cuts me off. "What he is referring to is Mom's side of the family which, according to Dad, doesn't know how to whisper."

129

"Yes, and we all consider that little cutesy name for us talking a bit rude." Julie glares at Mark and he puts his head down.

We climb the steps to the deck and the spread of food on the table looks amazing. There are, what appears to be, four different picnic salads, a dessert platter, and Kevin just placed a tray of burgers, hot dogs, and ribs on the table. It's just hitting me how hungry I am.

"Who's thirsty?" I look over at the door into the house and, well, damn. A taller, slightly darker skinned version of Grady has appeared in the doorway. He is carrying a large cooler out the door, with his biceps looking as if they are going to rip the sleeves of his shirt.

"You might want to lift your jaw off the floor if you want to survive this week," Grady sharply whispers into my ear. Is he acting jealous? Also, kinda hot.

"Hey cousin! How've you been?" He gives Grady a big hug. "And you must be James. I'm Danny." I go to shake his hand as he leans in to give me a hug, which just turns out to be an awkward exchange of my right arm pinned against his body.

Danny hands each of us a beer and we sit at the table. Things are quiet for a few minutes as people build their plates and start stuffing their faces. I feel bad about taking as much food as I did, but when I look around everyone's plate is just as full and there is still so much left over.

"Holy shit, these ribs are great Uncle Kev." Grady has sauce all over his face. I hand him a few napkins to clean his face off. I catch Danny's gaze, his eyes squinting a bit as he looks over at us.

"Homemade sauce Grady. That's the big secret. It can elevate even the cheapest cuts of meat. These are just some cheap pre-packaged ribs from Aldi we picked up on the way."

"Everything is really good. Thanks for cooking." I say, before ripping into a rib. And fuck Grady is right, these are delicious.

"It's no problem, James. I'm just glad we have someone outside our normal group who can enjoy it. I think these four take me for granted."

The table becomes livelier after dinner is over and we are picking at desserts. Julie talks, and also doesn't talk, about a case at work that is getting a lot of media attention. Danny talks about school, and how one of his articles got the attention of The New York Times and they have asked him to intern.

"And I hear you two had quite the season," Kevin says, reaching for another cookie. "You cannot tell me it's true James that you had never played football before."

"Very true. Just luck I was in gym class that day."

"And you helped Grady's college scholarship chances with that foot. Have you considered playing in college?" The whole table is staring at me, waiting on a response. The truth is, I had given it a bit of thought. I just hadn't really shared it with anyone. "Well Coach said scouts were at some of the games so I guess we'll see. I'm looking to go to school on the West Coast."

Grady coughs, choking on a brownie bite. Mark smacks his back. "Since when?"

131

"Since forever. You know I want to put distance between Penny and I."

"And Penny is?" Kevin asks.

"Oh, my mother. We aren't very close and don't see eye to eye on practically everything."

"To the point we rescued him so he could spend Christmas with us," Julie adds.

"Mom! Overstep much?"

"Grady it's fine," I say, "I have nothing to hide when it comes to Penny."

"Well son I'm sorry to hear that, but it sounds like you have a good plan in place. I say check out some colleges out there with good football programs. Bound to be one that needs a foot like yours. Might as well get some money out of it."

There is a collective grunt of agreement, but I can feel Grady's eyes on me. And I can see Danny's eyes on both of us.

From there the night gets a bit blurry. The beers kept coming out on the deck, until Grady and I retreated to the basement. Danny joins us for a bit, making us various drinks from the bar. We play arcade games for hours, having makeshift tournaments against each other. Eventually Danny leaves, which leads to Grady and I going to the bedroom. We sloppily rip each other's clothes off, fumbling around until we realize we are too drunk to do anything. Grady passes out wrapped around me.

I hear birds chirping outside the house. I look over at the clock and it's just after eight. How much did we drink last night? What time did we even go to bed? Grady is out cold still, his body leaning into me. I lift the sheet up and, yup, still very naked.

I lean back on the pillow and press my thumbs into my temples. I need to get up and at least get some coffee. Maybe some eggs. Bacon would be great right about now. Bacon would be really great.

The door to the bedroom opens and Danny stops half way into the room. His eyes go wide as he looks at me, then at Grady, at the pile of our clothes intertwined on the floor, back at me again. Shit. Shit this is bad. He just stands in the doorway, motionless other than his eyes darting back and forth between Grady and I.

Twenty-One

When Danny's eyes catch mine again, I quickly shake my head back and forth. I nod towards the main room and he slowly backs out, closing the door as he exits.

I need to go do some damage control before Danny leaves the basement. I slip out of bed quietly, throw on some gym shorts and a t-shirt, and head to the door. I turn and look at Grady, making sure he is still asleep, and sneak out of the room.

Danny is sitting on the couch facing me, his eyes locked with mine. "I knew it," he says, "I knew it. I knew it from dinner last night and the way you looked at him."

"Danny, you can't say anything. Not to him, not to any of them," I gesture towards the upstairs. I sit in the chair closest to the couch. "It's all still new, but we haven't really told anyone about it. There are like a handful of friends in our circle that know, and that's it. I'm not even sure what we are. We've never actually discussed it."

Danny leans in closer. "Look dude, it's fine. I'm not going to say anything to them, but I should at least talk to Grady. It'd probably be good for him to have someone from the family on his side. Probably won't be an issue really though. Mark and Julie are cool as shit."

"You're just...okay with it?"

"I'll say this. It probably seems hard now, but college makes it easier. You experience more shit there. It weeds out a lot of the assholes and people seem to be a bit more open. Well, I guess it's dependent on where you go to school. My roommate sophomore year was gay and, besides the few times he hit on me drunk or brought dudes back, I never would have known. I go to school in Boston which is probably one of the more liberal areas you can go. I just wouldn't advise going to like Kentucky or Mississippi, or some school in the backwoods of some midwestern state."

"Like I said at dinner, I want to go somewhere like California, so I've applied to a bunch of schools out there. I want to get away from my mom and her boyfriend, as far as I can. He kinda runs this cultish group and my mom has really bought into it. Half the reason I'm here this week is because I know I would have been forced to help him out if I was there."

"That makes California sound great. What about Grady?"

I sigh, sneaking a quick look at the closed bedroom door. I can still hear low snores behind the door. "We haven't talked about it much. He will probably have a lot more options than I will. He now knows my plan, but not sure what will happen if someone like LSU or Alabama or something offers him a scholarship."

"You should talk to him, James. You might have more sway than you think. But if it's okay with you, I'd like to take him on a hike this afternoon solo. Give us time to talk." The door behind me opens and Grady is running in the direction of the bathroom and slams the door shut. "Well, as long as he's up for it."

"Are you sure you don't want to come with us?" Grady's lacing up trail shoes in preparation for his hike with Danny.

"Nah. Spend some time with your cousin." I should probably come up with a plan for the day. Or not. A day lounging around the house while this hangover works itself out sounds fine.

"Honestly, I've never really spent much time with Danny one on one. We've never really had all that much in common. I think I'm just worried about it being a really awkward day with no way to escape."

"You probably have more in common than you even know Grady. Just because he's not into sports doesn't mean you have nothing in common. I really wasn't all that into sports until I was literally voluntold to be on the football team."

"Because that worked out so poorly for you, didn't it?" He leans in and kisses me, pushing me back on the bed. He starts to lift the corner of my shirt up, but I push him off and stand up. He pouts at me.

"You are supposed to leave with Danny in five minutes. Don't get me all riled up and don't be late."

We leave the basement and Danny is sitting on one of the couches upstairs. "Hey cuz! I packed us some snacks and a few waters for the hike. Let's head out while the sun's still out. I think it's supposed to rain tonight."

"Is it? Shit," Julie says from the kitchen. She opens the fridge door and starts moving things around. "Going to need a plan b dinner option for tonight then."

"Let's go before that unfolds," Grady says, grabbing one of the backpacks next to Danny. He turns to me and mouths *last chance* and I roll my eyes. The two exit the front door and I'm now alone with Julie. I take a seat at one of the kitchen counter stools as Julie emerges from the fridge, which is packed. Julie looks up and jumps back.

"Oh Jesus! I didn't even know you were there. I thought you left with Grady and Danny." She laughs and puts her phone down on the counter. She pulls a stool opposite me and flips her phone towards me. "I was trying to figure out what to make for dinner tonight now that we will be housebound. I was thinking of making a version of my mother's lasagna and chicken parm, maybe with some homemade garlic bread or garlic knots or something. What do you think?"

"I mean I think that sounds great. Other than a restaurant I've never had homemade Italian food. Penny usually throws a jar of sauce with some boxed pasta, and heats up a frozen chicken patty or sometimes frozen meatballs to go with it."

"I...I don't know what to say to that. Other than we are absolutely having Italian for dinner tonight. It works well because a lot of the prep can be done ahead of time."

"I don't think the idea of meal prep really came to Penny. She relied heavily on frozen meals, or things that came together quick like mac and cheese or ramen or chicken nuggets and fries. Frozen burger patties and stuff. I started cooking a bit for myself when she started working nights and still do now when she's at Ralph's."

"Would you want to help me put together tonight's meal? It's not all that hard to do and definitely something you could learn to make at home. But James, you are always welcome to come to our house for dinner. Even on the few nights of the week you aren't already there." She winks at me, and starts piling things on the counter from the fridge.

"We'll start with the chicken cutlets for the chicken parm. I bought thin chicken breasts when we were at the store, which saves a lot of time and effort. Usually, you have to flatten the chicken out with a rolling pin or meat tenderizer. To start, grab three bowls from the cabinet. Put a cup or so of flour in the first bowl, crack four eggs in the second bowl, and put like two cups of the breadcrumbs in the third bowl."

I get to work on setting up the bowls while Julie dumps a bunch of ground beef and sausage in a pan. Once I have the bowls set up, she flies by and dumps a bunch of seasonings into the flour and the bread crumbs. "I'll write down for you what I just added. It's not necessary but just kicks the flavor up a notch. My mother-in-law doesn't put seasoning in her food and I used to dread going to her house to eat. That is something I always pay special attention to. Anyways, you are going to want to take each cutlet and coat it in the flour, then the egg, and then flip it a couple of times in the bread crumbs to get them coated. Using a fork will make it easier and less of a mess. Place them on this tray and we will fry them up when they're ready."

After I finish the cutlets, she starts guiding me through the steps of the lasagna. Adding the garlic and onions to the meat mixture along with the tomatoes and a whole bunch of things I didn't catch to make the sauce. She has me make the cheese mixture while she finishes the meat sauce. "Okay, now we are going to layer the dish and you will not repeat the following. I almost always use fresh noodles for the lasagna but I didn't know what time I'd have here. So, we will be using no-boil lasagna noodles that just cook in the oven with the rest of the dish. Again, do not repeat this later." The lasagna comes together quickly, as does frying the cutlets. The kitchen is starting to smell amazing, and my stomach gurgles in response.

Julie's looks surprised. "We never ate lunch! Here we've been working away and you've probably been starving. The food's prepped so let me get something together and we can sit and relax."

I take a seat at a small table off of the kitchen. In what seems like seconds, Julie is over with a plate of cheeses and small sandwiches, and a bottle of wine tucked under her arm. "I know your mom would probably kill me if she found out we knew you guys were drinking up here. But you guys are graduating soon, and Mark and I believe it's better for you to be a bit prepared. Too many kids are sheltered in high school and then get their stomach pumped after arriving at the college party scene." She pours two glasses of wine, her glass larger than mine, and we start snacking.

I take a sip of wine and, well, it's delicious. Usually when there's wine at parties it comes from a box or a jug. I spin the bottle around to look at the label. "I can guarantee you this is something you haven't had before. It's a Sancerre, which comes from the Loire Valley in France. It's along the lines of a Sav Blanc but a bit more tasty. And often a bit more pricey."

"It's really good. It seems like something you actually sit back and enjoy." I pop a few more pieces of cheese in my mouth. It's weird and not weird to be hanging out with just Julie. I can't imagine having the same type of relationship with Penny, but it's nice being treated like an adult. I then notice, sticking out of a tote bag on the floor, a copy of *Breaking the Moon*. "Is that your book?"

"Oh. Yes, yes it is. I saw that the movie was coming out and people were going crazy about it, but I'm someone who has to read the book before seeing the movie. I just finished it last night while you guys were hanging out with Danny downstairs."

"It's one of my favorites. I've read it at least four times. Grady actually got me an autographed copy with a note from the author for Christmas. I keep telling Grady he should read it, or at least watch the movie. But he hasn't seemed interested in either, despite how much I've talked about it."

Julie is looking at me oddly. She takes a sip and leans in, and opens her mouth but doesn't say anything. She leans back in her chair, but keeps her gaze on me. "I want to ask you something but you can choose not to answer, or ask me to move on to a new topic."

"Okay."

"Do you...is there a reason why *Breaking the Moon* is one of your favorite books? Do you connect with one of the lead characters?"

I start fidgeting with the wine glass. Why did I have to talk about *Breaking the Moon* with her? Of course she was able to put two and two together. I feel the sweat beading on my forehead and my palms are sweaty. She is still staring at me. I look down, but slightly nod up and down. How did this day get here? I was pushing Grady to go on a hike with Danny to talk things through, and now I've just come out for the first time to an adult.

I feel a hand grasp mine, despite the sweatiness. I look up and see that her look has softened a bit. I am now just realizing I've started crying. Julie gets up from the table and leans in and gives me a tight hug. It seems like the hug lasts for minutes before she lets go and returns to her chair. I wipe my eyes and grab my wine glass, finishing it in one gulp. Julie almost immediately refills it.

"Everything's fine James. Nothing has changed here, and I am sorry if it seemed like I was prying. When you pointed out the book it for some reason made me think you were trying to talk about it. But you can trust me completely that I won't tell

Mark or Grady or…" Julie's face just goes blank. She looks from me, to the book, and back at me. "How did I not see this before?" All I can do is just sit there and blankly stare at her as I can see her working through it in her head. "He's never had such a close friend over at our house as much before, and has never wanted to bring someone along on a trip to the cabin. Or the holidays, and the gift he gave you."

"I…," I stammer, trying to figure out how to pick my words. The day started with Danny finding me in bed with Grady, but this one is all on me. "I don't know what to say. I don't know what to say without lying, or what to say without saying too much."

Again, she grabs my hand and leans in closer to me. "James, you don't have to say anything. All I will say is this. I have in the past couple years had some suspicions on where Grady's…attention focuses. Nothing really to point to, but a mother knows things about her children. And I know it's not your place to say anything on his behalf, to confirm my suspicions. But know that we really enjoy having you around, and you have seemed to open Grady up in ways we hadn't seen until this year. And I want you to know that I would be quite upset if anything were to change, if you didn't spend time at our house and with Grady. So just keep that in your mind as I can tell by looking at you this was a very tough conversation to have. And I already know this is something you can't talk to Penny about, but you need to know you can always come to me if you need to talk. I have to imagine there are some topics I would prefer not to address, but my door is always open."

There is a silence in the room, and I feel like the conversation took as much out of her as it did me. And yet all I can think about is how the hike is going with Grady and Danny. I look out the window and it's starting to look a bit cloudy. Hopefully they get back before the rain starts.

"Well," Julie says, breaking the silence, "since dinner is prepped, should we watch a movie or something?"

The credits are rolling on *Bridesmaids* as the door flies open. Grady and Danny, followed by Mark and Kevin, fill the entryway. And they all look absolutely soaked. I had been so focused on the movie that I hadn't even noticed it started raining.

"Why don't you boys get changed and I'll finish getting dinner ready." Julie gets off the couch and heads to the kitchen, and I stand to follow her. "James you already helped enough! I only need to warm things up at this point."

Grady is looking at me funny. "I helped make dinner," I add, to clear the confusion. We both head down to the basement, Grady stripping down to nothing as he enters the bedroom.

"I'm going to jump in the shower. That rain was freezing." Grady pulls his Giants shirt and sweatpants out of his dresser and starts heading to the bathroom.

"You good?" I ask, grabbing his arm as he passes by.

"It's been…a day. We can talk later about it," Grady frees himself from my grip and closes the bathroom door behind him. It doesn't look like it went well.

144

I head back upstairs and Julie is topping the cutlets with sauce and mozzarella on a tray. I plop down on one of the counter stools as Julie is putting the tray in the oven.

"Glad you weren't on that hike?"

I laugh, but it almost sounds like nervous laughter. It's like things are weird but not with Julie right now. Everything went as well as it could in that conversation, but it's a weird spot to be in where I know she knows, but Grady doesn't know she knows.

"You don't have to say anything to him about our conversation. I don't plan on bringing it up with him either. I think it's important that he gets there on his own, and I don't want him to think you took that from him."

"I wasn't planning on it. That's a level of discomfort I don't want to go to."

Mark emerges from the hall and Grady comes up from the basement at the same time. They occupy the stools on either side of me and Mark grabs a piece of mozzarella from the cutting board.

Julie smacks his hand and he drops it. "Dinner will be ready in like five minutes."

And it was practically five minutes. We are all seated around the table, with Danny and Kevin joining us. Grady seems off, and I haven't noticed him look in Danny's direction once. I try to get Danny's attention but he seems to be focused on getting Grady's.

"James," Kevin says, "did I hear correctly that you helped make dinner? Jules actually shared Gran's secret recipes with an outsider?"

"Oh stop Kev. And yes, I showed him how to make both the lasagna and cutlets. Grady's never shown much interest in the kitchen and James offered his help."

"Well, it all tastes great," Mark adds.

For a bit all you can hear is the scraping of silverware on plates, and in a flash dinner is over. I help Julie with the dishes while the guys finish clearing the table and collect on the couch. I hear the sounds of football from the TV, college football I'm guessing.

While I'm drying my hands Grady comes back into the kitchen. "Hey I'm going to go lay down. I think the hike took a lot out of me and I'm feeling tired."

"Okay sweetie. Let me know if you need anything." Grady gives her a hug and heads for the basement door. I see Danny looking towards the door as Grady closes it, and turns back to the TV.

"Is he alright? He's seemed a bit off all night." I know Julie and I had a pretty frank conversation earlier, but I also know that telling her why Grady was quiet and acting weird would be a bit too much for her.

"I'll head down there and see what's going on." Mark and Kevin are cursing at some play while I make my exit to the basement. When I hit the bottom of the stairs, I notice the main room is empty and the bedroom door is closed. I knock on the door before entering, which then strikes me as odd given it's also my bedroom for the week. Grady is laying in his bed on top of the covers, just staring at the ceiling.

"Why didn't you warn me about the hike? And the real reason you didn't want to go?" His gaze still hasn't left the ceiling. I lay down on the other bed and do the same.

"He said he wanted to talk to you, and I think we both know you wouldn't have gone on the hike if you knew about this morning ahead of time."

"How much did you tell him?"

I sigh. "Not that much. He had kinda put it together on his own. You know, before he walked in on us sleeping in bed together this morning. There really wasn't any way to deny it when he said he knew."

The gaps in the conversation create an uncomfortable silence. I can tell Grady is pissed off. I'm not sure if it's at me, that we put ourselves in a position to get caught, or something else. If he only knew the conversation Julie and I had earlier it would probably be a full meltdown.

"It's just kinda shitty you didn't warn me beforehand. You had all morning."

I roll over on my side, facing him. This argument would go nowhere with the back and forth of him accusing me and me apologizing in a circle. "So how did it go?"

"Fine. He told me about his roommate at school and he told me things are much different once you leave high school. He also said I should tell Mom and Dad because they would be understanding, and I told him it's not his place to tell me who and when I should tell."

147

"Do you want to tell them?"

He turns to face me. He looks much less angry now. "Yes? Maybe? I don't know. I have tried imagining having that conversation with them and I just can't see it. I picture lectures from Dad about my football career and Mom freaking out about things that she shouldn't even be thinking about now. Marriage. Grandkids."

There is a knock on the door. "Can I come in guys?" I look over at Grady and he nods.

"Come in Danny."

Grady sits up in bed and Danny takes a seat next to him. "Grady, you need to know I didn't want to make things awkward today. After what I saw this morning, and James telling me no one in the family knew, I thought it was important for you to have someone in the family that knows. Like when I realized I wanted to stop playing football but was worried it would crush my dad. You helped me then and reassured me that the decision was mine, not his. And he ended up being fine with it after we talked it out."

"I get it, but this will be a much different conversation. One that has much longer repercussions than stopping playing football."

"No one is telling you when to tell them," I say, sitting up in bed, "but I think they will take it easier than you think. It's not like you're dealing with a situation like Penny or Ralph. It'll be hard, for sure. But you'll know when the right time is to tell them."

There is another knock on the door. Mark pops his head in. "Wow looks like a serious powwow going on in here. We were thinking of taking a family walk down the hill to Fields Ice Cream Stand. You guys down?"

Danny and I both look at Grady. "Yeah, we'll be up in a minute."

"Great! Mountain Top here I come!" Mark leaves the door open and heads back upstairs.

"Mountain Top?" I ask.

Grady rolls his eyes. "It's like some giant bowl with 6 or 8 different scoops of ice cream. It's gross. Let's go."

"Wait, why is an ice cream place in the middle of nowhere open during the winter?"

"Because what else are people supposed to do around here?" He's got a point.

I'm glad he's snapped out of his funk.

The rest of the week flies by, filled with movies and board games, college football and New Year's Eve celebrations. Grady and I even had a chance to sneak out of the room a little after midnight for our own midnight kiss. I never had someone to kiss at midnight before.

By nine on New Year's Day morning the car is fully packed up. Kevin and Danny also decide to leave this morning and we are all standing outside by the cars. The rain stopped at some point overnight, and today looks like it will be much more pleasant for the ride home.

"We really should do this more often," Kevin says. "And bring James back with you too. I think having someone outside of our little circle changed the dynamic a bit."

"Maybe we can do a trip shortly after graduation?" Grady says.

"We can probably make that work!" Julie leans in and gives Kevin a hug, then Danny. Mark waves to them as he and Julie get in the car. Danny and Kevin are in their car and gone in a matter of seconds.

"So," Grady leans in, "did you have a good trip? I'm sorry about the bit of drama at the beginning."

"I had a great time, and you don't need to apologize. It was a stressful situation."

"Well, I will make sure next time is stress and drama free."

Next time.

Twenty-Two

The Beacon High Winter Formal dance, I've been told, is almost as revered as prom. And, because of this, it becomes a whole weekend event. Which involves Kyle and Patty hosting the first party.

The party's animal themed, so we all came in our best attire. Grady and I went to Target and found animal onesies for us, Davis, and Rob. Sharks, in particular, of various colors. Mark drops us off down the street from the twins' house. "I was going to make a joke about hunting for blood in the water but realized how gross that sounded."

Grady groans. "Yeah. On that note, bye."

The party is already in full swing by the time we walk through the door. I grab a cup of beer from the table and head for the backyard, where Chloe and the girls are waiting for us.

"My goodness! Who is that? Is that, what's his name...Jameson? Jorge? Yes. I do believe it's Jorge."

"Real funny Chloe," I say, collapsing into an Adirondack chair.

"You have really been MIA lately. Both you and Grady have," Dana adds, leaning in. "What gives?"

I pause, trying to think of a good answer. "Well, I have been picking up more shifts at work with football done. Can't speak to Grady's deal." Well, except almost any waking moment I'm not at work I'm hanging out with Grady.

"Let's make up for lost time and get absolutely shitfaced," Rob says, holding six more cups of beer.

And we do, in fact, make up for lost time. As the night progresses, we continue to plow through the keg. The party eventually moves inside as it gets later, and Grady and I find ourselves alone in the downstairs bathroom.

Immediately he presses me against the wall, my head knocking a small shelf off the wall. He laughs, picking me up off the ground and placing me on the vanity. I unzip the front of his shark onesie, my hands trailing down his body to the waistband of his boxer briefs.

"Where did they go? We need to get Davis home before curfew." We freeze at the sound of Dana's voice, but Grady's lips start caressing my neck after it's silent for a bit.

Suddenly we are surrounded by light, with Dana, Rob, and Chloe in the doorway. Chloe just bursts out laughing looking at us, leaning against the doorframe.

"Holy shit!" Rob says, staring at us but also trying not to stare.

"Holy shit is right!" Dana says. "Of course they haven't been around. Look at how hot this is! And you obviously knew you bitch!" Dana pushes Chloe lightly, which causes her to tumble onto the ground.

"I would love to come up with some sort of explanation but I literally have my hands in his pants." Grady's face flushes and suddenly we are all laughing. "We did plan on telling all of you but...umm...surprise?"

"And no one speaks of this to anyone, blah blah blah," Chloe says, Rob pulling her off the ground. "Let's get home because I at least need to pretend to sneak by my parents when I get home."

When Julie rolls up to pick us up, Grady and I take the middle row and Davis and Rob take the back. "Good night boys?"

"Great night," I say.

My phone buzzes as I'm trying to sleep off last night's hangover.

CHLOE: I need food I feel like I'm dying
GRADY: Someone told you to stick to beer - you moved to the jungle juice
CHLOE: Please don't talk about it
DAVIS: It wasn't that bad. I saw Kyle make it. Or Patty made it? It was only like two handles of vodka
CHLOE: STOP
DANA: You assholes woke me up from my nap

JAMES: Anthony's or Big Bite Burgers? I think BBB would be better.

ROB: You want me to pick u guys up?

GRADY: omg Rob's alive

DANA: Yeah if we thought Chloe drank a lot of juice

CHLOE: Like really stop

DANA: Rob was trying to outpace her

GRADY: Who forgets that Chloe can probably outdrink all of us

CHLOE: I'm going to kick you all in the balls when I see you.

DANA: I don't have balls.

CHLOE: Then a vag slap for you.

ROB: I'm leaving so u all better be ready.

I live the furthest from Rob so I have a bit more time. I make my way to the bathroom and pop three Advil and brush my teeth quickly.

As I'm leaving the bathroom Penny emerges from her bedroom. "Where are you off to?"

"Just grabbing some lunch with Chloe and the group."

"Will you be at Ralph's for pictures before the dance?" Again with this. She's been pushing this all week.

"No. I told you we're doing photos at Grady's house. That's where we're meeting up before leaving."

"Then you won't get any pictures with Virtue."

"Virtue isn't in our group so she wouldn't be in our pictures anyways."

"You need to be nicer to her. You are like a brother to her." She can't honestly believe that. Virtue and I pretty much avoid each other both in and outside of school. We don't even really talk when it's just the three of us and Ralph in a room.

"She can take photos with her friends. And, if you really need a photo of us together, I'm sure someone at the dance can take one. There isn't enough time to make multiple stops. Wait, is she even going to the dance? I've never heard her talk about it and it doesn't really seem like something Ralph would go for."

"It's Mr. Dursten James, not Ralph. Show some respect. And he knows she is going. She's going with some friends from Wishing Well. They are going to make sure the dance is safe."

"That sounds like buckets of fun."

"You could learn a thing or two about manners from her. Maybe see if she wants to go to lunch with you."

Absolutely not. "Rob already left to pick us up and there isn't enough room in the car for another person. But he should be here any second so I've gotta go."

As I'm closing the apartment door, I hear her say "I'm leaving to go over there now. Try and stop by!" Yeah, like that's going to happen. Luckily Rob's pulling in the parking lot as I jog down the stairs.

"Rough night?" Tammy, our waitress, is standing at the table. I look around at us. Chloe is slumped against Rob. Grady's head is literally on the table. My headache luckily seems to be going away. "It's been a while, but I'm pretty sure kids usually party on the night of the dance. Not the night before. Do you need a few minutes?"

"Water. Another water. Double Double extra bacon. No tomato. Fries and tots." Grady's head never moves off the table as the waitress scribbles down his order. The rest of the table orders.

"I'll do the same as his Tammy, but make one of those waters a Diet Coke." She takes the menus and we are left to our own misery.

"She has a point. Why did we drink so much last night? Now we all look like shit and we have to be in photos in like six hours. Oh god. I have to sit in a chair getting my hair and makeup done for like two hours."

"Barf to that," Grady says, finally lifting his head off the table. There is an imprint of the checkered tablecloth on his face.

"Move Rob, like now." Rob stands up and Chloe runs to the bathroom.

"We need to talk logistics," Dana states. "We have to be at Grady's for photos at five. Chloe and I should be done at the salon around 3:30. Rob, can you pick us up at like 4:15?" Rob nods in approval. "Are we all coupling off and taking our own cars?"

Tammy drops the drinks at the table. "I was going to keep it a surprise but my parents hired a limo to take us to the dance, and then to Davis's party after. The limo should be at the house for 5:30. They even stuck fake sparkling juice labels on some champagne bottles to hide it from the driver."

156

Mark and Julie always think of everything. And this is why Virtue could not be invited along with us. That limo would never make it to the dance.

"Sweet," Davis says. "Do we need anything other than the champagne or will we be good?"

"Let's not get to last night's level before we get to the afterparty," Dana responds, picking at her straw wrapper. "I want to somewhat remember our last winter formal."

Chloe is back at the table. "You better not be talking about drinking. I'm feeling better but not that much better."

"We were just discussing our limo transportation to the West Beacon Society Room actually."

"A limo? Oh, how fancy."

"So," I add, changing the topic, "my mom was really on us to stop at Ralph's and take photos with Virtue and her cult friends. And she really wanted me to bring her to lunch today."

"No to all of that," Dana says. "Do you remember when she went to that party at Keegan's last year? She walked around for like ten minutes or something, went home and told Ralph about it, and the cops were there like fifteen minutes later to break it up."

"Then she had the nerve to try and recruit Quentin and I that next Monday for her dad's cult. Uh, no thanks." Grady had never mentioned before that Virtue tried to recruit him.

"Not to be nosy but are you talking about Ralph Dursten?" Tammy is back at the table, carrying a tray of our food. "I went to school with Ralph and," she leans closer to the table, "he's a fucking weirdo. And his daughter is off too. They

157

came in here a couple of times and really made the whole staff feel awkward. The last time he was here he stood on one of the booths and openly invited everyone to come join Wishing Well, in order for us to get back on the correct path of life. If that's the correct path then I will not have what he's having."

"Try being the son of the woman dating him. Oh wait, that's you!" Dana laughs, pointing at me. I throw a french fry at her.

"Oh, bless your heart kid. That's got to be rough. Well, if you go on any family dinners, try not to come here!" Tammy chuckles to herself as leaves the table.

"Thank you for that Dana, really. I love being associated with the town weirdo."

"Guys. Food. Stop talking." Chloe grunts.

Rob waves towards Grady's house as he drops us off. "Hi Mark and Julie! I'll be over later. Thanks again for the limo!" They wave back and Rob is gone.

"What time do we need to pick up our tuxes?" Grady asks. Mark and Julie are walking down the sidewalk towards us.

"Around three. Why?"

"Well, it's only 1:30 now," Grady says, then leans in close to my ear, "and I believe you said your mom is already over at Ralph's?"

"Hey boys," Julie says, "getting excited for tonight? And way to ruin the limo surprise!" She playfully pushes Grady and he fakes a stumble back.

"It's very nice Mark and Julie, thank you. It will sure make some people jealous."

"Did you invite Penny over for pictures James?" Mark asks. "We would have asked ourselves but we didn't have her number. We figured the other parents could stay and have some drinks while Julie and the other moms cry about everyone being so grown up now."

"Oh really, Dad? Like you won't be crying along with them."

I nudge Grady. "Be nice. Penny will be at Ralph's for pictures of Virtue and her friends."

Mark nods, seemingly pleased by not having to entertain Penny. "What are you guys doing beforehand?"

"We need to go pick up our tuxes and I need to play chauffeur to James while he runs some errands."

"I still can't believe neither of you found dates for the dance. What quarterback of the state champion football team doesn't have a date to a dance? Oh and of course, more importantly, the star kicker of the football team. The kicker! TV has really failed us with expectations."

"Honey, I am sure they could have brought their pick of the whole class. Maybe they don't want dates. Too locked down, save some money too!" Julie winks at me. "Okay Mark, we've bothered them enough. We'll see you boys later on for the big night!"

"Did you think for a second she was hinting that we were going to the dance together?" I ask Grady, watching Julie hop on Mark's back and him carrying her up the stairs.

"No way," Grady shakes his head, "they're just weird."

We fall back on the bed. Grady is breathing heavily next to me, and he moves closer and puts his head on my arm. "That was different," he says, "should I be concerned?"

"Let's just say I have been doing some research and no one should look at my browser history." I look at him while we lay there. He looks the same as that first day of school. How does he stay in the same shape as he was during football? Does he really work out all the time? But when? We are at school all day and I'm over his house almost every day after school.

"Why are you looking at me like that?"

"When do you find time to work out?"

"Random. Usually in the morning I do weights and at night, before bed, I go for a run. Sometimes Davis comes over before school and we lift together. Why?"

"I, umm, was looking at your body and just noticed you pretty much look the same from football."

"Oh you JUST noticed, did you?" He leans his head in and kisses me, his hand moving down my arm and onto my stomach.

"While I'd love to continue this, we have to get going. Maybe we should shower first."

"Good call."

You never realize how small an apartment shower can be until you try and use it with someone else. But with some assistance on both of our parts we made it work, just like back at the hotel in New York. "I get the whole showering with someone else is kinda hot but do you think that's just for, like, normal sized showers?"

"Yeah, something is telling me right now that it doesn't matter the shower size." I reach for the shampoo and almost punch Grady in the face. Maybe he has a point. Wait, was that the apartment door opening? I whisper, "Did you hear that?"

"James are you home? I had to run back and get some shoes for Virtue to go with her dress. Do you want to come over with me after?"

Fuckkkkk, Grady mouths. We never should have come back here, or at least showered one at a time. "I still have some errands to run before the dance so I'll pass."

"You need a ride? You can get errands done quicker if you have a car to do them."

"No, it's fine. Grady is coming by in a little bit to pick me up." Grady starts to laugh and I give him a look.

"Don't you think you spend too much time with Grady? Honestly James, you need to branch out a bit more. He's a bad influence on you."

"What?" Grady whispers, face scrunching up.

"What do you mean?" I prod. Grady rolls his eyes.

"You know that Virtue tells me things about school, things that I know I won't hear from you. Things like Grady is a womanizer, dates all sorts of types at school. That's not a good path to be on in life James, and I worry that you might pick up some of his habits."

A womanizer? Grady mouths, grabbing my ass. I burst out laughing.

161

"It's not funny James. You really should spend more time with Ralph. It'd be good to have a father figure in your life with good morals."

"Okay Penny, I will try and spend a little less time with Grady but don't really have a choice today."

"Alright well have fun tonight. I'll be over at Ralph's. Don't stay out too late and stay out of trouble. Make sure to talk to Virtue and maybe invite her and her friends to hang out with you guys." The door to the apartment slams.

"Okay, really? A womanizer? Really Virtue? I literally had your dick in my hand like twenty minutes ago and, oh look! There it is again!"

"Calm down Romeo, and don't do that right now. We don't have time. Let's get out and go get our tuxes."

Twenty-Three

We are in Grady's room getting changed into our tuxes. Our group decided to do anything other than black, because we knew everyone else would most likely go traditional. We wanted to stand out. I went with royal blue with black trim, and Grady's is a deep purple. I look in the mirror and I have to admit...I look good.

"Ready to do this? Oh wow. You umm...yeah. Okay so maybe we have time for a quick umm."

"And you look great too. Let's hope you can keep your shit together a bit more in front of your parents." I lean in and kiss him.

"You just look so...hot in that tux."

I look out the window and see that both Rob's and Davis's cars are in the driveway. "The gang's here. Let's head down."

Julie and Mark are waiting at the bottom of the stairs when we hit the front hall. "Oh wow. Interesting color choices gentleman. But you both look very handsome." Julie gives my shoulder a squeeze and Mark wipes a tear from his eye.

"Told you he'd cry first," Grady says, leaning in to give Mark a hug.

"No one's crying. I think the rest of your friends are here." Mark opens the door and, wow. Those are some bright tuxes.

Davis is wearing what could only be described as a banana yellow colored tux, with Rob in a bright green tux. What I didn't know was the girls actually worked to match us. Chloe's dress is purple and royal blue, and Dana's is green and yellow.

"Look at the girls!" Julie squeals. "How on earth did they find those dresses to match your ridiculous tuxes!" In a way, they only helped it appear like we were all going together as friends.

"Shit, I forgot something upstairs. James, can you come with me for a second?" We head back upstairs to Grady's room. "I almost forgot I bought you something for tonight. Well, I bought both of us something." He reaches into his top dresser drawer and hands me a small box.

"Grady...I didn't get you anything."

"And there was no expectation for us to get each other gifts. But I had this idea come to me one day and I knew I had to find them and buy them." I open the box and inside are a set of cufflinks, one in the shape of a G and one in the shape of a J. "We know we can't go to the dance together, technically. But I wanted us to feel like we were going together, and I hope that each of us wearing a set of these cufflinks will help with that."

"Thank you. I love them." I give Grady a big hug, just as Davis comes into the room.

"Hey guys. Hate to break up whatever cute moment you're having here, but all the parents are here now. Well, not yours James, but the rest. Let's go. You'll have plenty of cute moments later."

As the photo taking continues, the parents cannot get over our tuxes and the girls' dresses. After the group shots, Chloe's parents ask for a couple of photos of just Chloe and Rob. The limo is pulling up the driveway as Chloe and Rob finish up, so we start walking down the lawn to meet it. "Hey Grady? James? Can I get a few pictures of you guys?" Julie holds her phone up and gestures us back to the top of the lawn.

"You still sure they don't suspect anything?" Grady responds by raising an eyebrow.

"Just a couple. Let's start with one with your arms around each other's shoulders." Julie snaps a few photos. "Okay, now do a couple of you just standing there. Okay, good. Alright, go off with your friends. Have fun tonight. Be moderately safe and call if you need a ride home from anywhere after!"

"You might need to have that talk with them," I said, clapping a hand on Grady's back. We join everyone in the limo and take off to the winter formal.

The winter formal is…weird. It wasn't as coupley as I expected. The only time the couples truly broke off was during

165

slow dances, and the DJ wasn't really pushing a lot of slow songs. Grady and I stood off to the side at a table, chatting while the slow dance songs played. I see Virtue with her friends off to the side. For some reason she keeps glaring at me. Maybe because I didn't invite her to hang with my friends, or take the photo my mom requested with her.

"We could dance if you want," Grady offers, leaning against the wall.

"Oh okay. I'll get right on that."

"What I meant was that this isn't the only room in this place. We could find a private room. A bathroom, janitor's closet."

"Your solution is to go dance next to either some urinals or some gross mops? You really are quite the romantic Grady."

He laughs. "I get it. But other than Virtue and her weird friends, it's pretty much just you and I on the sidelines right now." His hand finds mine under the table.

"Grady! What are you doing? What if someone sees?"

"Yes James. Under the table and through the tablecloth in this dark room. Someone is going to see." He gives me his little smirk, and it makes me regret not taking him up on that janitor's closet.

Chloe and Dana come back to the table, followed by Rob and Davis. The DJ goes right into another slow song and Grady lets out a groan. "Hey, why don't Rob and Davis sit this one out and we take you two out for a dance?"

"Please," Rob pleads, "my feet are killing me."

I go to walk up to Chloe, but she takes Grady's hand and Dana grabs mine. "You're stuck with me handsome."

There is a weird attention shift in the crowd. Most are looking from Chloe and Grady to Dana and I. Do Chloe and I really give off that much of a vibe that people think we are dating? Are people thinking this is scandalous in some way?

"Yes, I notice them too. I'm trying to figure out if they think Chloe should be dancing with you, or if it should be Grady."

"It's definitely Chloe," I say. Looking at Grady and Chloe, they would make a cute couple if it weren't for some obvious road blocks.

"I'm not 100% sold on that. I know what I know, and I haven't heard anything. But the two of you spend a lot of time together, and somehow there are only two football players at the whole dance without dates. Again, not saying you guys are making it obvious, but you definitely are not helping your case if anyone suspects. That's why Chloe and I came over to dance with you guys...she had the same thought I did."

"Well regardless if that is the case or not, thank you for thinking of us. I don't mean to pry, but you and Davis?"

She smiles. "No, it's not like that. I think it could be, if he wanted me. The whole thing. A relationship."

"Oh c'mon Dana! He is constantly flirting with you and pretty much pushes people out of the way to get a seat next to you at lunch."

"Well, I'm not going to make the move. It's up to him to grow a pair."

Looking around, whoever was on the winter formal committee really threw in the towel on this year's theme. It was Out of This World or something. It's just a bunch of purple lights and star-shaped string lights. Maybe the venue cost a lot to rent, and the budget for decorations was the first casualty.

"You know James, I had a crush on Grady for the longest time in middle school and the first few years of high school."

"How'd that end up working out for you?"

She gives my shoulder a little punch. "I did get dared to kiss him at a party freshman year. And I did. The kiss was bad. I didn't have a lot to compare it to at the time, but from what I knew it was bad. I thought it was because I caught him off guard, but I think we know the real reason now."

"But I've heard he dated his fair share of girls over the years, so he must have just been inexperienced"

"Are you kidding me? Grady dated like half of our class and dipped into the pool of juniors too. But I don't think it was him that really initiated any of it. I think he let girls come to him, flirt with him and ask him out. But it's so odd that he hasn't dated a single girl his senior year!"

I let out a laugh. "Okay so this all makes sense now. My mom came home today and was talking to me while Grady and I were in the shower." Dana's eyes go big. "No, she didn't know he was in there. Calm down. Anyways, she had told me that I should spend less time with Grady because Virtue said he's a womanizer. That he's a bad influence on me. All while he's literally standing butt ass naked in the shower with me."

Dana laughs so hard she snorts. "Oh, that was not pretty of me. But fuck, that's funny."

"What the fuck is he doing?" Chloe says a bit too loudly, people turning their attention to her. I look in the direction of Chloe's gaze and Rob is leaning in close with some girl who has her hand on his shoulder. Rob has a big smile on his face as he's talking to her.

"Oh shit. Why is Rob talking to his ex THAT close?"

"What the fuck are you doing Rob? Heather, if you don't take your fucking hand off him I will remove it for you."

"Oh fuck off Chloe. We were just talking." Heather says. She smiles and tilts her head. "Maybe if you weren't dancing with another man."

"Say that a little closer to my face so I can slap the shit out of you, you twat."

"That is enough Miss Jenkins," a chaperone says. He must be a teacher for the underclassmen because I don't recognize him at all. "You need to leave. Now."

"Do you have nothing to say Rob?" Chloe says, as she is escorted out of the room. Rob just stands there staring at Chloe as she goes through the doorway.

"Well, that escalated quickly," I say to Dana. "With the limo, do you think we should also go? She doesn't really have a way home."

"I'm down," Davis appears next to the three of us still on the dance floor. "I mean I should probably get the house ready for the party anyways. I talked to Quentin and he'll give

Rob a ride to the party. Probably shouldn't be in the same car as Chloe right now."

I look over at Rob, who is just staring at the floor. Heather was no longer anywhere in sight. As I walk by him, I clap his shoulder. "I'll talk to her Rob." He nods, and just like that we are out the door.

That's a wrap on the winter formal.

Twenty-Four

Chloe pulls up to Sam and Mitch's condo and cuts the engine. "Here's to hoping the rest of your night goes better than mine." The limo had dropped Chloe and I off at her house, and she volunteered to drive me over to the condo.

"Maybe he wasn't flirting with her. He had a lot to drink before and at the dance. Rob seems to just talk a lot more when he's drunk."

"Yeah sure. But out of everyone there he chose Heather to latch onto. It just feels...shitty."

"You sure you don't wanna go to Davis's party? I know he'll be there but so will almost everyone else. Hang out with Dana. Flirt with another dude. Make him jealous, or at least make him see what he did was wrong."

"I think I'll just head home. I'd just drag anyone around me down. You have everything you need?"

"Yeah. I had dropped a bag of stuff off earlier this week so I didn't have to think about it tonight."

Chloe starts picking at her finger nail, chipping off some of the polish. "Where did Uncle Mitch and Uncle Sam even go tonight? But it's super nice of them to give you the condo."

"They had to work at Tipsy Mic tonight but I think they said they were heading up to Narragansett after, to a friend's beach house. They closed the bar tomorrow but we've been pretty slow on Sundays anyways. No football and no beach goers." My pocket vibrates.

MITCH: Have fun tonight! Don't break anything and clean up after yourselves!
SAM: What he means is don't leave your used condoms and wrappers on the ground
MITCH: Sam…just no. stop
MITCH: Hope you're there or almost are! Don't want the condo to burn down
JAMES: Thanks guys. About to head in.
SAM: Key's under the mat.

"Grady?"

"No, just Mitch and Sam. But I better head in. They are concerned that the place may burn down?"

"Maybe some mood setting candles? Oh how romanticcccc," Chloe feigns falling back, rolling her eyes.

"Thanks for the ride. Consider going to Davis's. You know I'd be there with you otherwise."

"Have LOTS of fun." Chloe says as I close the car door. She is pulling away as I unlock the door.

Wow. The living room looks amazing. There are candles lit everywhere, with string lights filling almost the whole ceiling. Flower petals are all around the sofa bed and on top of the sheets. An ice bucket sits on the table next to the sofa with two bottles of champagne, along with a note:

Your clothes are on the vanity in the bathroom. Your bag of decorations wasn't going to cut it so hope you like what we did with the place. Left some snacks in the fridge. Have fun tonight kid. -Mitch and Sam

I find the bag with my clothes, toothbrush, and deodorant sitting on the vanity, just like they said it would be. I jump in the shower for a quick rinse off. Okay so, between sitting outside with Chloe and being here, it's been about fifteen minutes. Grady was going to do a quick loop of the party, which he said should take about a half hour. That gives me a little time to finish getting the living room settled.

Out of the shower, I brush my teeth and get dressed. Earlier this week I looked back at photos of the team's trip to New York City, specifically the photos of Grady and I from our late-night walk in Times Square. I wanted to recreate some of that night tonight, so I packed the same clothes I wore in the pictures to change into tonight. A Beacon Colts t-shirt and navy shorts.

The kitchen clock says 11:30. Grady should be here by probably midnight. I open the fridge to see what snacks Sam and Mitch left. Inside there is this giant platter of cheeses, crackers, chocolate-covered strawberries, and other fruit. I suddenly feel starving, but don't want to ruin the surprise for

Grady. I take a few pieces of cheese and fruit, then rearrange the rest on the platter so nothing looks missing.

I turn on the TV and settle in on an American Dad rerun. I open the bottle of champagne and pour two glasses and place them on the table.

The episode ends and, like clockwork, I hear a car door slam outside. I run over to the window and peek outside. Not Grady, just some neighbor with some grocery bags. The clock says 12:02. Where's Grady?

JAMES: Hey just want to make sure you're on the way.

A third episode of American Dad has just started. I start to worry that something happened to Grady. I check my phone for, like, the ninetieth time. Nothing.

I grab one of the champagne glasses and drain it.

The first bottle of champagne is gone. I look at my phone. 1:30, no texts.

JAMES: Grady this is really fucked up
JAMES: What happened to 30 min
JAMES: Just don't bother. Don't bother texting me. I know where I stand

It's just before two when I finish cleaning up the condo and blowing out the candles. I don't know what to do about the string lights so I leave them. I just don't want to be here anymore. I leave the condo and start the walk home.

My alarm clock says 2:42 when I finally lay down in bed, alone in the apartment. I plug my phone in to charge and roll over. And just sob into my pillow.

Twenty-Five

I wake up around nine and the apartment is quiet. Penny must still be over at Ralph's. I feel exhausted, but a mile and a half walk at two in the morning probably didn't help.

I grab my phone. 12 missed calls and 9 text messages, all from Grady.

GRADY (3:10am): Hey I lost track of time at the party. otw

GRADY (3:21am): Hey I'm here. I knocked but you didn't come to the door. I tried calling

GRADY (3:23am): Are you still here? I tried calling again

GRADY (3:26am): Can you please respond

GRADY (3:29am): Okay so I'm guessing you fell asleep

GRADY (3:33am): I'm heading home. Text me if you wake up

GRADY (8:41am): You awake?

GRADY (8:52am): Are you mad at me

GRADY (8:54am): Are you really not texting me back

I put my phone down on the bed. Not only did Grady blow me off last night, but he had what appears to be twenty-one opportunities to apologize. Not one. My phone lights up.

CHLOE: Hey Grady's been texting me all morning asking about you. What happened last night?
JAMES: He never showed. Well he may have but it wasn't until after three
JAMES: I left and went home around two. I couldn't sit there any longer waiting
CHLOE: WTF
JAMES: I woke up to a ton of missed calls and texts from him. Not a single apology
CHLOE: What a shitty night. What a shit night for both of us. Dances suck
JAMES: I'll text you later. I need to figure out my response

I sit up in bed. I feel like shit. But I also know I need to get ready and leave the apartment. I can't deal with Penny if she comes back. Or, worse yet, if I get invited over to Ralph's for dinner or something. I check the weather app, forty-eight degrees. I throw on sweats and grab a blanket out of the hallway closet. Laying on the beach sounds good right now.

JAMES: I'm heading down to our spot on the beach. If ur bored feel free to join
CHLOE: I'll grab Beacon Donuts on the way. C U soon

When I get to the beach it's completely empty. The sun is starting to come out from behind the clouds, but it's still winter. I've been told the beach season here really doesn't kick off until the weekend of Memorial Day. Well, that's at least what Chloe told me.

I had grabbed the mail on my way out, noticing our mailbox was looking a bit overstuffed. I set up the blanket and sprawl across it, starting to cycle through the mail when I notice a letter from UCLA in the pile. My heart skips a beat as I rip open the envelope, unfolding the letter inside:

Dear James,

As the head coach of the UCLA Bruins, I wanted to write you to let you know how impressed our coaching staff was with your play this season. In particular, your extraordinary play in the Rhode Island State Championship game. We are always looking to recruit the best talent in the nation, and I want to confirm to you in writing my offer of an athletic scholarship to the University of California, Los Angeles. Your scholarship will include the cost of your tuition fees, books, supplies, room and board, and travel expenses.

I stop reading the rest of the letter. I don't believe it. I actually have a way out. And I should be celebrating this right now. I should be celebrating with Grady, but instead I'm sitting alone on this beach.

I pull out my phone and pull up Grady's and my text chain. He hasn't sent anything since asking if I was mad at him. Of course I'm mad at you Grady. I'm also mad at myself. I'm mad that I built this image of the dance in my head that maybe was unrealistic. Maybe I should have known that Grady wasn't going to take it seriously. But what about the cufflinks? When he put the cufflinks on me, I almost told him I loved him in that instant, but stopped myself. I didn't want to freak Grady out right before the dance in case he didn't feel the same way. Maybe he doesn't. He couldn't even bother to show up when they had planned last night for weeks.

JAMES: Of course I'm mad. You blew me off Grady.
JAMES: You lied to me and couldn't be bothered to even text me to say you weren't coming
JAMES: But I bet you don't care how it felt to sit in that condo alone for hours waiting for you. While you had fun with your friends
JAMES: I need time and some space. I'm clearly not a priority to you and need to figure out if I can be
JAMES: Don't text back

Twenty-Six

Tipsy Mic is busy for this early on a Friday night, but it's mostly concentrated at the bar. It's been almost a full week since the dance and work was one of the few things that had been a helpful distraction. Sam is setting up the stage for open mic, and clearly hasn't noticed how slammed Mitch is. I throw my coat under the host stand and hurry behind the bar. "What do you need me to make?"

"Oh thank god," Mitch hands me a strip of drink tickets. "I think I should be able to catch up the bar guests but can you make Sarah's drinks for her tables?"

Most of it is quick beers, so I knock those out right away. A couple cosmos and a vodka soda are left. I get to work on the cosmos when Sarah walks up to the service bar. "I think Mitch is losing his mind. Can't wait to see the fight between him and Sam later." She grabs six beers off the bar top and heads off to her tables. Cosmos are done, and I quickly pour the vodka soda.

"Mitch, do you need any help?" He doesn't even turn around. Probably didn't hear me. I take a quick inventory of the beer fridge and head to the cooler to grab some cases to refill. Walking through the dish room I notice things are getting a bit backed up. "Hey Dan?" I call into the kitchen, "where's Miguel?"

"Didn't show up yet," I hear from behind the wall. I continue to the cooler, grabbing a case each of Corona and Michelob Ultra to bring back to the bar. On the way back I stop at the dish station. This is going to get bad if it gets any more backed up. I fill up a tray of plates and push it through the washer. I notice two of the glass racks are full so I send those through the machine as well.

The bar has calmed down a bit since I left to grab beer. Mitch is leaning against the back counter when I enter the bar. "That was a bit wild for this early. I guess there is some drive-in movie being set up on the beach since it's unseasonably warm. A bunch of people saw us and stopped in for a drink on the way."

"I think you might be in trouble because Miguel isn't here yet and stuff is starting to pile up. I sent a few things through to get washed on my way back from the cooler."

"Really? Shit. Okay, I'll go call him and see what the deal is. If not, Sam is on dish duty until open mic starts. Man the bar for a bit."

I had been working at the Tipsy Mic for the last five months but had never been left to work the bar by myself. No one new comes in for a bit, so I just spend my time prepping fruit for the later rush and making sure the beers and popcorn remain full for the few people at the bar.

"Hey James." I freeze, then turn around to see Mark and Julie settle into the two stools closest to the service bar. They look dressed up, really nice. I'm so used to seeing them in sweats and t-shirts. I know a lot of parents keep up appearances when guests are over, but I was over there so much that they let their guard down. Well, had been over there so much.

"Hey guys! You look nice. Big date tonight?"

"We're heading up to Providence to see a show," Julie responded. "Hey James, is everything all right?"

"What do you mean?"

"Well, we wanted to stop in because we hadn't seen you all week."

"Has it been that long?" Shit, they know something's up.

"James," Mark leaned in, "did you and Grady get in a fight or something? Or did something happen to him at school? We've both tried asking him but he just says he's fine. He just comes home and goes right to his room. We've pretty much only seen him for dinner and when he is coming from or going to school. And it's quiet James. You know Grady. Quiet is not really a Grady mood."

I love Mark and Julie. But I couldn't tell them what caused the fight between Grady and I.

"We got into an argument after winter formal. It's not really for me to say what about. I think he's just under a lot of pressure and stuff." Their expressions looked a bit sad. Maybe

Mark had figured Grady and I out. Or maybe he's just concerned for Grady. I need to not get myself worked up during a work shift.

"Well, I hope you and Grady figure it out. I hate to see you two fighting. It's not a way to end things the last few months of senior year." They stood up from their seats at the bar. "Hope to see you soon James." Julie reached out and grabs my hand, gives it a little squeeze, and then they are walking out of the bar.

"What were the boyfriend's parents up to?" Mitch asked. I hadn't even realized he was back behind the bar.

"Ex-boyfriend's parents. Just checking in on me since they haven't seen me all week."

"If you say so. You can act moody as hell but you aren't over him. And I bet he isn't over you. He just got scared about everyone finding out about you two and chose to not leave that party. Was it shitty of him to not text you? That he didn't see the effort you put into making the night special after the formal, having a little spot just for you two? Yeah. But mark my words…you'll get over it."

I wanted to believe him, but Grady hasn't even tried to apologize. I mean, maybe he thought he did but it was more of an excuse.

The night began to pick back up. Mitch wanted me to learn how to manage the bar a bit better, so we switched spots and he worked the service bar and I handled guests. Once you got into a rhythm it wasn't bad, especially with Mitch helping out as needed. A lot of the patrons at the bar, like most Fridays, were Sam and Mitch's friends. Since Mitch had told them I was 18 they shamelessly flirted with me. It did help to lift my spirits a bit.

"Just remember this young man's heart was broken this week, so tip generously when you leave," Mitch calls out to the bar, winking at me.

"Heartbroken? That's good news for the rest of us." Oh no. I look over and Henry is sitting at the end of the bar. Really Mitch? That was the one moment you chose to announce to the bar I'm single? Now I have to deal with creepy Henry all night. I turned to Mitch and he mouths *I'm so sorry*.

"Hi Henry. What can I get you?" He looks me over. Gross.

"I guess, for now, a martini. Dirty. Extra dirty. Might get a little hungry later." I walk away and start making his martini at the other end of the bar.

"At least my friends are younger and more attractive, and just kidding around when they flirt with you. That man is just disgusting."

"What would you guess? Thirty-five? Forty years older than me?"

"At least. If he gets to be too much let me know, and we can always switch you over to service bar. You've been doing a great job tonight. Simon and Xander pretty much told me my service was shit in comparison."

I laugh. "It's probably because you get that pissy look on your face. You don't have a good poker face." I bring Henry over his martini. "Do you want some popcorn?"

"None for me. I'm trying to watch my figure." He leans back in his chair and rubs his hands down the front of his body. "So why did you and your little boyfriend break up?"

"I'm sure it's just a fight Henry. I bet we'll be back together next week." Literally anything to steer the conversation.

"Don't you think it would be smart to explore your other options? Play the field a bit while single? You're attractive enough to probably get anyone you want."

God. Make. This. Stop. "There really aren't any other options at school. It'll be him or someone at college next year."

"Who says they have to be from your school?" Henry smirks, leaning his elbows on the bar top. "You should probably pursue someone with a bit more experience before you go off to college."

"Good evening, everyone!" Thank God, an interruption. "For those of you who don't know me, but I think most of you do, I'm Sam. I will be your guide on Open Mic Night, performing a bit myself and maybe joining others. I'm going to start things off with one of my normal kick off the night songs."

I use the distraction to retreat back to the service bar and pour myself a Diet Coke. Mitch had told me before I could put a little something in my soda if I wanted to take the edge off, but Sam shot him down because it makes them a liability. I honestly don't know how Mitch drinks during most of his

186

shifts. I feel it would make me sluggish, let alone remembering what people ordered.

Sam finishes his song and a younger blonde girl takes his spot on the stage, claiming she is going to sing an original song. Her voice is nice, but the song itself sounds pretty stupid.

The tables are really starting to fill up around the stage and the service bar tickets are piling up. Sarah is making constant trips back and forth from the bar. Miguel pops his head into the bar. "Hey James, have you seen Mitch? I got my jobs mixed up and had to wait to get a ride over here."

"He just ran back to grab some wine from the back, but I'll let him know you're here. You've probably got your work cut out for you." He nods and heads over to the dish room.

"Oh bartender? Another martini please." I go ahead and start making another dirty martini. "And make one for yourself too!"

"Henry, you know I can't do that. In case you forgot I'm eighteen." I bring him his drink and go to take the empty glass away.

"Oh, how could I ever forget that. Wait," he grabs the sword of olives from the glass. He stares at me as he eats each olive one by one. I guess reminding him I'm only eighteen was the opposite of a deterrent.

I take the glass and place it in the bar's dishwasher and start loading it with other glassware. I take a sip of my soda and place it on the corner of the bar top. I take survey of the stock and it looks like we need some vodka and bourbon from the back. I grab Mitch's key on the bar wall and head back to the liquor locker. I grab a crate and start filling it with bottles.

"Hey James? I think Sam is going to want me on stage in a few songs so you will be solo on the bar for a bit."

"Got it Mitch. Be right there."

I lock the cage and head back behind the bar. A few people are starting to sit down as I put the crate on the ground. I grab a quick sip of my soda and walk over. "Hey ladies, what can I get for you?" They order a few glasses of wine, so I go about pouring them. Mitch is joining Sam on stage and they start singing some sappy love song to each other.

I bring the ladies their wine, check on my guests other than Henry, and head back to the service bar. There are a few tickets so I get to work. I place them on the bar and stumble back into one of the beer fridges. I suddenly feel quite dizzy. The room's spinning a bit.

"Hey Sarah, can you watch the bar for a minute?" She nods and I head towards the bathroom. I lose my footing and grab a table to hold myself up. Did Mitch sneak booze into my soda? Wait, why would Mitch put booze in my drink? I crash into the bathroom door and fall onto the ground. There is a wadded-up bunch of toilet paper next to my face. Gross.

I try to pull myself up on the sink but my head feels so heavy. The door opens behind me and I can see Henry filling the doorway. He's enormous, blocking any way out the door. It then hits me. I had put my soda on the bar top and not the service bar. Did Henry put something in my drink?

"I told you that someone with experience could help you."

Twenty-Seven

Henry is grabbing the back of my shirt and pulling me up. He pushes me against the bathroom wall, holding me against it with his left hand. He reaches around me and starts unbuckling my pants. I try to push against him, try to get out of his grip but he's too strong. My pants fall to the ground.

"Help!" I scream, but he puts his other hand over my mouth.

"Now James, why would you want to go and ruin a good time?" He whispers into my ear, pressing himself against me. His left hand leaves my back and starts moving down the front of my body.

The room is spinning. Feeling more dizzy. I concentrate as much as I can and chomp down on one of his fingers.

He stumbles backwards into one of the stall doors and I fall to the ground. "You little piece of shit," he growls, coming for me again.

"Help! Please someone help! Help..." I can't tell if I'm yelling or not. I'm having trouble focusing. I feel Henry grab me again, pulling me up and against the wall again. I hear him start to unbuckle his belt when the bathroom door opens.

"What the fuck!" I lift my head as much as I can towards Sam and mouth *help*. Sam grabs Henry and throws him into one of the stall doors. I feel myself start to slide down the wall to the ground but Sam catches me. Mitch comes running into the bathroom just as Henry is running out, shoving Mitch aside. "Mitch! Catch him. Call the police. Do something!" Mitch's eyes go from Sam to me, with my pants around my ankles.

The spinning is too much, so I close my eyes as I feel myself being picked up off the ground.

Twenty-Eight

I'm suddenly aware my head is pounding, but I don't hear the sounds of the bar. I open my eyes and I'm in Mitch and Sam's living room, laying on their pullout couch. "Sam? Mitch?"

"Right here kid," Mitch says. He's sitting in a chair next to me, but gets up and takes a seat on the edge of the mattress.

"How did I get here?"

"What do you remember?" I think back to the bar. I remember carrying the crate of bottles from the liquor cage, pouring the wine for the ladies at the bar, checking on the other patrons except for Henry. *Henry.*

"What did he do to me?" I feel a tear falling down my cheek.

"We don't think anything happened. Almost, but we got there just in time. You still had your underwear on and he...he was in the process of undoing his pants."

"I tried to call out but I couldn't tell if I was loud enough," I wipe the tears from my face. Now that I'm focusing a bit more on Mitch his eyes look a bit red.

"We didn't hear you at all. I happened to look at the bar and notice people looking around, and also noticed Henry was missing. I told Sam to look in the bathroom and I started to head for the kitchen but stopped when I heard Sam yell."

"Did he get away?"

"Unfortunately, yes. We gave a description of him to the cops with his name. We don't know his last name so it may take a bit to find him. James…I shouldn't have let this happen."

"What do you mean you let it happen?"

"Henry has been a creep to you every time he's come in during one of your shifts, but seemed a bit more creepy than usual tonight. I should have just served him and kept you away from him."

"Still wouldn't have stopped him from putting something in my drink," I say. "Well, I'm assuming he put something in my drink."

"Do you want to go to the hospital? You seem like you are doing better but if it would make you more comfortable."

"No. I can't chance this getting back to Penny and Ralph." Mitch nods, understanding.

"Move over," Mitch says, and I slide over in the bed. He lays down on his back next to me. There's a long silence, both of us staring up at the ceiling. "James, you have to know it won't always be this hard. Tonight was traumatic, I know it was. But this isn't how things will be for you in life. And I know it must

194

be that much harder given how things are with Grady. Do you know many times Sam and I have called things off and gotten back together? More times than I can count on both hands. But things find a way to work themselves out in the end."

"Where is Sam by the way?"

"He headed back to the bar to make sure things were alright there. After making sure you were okay of course. We left Sarah in charge while we were gone, but it wasn't too busy when we left."

"Will this hurt business? The whole scene?"

"Do not worry about that James. At all. And it'll be fine. I don't think many people realized what was going on."

The front door clicks shut and Sam walks in, holding a bag of Wendy's. "How's our guy feeling? I picked you up a couple of Jr. Bacon Cheeseburgers if you are feeling hungry at all. And, of course, a fountain Diet Coke. Your favorite."

"Thanks Sam. My stomach feels a bit off but food might help."

"Did you happen to get anything for your FAVORITE guy?"

"I did get myself some spicy nuggets, thank you very much." Mitch throws a pillow at Sam, who ducks. Sam pulls out a Baconator and passes it to Mitch.

"You two fight like an old married couple."

"We've been together longer than a lot of married couples. Now sit up and eat. If you eat laying down, you're gonna get sick." Sam plops down on the other side of me, wrapping an arm around my shoulder. We sit on the sofa bed, in the quiet of the room, eating our Wendy's.

I wake up the next morning and the condo is quiet. I don't even remember falling asleep but do remember turning on some older movie, *Mean Girls*, that Sam and Mitch love. My jacket from the bar is folded nicely on the ottoman. On top of it is a rolled-up bunch of cash, a note attached:
Last night's tip share -Sam.
My phone vibrates in my pocket.

CHLOE: Breakfast.
JAMES: Is that a statement or a question?
CHLOE: I'll be there in a few minutes. Anthony's?
JAMES: Sure but I'm at Sam and Mitch's condo. Can you pock me up there?
CHLOE: Yes I can POCK you up there
JAMES: Rude.

Ten minutes later Chloe pulls in and I jump in the passenger seat.
"Did you stay over last night?"
"I did. I should probably text to let them know I left."

JAMES: Thanks guys. Not sure where you were this morning but Chloe picked me up for breakfast
SAM: np. Don't feel pressured to come back to work until you're ready. We already covered tonight's shift

Chloe gets a spot near the door at Anthony's. "Seems light for a Saturday."

The restaurant is, indeed, quite empty. We pick a table in the back corner, away from the other tables. "You need a few minutes?" The waitress holds out menus.

"Nah. Two egg bennies, two sides of bacon, two coffees, and two waters. Extra creamers for the coffees." The waitress pulls back the menus and walks away.

"What if I didn't want eggs benedict?" I asked Chloe.

"Oh please. You and I have ordered the same exact thing every time we've come here. You're just as boring as I am. What were you doing with the uncles?"

The waitress returns with our coffee and water. I add cream and sugar to my coffee, staring at the liquid in the cup swirling around. Spinning around. I tell Chloe about Henry, about his constant sexual comments and the way he looks at me, what he did to me in the bathroom. The waitress returns to the table and drops the plates of food in front of us. "Well don't you two look like a happy bunch," she says as she walks away.

"So, just to clarify, he only got as far as groping you. Nothing else happened, like physically?"

"Yeah."

"Thank God. Are you okay? I mean…mentally, are you okay?"

"I think so? I don't feel great, but I know things could have been much worse."

"I'm gonna kill him."

"I doubt we are going to see him again. We don't even know where he's from. I only know him as the creepy guy named Henry at the bar."

The table goes quiet for a bit as we eat breakfast. Anthony's has gotten a bit busier as the restaurant switches over to their lunch menu. The sun has started peeking out of the clouds, and more people are milling around on the street. "What's going on with you and Grady?"

I poke at a piece of egg. "I have nothing to report. He hasn't apologized to me and we really haven't talked since Sunday. And, as you know, I actively avoided him at school all week."

"Maybe you should reach out to him. Be the bigger man." The waitress floats by, stopping to top off our coffees, then moves on to the next table. "I know you love him. You haven't said it yet and he hasn't said it yet, but you and I both know it's true. Don't let one night ruin it."

"Maybe if he had intended on staying at the party, he could have told me that up front. At least then I would have just gone to the party. And hello, you're not speaking to Rob because he talked to some girl at the dance."

"He was, for one, flirting with her. Not talking. And second, it was his ex-girlfriend of many years. So, you know, it's a big deal."

"If he doesn't talk to me before the end of next week, I'll talk to him. But only if you talk to Rob too. If I can work things out with Grady, I want all of our little group back together.

"Fine."

Twenty-Nine

Walking into school on Friday morning I realize I need to make a game plan. Grady still hasn't reached out to me, although I probably haven't made it all that easy. I've avoided him in the halls and haven't once looked his way in the two classes we share. Is it really too much to ask that he be the one to initiate his own apology?

In Fiction Workshop we had recently finished reading *The Fault in Our Stars* and the latest assignment had been to write an epilogue chapter for the novel. Mr. Victorino had made copies of all our chapters and handled them out to us to read this week. The last part of the assignment, due yesterday, was to rank in order which chapters we thought worked best with the book.

"I have tallied the results and it would appear Griff's chapter barely beat out James's for the highest score. What I found particularly interesting is that the two chapters are wildly different. Griff's was a more uplifting turn for the characters where James took a more somber approach. In your packets, Griff's was the chapter marked five and James's was eight. I think this shows that most stories have the ability to change their trajectory with the smallest of tweaks, like adding a short epilogue chapter. What are some of your thoughts?"

"I had ranked those two as the top ones because they seemed to follow John Green's writing style and voice the best." Cassidy starts flipping through her packet. "Some of the others almost got there, but I realized after reading the other chapters that mine didn't really connect the way I meant it to."

"And there's nothing wrong with that. Over the duration of the semester many of you have shown you have a distinct writing style, and others also have the ability to adapt well to different genres. Or, in this case, fitting into someone else's writing style. It's why some fanfiction authors are wildly successful, and others do it more as a hobby. They can be successful in different ways. Some are invested solely in one book or series, and write endless side stories that closely connect to the original content. Others take fanfiction to a new level, like when Seth Grahame-Smith took Jane Austen's original work and infused it with zombie lore, creating *Pride and Prejudice and Zombies*. Grahame-Smith even credited Austen as a co-author of the novel and it was wildly popular. It brought a whole new group of readers who most likely wouldn't have read the original work."

"I loved *Pride and Prejudice and Zombies* and found myself jealous that I didn't think of it first," Chloe said. Chloe read a lot in her spare time. I mean...a lot. One wall in her bedroom was floor to ceiling bookcases overflowing with books. Which makes sense with her parents owning a bookstore and all.

"And it was a good example of what some authors can do when books hit public domain status. Which brings me to going over your next assignment. I want each of you to pick a novel that is part of the public domain and rewrite the first two chapters in your own reimagining of the story. You can use a book we've already covered during our public domain lesson, one you've read on your own, or something new you want to read. I caution you that, if you choose to pick a book you haven't read yet, make sure you have the time to both read the book and write your chapters." Mr. Victorino hands a stack of papers to the first desk in each row, with people taking one and passing the rest back.

"This is a list of common public domain novels or novellas that can help you choose for your assignment. I would advise if you are picking a book not on this list that you run it past me first, to make sure it truly is public domain content. Chapters using a non-public domain work as the foundation will not be accepted and you will get an incomplete on the assignment."

One of the first novels on the list is The Great Gatsby. Between the book and the number of movies that have been made, it probably would be one of the easier ones to use. The bell rings, leading to the class hurrying out of the room to get to lunch. "Have a great weekend! If you want to get ahead on the assignment over the weekend and want to run books by me, send an email! James, could you hang back a minute?"

"Sure thing. Chloe, can you grab me two slices of pizza and a Diet Coke?"

I hand her a twenty-dollar bill and she's out the door. "And a Klondike bar for Chloe!"

"What's up Mr. Victorino?"

"I just wanted to make sure everything's okay with you. You haven't been as active in class the past couple weeks and that chapter you turned in was, well...depressing."

I like Mr. Victorino. He's probably my favorite teacher I've had this year, but not someone I'd choose to confide in. "I'm fine Mr. Victorino, just a bit stressed with workload and college next year and all."

"That's normal senior behavior James. But if you ever do need to talk about something my door is always open. Go get your pizza before it gets cold and the rest of your money before Miss Jenkins spends it all."

I find Chloe sitting with Dana at the table closest to the back exit. I take an open seat in front of my pizza, diet coke, and two chocolate chip cookies. "Figured you could use the cookies. If not, I also figured that Dana and I could use the cookies."

"Thanks?" At least Chloe got my normal pizza order right. One pepperoni and one cheese.

"Have you talked to Grady yet?" Dana asks.

"No. I honestly haven't even seen him yet today." I did a quick scan of the cafeteria. Nope, not in here today. Maybe he's avoiding me now too.

"Remember our deal. You talk to Grady and I'll talk to Rob."

"Eww Chloe, really?" Dana side-eyes her. "After he was practically dry humping Heather at winter formal?"

"Calm down Dana. He was not DRY HUMPING her. He was just talking to her. Maybe flirting with her."

"Well don't go easy on him. Make sure he feels really guilty about it. Maybe force him to buy you something nice."

"You must be a gem to date Dana," I say, and they both laugh. I was hoping to catch Grady here but I still don't see him.

JAMES: We need to talk
GRADY: ok
JAMES: I'll meet you at your truck after school
GRADY: ok

"He sure is chatty." I turn my phone towards Dana and Chloe.

"Guys are so weird. I have great expectations for your chat this afternoon." Dana breaks off a piece of a cookie. Okay, so they weren't really for me after all.

"Hey," Davis takes a seat next to me, "some of the guys from the team are getting together tonight for some Madden and drinks at my house. You down James?"

I look at my phone on the table. "I don't know Davis. Maybe."

"Is this about Grady? Dude, who cares? The rest of the team will be there. Hell, maybe I won't invite him."

"Davis, you're his best friend. Of course you are inviting him."

"You guys need to figure shit out and stop bringing down the group. I can talk to him if you want."

"That's alright but thanks Davis. I actually made plans to talk to him after school."

"Great. Kiss and make up and then he can drive you to my house. Ladies, if you get bored later feel free to stop by." He winks at Dana, gets up and leaves.

"You could just let Davis handle Grady for you," Chloe says, "but that means he won't face the wrath of James."

"I do think I have a few things he needs to hear."

Thirty

I find Grady standing by his truck when I enter the parking lot. I have mixed emotions as I walk up to him. I miss him so much but I am still so angry with him.

"Hey," I say. Grady looks up at me. No smile for me it seems. He looks good. Focus James. You are here to let him know you are mad at him.

"Hey." I take the spot next to him, leaning against the tailgate. We stand there, quiet for a bit. The parking lot is busy, clearing out with the end of the school day. The track team is out running, the weather still holding up. I see Chloe and Dana talking at the other end of the parking lot, Chloe looking back and forth between Dana and I. Now that she sees me talking to Grady, she has no choice other than talking to Rob. "I haven't seen you around much."

"That was kinda on purpose Grady," I say, maybe a bit too snippy. This is a mission to work on getting him to apologize and patch things up, not dig the hole deeper.

205

"Is this still about the party?" His leg bounces up and down as he leans against the truck. Maybe he's nervous, but that's also a pretty stupid question.

"Do you still think you didn't do anything wrong, Grady? Honestly, when you think back to that night, you don't see anything you did or didn't do as wrong."

"I got hung up at Davis's party James, like I told you. The whole football team was there and we got to drinking. Davis had someone score a couple of kegs and I got stuck playing flip cup and lost track of time. But you really haven't given me any chance to talk to you since then and explain what happened."

"Because I was waiting for an apology, Grady. You've had about two weeks to apologize to me for that night and not once did you even think to do that. And that excuse about getting stuck playing a game is a real shitty excuse. Instead, I sat in Mitch and Sam's condo like an asshole for three hours waiting for you. For plans you and I made weeks ago, to have a nice night where we didn't have to be on guard and actually be with each other. Instead, you stayed at a party I'm guessing to keep your social status in check. You know how you could have fixed this from the start? Told me you didn't want to spend the night with me, that you would prefer to go to the party. Then at least I also could have gone to the party, or maybe hung out with Chloe. At least I would have a good memory of the night to look back on. Instead, it's me sitting alone in a room I know Sam and Mitch spent hours prepping for us."

"I went to the condo but you weren't there," Grady murmurs, his eyes squinting in the sun.

"Oh bullshit. Even if you did, was it at like three in the morning once the party disbanded and you needed somewhere to go? When I was convenient for you?"

"Fuck you James. I am under a lot of pressure right now. The next four years and maybe my future rides on what I decide to do in the next few months."

His future? "Are you talking about college, or are you talking about us?"

"Probably both James. I've worked my whole life to get where I am. I have offer letters from over three dozen schools to play football for them. But we know how these things work James. My career will be squashed if they find out about me. About us."

I turn away from him. I'm getting too worked up and I don't want him to see me cry, give him the upper hand. I look over and notice Chloe and Dana are gone. I clear my throat, refocus on angry energy. "Did you just come to realize this or did someone tell you this?"

"Does it really matter?"

Maybe it doesn't. What difference does it really make at this point? He's now chosen football over me but maybe that's how it always was going to be. He's right in a way. Football has been his passion almost his whole life. He's played it his entire life, Mark and Julie always have people over on Saturdays and Sundays to watch it, and he and his dad have mapped out all the schools with the best chances for him to play. I've been in his life for not even a year. But it's still not really an excuse for his behavior.

"If you knew this was how things would turn out, if you knew you would be going to college and would keep going on without being public with me, or any other guy if not me, then why string me along? Fuck Grady, we talked about going out to school in California together if you got offer letters for a school out there. And I bet you have a bunch that did offer you some sort of scholarship."

"But what if a California school isn't my best option? I have offers from Oklahoma, from Texas, from LSU to play football. On full scholarship. Those are the types of teams that get draft attention more than most."

"So now you've decided that you'd rather throw who you are aside, throw me aside, for the small possibility you could get drafted in the NFL someday? You go to a small school in Rhode Island Grady. Let's be real. You might be the best quarterback here in this state, but there are a lot more quarterbacks trying for the same thing you are. And they are from towns and states that live and breathe for Friday night lights."

"Okay, I get you're mad but you're just being fucking cruel."

"What's cruel is what you're doing to me right now, Grady. I have never felt about someone the way I feel about you. And now I'm learning you're just throwing it away because you're scared. Do you not think I'm scared? You hide because it could hurt your chances to play football. I hide because who knows what my mom and Ralph would do to me if they find out. So don't play that card with me because you will lose."

"You don't own the right to be the only one who can be scared."

"You want to talk scared? Last weekend at work I was almost raped in the bathroom by a customer. He put something in my drink, followed me into the Tipsy Mic bathroom, and held me up against the wall while pulling my pants down. Ran his hands all over me. He was starting to undo his pants when Sam luckily came into the bathroom and threw him off of me. And I couldn't go to the police or anything. You know why? Because of my fucking mother and Ralph. So yes, Grady, I get the chance to be a bit more scared than you."

"James, I-" Grady's eyes go big as he stops talking. I turn around and standing on the other side of the truck, with a smirk on her face, is Virtue.

Thirty-One

Shit. Shit shit shit shit.

I pull out my phone and call Chloe as I sprint out of the parking lot and onto the trail through the woods behind the school. "Yeah? This better be good. I was about to devour a burrito."

"I just got into a huge fight with Grady in the parking lot at school. He gave me the same shitty excuse about getting hung up at Davis's house. But I also told him about what happened at the bar last weekend--"

"--What did he have to say about that?" I barely miss falling on my face after tripping on a tree root, catching myself on the trunk of the tree.

"I didn't get to find out because Virtue popped out from behind Grady's truck. She claimed we were both bad seeds and needed help, especially me. That she was going to tell her dad so I can get fixed, whatever that means."

"Fuck. This is bad. Do you need to come over? I can come get you. I just need to see if I can get out of my shift at four."

"No need. I'm already cutting through the woods to your house. Should be there in like five minutes. See you soon." I look behind me and luckily there is no sign of Virtue following. Or maybe it's not lucky. Maybe she has already run off to Ralph who would then instantly go find Penny.

How did this happen? We were always so careful when talking about us in public, making sure no one was around that didn't already know. No, I definitely wasn't paying attention. I was too busy laying into Grady and trying to guilt trip him for the past two weeks.

I need to come up with a plan. It isn't going to be feasible to stay at the apartment. Not with Penny lost in Ralph's world and being within Ralph's grasp. They will send me away to his camp, whatever that is. I can't end up there. I stop and sit on a downed tree and pull my phone out again.

JAMES: Hey I may need to call in that favor
MITCH: What's going on? And of course. I'll let Sam know
JAMES: Virtue overheard a convo with Grady and probably on her way to tell Ralph and prob Penny
MITCH: Fuck. Ok what do u need from me?
JAMES: Hopefully just the couch until I figure some things out.
JAMES: I need to grab a few things from the apartment before Penny gets home from work

MITCH: Be quick. I'll put a key under the doormat before I leave for the bar. You never told her where we live?

JAMES: No. All she knows is that ur my boss

MITCH: Text me when you get to the condo. Don't worry about coming in for work. I can get Sam to work tables until open mic starts.

JAMES: Shit I forgot about work. I'll be there.

MITCH: What if she or Ralph show up?

JAMES: They won't. They won't make a scene in public. And I will make sure to leave with you or Sam

MITCH: Whatever you think is best. But the offer is there

MITCH: Good luck

I get up from the log and continue the trek through the woods. Thank God I took the job at Tipsy Mic and got to know Mitch and Sam. I'm sure I could have crashed for a night or two at Chloe's, but it would be one of the first places Penny would look for me. And that would probably have been game over for me.

Chloe is waiting outside the trail behind her house when I walk out of the woods. She starts running and embraces me in a big hug. "It's going to be okay," she whispers in my ear, "we will come up with a plan."

I slump into one of the chairs on her deck and she settles in the one next to me. "I texted Mitch. He said it would be alright if I stayed there and would tell Sam. Didn't say how long but I think I should be good for a while, given Mitch's history."

"Yeah, between my parents and him I've heard most of the story. I get it."

I just need to get through the next few hours. "You should probably get home soon to beat Penny there. I can drop you off on my way to work but just have to text my boss I'll be a little late."

"Thanks Chloe." Chloe disappears into the house. It has gotten significantly darker since I came from the woods. Shit. If it starts raining, I need to figure out how to get to Mitch and Sam's. I don't want to walk a few miles in the rain with all my stuff.

A loud meow shakes me back to the present. "Hey Baby, where did you come from?" Baby jumps into my lap and starts purring immediately and lays down. Still such a ridiculous name for a cat.

I'm going to need clothes, the cash saved in my desk, anything I need for school, and a few other things. The picture of my dad. I can grab Penny's luggage from her closet because it's bigger than mine. Then I will have only that and my backpack with my school shit in it.

Chloe emerges from the patio door. "Ready to go? Sandy said she had planned on staying a bit later anyways. I told her there was a minor family emergency but it shouldn't take long."

"Hate to bust your lie bubble, but can I drop you off so I can use your car to move my things to the condo? It looks like it's gonna rain and I don't want to get stuck in it lugging my bags. I can drop the car off at the bookstore before I go to work tonight."

"Didn't even think of all that. Of course. But let's get going."

It is a short, quiet ride to the bookstore. Rain did, in fact, start on the ride over. It was now coming down much harder and the wind was picking up. The streets closer to the beach flood quickly in heavy rains, so hopefully they hold out until I get back to the apartment.

I park in the closest spot to the door and throw the car in park. Man, I really should have bought my own car by now. Would have been really helpful in this scenario.

"Are you doing okay?"

"I think so," I respond, "as long as I can get out of the apartment quickly. I mean it's not like I have a lot of shit to pack up." Chloe laughs, and twists her hair in her fingers. I think it's a habit of hers when she's nervous, or maybe anxious. Maybe both. I see her glance at the clock. "Your shift starts soon. Go, please."

"Will you please, please, please text me when you are out of there and in the condo? Or even just when you leave the apartment?"

"Absolutely."

Thirty-Two

I don't see Penny's car anywhere when I pull up to the apartment. Either Ralph hasn't gotten to her yet or Penny got stuck at work. Another quick scan reveals Ralph's car isn't here either. Good.

I quickly run from the car to the overhang but still get drenched in the process. I take the steps two at a time to the second floor, turning right to go to the apartment when Mrs. Weddle pops out of her apartment.

"Hi James! Did you finally get a car? It's lovely! I've always wanted a Jeep but could never afford one. Always have a sedan ten or so years old. Harvey also was one to strike deals and get the cheapest car on the lot. Always a Chevy this or a Ford that, sometimes a Buick. Never a Japanese car, he didn't trust the manufacturing of them. Now I've got a Ford Taurus that is pushing twenty-five years old. Still runs great, but you knew that! They must be paying you well at that restaurant! I would come visit but being on a fixed income my type of a treat and night out is the two for five-dollar special at McDonald's!"

She talks a lot. And remembers everything, like how I had to frame it more to Penny I worked at a restaurant and not a bar. "Oh, it's not my car Mrs. Weddle. I'm borrowing it for the afternoon to grab a few things from the apartment, with it raining and all." Shit. Never give this woman more details than necessary.

"Are you going somewhere? Is Penny, sorry, your mom going to? I don't see her that much anymore as I'm guessing she spends most of her time between work and Ralph's. Doesn't leave much time for you!"

Okay, where would I be going? I can't give the normal spots because then she will tell Penny, and then she will go looking there. Got it. "I received a late scholarship offer to Syracuse for football. Their incoming kicker backed out and went with another school. Duke, I think."

"That's wonderful! But Penny told me you were staying local in order to help out with Ralph's group. University of Rhode Island I think she said, since they have the local branch. She was hoping you would go into leadership in Ralph's group if college didn't end up working out. She told me you had problems with some of your grades and wanted you to have a backup plan if college didn't work out."

Fucking Penny, always thinking for herself. I never told her I received the offer letter from UCLA for a full scholarship to be on their football team. "Oh Mrs. Weddle, I think you might be confused. My grades are great and will be fine at college, but it would be much better if I had a way to go to college that wouldn't cost us anything. I just haven't told her yet. I wanted it to be a surprise. I am heading up there with one of my teammates, Pete."

"The Cobb boy? Isn't he going to Kansas State? Something about his aunt and uncle living out there and having family nearby?"

I didn't realize her gossip extended outside this apartment building. "He got an offer too, so he just wants to check out all of his options. But I really should be going. I only have the car for like an hour and need to get over to his house by five. We're driving up tonight with his parents to go check out the campus tomorrow." Jesus, it's going to be hard to remember all the details to these lies. Because Mrs. Weddle will remember them all to regurgitate to Penny.

"And not tell your mother before? And where will you be staying? Are you going to call her or leave a note? She will worry about you, you know!"

"I'll leave a note for her with all the info. She's working late today so I don't want to disturb her and stress her out. But I really, really need to go pack and get on the road. It was good catching up with you Mrs. Weddle!" I turned around and start down the walkway to our apartment. Finally free.

I open the door and quickly move to my mom's bedroom, to grab the luggage out of her closet. It's not there. I also notice how little she actually has in her closet. A few shirts and a jacket on hangers, a pair of shoes on the ground, a pair of pants and an extra blanket on the top shelf. Shit, she must have

219

moved most of her stuff over to Ralph's and just kept a few things here as needed.

Wait, did she plan on having both of us move over there? It's true that Ralph had set up a small room for me in case I stayed there with Mom, but did she really expect to just move us there without asking me first? With Virtue there? No thank you.

Okay, new plan. I go to the hallway closet to grab my luggage but it's also missing. Did she really use both to move her stuff? It's fine. I still have my football bag under my bed. Luckily she hadn't taken this as well, so I drop it on top of the bed and start ripping clothes off hangers and throwing them in the bag. Once the hangers are empty, I move to the shelf and start grabbing jeans and shorts, and then empty the bins of socks and underwear. The football bag is full to the brim and I'm still not close to done. I run to the kitchen, looking for any sort of bags to use and settle on garbage bags. The first one gets stuffed with all of my shoes and sweatshirts, the second then filled with books and notepads from the top of my desk. I open my desk drawer and grab the copy of *Breaking the Moon* buried under a pile of random pens and markers. I flip through the book, relief flowing through me as I see my tip money tucked amongst the pages. In the bag it goes.

But the picture of my father is missing. I didn't realize it at first but I kept it under the stack of books on my desk. I go through the bag of books and it's not there, not stuck to the back of any of the books. I always suspected Penny searched my stuff but did she really come in and only take that one thing?

I run back to her room and start opening drawers, searching through them. Nothing in the dresser, nothing in the nightstand. She wouldn't have taken it and then hid it in a common area like the kitchen or the living room. She either has it with her, or she got rid of it.

I return back to my room and zip up the football bag and throw it over my shoulder. I grab the two garbage bags and give the room one last look over, checking if there's anything I will miss. This is likely the last time I'll be here. But the room is practically empty. Like I said to Chloe, there wasn't much to pack up. When you don't have a lot of money, and move around a lot, you don't accumulate a lot of stuff.

As I exit the bedroom and start crossing the living room, I hear the entry door click shut. Penny is standing there, and her eyes turn to slits when she sees the bags in my hand.

"And where do you think you're going?"

Thirty-Three

She is standing in front of the door, blocking my one and only exit. Well, excluding jumping from the balcony. Could work, but if I hurt myself I'm basically fucked.

"What did you do with my picture of Dad"

She moves forward slightly, but still blocking the exit. "Ralph came to visit me at work this afternoon. He let me know some very interesting things that Virtue told him. About you and Grady. Did you not learn anything from your disgusting friendship with Andy? Why we moved here? And then you have the nerve to have disgusting relations with a stranger at the BAR you work at. You told me it was a restaurant, not some establishment filled with sick, disillusioned people."

"I was attacked by a customer who tried to rape me. And nothing happened other than the fact he drugged my drink."

"You won't be going back there. Virtue also told us that you stayed at the owner's condo that night, those pedophiles taking advantage of you."

"They aren't pedophiles! Jesus Christ Penny, they let me stay there because they knew how you'd react given the situation. How you've blown things out of proportion before."

She actually smirks in response. "So where are you going, huh? I see you pretty much have your whole life there. I guess you can throw that in the car and bring it to Ralph's, since I canceled the remaining part of the lease on the apartment. We have to be out by Monday."

"There is no fucking way I am moving in with that psychopath. But you don't get to know where I'm going because you're just as crazy as he is."

Penny moved her body ever so slightly to the left, one foot in the kitchen but still blocking the door. She pulls the closest drawer open, grabs something, and closes it quickly. What could she be grabbing? Wait, is that the knife drawer?

"You won't be moving in right away to Ralph's. Given what we've learned today, we have already set up a spot for you at Wishing Well's camp. We'll get you there this evening to start your reformation process. Fix you right up like we're doing with Andy."

My heart stops. All of the unanswered texts to Andy. It all makes sense now. "What did you let Ralph do to Andy? Oh my god. It was you. You caught Andy and I, and you brought Andy to Ralph. You're a monster."

"The camp offers many programs to help those who strayed from the right path of life, and your current situation is just one of them," she moves her hand in front of her, which is holding a knife. "You will be going to get right in the head."

"Like you're one to talk about being right in the head, holding a fucking knife. Where is my picture of Dad?"

She, for a moment, just stares at me with a blank expression on her face. "Why do you care so much about him? You never even knew him. He is just some fantasized memory in your head when truly he was a terrible man, a terrible influence on you. So, I had to make sure he wouldn't be around you any longer to continue corrupting you."

"What do you mean you made sure...you told me Dad left us after a business trip when I was two. Were you the one who left? Or did something happen to Dad?"

"It doesn't matter James. Now, drop those bags and let's go. I will come back and get them after we bring you to camp tonight"

I need an escape plan. If I grab the book with the money, I don't really need the bags. Worst case scenario is that I need to buy some new clothes. The book is still on top of the bag, so I drop the bags to the ground and pick it up. "There's no fucking way I am going to that camp. Get out of the way Penny. I'm an adult. You can't make me do anything."

"Oh sweetie. No one at camp cares how old you are or how you got there. They just care about reforming you to fit the correct way of life. And you constantly disrespect your own mother by calling her by her name. We'll make sure to fix that too."

I run for the door, aiming for the door handle beneath her right arm but she reaches out with her left to block me. I feel a burning sensation down my right arm, seeing the blade pull away covered in red. Blood. I stumble backwards and fall onto the ground. "Fuck. What the fuck." The pain is excruciating. Wow, that's a lot of blood. Shit that's a lot of blood. I feel woozy at the sight of it.

"We'll get that patched up, but it looks like you won't be going anywhere dear."

I start crawling backwards away from her, pain surging up my arm as I move. I hit the cool bathroom tile, and with all my strength roll my body onto the bathroom floor. I see her moving towards me so I turn around and slam my back into the door, shutting it behind me. I reach up to turn the lock right before I hear her hit the door. "OPEN THIS DOOR IMMEDIATELY JAMES."

I feel tired. There is a red puddle pooling on the tile. My head feels light. I don't like the sight of blood. I need help. That's a lot of blood. Can't be good. I struggle to pull my left arm over my lap. I fumble in my right jeans pocket to grab my phone.

When my phone screen lights up, I slowly type in the passcode. Things are starting to get a bit hazy. A bit blurry. I go to my recent messages, find his name.

JAMES: waffle

Thirty-Four

My head feels heavy, especially my eyelids. I hear the noises of machines, the beeps and boops, all around me. I open my eyes but the brightness of the room is too much. I can tell I am laying down in bed, but where am I? I feel tied down, connected to the bed somehow. She succeeded. She actually got me to Ralph's camp.

I hear other noises, other voices around me in addition to the machines. *Wait. It must be a hospital room, not camp. Thank God.*

But how did I get here? The last place I remember being is at the apartment. Sitting on the bathroom floor, hiding from Penny. The blood. The cut on my right arm.

I try to open my eyes again, and this time it's a bit easier. A chair squeaks in the room. I look to the right to see a man with his head slightly bent down. It's Mark, and he looks exhausted. "Mark?" I croak, sounding more like a whisper.

"Oh James. Thank God." He reaches out and places his hand on mine. He looks like he is about to continue talking, but starts sobbing. His eyes are bloodshot, but he has a small smile creeping up on his face.

"How long have I been here?" Oh gross. I just realized I have a catheter attached to me. Have I just been laying here pissing the bed? Well, I guess it's not exactly pissing the bed.

"Almost two days. You were brought in Friday afternoon, and it's just about noon on Sunday. Things were touch and go there for a bit. They said...they said you lost a lot of blood. Do you remember what happened?"

I nod, and start crying. He squeezes my hand and we sit in silence again for a short time. When I go to speak again, I suddenly feel very tired and drift off back to sleep.

Thirty-Five

I awoke again to much of the same, the sounds of the machines and Mark sitting by my side. "Sorry. I must have fallen back asleep," I say, as a nurse comes walking in.

"Only for a couple hours." Mark looked a little better than before, possibly he took a nap when I dozed off.

"Hello James. My name's Kelly, and I'm one of the nurses who has been taking care of you. How are you feeling?"

I try to lift my right arm again, but it still won't move. This time, however, I did feel a bit of pain. "Like shit. Pretty tired. My right arm's hurting a bit."

She smiles back at me. It was one of those smiles where you know it's the sympathetic type, probably knowing what put me here. "We can get you some more pain medication to help ease the pain in your arm. I saw you look at it…were you trying to lift it?" I nod, confirming. "Try not to move it for at least the next day. It suffered some pretty big trauma and needs

229

time to heal, and for your blood fully circulating after the transfusions you've had the past two days."

"What happened to Penny?" It was more a question for the room, rather than directed at Nurse Kelly.

She turns to Mark, nods, and looks back at me. "I think Mr. Tomlinson would be best to go over those details. I know some, but not all. You should try eating something. I'll come back a little before dinner with some light foods for you to eat." She brings over a little cup with two pills in it, and another cup with water. She assists me with taking the pills.

"Thank you," I lean further back and try to relax, as much as I can. Nurse Kelly leaves the room and shuts the door behind her. "Mark...does Penny know I'm here?"

Mark lets out a deep breath. "To my knowledge, no. But I don't believe she's in any position to get over here anyways." I let out a sigh of relief.

"Your neighbor, I think her name is Mrs. Weddle, told the cops and myself everything she knew about what happened. She had seen Penny when she was heading up the stairs to your apartment. I think she tried to flag her down to tell her something, but Penny went past her and headed straight for the apartment. It's my assumption from the amount of detail she was able to give the cops that she must have been standing with her ear to the door when you and Penny were fighting. She was able to pick up on details about something Penny did to keep your father out of your life, what happened to someone named Andy, sending you off to be reformed at some camp, and you not having a choice about it. She heard some altercation inside and slamming of doors, Penny screaming, and backed away just in time when Penny flung the apartment door open and ran past her. Mrs. Weddle had noticed a large red stain on her shirt, so she tried to get into the apartment but the door was locked. She immediately called 911."

Bless that woman. Her being a nuisance may have saved my life. "And then the cops came and got me, and brought me to the hospital? What about Penny?"

"Not exactly," Mark started. "Mrs. Weddle was able to give the details to the operator so they could send cops to find Penny, and an ambulance to the apartment to get you. Mrs. Weddle gave them the make, model, and license plate number of Penny's car, as well as Ralph's address. The cops found her car there, with Ralph screaming something about religious protections out a window and that they couldn't enter his home since it was a house of worship. Nothing that made sense. One of the cops saw him move in the window and grab a gun. A shotgun I think they said. He started to turn back with it and one of the cops shot him through the window. When the cops went into the house, they found blood splatter and a trail leading out the back door. There is an active manhunt going on for him."

I'm pretty sure my mouth was hanging open at that point. Ralph was crazy, but this was a whole new level. "And Penny?"

"I'm getting there. There are a few more details you need to know. When the cops entered the house, they noticed a door with like three or four deadbolt locks on it. Given the rumors swirling around town, and the details about Andy that Mrs. Weddle had relayed to them, they broke the door down. The door led down to the basement. There were five teenage boys handcuffed to beds down there, with Virtue standing there holding a knife. One of the cops disarmed and handcuffed her. Most of the boys down there were in shock, but one was able to talk about the things Ralph did to them. That Virtue was down there telling them to be quiet or she would kill them. James...there is no camp. Camp was the basement, and one of the five boys down there was Andy. The cops said the whole basement was soundproofed up to the staircase."

I was almost kidnapped and locked in the basement of Ralph's house, if not for being able to escape Penny. It would have been that much easier for her to do if all of this had happened after I already lived there.

My eyes suddenly feel heavy and I drift back off to sleep.

Thirty-Six

I come to and Mark is scrolling on his phone. "You still owe me the rest of the story. About what happened to Penny"

Mark puts his phone down. "Ahh yes. So, your mother had run up to one of the bedrooms upstairs and tried to barricade herself inside. The cops were able to get in and handcuff her. She's in custody with pending charges of murder, attempted murder, and kidnapping."

"Murder? Who did she murder?"

Mark shrugs. "That is the one detail of all this I don't know. But James, you have to realize how lucky you are to be here. Without your quick thinking you would have probably bled out in that basement or on the way there."

There was one thing still bothering me. "One more question. You detailed what the cops did, but you never said what happened when the ambulance got to the apartment building. I'm assuming they broke in and found me?"

"That's not quite what happened," Mark says. "Someone beat them there and was able to find you first."

"Who?" I ask. Mark points to the right side of the bed. In all the times being awake, I had never looked to the right side of the room, as Mark and the nurse were always on the left. Slumped over and sleeping in the chair was Grady, with a single pink balloon tied to his wrist.

I look over and Mark is crying, and now I'm crying. Actually sobbing. Grady and I had left things so poorly yesterday. Or the other day. Time is tricky right now. That's right. Waffle. He knew when our codeword came via text I needed help. And he beat the ambulance there. "What's with the pink balloon?"

Mark's sniffling turns into laughter. "He felt stupid being in the room and not having something. He didn't want to do flowers or a stuffed bear. He thought a get well soon balloon or something would work, except all the gift shop had left was that pink balloon. He's barely left that chair other than the occasional bathroom run. I think this afternoon is the second time he has slept since getting here."

I have Grady back now, I think, but what now? "What do I do now? I was supposed to stay with Mitch and Sam for a little bit until things blew over with Penny, but are they still going to take me in now that I'm a mess? What about school? I'm guessing I'm going to be here for a bit, but what about classes?"

"You don't have to worry about any of that. You will stay with us, and we will make sure everything is sorted out with school. I think I also need to apologize to you James."

My head tilts. "What could you possibly be sorry for?"

"I know we haven't known each other for long, just these last six months or so. But I think I've come to see you like a son over that time. Partially because of how often you were at our house, but I think also because in my mind you needed that in your life. Grady has friends, but he's never gravitated towards one the same way as you, or made sure that Julie and I were as involved. But I feel like I may have been at fault for the falling out you two had right before the incident with Penny."

He pauses to take a sip of water. "I think you know that Grady has received a lot of college acceptance letters, and a lot of those letters have full ride scholarships to play quarterback. Or be a backup to start. About a week ago I saw him in his room with all the letters fanned out on his bed. He had told me he didn't know what to do. He had letters from big football schools like Tennessee and Oklahoma, Texas and Florida State, but also from some West Coast schools like USC and UCLA. He knew he would have a better chance starting at Texas or Florida State compared to Oklahoma and Tennessee. But he also was considering USC and UCLA because he knew you were planning on going out to school in California. I told him he needs to think carefully about his decision and what's most important to him. Not to make any rash decisions based on his current situation but to look to the future. I think he took that as me telling him to not think of you, but think only about his

235

football career and nothing else. That's not what I was saying at all. I just want my son to be happy and for him to think about what would be the best for him in the long run."

I hesitate. "Which is?"

Mark leans in. "Honestly, I didn't want him to go to a school in the Deep South. I know the looks people gave his mother and I when passing through, especially in smaller towns. I don't want that for my son. And now, given the situation between you two, it's even more reason to steer him away from those schools. Their fans can be so unforgiving, and I think I just didn't put it as eloquently. He may have said one thing, but I think the answer was always going to be you, James. For him."

"I hadn't told him yet, but I got a full scholarship to UCLA to be their kicker. I mean, I hope I will be able to rebound from this."

"Then I guess I'm going to UCLA," Grady says. I look over and he is wiping the sleep from his eyes, but not the bags underneath them. He removes the balloon from his wrist and ties it to the bed frame. "So, you want to know what happened on Friday?"

"It's the only thing I don't know." I say, as Grady slides the chair closer to the bed.

"Dad, can you give us a minute? I need no distractions when I tell Jamie here what should be the start of an epic love story."

Thirty-Seven
GRADY

James's eyes are wide and his face goes pale when he sees Virtue. She has this look of satisfaction on her face, like her plan the whole time was to find something wrong with James, something to come between her father and Penny. And now she has it.

"Wait 'til my father hears about this. They send bad seeds like you away to camp for sure!" Before either of us can respond, she is off running into Marjorie's car and they are out of the parking lot.

I turn to talk to James, but he is already running into the woods. Fuck. This is bad. Like REALLY bad. I slump against the truck. He's got to be going to Chloe's but I can't go near there right now. Not after what I just said to him about college and what he told me about the bar. How did I mess this up so badly?

"Hey bro, what's up? You look like a truck hit you." Davis leans against the truck next to me.

"Man, I really fucked up Davis. I told James I couldn't throw away everything I've worked towards with football just for a high school fling. But I don't think it's a fling. I didn't think it before I said it and I sure as hell don't think it now. And then he told me some customer drugged him and tried to rape him at work, but his boss stopped it just in time."

"Fucking A man."

"That's not the worst of it. Virtue popped up from behind the truck after all of this. She heard it all and is off to go tell her dad about it. You've heard the stories, what Ralph Dursten does. I can't let that happen to James."

"What can we do? Should we go to your house and talk to your parents?"

"I'll head home. I'll text you if I need anything. Thanks buddy." I give Davis a half hug and jump in the truck and race out of the parking lot. It's starting to rain a bit, my wipers leaving awful streaks across the windshield. Shitty old wipers. If James were here, he would remind me the ones he bought me are still sitting in my room.

I sigh in relief to see Dad's car in the driveway. I run into the house and sprint up the stairs, opening his study's door. He looks up from his desk and points at the phone pressed to his ear. *It's important*, I mouth to him. "Hey Randall, can I give you a call back in a bit? The school is calling my other line so I want to make sure everything's fine with Grady. Thank you, talk soon." He put the phone down and sits back in his chair. "Okay my son. What is so important that you came in and interrupted my call with the President of Rhode Island College?"

I plop down in one of the chairs in front of his desk. "Dad I've fucked up." Dad's eyebrows furrow at the language, but I ignore it. "I need to tell you something and then give you the problem."

"Go on," Dad says, coming around the desk and taking the seat next to me.

I feel a bead of sweat drip off my temple. "Okay. So. I've...I've been dating James for the better part of this year. Maybe it wasn't serious at first, but it might be. No, it's definitely serious. But then I messed up with the winter formal. He put together this really nice after event thing for us and I didn't go. I went to Davis's house instead because I thought it would hurt my reputation not to. But Davis told me later in the night I made the wrong choice and I went to make it right, but James had already left. I ruined things. Then you and I had our talk about schools and I got scared about not making you and Mom proud by not going for one of the bigger football schools. You guys have helped me so much over the years, put so much into developing me as a football player. So, I told James I couldn't make a decision on something like him and I, something that could change the whole trajectory of my life. And then James said that some customer drugged him and tried to rape him at work last weekend. After I pretty much told him we weren't going to work even though I told him I would consider California if he got into a school there. And now crazy Virtue Dursten heard all of this and is going to tell Ralph. And she said that James would go to camp, whatever that really is.

And I don't know if I could live with the fact that I destroyed his life because I couldn't fucking deal with how I felt."

I sit back and take a deep breath. The last few weeks had been so stressful that, while I had been able to vent to Davis, it was never 100% of what was going on in my head. It wasn't until today I told Davis it was more than a fling. Oh my god I just told my Dad I have...had been dating a dude.

"I'm not going to lie Grady. This is a lot to process. However, if it's any consolation, I already had my suspicions about you and James. Not any one thing, but you're different around him than your other friends. Even than around us. It's almost like you're less guarded. You seem more happy kid. And your mother really believed it and pointed out various things to try and convince me."

I shake my head. I was trying really hard to keep my emotions in check. I feel like I could cry out of relief at any second.

"I've heard the rumors about Ralph Dursten and his weird cult-like group, his camp. There are many families in this town, and surrounding towns, that belong to his way of life. I personally do not get it. That man is about as stale as week-old bread, except for that slight crazy streak you mentioned."

"Dad, what do I do? He's not going to listen to me right now and who knows if Virtue has reached Ralph and Penny and..." my phone vibrates in my pocket.

JAMES: waffle

"No, no, no. Dad, I've got to go. Wait, we have to go. Can you take me to James's apartment?"

"What's going on? What was that text?"

"When James was going to dinner at Ralph's for the first time, we joked about him needing a codeword if he was in trouble and needed help. But then we actually came up with one because we knew how crazy Ralph was. And he just texted it."

"Go. Let's go. I trust ya kid and know you wouldn't act on something like this if it wasn't serious. Out the door. Go!"

It's pouring when we pull up to James's apartment, the parking lot in front is starting to flood a bit. I can see one of James's neighbors pacing outside his apartment on the walkway. Before Dad's car comes to a stop I'm already out the door, running up the stairs to the second floor. The neighbor grabs my arm to stop me. "It's locked. I don't know what happened but there was a lot of yelling and commotion, and Penny ran out of here with a big red stain on her shirt. I...I think it was blood. I've called 911 and there are people looking for her. An ambulance is on the way."

Blood? I get out of her grasp and try the handle. Sure enough, locked. I pull out my keys and find the key James gave me months ago. The door unlocks and there is blood all over the carpet, next to James's football bag and two garbage bags overflowing with stuff. The blood trails to the bathroom door, spread thick across the bottom of the door.

I reach for the knob but the door is locked. "James, are you okay?" I knock on the door, quietly at first but growing louder with each knock. "James! Please respond. Are you okay in there? James! JAMES!"

"Is he not responding? I didn't see him leave so he has to be in there." The neighbor has appeared in the doorway, but doesn't enter the apartment. "Is that your father down there? I'll go let him know what's going on.

"I'm going to break down the door. James, I'm going to break it down. If you can hear me, you need to move out of the way." All I hear is the rain pouring down outside. I step back, lean my shoulder down, and run as hard as I can into the door. It gives immediately, and I slip when I hit the bathroom floor, but am able to stop myself from falling by grabbing onto the sink.

James is crumpled on the floor next to the tub, blood all over his clothes and the tile around him. "No. No no no no. James, can you hear me?" I shake his shoulder and he doesn't move. I see a long cut on his right arm, which is still bleeding. "Oh my god…James, please please wake up. PLEASE!" I check his left wrist for a pulse and I finally find it, but it doesn't seem very strong. Tears are blurring my vision as I reach under him and lift him off the ground. I brace myself to not slip on the floor, his head rolling over and pressing into my chest.

I walk out of the apartment and get to the stairs. My legs are shaking but I manage to carry him slowly down the stairs, just as the ambulance pulls into the parking lot. Dad is talking to the neighbor by the car as I walk out into the rain. I continue to carry James to the EMTs, who are rushing out of the vehicle.

"Oh my god," I hear the neighbor say, and I feel the pressure on my arms lighten as Dad grabs James's legs. It's only a matter of seconds until the EMTs have brought the stretcher out and James is loaded in and taken away.

I turn and just lean into Dad's chest, sobbing uncontrollably. "There was so much blood Dad," I manage between sobs. "I don't know if he's going to be okay."

Thirty-Eight
GRADY

When we get to the hospital, they tell us James should be out of surgery soon but that only close family will be able to visit him. That the first couple days of recovery would likely be rough and we aren't out of the woods yet.

Dad looks at me, his face scowls, and he turns to the nurse. "Here's what is going to happen. That kid in surgery only has one family member to his name, his mother. Who, as a matter of fact, is the one who put him on that operating table. This young man over here is his boyfriend, who found James bleeding out and probably would not have survived if not for my son picking him up and carrying him out to the EMTs. I think you are going to make a damn exception in this case and let my son and I in his recovery room because we are the closest thing he has to a true family. And, if not, I will go above you and above the next to make sure it happens."

The nurse nods, and responds, "I think we can work something out."

I wake up because Dad shakes my shoulder. "They said he is out of surgery. The doctor believes they were able to help him just in time for potentially no long-term medical issues. We should be able to see him in a couple of hours."

I didn't even realize I had drifted off to sleep. It wasn't even that late, but I feel exhausted. "Dad, I might go grab a coffee or a soda. Do you want anything?"

"A coffee. Here's two twenties. Make sure to grab some snacks. I think we might be here for a bit." I take the bills and start to walk away. "Hey Grady, do you want me to see if they have a shirt for you to change into?

"I'll be fine." I walk aimlessly down the hall, looking for an elevator. The hospital is so busy at the moment no one notices me walking randomly down various hallways. I finally get to the elevators and hit the button for the main floor.

The door opens and it's somehow quite calm on the main floor. I walk over to what appears to be the combined gift shop and mini-convenience store in the front of the building. But my pocket vibrates before I walk-in, so I stand outside and pull out my phone.

CHLOE: Not sure if this is appropriate but have you heard from James?

CHLOE: He was supposed to drop my car off at work and it's not here

CHLOE: I texted Mitch and he said he never showed up to work but could be at their condo

CHLOE: No one is answering at the condo

GRADY: He's in the hospital

CHLOE: WHAT

GRADY: His mom found him packing up his stuff at home

GRADY: So he tried to leave and his mom stabbed him

GRADY: With a knife

CHLOE: She stabbed him?!?!

GRADY: He texted me from the apartment and I found him locked in the bathroom.

GRADY: So much blood

CHLOE: Is he OK?

GRADY: He's out of surgery and should be OK.

GRADY: They aren't letting anyone see him yet

CHLOE: I'm leaving now

GRADY: Don't.

GRADY: They said only immediate family could see him for a few days

CHLOE: How are you there?

GRADY: Dad gave an impassioned speech to the nurse

CHLOE: You are part of the reason he's there. How is that fair

CHLOE: Sorry. That's uncalled for

CHLOE: You had no way of knowing this would happen. JFC Grady. What happened to cause that fight?

GRADY: I was confused. It was a mistake

GRADY: I carried him out of that bathroom. His blood is all over me

CHLOE: fuck.

CHLOE: I'll text you in the morning for an update. I need time to cool off

CHLOE: But if anything changes or he wakes up, you better text me

GRADY: ok

Fuck she is mad. I put my phone away and walk into the shop. No one is inside except an older man working the counter. I don't notice any hot coffee being sold so I grab two canned espresso drinks from the fridge, along with two packs of peanut butter M&Ms and a bag of beef jerky. I start to head to the register but my eye catches the gift section. Most of it is flower arrangements and teddy bears or other stuffed animals. I notice there is a spot for balloons but there is only one lonely pink balloon with nothing written on it or any pictures. "Excuse me, do you have any other balloons?"

The man looks at me, his eyes go wide when he sees my bloodstained clothes. "I'm sorry but our shipment of balloons got lost, so we won't have anything until after the weekend most likely."

"It's okay." I grab the pink balloon and bring everything up to the register. The man is staring hard at me, and hasn't started ringing anything up. His hands are on the counter and I see that he has a tattoo on his left hand. It's a ring around his finger. It's rainbow colored.

"Are they okay? Are you okay?"

The question catches me off guard for some reason. I found myself staring at him for what seemed forever. "My boyfriend's mom tried to kill him and I found him."

The man just shook his head in response, and pushed the items back towards me. "Don't worry about this. Keep your money. You've certainly had a rough day. Is anyone here with you?"

"My dad."

"Okay, that's good. That's really good of him Grady."

"You know who I am?"

"You're our star quarterback. My son's on the team, Manny Lillard. He told my husband and I that you pretty much have the pick of colleges to play football at. That was some play you guys pulled off in the championship."

"I was waiting to see where James chose to go to decide." The tears are falling down my face again, and Mr. Lillard comes out from behind the counter and gives me a hug.

"I don't know what happened but I can tell you whatever it is, it will get easier. Okay? Why don't you take this stuff back up to your dad, tell him I'm going to order a pizza for the two of you, and it will be down here in about an hour. Consider it a thank you for turning our football program into something to be proud of the past few years."

"Thank you, Mr. Lillard." I grab the snacks and drinks and leave the store, with the balloon string wrapped around my wrist.

Thirty-Nine

GRADY

Mom arrives at the hospital early Saturday morning, with breakfast and a change of clothes. I initially objected but she told me I needed to change for the mere fact of sanitation, that I was starting to scare off the staff with my stench. She passes me the bag and I go into the bathroom after removing the balloon and handing it to Dad. Inside she had put, with the clothes, deodorant, body spray, body wipes, and a toothbrush with toothpaste.

After cleaning myself up and changing, I look at myself closely in the mirror. I look terrible. My eyes look slightly bloodshot and have bags under them. I gather my old clothes and throw them in the bathroom trash. They are unsalvageable. Even if they were, who would ever want to wear them again.

When I get back the doctor is standing outside the room talking to my parents. They are talking close and I can see Dad's serious face and nodding along with the doctor. When the doctor leaves, he turns to Mom and they appear to be debating back and forth.

"What's going on?" They stop talking and Mom turns to face me.

"The doctor was just giving us an update. James isn't awake yet but she thinks it's likely he will wake up by tomorrow or Monday at the latest."

"Anything else?"

Dad steps forward. "The doctor wanted to know what the plan is here on out. Meaning, after the hospital. They are aware of James's home situation and they were worried for his after-care once he is released from the hospital."

"And?"

"Well, your mother and I were talking and we think it's best that James come to stay with us. I think at this point we are the closest thing he can call family that truly cares for his well-being. However, with James staying in the house, we will need to lay some ground rules."

"I'm guessing you have brought Mom up to speed on our conversation from yesterday." I look at her and she smiles.

"Sweetie I already knew. A mother has these types of intuitions, but I wanted you to figure it out on our own. You don't need someone telling you who to be or who to love, or nudge you one way or the other. But I tried my best to hint it to you the best I could. Like asking you and James to take some photos with just the two of you before winter formal. I'm just sad that James didn't have the same support system in place and it came to this. And, don't be mad at me or him, James and I had a talk about it at the cabin. I brought it up, not him, so don't hold it against him. I think he was relieved to have a parental figure be understanding for once."

She's known for like two months. I never would have known. Nothing has seemed different since the cabin. But when would they have had time to talk openly, just the two of them? *The hike.* Dad and Uncle Kev had been off fishing while we were on the hike.

"Wait, how did you not tell me?" Dad didn't look mad. Was it a look of disappointment that he wasn't the first to know?

"Mark, like I said, it wasn't my place to say anything to you or Grady. James talked to me in confidence and I couldn't break his trust. It was a very emotional convo and I know it was hard for him to talk about so openly."

Dad nods, seeming to understand. What did James even tell her? "Anyways," Dad turns to me, "the doctor also said we can go into the room. We don't have to leave, even when visiting hours are over."

A surge of relief flows through me. "How did you swing that?"

"When you know the President of Rhode Island College, who provides about 50% of the hospital's nursing interns, I guess you can say I had a bit of an upper-hand."

"I guess it pays to have a dad in high places once and awhile."

When we enter the room, it's like the air is immediately sucked out of it. James is looking a bit rough for wear, with so many tubes and sensors attached to him. I lean into Mom and just cry, feeling her shake in my arms as well. "It looks so bad," I say.

"I know. I know," Mom says, rubbing her hand on my back. I feel Dad's arms wrap around both of us.

"He's a strong kid." Dad pulls his hug tighter. "We just need to be patient and just be here for him."

I can't figure out how long we've been sitting in the room, but I need some air. Or a distraction of some sort. "I'm going to head down to the gift shop to find a book to read or something. I can't just sit here."

I wave at Mr. Lillard as I enter the gift shop. There is a small bookcase in the corner, filled with used books at a discount. Most of it is your standard thrillers and romance novels, but I notice on the bottom shelf a copy of *Breaking the Moon*. James's favorite novel. This is clearly a sign.

I bring the book up to the register, along with another bag of peanut butter M&Ms. Mr. Lillard puts the book down after picking it up. "Are you sure you want to read this?"

"I think so," I say, "it's James's favorite book."

"Okay, but I'm going to warn you. It's not a happy ending type of book, and I know what you're going through right now. But I understand."

When I get back upstairs my parents are nowhere to be found. I settle into my chair at James's side, the one with the pink balloon tied to it, and start to read.

Forty
GRADY

"How can you like Felix? He pretty much ruins this book completely. You're right. I'm not watching the movie."

"Grady, did you say something?"

"Sorry Dad. I'm complaining to James when he can't respond about how terrible this book is that he loves."

"Should I be worried about Teddy? Is this someone you are comparing me to, that I'm supposed to live up to? It's unrealistic James. It's all outlandish and unrealistic."

Dad's eyebrow lifts slightly. "Okay crazy. I'm running out to get us dinner. You need a break from that book when I'm back."

"He dies? What monster's favorite book is this sad? Who reads sad books for fun? And why would you make me read this when you are lying in a hospital unconscious after almost dying?"

I throw the book on the floor and it slides to the corner. Dad is out cold in the chair to the left of the bed, unfazed.

I turn to James and put my hand on his. "James, I just want to say I'm sorry. I'm sorry for not coming to Mitch and Sam's after the dance, for not being there for you after what happened at Tipsy Mic, and for what I said about football and school. I didn't mean it at all. I never should have, never would, put football before you. I know what I said but I wasn't thinking right."

The hospital is eerily quiet. Just the sounds of the machines next to the bed and light breathing noises from Dad.

"I never said it to you before. Hell, I don't think I've ever said it to anyone ever other than my parents. But, James, I love you. I really do. And I need you to wake up. I need us to get out of this room. If you still want to go to California, we can go to California. If you don't, now that your mom and Ralph are out of the picture, that's fine. Just tell me where and I'll finally commit to a school. But you need to wake up for me. They told us probably tomorrow, so let's try for that...yeah?"

I lean forward and kiss him, but it makes me feel worse. It feels so one-sided. I'm crying again, and I feel like all I've done is cry and pace this room the past few days. I should really try to get some sleep. I realize I never had removed the balloon from the back of the chair, and now it's floating close to the edges of the window blinds. I can't be empty handed when James wakes up, so I tie it back to my wrist and curl up in the chair.

I don't say anything, but I notice Dad slowly wiping a tear from his cheek in the corner. Guess he wasn't dead asleep after all.

I wake up feeling a bit rested, but sit there with my eyes closed. I don't think I'm quite ready to face another day in this room. But I realize Dad is talking to someone quietly in the room.

"...I told him he needs to think carefully about his decision and what is most important to him. Not to make any rash decisions based on his current situation but to look to the future. I think he took that as me telling him to not think of you, but think only about his football career and nothing else. That's not what I was saying at all. I just want my son to be happy and for him to think about what would be the best for him in the long run."

I'm not sure how I ended up with such a great dad, but I can't believe how easy this all was with him. I don't have much to compare it to, but you always hear the horror stories. Wait, who is he talking to? Is James awake?"

"Which is?" James says quietly.

"Honestly, I didn't want him to go to a school in the Deep South. I know the looks people gave his mother and I when passing through, especially in smaller towns. I don't want that for my son. And now, given the situation between you two, it's even more reason to steer him away from those deep south schools. Their fans can be so unforgiving, and I think I just didn't put it as eloquently. He may have said one thing, but I think the answer was always going to be you, James, for him."

There is a pause. "I hadn't told him yet, but I got a full scholarship to UCLA to be their kicker. I mean, I hope I will be able to rebound from this." He's awake!

"Then I guess I'm going to UCLA," I say. I wipe the sleep and tears from my eyes. I remove the balloon from my wrist and tie it to the bed frame. "So, you want to know what happened on Friday?"

"It's the only thing I don't know." James says. I slide the chair closer to the bed.

"Dad, can you give us a minute? I need no distractions when I tell Jamie here what should be the start of an epic love story."

Forty-One

It's Tuesday and the doctor says I should be able to go home tomorrow. Oh, and Grady still hasn't gone home. Neither has Mark. I overheard Mark making a few phone calls in the hallway. One was to our school to let them know some details of what happened, and that we wouldn't be in school for the rest of the week. The other was to Rhode Island College to let them know his TA would be teaching his night class for the week, and assuring whoever it was on the phone that the TA was more than qualified.

The thought of going to school seems like too much. Not only because I feel exhausted, but I'm sure word has spread quickly about what happened between Grady and I, what happened to me, and what happened at Ralph's. Oh shit.

Mark reappears in the doorway. "Hey Mark? What happened to Virtue? I just realized you told me what happened in the basement, but never what happened with her."

Mark takes a seat next to me. "I'm not 100% sure but I think she was brought in for a psych eval and will probably be sent somewhere for treatment. I think they are trying to determine if her actions were her own, or if she had been groomed by her father over the years to do whatever he said."

"They should lock her up for good," Grady says. "She doesn't deserve anything after what happened to James."

"It's not that simple. Ralph was a bit messed up. Very messed up in the head. He was able to bring others in and believe his cause, let alone his own daughter who was around him all the time. It might take time but she may be able to learn what he was doing was wrong."

"Mark, what happened to Andy and the other guys in the basement?"

Mark looks at the door, then back at us. "They've been keeping this pretty quiet, but Andy and one other boy are staying here. The others are back with either family or friends. The cops have vetted all their parents to find out if they knew what they were doing sending their kids to Ralph. Outside of that I don't know much more, I have just overhead that much when walking the halls during the day."

"Can you find out if they would let me visit with Andy? We have some history and things must have been pretty lonely in the basement for him. I think he…he may have been down there as long as I've been in Beacon."

"I'll see what I can do, but's almost lunch time. What do you guys want? I'll run down to the cafeteria or out somewhere?"

"Whatever works for me, Dad. But I need a Mountain Dew or something with caffeine."

"Got it. James?"

"I'm good Mark, thank you. The pain meds make me feel off. I'll just eat Jell-O or whatever they bring me for lunch."

With Mark gone, Grady leans in and kisses me. I place my left arm behind his head but he pulls back. "As much as I'd like to do this, I will not be responsible for hurting you. I love you too much. Want to make sure you go home tomorrow."

"Did you just say you love me too much? I don't think we've used that word yet."

"Shit," Grady says, "I forgot when I did say it you were passed out in this bed."

"You waited until I was practically in a coma to say it? I love you too, even if you make some shit decisions sometimes." He leans in to kiss me again. "Is it going to be weird that I will be living with you guys?"

"Nah, but we will have to be probably even more stealthy than before if we are gonna mess around."

"That's an understatement." Mark is in the doorway, and now my cheeks are burning and Grady's face flushes. "Anyways, sorry to interrupt but you have visitors. I ran into them on the way to get lunch. Grady, why don't you come with me and help get lunch. This is probably going to take a while.

"Oh shit. I was supposed to tell Chloe when you woke up so she could come visit." Grady pulls out his phone but Mark grabs his wrist.

"That won't be necessary."

The whole football team is outside the room, with Coach Peters entering the room first. "Hey Stockton. The hospital said you could have visitors and, when they heard, the whole team wanted to come visit. We got permission from Principal Gupta to let the team leave for an extended lunch period to visit."

"The whole team?" I asked. "Even Darius?"

"Even Darius. Look kid, I'm not great with words. But this is some shit you've been through. And I'm sorry that with everything that happened you and Tomlinson weren't comfortable around the team to be yourselves. I get it, I truly do. I played in college with a few guys who came out as gay almost twenty-five years after graduation. I guess not much has changed but I hope it does. You are a helluva kicker. Oh! I heard from the UCLA recruiter. Congrats on the scholarship! He said the sell was the trick play you pulled off in the championship game. Saves them a roster spot if they know their kicker can throw the ball too."

"Grady, Davis, and I must have practiced that play for weeks."

"And it showed. Again, congrats. But I don't want to eat anymore into the team's time to visit. See ya back at school."

The team started walking in one at a time after Coach left the room.

Griff: "Feel better bud."

Sammy: "Dude that's a big bandage."

Jeremy: "You and Grady huh? I always thought you had a thing for Chloe."

Pete: "My dad told me that Mrs. Weddle said you and I got into Syracuse. I didn't get into Syracuse."

Patty and Kyle: "We didn't want you to mix us up, so we both came in together to say feel better."

Alex: "I got a scholarship offer from Arizona so looks like I'll be seeing you on the field next year."

Dom: "Uhh I don't know what to say. Good luck."

Clayton: "I hope that bitch Virtue gets what she deserves."

Benji: "Here. We got the Fiction Workshop class to sign this card. Ignore Sammi's note."

Manny: "My Dad told me what happened to you. Dude, you could have told me you were gay. I have two dads and no one has ever gotten on my case. They are literally the loudest fans in the stadium on game day, so it's not a secret. I'm here if you need to chat."

Daniel: "Hope you feel better. I was flirting with the nurse, and I think she's into me. But she said you're doing great."

Mike C.: "I overheard Daniel. He's an idiot. Can you get me that nurse's number though?"

Cody: "Feel better James."

Butch: "You're coming back to school soon, right? I need help with Calculus."

Frank: "You going to have a cool scar or what?"

Darius: "I know I've been a complete dick to you all year. It's just that Grady always gets all the attention and it's easy to get mad about it."

Quentin: "You should have seen Mrs. Frams in Health class, going off on the class about skipping class. How you and Grady were going to be suspended. Chloe told her to stop being such a fucking bitch all the time and that you almost died, that Grady was here with you. Mrs. Frams just looked shocked. I don't think any student has ever talked to her like that before. Chloe didn't even get in trouble."

Keegan: "Hey umm...see ya at school."

Mike S.: "You and Tomlinson, really?" He leans in and whispers, "If you ever need a third you know where to find me."

Damian: "I heard they put Virtue in some psych ward. Did she really kidnap people and lock them in her basement?"

Kam: "Hope you're feeling better."

Devon: "Your mom did this? I thought my mom was fucked up, but damn."

Philip: "If you ever need to talk, let me know. My mom was part of Ralph's group, and she's a mess now after learning about what he did to those guys in the basement. What happened to you. I think she is just regretting ever getting involved with them."

Adam: "Feel free to text if you need anything."

Rob: "When Chloe texted me Friday that she was worried I brushed it off. Dude, I was off. She has been a mess all weekend. My mom let her stay over because her parents were out of town this weekend and she didn't want to be alone. But I'm glad you're doing okay. See you when you're back home."

Davis: "Hey James. Glad you're doing good. Well, not good but better than what could have been. Look, I don't know what you and Grady have talked about. But he feels terrible. I talked to him right after your fight and he knew he fucked up right then and there. I offered to help however I could but told me he would take care of it. I haven't had a chance to talk to him since Friday afternoon, but I heard what happened. Did he really pick you up out of a pool of blood and save you? I know you might be mad at him, but that's some Prince Fucking Charming shit right there."

Davis leaves the room, and I lean back into my pillows. That was exhausting. It was nice but difficult to sit through, especially the ones who clearly came only because the whole team did.

"I hope you don't think I forgot about you." Chloe enters the room, looks at my arm and the machines hooked up to me. Then it's like a waterfall is running down her face. "Oh James, I'm so glad you're okay!" She leans in and hugs me, then sits back in Mark's chair.

"Sorry about stranding you at the bookstore on Friday." I say, giving her a quick smile.

"Really? That's what you have to say? Fuck James, you almost died. I've been a wreck for days. Thank God Rob let me come over and Mrs. Holmes let me stay over. My parents were at my grandma's taking care of her. And Dana's in New York City for the weekend because her parents are thinking of moving there if she goes to NYU."

"Would it be better if I told you that Salinger just proposed a threesome with Grady and I?"

"That didn't happen." I give her a deadpan look. "O.M.G. that did happen! He's disgusting. Well, not disgusting to look at, but pretty disgusting."

"You and Rob are back on, I take it?"

She glances out the door. Rob is standing out of earshot talking to Keegan. "I didn't know I wanted it, but he was the only one I could turn to. He was there for me, no questions asked. He never brought up anything from the dance or how I ignored him after. I know we need to talk about it, but I think he also knew I needed him. I didn't realize how good he really was to me. And still is."

"Mark and Julie told me I'll be living with them, now that Penny is essentially out of the picture."

"What's going to happen to her? There are rumors going around school that she murdered someone. I normally don't listen to rumors like that, but I also heard it came from Jimmy. You know, Jimmy Quaid? His dad's a cop in town."

"Mark said something similar. He wasn't sure of the details either, but it wasn't any of the kids locked in the basement at Ralph's. Unless there were others before and my mom was somehow involved. She was pretty much living there, so how could she not at least have known about it?"

Rob pops in the room. "Hey babe? Coach says it's time for us to head back. I can bring you after school if you want to come back."

I grab Chloe's hand. "Thank you for everything. If you hadn't let me borrow the Jeep, I would have gotten back to the apartment that much later and she probably would've ambushed me. Maybe even with Ralph. Don't feel pressured to come back later. I should be getting out tomorrow, and then we can just hang out at Grady's.

"It's not Grady's now James. You live there too." She winks at me, and she's out the door.

Forty-Two

The movie credits roll on Grady's iPad for *Breaking the Moon*. I insisted we watch it after Grady told me he read it Saturday night, and when I had noticed earlier that it was already available to stream. He begrudgingly rented it, but only because I had the upper hand by being in the hospital.

"This is shit. This movie is shit and that book was also shit. Why do you enjoy that? It's just sad." Grady's wiping tears quickly from his face, but doing it facing away from me.

"Not everything has to be action filled or scary or funny. Sometimes it's good to read or watch something with a good story, even if it's a bit sad."

"It's a high school love story where one of them dies James. It may just be hitting a little too close to home right now."

"Alright. I'll give you that." There's a knock at the door. Two cops are standing at the door, with Mark right behind them.

"James Stockton? My name is Officer Quaid. We have some questions we need to ask you. Are you feeling up to it?"

Grady sits back in his chair and I sit up a bit in bed. I could tell our closeness was making the other cop a bit uncomfortable. "Of course."

"Mr. Tomlinson, will you and your son give us a bit of privacy with James?"

"No." The cops just stare at me. "They have been here since Friday. Both were part of getting me here. They stay." I feel Grady's hand slip into mine.

"I think that should be fine." Officer Quaid pulls up a chair next to the bed, Mark takes his normal seat, and the second cop stands in the doorway. "James, I know we've confirmed through multiple sources your mother attacked you, along with Ralph and Virtue Dursten's involvement. We are missing some bits and pieces of the conversation with your mother during the altercation. Can you give us a bit more detail about how everything escalated before the attack?"

I go into detail on what Virtue told my mother, the discussion about Andy and the camp, and what she had said about my father. "She mentioned that she made sure he wouldn't be in my life, but up until then she always said he abandoned us when I was young."

Officer Quaid sighs. "So that's really the reason why I'm here. When your father disappeared, I am guessing you and your mom moved out of the house?"

"I think so, but I never knew why we moved."

"From what we can tell we believe your mom became involved with Ralph Dursten around that time."

My jaw drops. "No way. I didn't even meet Ralph until last year."

"Did you move around a lot growing up?"

"I did. Almost every year I was in a new school, a new state."

"Ralph's group was a bit more widespread than people knew about, than we even initially knew about. There are pocket communities that push as far west as Colorado. We haven't questioned your mother on the topic and obviously, given what you just said, you also had no idea. But we believe Ralph was moving you and your mother from community to community, some more rural than others."

"But why?"

"James, this may be hard to hear, but your father's last name wasn't Stockton. Hell, it wasn't even your mother's maiden name. Your father's last name was Diaz. And when we ran fingerprints on your mother down at the station, we got a hit on them. For Penelope Diaz. She has been wanted for the murder of your father, Bobby Diaz, for close to fifteen years. They found his body buried behind your old house, with the murder weapon close by with your mom's fingerprints on it. We believe Ralph somehow secured documents for you and your mother, giving you new last names. We believe he assisted her in alluding authorities looking for her by utilizing all of his Wishing Well community connections."

Officer Quaid hands me a photo and it's clearly my mother. But she looks so much different. Her hair color and style are much different, she's much heavier, and she has brown eyes instead of her blue. Looking at it closer, I can tell it's her but I don't think most people would know it's the same woman. "This is the photo they have been using to find her for years. But, after meeting your mom at the station and how far you are from your childhood home, I can see how she has been able to hide all these years."

Now that Officer Quaid mentioned it, I vaguely remember my childhood home and my mom had mentioned it was in New Hampshire. "Where was my childhood home?"

"Nebraska."

Tears fill my eyes. She's always been a liar, a monster. It wasn't just Ralph that molded her that way. He just helped her justify her actions. Now I'll never get to know my father. All I have left are some of his Latin features, since she took the one photo of him. The photo.

"Officer Quaid, I'm sure it's still a crime scene. But my mother took the one photo I had of my father, and she either kept it at Ralph's house or she tossed it. Do you think I would be able to go to Ralph's house to look for it, or one of the cops could? It's a photo from a lakefront of me and him."

"I can't allow you into the house, but I can make sure to stop this week and give the house a look over for it. Do you have any questions for us?"

"Am I able to see her?" Mark's face scrunches up and I feel Grady's grip on my hand tighten. "I feel like there are a few things I need to get off my chest."

"She's being brought back to Nebraska on Friday to face murder charges. We can arrange for you to see her on Thursday before her transport."

"Looking forward to it."

Forty-Three

Mitch and Sam stop by that night with dinner from Tipsy Mic. They assured me they had people covering the bar for a bit when I questioned how they were both here.

"I'm so sorry we couldn't get here sooner. We weren't sure when visitors were allowed until Chloe stopped by this afternoon. We were so worried when you didn't show up to work or the condo."

"And heartbroken when we heard what happened," Sam adds, placing a hand on Mitch's shoulder. "You've had a rough few weeks kid."

"Grady told us about how Mark and Julie are taking you in. They're good people."

"And James," Sam says, "our door is always open. We offered it up to you before this happened, and it will always be available to you if needed. We also understand you won't be able to serve tables or bartend for a while, but we can find something for you to do if you still want to work."

"Thanks guys, I really appreciate it. You guys have been so good to me, always looking out for me. Kinda like the big brothers I never had."

"Thank you for that age-related compliment. I think it's time for us to go out on a high note. We'll stop by Grady's to visit later in the week. Enjoy the burgers.

After we eat Mark tells me he spoke with the doctors and got permission for me, and only me, to visit Andy in his room. Mark, with the help of a nurse, get me from the bed into a wheelchair they brought in. Grady grabs my hand. "Good luck. I'll be here when you get back."

"You don't have any problem with me seeing Andy, given our history?"

"I'm pretty confident I'll be fine. And it would be a dick move to say anything otherwise." Grady pops in his headphones and turns his focus to his iPad.

Mark wheels me out of the elevator and stops outside the last door of the hallway. "Andy's still a little out of it. He also looks a little worse for wear, more than you do, so I just want to make sure you're prepared." He opens the door, pushes me up to the bed, and steps back to the door. "I'll be right outside."

Mark wasn't lying. Andy looks awful. His face is sunken in and he just looks so frail. Nothing like what I remembered from last summer. Were they starving him? Was he refusing to eat? Andy opens his eyes and looks over at me, his eyes going wide.

"Oh Andy," I say, "I'm so, so sorry. I was so mad at you for ignoring me last summer and now realize I'm a fucking idiot."

"I want to apologize on behalf of Ralph and Virtue for what they did to you. And for, if anything, my mother may have done to help them. I know she must have helped get you there. I'm not sure how much the cops have told you, or what you've told them. But here is what I know."

"I know you have been through a lot, and I know you've had to endure whatever they did to you for months. I know that you and the other guys locked down there all survived and were able to leave that basement. The police are actively looking for anyone involved in Wishing Well and are questioning them, and some of the parents are in custody. Ralph Dursten is missing, Virtue Dursten is being given a psych evaluation, and my mother is in jail. She tried to send me to that basement, and tried to kill me when I fought back. I want you to know that, despite how you feel, things should get better. It might be hard. But I will be here for you if you need to talk, if you just need to vent. I wasn't in that basement with you, but you and I know each other. I've missed you, and I'm glad to have you back in my life. You're not alone." Andy has the same look on his face from when I first started talking, but his face is streaked with tears.

Mark and a nurse come into the room at that point. "Okay James, that may be enough for Andy for the day."

"Nurse? Do you have a piece of paper and a pen, or something?"

"Sure." He pulls out a marker and a small notepad and hands it to me.

"Mark, can you write my phone number on a piece of this? I don't want to attempt to write left-handed. I'm guessing Andy lost his phone at some point." Mark scribbles down my name and number and rips off the paper, handing it to me. I place it on the table next to Andy's bed. "When you are ready, please call or text me. I'm being released tomorrow from the hospital but will be staying with Mark."

Mark grabs the back of the chair and rolls me to the door. As I hit the threshold, Andy quietly says "Thank you James."

Forty-Four

The day after being released from the hospital, Mark and I are about to leave to go where they are holding Penny.

"Do you want me to go with you?" I knew Grady felt uncomfortable asking. He just looks uneasy.

"Only if you want to, but I know you don't. And that's fine. I don't even really want to see her but I think she needs to see my face one more time before she disappears forever."

"She's not disappearing forever Jamie. She's likely just going to prison in another state."

"Okay. One, stop trying to make Jamie happen. It's not a thing. Two, she will be disappearing for me. This is the last time I intend on seeing her if I can help it."

The drive to the prison takes about forty-five minutes but it seems like hours. Mark and I try to make small talk like normal, but I think the anxiety of the visit was taking a toll on both of us.

When we finally arrive, Mark checks in with the guard and the gate opens. We park somewhat close to the door. To the right of us there is a fenced in yard, where a few women are doing laps along the fence line. Must be an exercise break.

Once in the building, a guard takes us down a long hallway to the visitation room. It takes me a while to get out of the chair, as I'm still feeling a bit tired. They said it should last a few weeks and I should keep off my feet at first as much as possible. Mark and Grady pleaded with me to use the wheelchair today. I agreed, but refused to use it going in and out of the visitation room. She needed to see she didn't succeed in breaking me.

"Do you want me to go in there with you?"

"Only if you want to. But I'd like to be alone at the table with her."

"That's fine. I'll stand by the door with the guard, if that's alright." The guard nods in response. Mark reaches in and gives me a hug, taking caution to loop under my right arm. "Whatever happens here, whatever you can and cannot say, I'm proud of you. This takes a lot of guts James."

The room has about a dozen tables in it, and only two are currently occupied. I sit at a table on the far left, away from the other inmates and visitors. The room just makes me feel sad. Everything is so gray, so dull. I had imagined the visitation room would be spruced up a bit, liven up the visitation experience and shield visitors from what their family and friends were experiencing.

A door opens on the back wall and a prison guard walks in, with an arm looped around Penny's. She looks tired, but she also is starting in some ways to resemble the photo that Officer Quaid had shown me. I can see it now.

"There is a fifteen-minute limit on visitation today," the guard says. He takes out a set of handcuffs and loops them into an opening on the table, something I hadn't even noticed. "We don't normally handcuff inmates to the table, but this is a bit of a unique situation. Feel free to get my attention if you want to end the visit early."

The guard walks away from the table, leaving Penny and I alone staring at each other. The silence is almost deafening at first, her now unfamiliar brown eyes staring back at me.

"Why'd you do it?"

"It's not like you were willing to go with me to Ralph's, so I had to improvise. Although I didn't intend on the cut being that deep. Just something to make things easier."

It wasn't accidental. "No. Why did you kill Dad? And don't be stupid Penny. I know they found his body buried at our old house. Along with the murder weapon."

"Your father wasn't a good man, and he wasn't a good influence on you. He was having sex with my cousin Greg almost immediately after our wedding, and did for years. I was so blind to it. He went on all these business trips. I found out that Greg always tagged along on his business trips, and had to find this out from Greg's mother. My Aunt Michelle, bless her, found some reservation for the two of them and brought it to me. I should have known better. I'm pretty sure the last time I had sex with him was when I got pregnant with you, but never put it together. Greg was a groomsman in the wedding. Hell, it was probably going on before the wedding."

I noticed that one of the inmates and her visitor were no longer talking and appeared to be listening in. Visibly leaning in.

"I'm not stupid enough to tell you what happened to him, but whatever happened is something that man deserved."

"So instead of divorcing him, or leaving him, anything…your go-to was to kill him? You married a closeted gay man who probably was getting pressure from his family to settle down and get married. You then uproot your whole life, my whole life, and create this giant lie for what? End up with fucking Ralph? A low-rent version of a cult leader?"

"Shut your mouth about Ralph. Ralph is a good man and has a great vision for how the world should be. How it will be!"

I smirk. "Well, probably not for long. He's on the run, you see, and the cops are fully aware of where his other communities are. It's over. It's done. Virtue? Probably locked up in a psych ward, if not prison, for the rest of her life. The basement? It's empty. The boys are free from what you called camp."

She's crying, and shaking. But between the tears her eyes show rage. I have learned that look over the years. "You are…such…a disappointment. You will turn out…just like your father."

"Well, not just like him, since you'll be locked up for the rest of your life." She tries to lift her hands up towards me, seeming to forget she's shackled to the table.

"You failed me, but you also failed in your attempts to change me. Because you know who saved my life? Grady. He had a key to our apartment because I gave him one months ago, so he could visit when you were at Ralph's. He bust down that bathroom door that you failed to open and carried me to safety. Stabbing your own son with a knife because he didn't fit some fucking delusion you had put together in your head. If Grady hadn't come, I would've been dead on that bathroom floor you crazy bitch."

The other inmates and guests have also gone quiet. The guard and Mark are keeping an eye on us.

"You see that man standing in the back of the room, in the Beacon Football shirt? That's Grady's father, Mark. Mark didn't leave my side for over three days in the hospital. Mark and Julie have invited me to live in their home, with Grady. And, guess what? Grady and I are going to school TOGETHER next year at UCLA. Mark and his family, in the matter of days, have shown me more love than you ever had in my whole life. So just remember when I'm off living life the way I want, not the way you wanted, you'll be locked in a place like this taking group showers with a bunch of women. Trying to avoid their advances. The ultimate fuck you to both you and Ralph, and your beloved camp and reformation."

I stand up a bit too quickly and have to brace myself on the table. "Oh, and I think I might drop Stockton. Go by James Diaz." The look of rage is back on her face.

"Guard? I'm ready."

Forty-Five
THREE MONTHS LATER

It's the Friday before finals week, and thank God. The road to get here has been exhausting, and so has all the attention. Everyone in class wants to talk to me, check how I'm doing, ask if all the stories of what happened were true. Even the teachers couldn't control it, or maybe they didn't want to. Maybe they were just as curious as my classmates were.

The cafeteria was chaotic so our group decides to eat outside. We were all paired off...wait, Davis and Dana?

I lean into Chloe's ear. "Why didn't you tell me about that?"

"Ask your boyfriend. I had no idea about it."

"Grady."

He laughs. "I just found out about it yesterday so relax."

"You know we can hear you, right?" Davis throws a chicken nugget at Grady's head, who leans in and catches it in his mouth. "It's going to sound super cheesy, but after what happened to you and seeing Grady's response it woke something up in me. I've always had a crush on Dana, and it scared me that something could happen that would stop me from ever having the chance to pursue it. And we've just been seeing where things go the last couple of months."

"And, weirdly, I also always had a crush on Davis. It wasn't just the four of you I was watching on the field on Friday nights."

Davis leans in and kisses Dana. "Oh god that's going to take time to get used to," Chloe says, making a gagging motion.

I lean against Grady, taking a bite of my sandwich. All of this is still taking time to get used to.

At the end of the day, I swing by Principal Gupta's office. Mary the secretary had approached me before lunch to ask that I stop by after seventh period. I knock quietly on the doorframe. "Principal Gupta?"

"James, yes! Please come and sit down." I take a seat at one of the chairs in front of his desk, placing my backpack on the ground. "I apologize that this is the first time I've sat down and spoken with you since, well, everything."

"Really Principal Gupta, it's fine."

"As leader and advocate of the student body I absolutely should have done this sooner. I was able to get the whole football team over to the hospital to visit you, but I was somehow unable to visit or at least tag along. What you went through is something this school has never seen before. What those other boys went through, something that no child should ever experience. I can't believe all of that was happening right

286

in our small little town. You can be open and honest in this space with me. How are things going?"

"Probably better than anyone is giving me credit for. Emotionally, that is. My body could be better, but I've been getting better and better every week. I think with what happened with my mother, I think it was past a breaking point of trying to rationalize it in my head. Where most people would try to cling to that notion that she's family and make excuses, I don't. She killed my father and came very close to killing me. That's not what family is, that's what a disease is."

Principal Gupta had been very quiet, nodding occasionally. "And things have been going well staying with the Tomlinsons?"

"They have been better parental figures in the past few weeks than I've experienced in my whole life."

"And is it weird at all having that type of relationship with them, given your relationship with Grady?"

"Principal Gupta if I didn't know any better, I think we could confuse this with a therapy session."

He laughs. "I do have a background in psychology, so I might just be accidentally falling into old habits. I just want to make sure, after everything you've been through, that you are in the right place for you. You just learned how unstable your home life truly was, and it can be a lot to digest."

"I guarantee I am in the right place for me. And it's not going to be for long. I'll be leaving for college in like two months."

"Ahh yes, UCLA, right? And Grady too?

"Yes sir."

"I think that will be good for you. It will be good to get away from here and what happened, but also good to have something stable around you to fall back on. Speaking of graduation and the next steps, that is why I actually called you in for a meeting today."

He slides a piece of paper across the desk. It's the program for next Friday's graduation. The speeches section is listed in order as: Class Advisor, Valedictorian, Superintendent Lang, Salutatorian, Principal Gupta, and Class Representative. Under the Class Representative title is my name. "What is this?"

"James, many schools do something called the Every Man speech, or something similar. It's a speech not necessarily based on academics, in which you are in fact a stellar student, but someone who the graduating class votes to represent them. It's widely thought that the person giving this speech can relate better to most of the student body."

"Principal Gupta, I've only been a student here for a year. How could I be the one to represent the class?"

"Ask your classmates James. It's something that's voted on, and you won by a very large margin. It could be attributed to what you just experienced. It could be attributed to dating the quarterback of the football team. Or, more likely, it could be attributed to the fact you have made such a strong impression on people in a very short period of time."

"I don't know what to say."

"That's why I called you in. You don't have to accept it. It hasn't been announced yet to the student body. I do think they already know who won, given the voting results. But I want you to think about it. Most of your electives this year focused around writing, or reading heavy courses with essay writing. It's not that you can't do it. You just need to find the right voice for this speech."

I stare at the paper on the desk, at my name on the paper. I think about those who wouldn't want me to do this, or tried to keep me from getting here.

"I'll do it."

I walk out of my English final, feeling pretty good about the final essay portion. Grady and Davis are waiting outside the classroom. "That was your last final, right?" Grady walks over and kisses me.

"Yup. Now to work on my speech for tomorrow."

"Are you're saying we can't go off to the beach for a bit?" Davis asks. "The girls have the car packed up already for a beach day James! C'mon, you can work on the speech there. Run lines past us between jumps in the water. Beach, beach, beach, beach!"

"Dude, it's barely June. That water's going to be freezing." Grady says.

"Don't be a little bitch. You jumped in that ocean in January!"

"When drunk and on a dare!"

"Guys, you are more than welcome to jump in the water. I'm not quite there yet." I point at my arm, and I can tell they both look a bit deflated. "Oh stop. Just because I can't go in doesn't mean you guys can't.

I actually at this point could go without bandaging my arm, but choose not to. At least for now when in public, as the scar looks pretty gross at the moment. Julie brought home anti-scar cream from some fancy body shop last week and gave it to me. She was told it was the best one available but not to get my hopes too far up. But I'm actually seeing some improvement in it, but not enough to subject everyone to see it.

The beach is mostly empty when we get there. A few older couples spot the sand, along with a few other seniors who wave when we start setting up.

I watch as Grady strips down to his bathing suit and sprints with Davis and Rob down to the water. Grady and Rob stop dead in their tracks when they hit the water, but Davis does not. I think the yelp could have been heard two states over when Davis emerges from the water. "You assholes!" Davis runs at Grady and grabs him, wrestling him into the water as Rob runs a safe distance away.

"Idiots," Chloe says, looking up from her book. "Rhode Island has like a two-month window where the water is a mildly enjoyable temperature."

"I wish I could go in. Until I moved here, I had never even seen the ocean. No lake or anything compares to it. But," pointing at my arm, "it might be a bit until I'm ocean bound."

"Well, then it's lucky you are off to sunny California and will have limitless options," Dana says. Dana's parents had convinced her to follow the family legacy of going to the

University of Michigan, which she seemed not too pleased about. But maybe not. She wouldn't say it, but she hated the NYU campus when she visited it.

At some point they must have trapped Rob, because they're all in the water now. They are looking towards us and waving, just as a giant wave crashes into them. We all laugh at them.

"We've got some sandwiches and some pre-made margaritas and vodka-lemonades. What do you want James?"

"Lemonade sounds good." I guess Rob had volunteered to be the designated driver at Chloe's request. Although I had been very careful lately, given my arm and that I was still kinda recovering, this was a time to celebrate.

I jot a few notes but nothing is coming together on this speech. Everything seems too personal and I fear it wouldn't be able to connect to the audience. My mind just keeps going back to Penny and Ralph and where I was now.

"Hi James. Hi Chloe. Hi Dana." I turn around and Andy is standing there, on the beach in a hoodie. He looks noticeably better, not completely back but definitely better. It turned out Andy's parents had helped Penny get him to Ralph's and the basement, and now are awaiting trial. Andy has no other family to speak of, much like me. When one of the parents in town heard his story, they opened their home to him for the remainder of the school year.

"Hey Andy. Whatcha doin?" Chloe smiles at him.

"I sometimes come here after school to think, when it's pretty quiet. The sound of the waves quiets my brain. Makes me feel better."

Chloe squeezes my hand slightly and gives me a small nod. "Andy," I say, "do you want to join us?"

"I don't want to bother you guys. You seem like you're having a nice day and I don't think I'm all that fun."

"Andy, if you don't sit your ass down on this blanket, I will get the three assholes in the water to do it for me." Andy hurries over to the blanket and takes a seat next to me. After a few moments he takes off his hoodie. He still looks so skinny, but better than at the hospital.

"What are you going to say in your speech?" Andy asks.

"I'm really struggling coming up with the words, whatever message I should be conveying to the class. And then I get stuck in my own head because it's not just the kids, but all of the families and the teachers and staff. It's hard to pinpoint what is appropriate to talk about."

"James, my opinion? Don't hold anything back. You have experiences that maybe most haven't lived through, but there are things that can be learned from it. Look at Grady. You came to town and the most admired person in the school gravitated right to you. That makes you now one of, if not, the most admired people too. All of these friends you've made and how you've changed. You are the same person I knew last summer, but also so different at the same time. This place, for better or worse, made you who you are today."

It's partially my fault Andy ended up under Ralph's roof, and here he is being my biggest motivator. Thank God Grady is still down in the water.

"I've mostly been keeping to myself at school, just trying to get through this year and hope that I can start senior year fresh. Wherever that is. Work on getting better with people again over the summer, to trust most people again. Do you know what they did to us there? They would spend half the time preaching something religious out of a hand-written book, and the other half was what they called Reformation Time. They would switch back and forth between these presentations of naked women and presentations of naked men. If I got hard when the naked men were on screen, or didn't get hard when the naked women were on screen, they would beat me with a belt and withhold food for the day. I honestly don't know how much more I would have been able to take, and it's like someone heard my pleas. The cops stormed into the house and saved us."

"Fuck." Dana says, finishing her lemonade and grabbing two more out of the cooler. She hands one to Andy and he accepts.

"But James, you are who I have to thank for getting me out of there. If you hadn't fought with Virtue that day, she never would have gone and told your mom and you never would have gone back to the apartment. The cops never would have been called by your neighbor and I would still be in that basement, probably dead. Discarded and having that bed filled by the next person they convinced a parent to turn over to their care."

I put my arm around him. He flinches, but then relaxes. "James, if you hadn't come to the hospital room that day_ I wouldn't be sitting here today. You had almost just died, and you took the time to visit me and remind me that life could be worth living. It meant so much to me in that moment. And that is what gave me the confidence to come over to you guys in the first place."

"And I meant it. I'm only here for a couple more months but I can help you keep working on getting closer to feeling normal. I don't want to speak for the group, but I think the rest of them will too. You just have to put up with maybe some competing attitudes."

"Hey Andy!" Grady says, as the guys walk back to the blanket. "Do I need to worry about you moving in on my man?"

And Andy just smiles.

Forty-Six

The crowd applauds Principal Gupta as his speech wraps up. My nerves feel like they are at an all-time high. I scan the crowd, looking for my targets. Grady had told me, during the speech, to only look at him, Davis, and Chloe. Maybe Rob and Dana if needed. But not Mark and Julie, because they would be a mess. Everyone was seated alphabetically, and they were all spaced out enough where I could be addressing the whole crowd by only looking at them. And everyone from our little beach group had given their blessing on the content of the speech.

"And our last speech today is from Class Representative James Stockton. James was a new student to our school in his senior year, but clearly has a grip on our graduating class as they voted him as the voice to represent them. So, without further delay, please welcome James to the stage."

Even being outside, inside an open football field, the sound of the clapping is thunderous. It's almost as loud as a

Beacon home game. It seems to go on forever, which isn't helping my nerves at all. Finally, the clapping dies down. I place my speech on the podium in front of me, and take a deep breath.

"Graduates, parents, family, friends, teachers, administration, and staff. I want to start out by saying I'm terrified of public speaking, and apologize if it seems like I'm reading straight off of a piece of paper. I want to make sure I come across as making sense and not make an ass of myself in the process." A couple of laughs pop up in the crowd.

"I was quite honored, and quite honestly surprised, to be chosen to be the voice of my classmates. I have moved around quite a bit throughout my school years, which made it difficult to establish connections with classmates and teachers. And, in turn, I was expecting much of the same in my senior year. Which was fine, because it was what I was accustomed to and what was normal to me. Boy, was I wrong."

"That was very apparent on the very first day of school. In gym class, of all places. Coach Peters took over class and told us he didn't have any kickers for the football team this year, and we would be informally conducting team tryouts. I never really played any sports growing up. I was never in one place long enough early on to sign up and be part of a team. This led to missing out on a lot of the fundamental skills you learn in any sport. I also didn't have a father figure in my life to help push me towards a particular sport he played as a kid, and a mother who didn't care to spend her free time carting her kid off all over the place for a game. So, as I got older, I was often picked last or close to last in any gym class. I could run, but if it came to shooting, defending, hitting…whatever the skill of that particular sport was, I was awful. It also probably didn't help with making friends with other boys my age."

I could tell I was starting to talk faster so I paused, took a breath, and found Chloe in the audience. "But that first gym class at Beacon High I lined up with all the other kids. Well, all the other kids not already on the football team, and we did kicking drills. And it was in that line that I met my first friend at Beacon, Chloe Jenkins. Her sass and commentary on everyone in class immediately won me over, and it seemed possible I could gain a friend out of it. Well, maybe it was fate, but somehow both her and I were gifted with some very specific skills that made us perfect to be special teams players on the football team. She the punter, I the kicker. With the amount of time we would be spending in practice together, our friendship was destiny. And it was, and still is, thick as thieves. Chloe was the person I knew I could go to with any problem, talk to about anything. Chloe taught me the true meaning, and feeling, of friendship."

Chloe stands up, takes a bow, and blows a kiss to me. Again, inciting laughs and a few more claps. "Penny, my mother, moved us last summer from Vermont after discovering my romantic relationship with a male friend of mine. But, little did she know, a budding romance was developing between her son and the new school's star quarterback. Someone adored by the masses, Grady Tomlinson." Whistles break out from the scattered football players in attendance.

"Now, if Hollywood and high school romantic comedies have taught us anything, you do not ignore something like that. But it wasn't very clear at first, being new and all, I thought Grady was just being nice and welcoming me to the school. Then we went through that awkward will they, won't they phase. Complaining to Chloe about what to do about it. But I would love to give a shout out to the PTA, Coach Peters, and the faculty who helped plan our road trip to see the Giants game with an overnight trip in New York City. And maybe Grady's late-night craving for McDonald's. Because it was there, standing in the middle of Times Square that Grady Tomlinson, our team's quarterback and captain, first kissed me."

A chorus of oohs and ahhs burst out from the crowd, with parents and faculty making shushing noises. "But I bring this up for two reasons, not just to make you all feel squeamish and uncomfortable. You see, Grady and I kept this very much under wraps. Only a few of our friends knew about us. But the situation wasn't ideal for a football player, let alone a star football player with a mountain of acceptance letters from top football colleges. So, we dated in secret. Can you imagine how surprised we were when the yearbooks were distributed two weeks ago and we were voted as Best Couple in the class? We were dubbed The Kings of Beacon. Well, it appears it wasn't as secret as we thought it was. Someone saw us in Times Square and it circulated through the football team and the other various cliques in school. I mention this because this was the opposite of what I had experienced before. Last year I was pulled out of school for kissing a guy, and this year I was voted as the best couple in the class. It was honestly the most accepted and one of the happiest moments I have experienced in my life to date."

I notice Chloe ugly crying. "I have an unforgiving mother, who dated an even more unforgiving man. Yet she was the one who tried to kill me, until Grady saved my life. His parents, Mark and Julie, offered to take me in because I had nowhere to go. This taught a valuable life lesson. If you are in a bad situation, you don't have to stay with the family you are born into. Find someone, or some people, that care about you, no strings attached. Someone who will quite literally pick you up when you are down and carry you, so that you can be happy and find your own people to call family."

Mark, Julie, and Grady crying. Check, check, and check. "But sometimes, one must endure pain and suffering to help others in need. Through that pain we helped rid this town of an evil man. I know what I went through was worth it because it saved the boys Ralph locked up in that basement. Yes, I endured pain and still do, but it stopped a chain of torture. One of those boys taught me the life lesson that it's okay to suffer a bit when it will help someone else, and others, to a better life."

I catch Andy in the back row, smiling. He knows he is the one that inspired this whole speech. But I don't need to find any of my guideposts. The crowd is invested, many crying. It feels so...freeing, to get all of this out.

"I know I have taken much more time than I was supposed to, and apologies Principal Gupta for going slightly off script from what you received last night. But I want to thank Beacon High for, again, teaching me the experience of friendship, of love, of having a true family, and the notion of true individual sacrifice in helping others. And I hope, if you take anything from today, it's one of these life experiences that you can apply going forward. Because the world can always use a little more friendship, love, understanding, compassion, and selflessness. Thank you.

I do a little bow before heading back to my seat, in the direction of Grady, revealing the artwork on the top of my cap.

A single pink balloon.

Forty-Seven

PENNY: FIFTEEN YEARS AGO

Penny drops James off at Cindy's house. "Thanks for taking him, Cindy! We should have the carpet ripped up and out by tomorrow afternoon and I can come grab him then. Sweetie? Behave for Mrs. Nelson!"

She parks just out of sight of their house, on a side street. The papers Aunt Michelle had given her this morning sit neatly on the passenger seat. The receipt for two one-day tickets to Disney. An invoice for a three-night cruise from Florida to the Bahamas and back. The invoice includes an upgrade for a couples massage and spa package. Aunt Michelle had found them all on Greg's desk. All from Bobby's email address. All the activities taking place in the past week. While Bobby was supposedly in Florida for an insurance conference.

The house is dark when she walks up to it. Good. He isn't home yet. She keeps the papers tucked under her jacket to avoid the rain. She goes in through the back door and settles in at the kitchen table, fanning out the receipts in front of her. How would she address the situation with Bobby? Would she question him and corner him into admitting it? Or just throw it all at him at once?

The kitchen clock ticks away as she sits in the quiet, the only light on in the house being the one over the kitchen table. She hates the clock. She now hates this house. She hates everything that reminds her of Bobby. Yes, she wanted to get James out of the house so he wouldn't hear the conversation she was about to have with Bobby. But honestly, she couldn't stand looking at his little face while he pestered her with questions. He looks just like his father.

The front door opens, bringing her back to the present. "Penny, you home? I didn't see the car in the driveway but saw the kitchen light on." His bags drop to the ground and she hears him walk down the hall.

He emerges in the doorway, with a big smile on his face. "What are you doing sitting back here? Where's James? I picked him up a couple of things down in Florida. Got him these touristy key lime chocolate things, and some sand from the beach, and–" he stops when he sees the papers on the table. His eyes get wider and wider when he moves from one to the next, seeing that she had circled Greg's name on each of them. "Honey, I can explain…"

"Do," she says, pointing her finger at him. "Do explain why my cousin is going with you on your business trips. Getting couples massages and heading to the Bahamas and fine dining." She pulls papers out of her purse. His credit card statements from the past three months. "And why you are booking random hotels in Omaha when you tell us you had to stay late at the office. When did you exactly start fucking my cousin? Was it three months ago Bobby? Was it a year ago? Five years ago? Was it before the wedding?"

"I...I wanted to tell you Pen, I really did. But I didn't know how, and now we have James. Greg said we couldn't say anything with him living at home, that it would have to wait."

"You were planning on leaving me for him. What kind of a father abandons his wife and child for some fucking fling. With a man, you disgusting pig. That does not align with the path of life we are supposed to be on."

"Path of life? Is that more of that bullshit you've been reading on the internet? That man is filling your head with crazy Penny."

"You don't get to tell me what is and what's not crazy Bobby." She slides the chair across the floor and leaves the kitchen, wandering into the living room. "You need to pack your things and leave. I don't care where you go but it won't be here. But it better be far away so I don't have to see your face."

Bobby follows her into the living room. "We have a son together. You can't expect me to leave him."

"That is EXACTLY what I am saying to you. You're a pervert Bobby, and I will not have you corrupting our son to be like you."

"That's not how it works, Pen, and you know that. Unless that's what that preacher man has been feeding you. If this is how it's going to go fine, but we can let the courts decide how custody lands. I'm sure I can dig up some dirt on you-"

The fireplace poker connects with the side of Bobby's head. Penny gasps as he crumples to the ground.

She stands there for what seems like hours, starting at his lifeless body while holding the fireplace poker. Watching the blood pool on top of the floor around him. She needs to consider next steps. Penny heads to the garage and finds the tarp they use to clean up leaves in the fall. Used to use. She grabs that, along with a roll of duct tape, and heads back to the living room.

Getting Bobby onto the tarp and rolling him up wasn't too much of a struggle, neither was taping the tarp shut. The problem now was what to do with his body. She goes out the back door, into the rain, heading to the shed. She is careful not to turn on the light, to draw unwanted attention to herself. Against the left wall there's a large shovel.

About an hour later, she has a deep and wide enough hole to put the tarp in. And about twenty feet from the large hole is a smaller hole, the same length of the fireplace poker. She leans the shovel against a tree and heads back to the house.

The sound of Bobby's head smashing on each step seems deafening to her, but she assures herself the sound of the rain covers it. She struggles to pull the tarp over the driveway, then the grass, then the floor of the woods. The tarp, occasionally getting stuck on a random downed branch or tree root, finally makes it to the open grave. She pushes the tarp in, Bobby's arm flailing out of it as it hits the bottom of the hole. His wedding band catching a bit of the moonlight. She begins the slow task of filling the hole, the dirt heavier than before because of the rain.

Once she has also buried the fireplace poker, she gathers some of the random brush from deeper in the woods and places it on top of the fresh dirt, camouflaging it with the rest of the forest floor. Penny picks up the shovel and heaves it as hard as she can, out of sight and away from the freshly dug holes.

Back in the house, she again notices the pool of blood staining the hardwood floors. It doesn't matter. She cannot stay here. She pulls out her phone. She needs help.

PENNY: He came home and wasn't being reasonable. He won't be a problem for us anymore

PENNY: But I need help

RALPH: Of course, anything for you.

RALPH: Here's what you do. Pack up what you need for yourself from the house, anything you want to keep. Do the same for James.

RALPH: In the morning, go to the bank and take out as much money from your accounts as you can without drawing suspicion. Pick up James and start driving to Tennessee. I have a cabin there you can stay in

PENNY: Thank you Ralph

RALPH: I'll send you the address once I'm home.

PENNY: Talk soon

"Cindy, thank you again so much for watching him! We were able to take the carpet out and it's being hauled away tomorrow! I hope he wasn't too much trouble."

"Not at all, he was an angel," Cindy said, letting go of James's hand as Penny picked him up. "I'd love to do it again some time!"

"You'll be the first person I call. Talk soon." Penny opens the back seat and buckles James into the car seat as Cindy closes the front door.

"Mommy, why so much stuff in car?"

"Well little man," Penny said, "you and I are going on a little adventure. How does that sound?"

Acknowledgements

I have always wanted to write a book. I think it was because I was a big reader as a kid. I have talked about writing a book for as long as I can remember. As a little kid I would write stories in between readings of the latest *Goosebumps* or *Boxcar Children* book. I have my parents, Linda and John, and my Aunt Donna to thank for helping keep that love of reading alive.

I remember as a child being brought to our tiny town library, now a daycare facility, to pick up stacks of books. Participating in summer reading challenges, feeling triumphant winning a sticker or a coupon for a free ice cream. I remember visiting Donna at her apartment in Wethersfield, her taking me to a now shuttered bookstore in Rocky Hill. I used to spend hours in that store, but ultimately always left with the newest *Goosebumps* release by R.L. Stine.

This book would not have taken off without the help of my husband Brendan. When one goes almost thirty years talking of writing a book, and has nothing to show for it, sometimes they need a push. For my birthday in 2019, I was gifted a future week-long stay at an Airbnb so I could have the peace and quiet I needed to finally write. I set up the booking for April 2020. It was finally happening.

And then the pandemic hit. Looking back, the Airbnb probably would have been fine. But this was supposed to happen in month number one of the pandemic, at least the first month it started to surge in the United States. This was at the time where everyone thought the virus lived on surfaces, people wiping down their mail and groceries. Quarantining their forty-eight pack of toilet paper in the garage for three days. No way was I going to a complete stranger's house without knowing what their post-guest cleaning protocols were.

Alas, I did end up rescheduling and did book a five-night hotel stay in coastal Maine in May of 2021. In that hotel room in Scarborough, Maine, was where the idea of James, Grady, and all of Beacon was born (although the town had a different name at first).

I picked up the working draft of this book on and off so many times in the coming years, but decided in the beginning of 2023 it needed to be finished by year's end. And I did it.

I then needed to find my peer review group. A group of trusted friends who I knew could be brutal with me if the book sucked. What needed changing, what didn't work, what characters were too much of an asshole. I named them my "Donut Readers" due to my love of a certain treat.

Sarah, Betsy, Lynn, Kim, Jess, Shar...I cannot thank you enough for volunteering your time and giving the first draft a read and providing the feedback you did. It was scary, putting out the longest thing you've written to date for critique, but I thought I might have something halfway decent when a few of you read it in a day or two. You helped shape the town of Beacon and the characters who called Beacon home. And helped me name this book *The Kings of Beacon*.

And an extra shout out to Sarah and Betsy. Betsy, our resident artist, painting what became the cover of this book. Sarah, graphic designer extraordinaire, designing and formatting it all into the beautiful package you see today. I apologize in advance for hitting you up on the next book. And the next. And so on.

As for the dedication of this book, it was to our cat Rocco. We lost Rocco at the end of October 2023 at the age of fourteen. The night before his vet appointment, where Brendan and I both knew he wouldn't be coming back home with us, I finished writing *The Kings of Beacon*. Dedicating this book to anyone else would have felt wrong.

And last, but not least, thank you to the readers joining me on this journey. I hope you've enjoyed *The Kings of Beacon* as much as I did writing it. If you did enjoy it, I ask just one more thing of you and that is to review it on Goodreads and, if you purchased a copy, wherever you bought it from. Self-published authors have success by word of mouth and positive reviews.

This won't be the last you will hear from James and Grady, or Beacon. Beacon hopes to see you again soon.

About The Author - Mike Jakubowski

Mike lives in Connecticut with his husband Brendan. He spends his days binge watching television, reading books, drinking wine with friends, and counting dogs while running road races around the state.

Oh, and he sometimes does a bit of writing.

You can visit Mike at
mikejakubowskithewriter.com

Or follow him on Instagram and TikTok
@mikejakubowskithewriter

DAVID BARR KIRTLEY

HOST OF *GEEK'S GUIDE TO THE GALAXY*

**Geek's
Guide
Press**

This book is dedicated to my four biggest supporters—
Kathryn Barr Kirtley, John R. Kirtley, John Joseph Adams,
and Steph Grossman.

You are always there when I need saving.

Contents

Fantasy

Science Fiction

Horror

Introduction

As a short story writer, the most common question I get asked is, "What's a short story?" Most people have only a vague idea that short stories even exist, let alone that there are whole books and magazines devoted to them. I'm always taken aback by this. How can you go through life not reading short stories? Didn't these people ever read "The Tell-Tale Heart" in high school? Maybe they didn't do their homework, or they've forgotten the story, or it never sank in that "The Tell-Tale Heart" is this special thing called a "short story."

I feel really bad for those people. I love novels as much as anyone, and there are several long series that I've read over and over—Robert Asprin's *Myth* series, Roger Zelazny's *Amber* series, Gene Wolfe's *Book of the New Sun*, George R. R. Martin's *A Song of Ice and Fire*—but for me short stories are where it's at. I've always spent more time reading short stories than novels, and that trend has only accelerated as I've gotten older.

I can trace my interest in short stories to a few key moments. One was reading Isaac Asimov's *Foundation* and *The Caves of Steel*. In the author's introductions, Asimov recounts his conversations with legendary magazine editor John W. Campbell—how the two of them sketched out the ideas for the Foundation series and the Three Laws of Robotics. I couldn't imagine anything more exciting. Back then I mostly read novels because I didn't know where to find short stories, but occasionally I would come across an anthology like *The Super Hugos*, where I first read George R. R. Martin's fabulously creepy story "Sandkings," or Larry Niven's collection *N-Space*, where I first read his riveting story "Inconstant Moon."

But there are two events that really got me hooked on short stories. One was discovering *The Collected Stories of Philip K. Dick*. I couldn't believe it. Here was something I had never seen before—a five-volume set of short stories. I could read every story an author had ever published, over a hundred short stories, from his first published story to his last. I would sit at the dining room table, late into the night, eating bowl after bowl of cereal and reading story after story. The other big event that happened around that time was that my mom, who volunteered at the local library, pointed out to me that the library carried two science fiction magazines—*Asimov's* and *Analog*. They were flimsy little magazines encased in huge plastic sleeves. You weren't allowed to check them out, so I would sit for hours in the library and read them one after another.

I had always been writing and drawing, had created comics and picture books by the dozen. I had tried writing a few fantasy novels, but I always gave up after a few chapters because I had no idea where the story was going. But under the influence of *Asimov's* and *Analog* and Philip K. Dick, I developed a new ambition. I wanted to write short stories. I wanted to get them published. I dreamed of it the way other kids dreamed of being baseball players or rock stars. There was nothing I wanted more. And so for two decades, from the ages of 13 to 33, that's what I did. I wrote short stories. A lot of short stories. I gave it everything I had.

This book, *Save Me Plz and Other Stories*, collects 20 short stories that I wrote between 1999 and 2011, when I was between the ages of 21 and 33. All of these stories appeared in professional markets for fantasy & science fiction, and they include most of my best work. (I also wrote dozens of stories as a teenager, many of which received student writing awards or were published in magazines devoted to teen fiction. I think a lot of those stories are pretty good, and I may publish them in a future volume.)

Getting these 20 stories published required a lot of discipline and patience. I would print out a story, stuff it in a manila envelope along with a self-addressed stamped envelope, send it off, and then wait for a reply. It usually took magazines about three months to respond. Sometimes it took them over a year, or they wouldn't respond at all. An offhand comment I made once has become a popular meme—"Wanting to be a writer and not wanting to get rejected is like wanting to be a boxer and not wanting to get punched." I'm speaking from experience there. Getting these 20 stories published involved racking up well over 200 rejections. Even after I made my first pro sale—"The Black Bird," which appeared in *Gothic.net* in August 2000—I wrote 35 more stories which never sold at all.

I decided to break up this book into three categories—"Fantasy," "Science Fiction," and "Horror." That way people who don't like horror can skip those stories, and if you're more into science fiction than fantasy you can skip straight to the science fiction. "Save Me Plz" is arguably science fiction, but I decided to put it in the fantasy section because it draws so heavily on the iconography of fantasy role-playing games. "Three Deaths" is probably more fantasy than science fiction, but I decided to put it in the science fiction section because it falls squarely in the planetary romance genre, which is part of the science fiction tradition.

These stories aren't in any particular order. You can read whichever ones you want, as they're all standalone stories, with the exception of "The Skull-Faced Boy" and "The Skull-Faced City," which should definitely be read in sequence. But if you're curious, this is the order of composition: "The Second Rat," "The Black Bird," and "Beauty" were all written at the Clarion writers workshop in 1999, while I was still an undergrad at Colby College. "The Disciple" was written the summer after I graduated from Colby, when I moved back home to Katonah, New York. "The Skull-Faced Boy" and "The Prize" were written in the fall of 2000, when I was living in Austin, Texas. "They Go Bump" was written in the summer of 2001 at the Odyssey writers workshop, and "Seven Brothers, Cruel" was written shortly afterward in Katonah. In September of 2001 I moved to nearby Somers, New York. "Seeds-for-Brains" and "Veil of Ignorance" were written there in 2002 and 2003. In 2005 I moved to Los Angeles to study fiction and screenwriting at the University of Southern California. "Blood of Virgins," "Save Me Plz," "Transformations," "Red Road," and "Cats in Victory" were all written there. In 2009 I moved back to New York. By that time my friend John Joseph Adams had established himself as a top fantasy & science fiction editor, and would often encourage me to write stories for his theme anthologies. "The Skull-Faced City," "Family Tree," "The Ontological Factor," "Three Deaths," and "Power Armor: A Love Story" were all written for him. In 2010 John and I launched the *Geek's Guide to the*

Galaxy podcast, and in 2011 I took a break from writing fiction in order to devote myself full-time to the podcast, which was growing quickly in terms of both workload and popularity.

Many of these stories are responses to various books, movies, and TV shows, and you may enjoy exploring some of those connections. "Beauty" is a parody of the fairy tale "Beauty and the Beast." "The Black Bird" is a parody of Dashiell Hammet's novel *The Maltese Falcon* and Edgar Allan Poe's poem "The Raven." "Seven Brothers, Cruel" is a parody of the early modern ballad "The Douglas Tragedy." "Seeds-for-Brains" is a parody of Washington Irving's story "The Legend of Sleepy Hollow." "Red Road" is a parody of the *Redwall* series by Brian Jacques. "Save Me Plz" draws inspiration from the *Dungeons & Dragons* children's cartoon from the 1980s. "The Ontological Factor" is written in the style of Robert Asprin's *Myth* series. "Cats in Victory" and "Transformations" are parodies of the *ThunderCats* and *Transformers* children's cartoons from the 1980s. "Veil of Ignorance" is inspired by a thought experiment proposed by the philosopher John Rawls. "Three Deaths" is set in the same universe as the Edgar Rice Burroughs novel *A Princess of Mars*. "The Disciple" is set in the same universe as the H. P. Lovecraft story "The Call of Cthulhu." "The Skull-Faced Boy" and "The Skull-Faced City" are zombie horror stories in the vein of *Night of the Living Dead* and *Return of the Living Dead*.

Each story in the book is followed by an author's note describing how I came to write the story and get it published. Many of these contain spoilers, so definitely don't read them until after you finish the actual story. If you're not interested in the writing process or the publishing world, feel free to skip the notes and just read the stories. But I've always loved author's notes, so I wanted to make sure that my book was full of them.

I hope you enjoy the stories, and I hope they motivate you to read more short stories by other authors. Let's all spread the word. Maybe someday we can live in a world in which the standard response to a short story writer is not "What's a short story?" but rather "Oh great! I love short stories."

How I Met
John Joseph Adams

As you'll see throughout this book, John Joseph Adams has been a major figure in my life and career, so I'll take a moment to explain how we met.

In the summer of 2001, while I was a student at the Odyssey writers workshop, I attended a nearby science fiction convention called Readercon. One of the guests at the convention was Gordon Van Gelder, editor of *The Magazine of Fantasy & Science Fiction*. I had been submitting stories to him regularly for the past two years, all of which had been rejected. After one of his panels I walked up to him and said, "Hi Gordon. I'm David Kirtley. I don't know if you would remember, but I submit stories to *F&SF* all the time. I just wanted to introduce myself."

Gordon chatted with me for a few minutes, then said he had another panel to get to. The next time I submitted a story to *F&SF*, he remembered my name and mentioned meeting me at Readercon.

A year later, at a science fiction convention in San Jose, I met an author who had a few novels out from a major publisher. It turned out that we both lived in Westchester. He encouraged me to sign up for his newsletter, which I did, and a few weeks later I got an invite to attend his book launch at Barnes & Noble. "Come meet my friends and fans in Westchester!" it said. I was really excited. I'd lived in Westchester my whole life, and never knew there was any sort of science fiction scene there. I was looking forward to meeting up with a whole new community of like-minded people right in my own backyard.

I attended the signing, going so far as to read the entire book beforehand so I would be ready for the Q&A. There were only about seven people in the audience, which was disappointing, but I figured it was better than nothing.

The author read the first chapter of his novel, then asked if there were any questions. I raised my hand. He called on me, and I asked a hyper-specific question about the book, which he answered. "Any more questions?" he asked.

After a moment a man in the audience raised his hand.

"Yes?" said the author.

"I was wondering," the man said, "how do you get a book published?"

"Well, that depends," the author said. "Are you interested in publishing science fiction specifically, or something else?"

"I'm a photographer," the man said. "I take pictures of cities, and I want to publish a book of my photos."

"Oh," the author said. "I'm not really sure how you would go about doing that."

"Okay thanks," the man said. He stood up, along with his wife and kids, and walked out of the store. Now it was just me and one other family.

The father of the second family raised his hand.

"Yes?" the author said.

"My question is sort of along the same lines as the last question," the man said. The same process was repeated, and the second family walked out of the store.

I was left alone with the author. Clearly this was not going to be the night where I connected with a vibrant community of science fiction fans in Westchester. At the time I felt horribly embarrassed for the author, but I would later come to realize that this was a pretty typical book event.

Still, it ended up being one of the most important nights of my life, because of what happened next. The author asked me, "Are you going to the SFWA reception on Monday?"

SFWA is a professional organization for science fiction writers. I had recently become a member, but had never been to one of their events. I said, "I don't know. Maybe."

"Go," the author said. "It's the most important thing you can do for your career. Seriously, if you wake up on Monday morning with the flu and a broken leg, still go. It's that important,"

In fact I did wake up on Monday morning feeling pretty sick, and ordinarily I would have definitely stayed home that night. But because the author had been so adamant about this SFWA reception thing, I dragged myself down to the train station and took the Metro North train into Manhattan.

The reception was at the Society of Illustrators Building on East 63rd Street. It was a beautiful old white-brick building with framed artwork hanging everywhere. There were probably a hundred people there, and I didn't know any of them. Except one.

Gordon Van Gelder.

I figured he probably wasn't dying to talk to me, but I had come all that way, so I figured I might as well talk to *someone*. And after all, he *had* said "Thanks for coming up to say hi at that panel at Readercon" in one of his rejection letters. He was standing with a group of people. I walked up to him and said, "Hi Gordon. I'm David Kirtley. I don't know if you would remember, but I met you at Readercon."

"Oh hi," he said, plainly too busy to talk to me. "Hey, you should meet my assistant."

"Okay," I said, "sure." I found myself face-to-face with John. We had never met, but I recognized his name, and I knew that he had recently been hired as the assistant editor at *F&SF*. As soon as we started talking, it was like we were old friends, and it turned out that we shared many of the same tastes in fantasy & science fiction. Over the course of the evening a few other people I knew showed up, and I ended up having a really good time.

Two years later I attended a conference at SUNY New Paltz called Fantastic Genres, where various academics presented papers on fantasy & science fiction. I arrived at the conference and wandered over to the first event. I glanced around a packed lecture hall and realized that I didn't know a single person there. Except one.

John Joseph Adams.

He was sitting by himself. I went over and said hi and sat down next to him. We spent the whole weekend hanging out, and that's when we really got to know each other and became friends. After that we started meeting up all the time, going to movies and readings and conventions, making connections with an ever-widening circle of fellow science fiction fans in New York, which soon came to include Rob Bland, Andrea Kail, Douglas Cohen, Chris Cevasco, Matt London, Jordan Hamessley, Grady Hendrix, Theresa DeLucci, Matthew Kressel, Rajan Khanna, Bill Shunn, Carol Pinchefsky, and many others.

A lot of things had to fall into place for John and me to meet. I wouldn't have talked to him at the Fantastic Genres conference if we hadn't first spoken at the SFWA reception. I wouldn't have spoken to him at the SFWA reception if I hadn't first introduced myself to Gordon Van Gelder at Readercon. I wouldn't have even been at the SFWA reception if I hadn't gone to that disastrous reading at Barnes & Noble. I wouldn't have met Gordon Van Gelder at Readercon if I hadn't attended Odyssey. And so on. There are so many alternate timelines in which John and I never got to know each other and never became friends.

I shudder to even imagine what that would be like. Certainly much less interesting, and much, much less fun.

Publication History

The stories in this book previously appeared in the following publications:

"Beauty" first appeared in the March 2012 issue of *Lightspeed* magazine.

"The Black Bird" first appeared in the August 2000 issue of *Gothic.net*. It also appeared in *New Voices in Science Fiction*, edited by Mike Resnick, DAW books, December 2003, in *The Dragon Done It*, edited by Eric Flint and Mike Resnick, Baen books, March 2008, and in the October 2012 issue of *Lightspeed* magazine.

"Seven Brothers, Cruel" first appeared in the December 2002 issue of *Realms of Fantasy* magazine.

"Blood of Virgins" first appeared in the October 2006 issue of *Realms of Fantasy* magazine. It also appeared in Episode 88 of the *Escape Pod* podcast.

"Seeds-for-Brains" first appeared in the June 2003 issue of *Realms of Fantasy* magazine.

"Family Tree" first appeared in *The Way of the Wizard*, edited by John Joseph Adams, Prime Books, November 2010.

"Red Road" first appeared in the July 2008 issue of *Orson Scott Card's Intergalactic Medicine Show*. It also appeared in Episode 141 of the *Journey Into...* podcast.

"Save Me Plz" first appeared in the October 2007 issue of *Realms of Fantasy* magazine. It also appeared in *Fantasy: The Best of the Year, 2008 Edition*, edited by Rich Horton, Prime Books, August 2008, in *Press Start to Play*, edited by John Joseph Adams and Daniel H. Wilson, Vintage Books, August 2015, and in Episode 124 of the *Escape Pod* podcast.

"The Ontological Factor" first appeared in the September/October 2011 issue of *Cicada* magazine. It also appeared in *Other Worlds Than These*, edited by John Joseph Adams, Night Shade Books, July 2012.

"The Second Rat" first appeared in the Spring 2002 issue of *On Spec* magazine. It also appeared in the Spring 2006 issue of *MechMuse* audio magazine.

"They Go Bump" first appeared in *Empire of Dreams and Miracles: The Phobos Science Fiction Anthology*, edited by Orson Scott Card and Keith Olexa, Phobos Books, July 2002. It also appeared in Episode 382 of the *Escape Pod* podcast.

"The Prize" first appeared in *Empire of Dreams and Miracles: The Phobos Science Fiction Anthology*, edited by Orson Scott Card and Keith Olexa, Phobos Books, July 2002.

"Cats in Victory" first appeared in the June 2010 issue of *Lightspeed* magazine. It also appeared in *Lightspeed: Year One*, edited by John Joseph Adams, Prime Books, November 2011, and in Episode 141 of the *StarShipSofa* podcast.

"Transformations" first appeared in the December 2007 issue of *Realms of Fantasy* magazine.

"Veil of Ignorance" first appeared in *All the Rage This Year: The Phobos Science Fiction Anthology 3*, edited by Keith Olexa, Phobos Books, September 2004. It also appeared in the Spring 2006 issue of *MechMuse* audio magazine, and in the February 2015 issue of *Lightspeed* magazine.

"Power Armor: A Love Story" first appeared in *Armored*, edited by John Joseph Adams, Baen Books, March 2012. It also appeared in Episode 272 of the *Drabblecast* podcast, and in the December 2013 issue of *Lightspeed* magazine.

"Three Deaths" first appeared in *Under the Moons of Mars,* edited by John Joseph Adams, Simon & Schuster, February 2012.

"The Disciple" first appeared in *Dead But Dreaming*, edited by Kevin Ross and Keith Herber, DarkTales Publications, March 2002. It also appeared in the Summer 2002 issue of *Weird Tales* magazine, in *New Cthulhu*, edited by Paula Guran, Prime Books, October 2011, and in Episode 48 of the *Pseudopod* podcast.

"The Skull-Faced Boy" first appeared in the March 2002 issue of *Gothic.net*. It also appeared in *The Living Dead*, edited by John Joseph Adams, Night Shade Books, January 2008, in *Z: Zombie Stories*, edited by J. M. Lassen, Night Shade Books, September 2011, and in Episode 94 of the *Pseudopod* podcast.

"The Skull-Faced City" first appeared in *The Living Dead 2*, edited by John Joseph Adams, Night Shade Books, September 2010.

Illustration Credits

Some illustrations in this book have been cropped to fit this format. See the full-color originals at davidbarrkirtley.com.

"Beauty" illustration by Galen Dara. First appeared in the March 2012 issue of *Lightspeed* magazine.

"Seven Brothers, Cruel" illustration by Kyle Anderson and Mia Lee. First appeared in the December 2002 issue of *Realms of Fantasy* magazine.

"Blood of Virgins" illustration by Huan Tran. First appeared in the October 2006 issue of *Realms of Fantasy* magazine.

"Seeds-for-Brains" illustration by Scott Goto. First appeared in the June 2003 issue of *Realms of Fantasy* magazine.

"Family Tree" illustration by Michael J. DiMotta. First appeared on davidbarrkirtley.com.

"Red Road" illustration by Nick Greenwood. First appeared in the July 2008 issue of *Orson Scott Card's Intergalactic Medicine Show*.

"Save Me Plz" illustration by HyeJeong Park. First appeared in the October 2007 issue of *Realms of Fantasy* magazine.

"Cats in Victory" illustration by Jerome Jacinto. First appeared on davidbarrkirtley.com.

Galen Dara

Beauty

Nicole Sanders was beautiful. One night after work, she stopped off at a bar downtown, which is where she met the beast.

"Hi," the beast said, in a gentle voice. "Can I buy you a drink?"

He was a hulking, hairy creature. His spindly goat legs ended in a pair of cloven hooves. Massive sheep horns poked out of his forehead and curled around his gremlin ears. Instead of hands he had two furry paws. His demon eyes were bloodshot and sad.

Nicole studied him. He certainly wasn't the best-looking guy in the place, but he seemed so hopeful and shy, and she didn't want to hurt his feelings.

"Okay," she said. "A drink would be nice."

He bought two beers and carried them over. "I'm the beast," he said, sitting down beside her.

"I'm Nicole," she said.

He smelled sharp and fiery.

"That's an interesting cologne you're wearing," she said. "What is it?"

"It's brimstone," he said flatly, then added, "It isn't cologne."

"Oh."

The beast studied his drink.

"So what do you do?" she asked.

He shrugged. "Telemarketing."

"Do you like it?"

"It's all right." He gulped some beer. "Actually, I've been having some problems with my coworkers."

"I'm sorry to hear that."

"Yeah, I mean, things used to be a lot better there, before the whole, you know..." He gestured at his appearance.

"Oh," Nicole said. "So it's..."

"A spell." The beast nodded wearily. "Yeah. I actually used to be pretty handsome, if you can believe that."

"So what happened?"

He lowered his voice. "I was cursed by an evil sorceress." He held up his huge paws. "She turned me into this."

Nicole gasped. "That's horrible."

The beast sighed. "Oh, it's not so bad. I have some magic talking furniture that keeps me company. It's enough, most of the time..." He closed his eyes and shook his head. "Look, I'm sorry, I don't mean to...maybe I should go." He started to get up.

"Wait," Nicole said. "No. It's all right, really." She added, "I've never met anyone before who owned any magic talking furniture."

He glanced at her hopefully, then sat back down again.

They chatted for a long time, then she walked with him back to his apartment, and he invited her up for a drink. The apartment was small, and kind of a mess.

"I should straighten up a bit," said the beast.

"No, it's fine," Nicole assured him. She glanced through a doorway into the kitchen. "Where's the magic furniture?"

He lumbered into the living room and turned on his tiny television. "That's it."

She stared. "That's just a television."

"It talks," the beast said weakly.

"But...that's not magic at all."

He settled down on the couch and hung his head in his paws. "I know," he moaned, "I haven't got any magic furniture. I haven't got anything."

"Hey," Nicole said softly. "Don't worry. It'll be all right."

* * *

The beast called her the next day.

"I had a good time last night," he said. "You're such a good listener."

"It was nice," Nicole said. It had been a long time since a guy had opened himself up to her like that.

"Can I see you again?" he asked.

"All right."

They started going out together—to movies, to restaurants, and bars. Her friends didn't approve.

Her best friend Katie said, "I mean really, Nicki. The guy's a telemarketer. You could do so much better."

But she ignored them.

One night Nicole and the beast were relaxing in a local restaurant. Suddenly he gasped.

"What?" Nicole said.

"That's her," he whispered. "The evil sorceress I was telling you about. Over there, by the register."

Nicole sneaked a glance. The woman he'd indicated was in her mid-twenties, attractive, with curly red hair. "She doesn't look evil," Nicole said. "She looks pretty normal, actually."

"They always do." The beast sighed. "They always do."

Nicole dated the beast for a few more months. She began to really like him. His bloodshot eyes were soft and caring. His werewolf paws were strong and gentle. When he slept, he would fold his goblin ears in the most adorable way. He giggled whenever she poked him on his cute little doggie nose.

One night, as they sat on his couch watching TV, Nicole asked, "Is there any way the spell can ever be broken?"

"It'll never happen."

"Tell me."

He sighed. "For the spell to be broken, I must marry a beautiful girl who loves me for who I am."

"A beautiful girl?" Nicole echoed. "Only a beautiful one?"

"Yes."

She frowned. "Is that all I am to you? A way to break the spell?"

"No!" he said, wounded. "How can you think that? Yes, you are beautiful, Nicki—and smart, and sweet, and caring, and I love you."

She studied him for a moment, then took his paw and squeezed it tight. Of course he wanted to break the spell. Who wouldn't? That didn't mean he didn't love her.

17

He *did* love her, and she loved him. He was an honest, dependable, adorable creature.

And he wasn't shy about commitment either.

* * *

They got married in the spring.

The morning after their wedding, Nicole awoke to find a stranger in her bed—a gorgeous man with jet black hair.

"Beast?" she whispered.

He opened his eyes, which were bright blue.

"Beast no longer," he said, in a deep voice. "The spell is broken, Nicki. We did it."

He sprang from the bed and paced barefoot across the floor, studying himself in the full-length mirror. His shoulders were broad and toned, his calf muscles vividly defined. He stretched and flexed and laughed.

"Look at me!" he said, turning. "I'm my old self again."

"Beast..." she whispered.

"Brett," the man insisted happily. "That's my real name—Brett."

"Brett," she repeated, uncertainly.

He leaped back into the bed and kissed her over and over. "Thank you," he said. "Thank you for being who you are."

She studied this man, this stranger. He noticed her expression and said, "What's wrong?"

"I don't know, it's just...I've gotten to love you one way, and now you change."

"You're a beautiful woman, Nicki," he said. "You shouldn't have to live with some ugly monster. What kind of happy ending would that be?"

"It didn't matter to me," she said. "I didn't care how you looked."

He settled back, kneeling, troubled. "I don't know what to say."

After a moment she added, "I'm sorry." She pulled him close and embraced him. "I don't mean to be like this. You look great. Really."

* * *

Shortly afterward, Brett got promoted. He got his own office, and an assistant named Cindy. Then he started working late at the office more and more.

On weekends he'd recline shirtless on the front porch of their new house and play the guitar, and women from all over the neighborhood, who just happened to be walking or jogging by, would come over and talk to him.

One day Nicole came home early and found him relaxing in the living room, sharing a bottle of wine with her best friend Katie.

"Katie," Nicole said. "Could I talk to you for a minute?" She led Katie into the kitchen, and demanded, "What are you doing here?"

"It's not what you think," Katie said. "Brett's been teaching me to play the guitar, that's all."

"Katie," Nicole growled. "You were a music major. Brett only knows three songs."

Katie sighed dreamily. "But he's such a good teacher."

That night at dinner, Nicole said to him, "It's like I don't even know you anymore. These women hanging around all the time, your late nights at the office, you never call—"

"Nicki, calm down. You're not being fair."

"Oh, I'm not?"

"It's not easy, being attractive," he said, wrapping spaghetti around his fork. "You of all people should know that. I can't help it if women like me."

"You are *not* the man I married," she said. "The man I married was a kind, gentle—"

"Oh, come on, Nicki," he said. "Did you really think nothing would change? Nothing at all? If you woke up tomorrow and you were some ugly monster, would you still act exactly the same way? Feel exactly the same way about everything?"

"I'd still love you," she said. "Would you still love me?"

He glared. "I don't have to take this." He threw his napkin out on the table. "I'm going to bed," he said, as he stomped up the stairs.

* * *

The next morning Brett awoke with horns. There were two of them, stubby pale things, poking out of his temples like giant whiteheads.

"No!" he raged, pacing back and forth in front of the mirror. "No! This can't be happening."

Nicole watched from the bed. She said softly, "How?"

"I don't know. The spell was gone, broken, it—" He turned on her suddenly. "You! You did this to me."

"What? But I..."

He sat down beside her and took her by the hand. "Do you still love me?"

"Of course I do."

"With all your heart? Like you used to?"

She stared at the blanket.

After a moment, he stood. "I'm late for work."

When he returned home that night, he'd changed again. The stubs on his brow had grown into great horns nine inches long. His pant legs were shredded, and his knees bent backward when he walked. His smooth tanned arms now ended in a pair of jarringly incongruous werewolf paws.

At work, he had been demoted.

"Look at me!" he shrieked, grasping her by the shoulders and shaking her. "Look what you've done!"

"Get away from me!" she screamed. "Don't touch me!"

Later, he packed up a few belongings and disappeared into the night, slamming the door behind him.

* * *

He called the next day, but she hung up on him. He called her at home, at work. She wouldn't speak to him.

"These damn telemarketers," Katie said. "They never leave you alone."

He sent her roses, which she threw in the trash.

"I told you he was no good," Katie said. "I always said you could do a lot better."

One night he showed up at the front door, drunk. It was raining.

"Please, Nicki," he said. "Please. You have to take me back. No one will ever love me the way you can."

His ears were pointed and his face had grown into a half-snout. He gazed at her longingly, adoringly. He looked so much like the old beast that it was all she could do not to touch him on his cute little doggie nose, to tickle his adorable gremlin ears.

"I'm sorry," she told him sadly, "but this is the way it has to be."

* * *

Months passed. The paperwork for the divorce came through.

One night, on her way home from work, Nicole stopped by a bar to have a drink. As she squeezed through the crowd, she came face to face with him. He was beastly as ever, and had a pretty young girl at his side.

Nicole said awkwardly, "Hi."

He studied her with his bloodshot demon eyes. "Hi."

The girl glanced back and forth between them. Finally she said, "Beast? Who's this?"

He was silent a moment, then said wearily, "That's the evil sorceress I was telling you about."

Author's note: Beauty

"Beauty and the Beast" has always driven me crazy. It's the story of a beautiful woman who falls in love with an ugly monster because "it's what's on the inside that counts." So far so good. Except then the curse is broken and the beast transforms into a handsome prince. The end.

But doesn't that completely undercut the whole point of the story, which is that looks don't matter? Apparently looks *do* matter, or at least the story seems to think so.

I was in college when I wrote "Beauty." Around that time I had read a bunch of books about dating, along the lines of *Dating for Dummies* and *The Complete Idiot's Guide to Dating*. One of those books contained an idea that really stuck with me, which is that in every romantic relationship there's a balance of power, like conservation of energy. Maybe one person is smart and the other is popular, or one person is beautiful and the other is rich, in which case things balance out. But if things don't balance out in that way, they'll balance out in other ways. If one person is genuinely more desirable than the other, it's inevitable that the more desirable partner will have more leverage in the relationship, and will be the one calling the shots.

The book described a marriage between a beautiful woman and an average-looking man. Both of them knew that the wife was the more desirable of the two, and so the husband showered her with gifts and compliments, and generally let her have her way, because he didn't want to lose her. Then the wife was in a car accident in which she was badly disfigured. According to the book, it was basically inevitable that the husband would start making less of an effort to keep her happy. He didn't have to. Things always balance out. I found that idea both fascinating and horrifying—that the husband's level of affection would respond so predictably and inevitably to some hidden calculus of power and need.

And what would that mean for beauty and the beast? If you have a relationship between a beautiful woman and an ugly beast, where things exist in an equilibrium because the beast's kindness and devotion make up for his lack of looks, what happens when he becomes good-looking too? Is it inevitable that he'll become a little less devoted, a little less kind? In that case, maybe making him handsome would be the actual curse.

I've always liked the part in "Beauty" where the beast offers to show Nicole his "magic talking furniture," which turns out to be just an ordinary television. Obviously that's a reference to the talking furniture in the Disney cartoon *Beauty and the Beast*, but it works on multiple levels. It helps to set up that the beast is maybe a bit slippery right from the start, but at the same time a television *is* pretty magical. I lived alone for many years, and in those circumstances a television really does become a constant companion, as much as any magic clock or candlestick.

The Black Bird

The black bird on the mantelpiece spoke. It said, "Nevermore."

Spade looked up from cleaning his pistol. The bird, a black-lacquered falcon statuette, sat motionless. Spade placed the pistol down on his desk, pushed back the brim of his hat, and approached the bird. "You talk?"

The bird watched him with two small black eyes. "Yes," it answered. Its voice was eerily familiar somehow.

"How?" Spade demanded. "You're just a statue."

The bird's lacquered beak moved when it talked, as if the statue were alive. "Sounds like a mystery to me."

Spade lit a cigarette. "Well, I'm good with mysteries. I just solved one."

"You didn't solve squat." The bird sneered.

Spade was perplexed. He *had* solved the case. The black bird was a fake—a decoy. They'd scraped away a bit of its lacquered exterior and instead of priceless jewels they'd found nothing but worthless lead. He said suspiciously, "What do you mean?"

"You never did find the real falcon," the bird said. "Don't you wonder where it is?"

Spade shrugged. "The Russian has it, probably. Let Gutman and the others go after it if they want. They'll never find it."

"Wrong," said the bird. "The Russian doesn't have it. In fact, it's right around here somewhere."

Spade studied the bird. Finally he said, "All right, I'm listening."

"Good," said the bird. "Listen closely. Because this is a real mystery—not like your usual work, which is always about who killed who, or who's banging whose wife. That's not a mystery, Spade. That's hardly even a puzzle."

Spade frowned.

"Real mysteries," said the bird, "like—why do we exist? What's the nature of truth? Is there a higher power? They don't have solutions. That's what makes them mysteries."

Spade broke in. "So where's the real falcon?"

The bird sighed. "It's so obvious. I'd think you would have figured it out by now. You're the detective, after all."

"Tell me."

"Didn't you ever read 'The Purloined Letter'? The best place to hide something is in plain sight, where no one will think to look for it."

Spade walked across the room and lifted the black bird off the mantelpiece. It chuckled as he turned it all around. He walked over to his desk and set the bird down, then flicked open his pocketknife and began scraping off more of the black lacquer. Underneath, of course, was nothing but lead.

"You're getting warmer," said the bird.

Spade opened a drawer and took out an iron file. He began scraping away at the bird's leaden neck.

"Oh, even warmer now."

Spade scraped deeper and deeper. Then he took a deep breath and blew, sending filings flying away into the smoky air.

Beneath the lacquer and lead, the bird was made of gold and jewels, which sparkled even in the dim light of Spade's office. "Congratulations," cried the bird. "You solved the mystery! You're rich! Case closed."

"Something's not right here," Spade said.

He took up his pocketknife again, and used it to poke the largest jewel. The knife's tip sank a few centimeters in, as if the jewel were made of chocolate.

"Oh boy," said the bird. "Now you've done it. The plot thickens."

Carefully, Spade started scraping away at the jewel.

"I should warn you," the bird intoned ominously, "that if you keep digging into this matter, you may not like what you find."

Spade ignored him.

"Of course," the bird added, "people in mysteries always say that, don't they? And does it ever happen? No way. The hero goes right ahead, catches the killer, and gets the girl. He gets his picture in the paper, and a handshake from the mayor. So go ahead, Spade. Don't listen to me. Keep digging. Everything will probably turn out all right in the end."

The faux jewels fell away like dry scabs. Beneath lay cogs, flashing lights, an intricate network of tiny machines.

"What's this?" Spade said.

"Micro-circuitry," the bird explained. "That's what allows me to talk."

"There's no such thing."

"Well!" said the bird. "Look who knows so much! Just because you've never seen micro-circuitry, you presume it can't possibly exist. Read Hume some time, why don't you?"

Spade poked at the micro-circuitry with his knife. "What is all this?"

"Computers," said the bird. "Machines. That's what it's all about, Spade. Everything's a machine, in one way or another—your body, the universe. One day you'll probably be replaced by a machine. Who knows?"

"I don't think so."

"Sound improbable?" said the bird. "Why don't you try scraping away at your own outer layer? You might be surprised at what you find."

Absently, Spade ran a fingernail down the skin of his forearm.

"Leave well enough alone," said the bird. "Just this once."

"I think there's something more," Spade said. "A deeper layer." He began to scrape away at the micro-circuitry.

Circuits popped and sparked and fell away. Motors broke and oozed hydraulic fluid. Lights went dark.

"You're out of your league, Spade," said the bird. "Why don't you just go back to murder, adultery, that sort of thing. That's more up your alley."

"I've broken the machines," Spade observed, "and you're still talking."

The bird nodded reluctantly. "Perhaps it isn't the micro-circuitry after all."

Beneath the circuitry was a pink, porous surface.

"Looks like skin," Spade said.

"Maybe," said the bird.

Spade filed away at the falcon's beak, which cracked off and fell to the floor. He filed away its eyes, its throat. He scraped away tiny circuits and fake jewels, exposing more and more of the flesh.

"It's a face!" he said.

"Oh, it gets better," said the bird.

"It's my face," Spade said finally.

A living, miniature version of his own face stared back at him from the opening in the black bird's head.

"So you see," said the bird, "this is how I can talk. I'm actually alive, after all."

Spade realized with a start why the bird's voice sounded so familiar. It was his own. "Why do you look like me?"

"Because our perceptions of things, mysteries for example, are filtered through our own consciousness. If you keep digging for truth, eventually all you find is yourself."

"There must be something deeper," Spade insisted.

"I wouldn't count on it."

Spade raised his knife. The bird eyed it nervously. "Uh, Spade? What are you doing?"

Sam Spade had never failed to solve a mystery, and he didn't intend to start now. "I want the truth." With an unsteady hand he began to scrape away at the tiny face. Clear amber fluid oozed out. He scratched at the falcon's throat.

"That's the jugular vein," the bird whispered. "You might want to be careful around that."

"Will it kill you?"

"No."

Spade sliced it, and blood billowed forth, splattering across the desk.

Spade gasped. "Blood?"

"Blood," the bird confirmed. "That's as deep as you're going to get."

Spade set down the knife. "That's the answer to your mystery? Blood?"

"I never said there was an answer. Quite the opposite, in fact."

Spade scowled. "That's not a mystery."

"*Au contraire*," said the bird, "that is a true mystery. Real quests for the truth usually end in fits of self-destruction and bitter disappointment."

"I'm not finished yet."

"Oh no? What's left to do? You've already——" It paused. "Uh-oh, Spade," it added, "looks like you're bleeding."

"What?" Spade pressed his fingers to his neck, and his hand came away wet and sticky. He leapt to his feet, ran across the room, and looked in the mirror.

"I told you it wouldn't kill *me*," said the bird. "Beyond that, who's to say?"

Blood oozed from a gory section of Spade's cheek, and a deep gash ran across his throat. He seized a cloth to stanch the flow of blood from his neck, but the fabric soaked through instantly.

He spun around and stared at the bird.

"I said you might not like what you found," the bird said, almost apologetically, "but you didn't listen."

Spade sank to his knees, his blood dripping wide, wet spots across the carpet.

"No girl for you," the bird scolded. "No handshake from the mayor." It hopped from the desk and strode across the carpet toward him. "I told you you were out of your league." The bird shook its head ruefully. "But would you listen?"

Spade collapsed, his head striking the floor.

"Will Sam Spade live to solve another mystery?" the bird asked.

Spade watched as it loomed closer, its bleeding face a mirror of his own. Finally the bird stood before him, casting a long shadow over him.

"Nevermore," it answered, chuckling. "Nevermore!"

Author's note: The Black Bird

In the spring of 1999 I did a semester abroad in Cork, Ireland. The coursework was shockingly light compared to what I was used to at Colby, and I found myself with a lot of free time on my hands. I got a lot of writing done—three literary stories for class, and six science fiction stories that I wrote for fun—and I also read a ton of books. I would walk across town to the Waterstone's bookstore, pick up a book, then sit on the bank of the River Lee and read all afternoon. I was finishing a book every two or three days. I read a lot of Philip K. Dick, a bunch of Iain M. Banks, a smattering of philosophy, and a bunch of literary classics including, most notably, *The Maltese Falcon* by Dashiell Hammet.

So the book was still fresh in my mind when I arrived at Michigan State University that summer to attend the Clarion writers workshop. The format of the workshop is that you meet every morning and critique a few stories, break for lunch, then spend the rest of the day reading other people's stories and writing your own. You're encouraged to turn in a story every week, and it's all supposed to be fiction that you wrote at the workshop.

Writing six stories in six weeks while also reading and critiquing more than a hundred stories is a grueling experience, and it's typical for people to experience some degree of burnout. We were staying in a big three-story dormitory, and it was not the most conducive atmosphere for writing. Michigan in the summer was oppressively hot and humid, and the dorm had no air conditioning. The only way to get a bit of a breeze going was to open my door and window, but my neighbors across the hall (not Clarion students) were constantly having loud sex, which was incredibly distracting. Nevertheless I managed to churn out six stories, including "The Second Rat," "Beauty," and "The Black Bird."

I'm not sure where the idea for "The Black Bird" came from, but it's definitely the sort of thing you come up with when you're stressed out, overheated, and drifting in and out of sleep. I was afraid it was too weird, and didn't turn it in to the workshop, writing and submitting "Beauty" instead. But then my turn came around again and I hadn't come up with any new stories, so I was forced to submit "The Black Bird."

Our instructor that week was Mike Resnick, a grizzled old pro, blunt and cantankerous, who had published hundreds of novels. I had no idea what he would make of my weird little story. We went around the circle, and the workshop was pretty evenly divided between people who thought the story was interesting and original, people who thought it was amusing but nothing special, and people who thought it was pointless and pretentious. One student in particular gave a rousing defense of the story. "I wrote, 'This is almost perfect,'" he said. "Then I crossed out 'almost.'"

Mike Resnick went last. "Let me tell you something," he said. "I know Sam Spade. I know Sam Spade better than Humphrey Bogart does. And this story is brilliant." He gestured toward the students who had criticized the story. "These people are all wrong," he thundered. "Don't listen to them. If I were still editing, I'd buy this story in a New York minute. In fact, if you don't sell this to a pro market, I'll edit an anthology myself just so I can publish it."

I was floored. After Clarion I started sending the story out to pro markets. (Pro markets are markets that pay a certain amount. At the time it was 3 cents per word.) 1999 was probably the worst time to sell short stories in the history of science fiction, since the print magazines were quickly dying off and the online magazines were just getting started. There were only about seven or eight pro markets at the time, and several of them were clearly not going to publish a piece of surreal metafiction like "The Black Bird." But I dutifully sent the story off to the handful of magazines where I thought it stood a chance.

The story was eventually accepted at *Gothic.net*, one of the earliest online magazines to pay pro rates. I was ecstatic. My first pro sale! I emailed Mike Resnick to tell him the good news. "What?" he responded. "Why did you sell it there?" That took the wind out of my sails, but I wasn't sure what else I could have done.

A few years later Mike Resnick emailed me to say that he was putting together an anthology called *New Voices in Science Fiction* ("science fiction stars of tomorrow"), and he wanted "The Black Bird" for the lead slot. "We've got to get it away from that crappy little ezine you sold it to," he said. I was still proud of my sale to *Gothic.net*, but *New Voices in Science Fiction* was definitely a much bigger deal. I was thrilled to be in the book, which included stories by my Clarion classmates Tobias Buckell and Tom Gerencer, as well as rising stars such as Cory Doctorow, Kage Baker, Charles Stross, and Julie Czerneda. Mike also published "The Black Bird" in his anthology *The Dragon Done It*, a collection of speculative mystery stories.

Art is subjective, and sometimes you get lucky when a story really connects with a particular editor. I was fortunate that Mike Resnick just happened to be at Clarion that year, and that he happened to be such a big fan of Sam Spade and detective fiction. If not for him championing the story, it definitely would have gotten a lot less attention.

Kyle Anderson & Mia Lee

Seven Brothers, Cruel

The first time he kissed her was in a dark, dusty corner of the kitchen, behind a great clay oven.

The second time was on the stairs in the high north tower. Through tall window slits they could see patches of yellow and orange field broken by winding river, stretching below them.

The third time was in the courtyard, his back pressed tight against the stone well, while down in the darkness an old wooden bucket, hanging by a chain, swung back and forth, hitting against the sides, knock-knock.

Galan was in love with her. Her name was Sarei. The Lady Sarei. Her face was young and bright, her hair straight and black. She lived with her seven older brothers in a dark fortress at the edge of the world.

"I hate it here," she whispered into his ear, then glanced back over her shoulder toward the keep, where her brothers were feasting. "I hate *them*." Her seven brothers. "They're horrible," she said. "Ugly and cruel and they mistreat me. I'm nothing to them."

Galan followed her gaze, back to the keep.

He'd been out here a long time. He didn't want to leave her, not yet, but it was dangerous. "I should go back inside, before I'm missed."

"All right." She kissed him again, deeply. "Meet me after supper, by the stables."

"Yes," he said, drawing away, reluctantly.

He hurried across the yard. The fortress was cold and foreboding. Creeping vines grew out of the grime between the blue-black stones, and clusters of crows perched at odd angles along the rocky battlements. He passed below them, through a high arch.

In the great hall, Sarei's brothers sat together in the light of the hearth. Across the table from them sat Galan's own company, ten rowdy young men. He joined them on the bench.

Balthus was the oldest brother, and Douglas was the loudest, but they all looked the same—pale skin and black hair, except the twins, who were blond. Vassals, they were obligated to grant hospitality to knights, but they didn't like it. It had been a week, and they wanted their guests gone. But leaving here would mean leaving Sarei.

Galan noticed the brother named Douglas watching him.

You've never told me," said Douglas, stroking his long mustache. "Who's the best soldier in this bold company?" There was a mocking edge to his voice.

Out of the corner of his eye, Galan saw Sarei, carrying a heavy bucket, stop on the stairs. He said, "I am."

One of his companions laughed. "It's true."

Douglas said, "You're just a boy."

"But I'm strong," Galan said, "and fast. And deadly with a sword."

And I train constantly, he thought, with sword and lance and quarterstaff. I train until the master-at-arms retires bruised and weeping, and my practice sword shatters against its target, and the blood runs red down my wrist from a dozen cracked, dark blisters. I train through the night while the white stars wheel, until the rooster crows at the light. Because I dream of a lady to rescue. A lady to fall against my chest and whisper: *My brave knight, my love.*

A lady like Sarei. He glanced at her there on the stairs. Her eldest brother, Balthus, noticed his gaze and turned to look. Sarei fled up the steps.

"Well then," Douglas said, leaning back in his seat, "I'm glad I've never faced *you* in battle." Some of the brothers snickered.

Galan said, "You should be glad. Because I'd kill you."

They quickly fell silent.

Galan leaned forward and glared. "Because I never lose," he told them. "Never."

After supper, he met Sarei out behind the stables. The horses stamped and snorted. Clumps of wet straw spilled from the bales and across the dirt.

Her face was murky in the twilight. There was awe in her voice. "Is that true what you said tonight? About sword fighting?"

"Yes."

"You could take me away, then," she said, excited. "You could protect me." She shivered. "I hate it here. They're terrible to me here, they never let me leave. I'd do anything to get away. I'd leave tonight, if you'd take me."

"Where would you go?"

"With you," she said. "Back to your hall, to meet your lady mother. We'd marry and I'd stay with you forever."

Away in the night, Galan thought, the two of them—because he couldn't involve his company in this. But the two of them could ride fast, be back to his own lands within a few weeks, and married. "Your brothers might come after us."

He wondered how fast they could follow, and how well they could fight, and how badly they would want her back. She was their sister, after all, and there were seven of them. Seven against one.

She said, "Are you afraid of them?"

He stared at her, at her flushed cheeks and desperate eyes. She needed to be rescued from all this, he knew. And what was it for, the hard hours with sword and lance, the daydreams, the sad longings, if not for this?

"No," he told her. "I'm not afraid."

They went about the fortress, gathering belongings, then stole back to the stables. Sarei's mount was a milk-white steed, and his a dapple-grey.

They rode off into the night.

*　*　*

The morning sun shone bright across the dewed, yellow grass. Galan and Sarei splashed across a rocky stream, then rode up toward a line of trees on the far bank. The sky was huge and pale blue above them. It echoed the sound of hoofbeats.

They paused at the edge of the forest, to look back. A rider on a white and brown horse came over the hill behind them.

"My eldest brother," Sarei said. "Balthus."

Galan and Sarei spurred their mounts and fled through the trees, trampling the undergrowth. In a great gold meadow ringed with oaks, Galan wheeled his horse. "Go ahead," he shouted. "I'll meet you." Sarei's eyes were wide with concern, but she rode on.

Galan tossed back his cloak and drew his sword. Sunlight shone through the green branches all around, dappling the trunks of trees. To be alive, he thought, in the forest, in love, with a sword in your hand, and a foe to face. His horse took an anxious step back as Balthus burst into the clearing.

"Villain!" Balthus reined his steed. "Kidnapper!" His shoulders were wide, his jaw broad, his eyes dark.

Galan said, "Sarei wants to leave. She wants to come with me."

"She's a young girl. She doesn't know what she wants."

"I'll marry her."

"Liar. You'll dishonor her. And her family. And her name. Where is she?"

Galan motioned with his head. "Back there."

"Then move." Balthus drew his sword. "Or I'll ride over you."

"Go to her," Galan shouted. "If you can."

Balthus surged forward, sword held high. He beat at Galan's head with overhand blows. Galan parried. The horses passed and circled, snorting, misty breath glistening in the morning air.

Balthus backed away, then charged again, and Galan scampered aside. Their swords met, clanking in unsteady rhythm as the mounts swayed. Galan slashed. Balthus pulled warily out of range, hesitated a moment, then attacked again.

Galan met the man's sword and swept it aside, as their mounts stumbled close. The men were almost eye to eye. Then Galan smashed the pommel of his sword into Balthus's face.

The man dropped from the saddle and hit the ground hard. His horse turned, wary and confused, and Balthus gasped and held up his arms as one of its hooves came down, crushing his head.

Galan glanced back towards the forest. Sarei sat on her white steed, just inside the trees, watching. That was the last thing he wanted.

Balthus's horse trotted away, leaving a line of bloody prints in the wake of its red hooves.

Galan rode over to where Sarei was waiting. "I told you to go on ahead."

She said quietly, "I wanted to see."

He thought she might blame him, be angry and yell, or else fall weeping into his arms. She didn't. She simply sat there, still and silent, staring raptly at the lumpy mess that had once been a brother.

"Come on." Galan took her by the arm. "Let's go."

They rode away. Black-winged crows dropped out of the branches all around, settling lightly over the body, like autumn leaves.

* * *

"He was never strong," Sarei said. "Balthus. The others are more dangerous."

They followed a winding path through stony fields. Boulders loomed overhead, green with lichen.

"We'll make for the Briars," Galan said. "We'll have to dismount and lead the horses, but so will they. It'll be harder to follow."

At noon they crested a hill. Below, the Briars began, stretching to the horizon—looping branches thick as a man's arm, high as a castle wall, with wicked thorns. Galan and Sarei were halfway down the hill when they heard hoofbeats.

"Go," he shouted. "Hide in the Briars. I mean it."

But again she hung back. "It's Sebal," she said, when she saw the rider. The man was slender, with short-cropped hair, and his face was gaunt but handsome.

Galan met him. They fought among the boulders, swords ringing. Sebal tired quickly. He wheeled, to put some distance between them, but Galan pursued, forcing him back toward a boulder that jutted sharply out. Sebal parried blow after blow, just in time to keep Galan's blade away from his knee, his shoulder, his throat.

Then Galan reared his horse, and it leapt up, roaring, hooves wheeling in the air.

Sebal bolted. As the boulder's shadow fell across his face, he turned, just in time to see it smash into his cheek. He fell amid the rocks, neck broken.

Sarei laughed and cheered. "You did it! I knew you would." She applauded, then clasped her hands and squeezed them. "You got him."

Galan rode back to her, wiping grime from his brow with the back of his glove. Her pure glee angered him. "He was your brother. Show some respect."

Her smile fell away. "He was wicked. He *deserved* to die, for what he did to me." Angrily, she spurred her horse and rode off ahead of him.

Galan caught her quickly. "I'm sorry," he said, riding alongside her.

* * *

They entered the Briars.

Branches arched above, blotting out the sky. In some places the thorns pressed tight all around, and Galan and Sarei crouched and covered their faces, pulling the horses behind them through the fog.

And there were roses. Soft, white roses grew up and down the vines. The dirt was spotted with their petals.

Galan heard twigs snap, from near or far, it was hard to tell. Nearby branches were vague and ghostly, and everything beyond that was shrouded in white. He kept his sword in his hand.

They came to a spot where the vines were thick as tree trunks, the thorns long as daggers.

As Galan bent to rest, someone ran out from behind one thick stalk and slashed at him with a giant sword. Galan parried, but the blow sent him reeling back, arms quivering.

"Jait!" Sarei shrieked. "No!"

The brother was young and fierce. He carried a two-handed sword and swung it like a hammer. Galan blocked, teeth ringing. He blocked again. And once more. His sword cracked, its blade tumbling to the ground.

Galan hurled the hilt at Jait's eye. The boy turned aside and the broken sword spun harmlessly over his shoulder. Galan fled.

Jait followed, hacking back and forth with his enormous sword. Galan crouched low and scrambled through the branches as vines and thorns fell away behind him. Then he spun, his back pressed against a thick stalk, and watched as the great sword came hurtling toward his neck.

He dropped. The blade buried itself six inches into the wood above his head. Jait tugged at the handle, violently, but the sword was lodged. Galan leapt forward, seizing the boy by the shirtfront and running him back against the brambles. A giant thorn burst black and oozing through Jait's chest.

Galan gasped and fell away, and the boy hung there, impaled through the heart on one great thorn.

The vines drank him greedily. His blood leeched through the stems into the white roses that hung all around, and near his corpse their petals became dark crimson, and farther away they turned bright scarlet.

Sarei said, "Look at it. It's beautiful." She plucked a rose from near her dead brother's elbow.

Galan made his way over to the place where Jait's sword hung, buried in the wood. He set his foot against the stalk and ripped the heavy weapon free.

"Can you fight with that thing?" Sarei asked.

"I can fight with anything," he said. She smiled.

That night, as they lay on his cloak against the hard ground, Sarei slipped out of her dress. She tore at his belt, and climbed on top of him. As she swayed there, lowering herself down onto him, then up, then down again, she threw back her head and screamed. And when she looked at him, her eyes were aflame with lust and desire, with terrible pleasure.

Like when she watched her brothers die.

* * *

Galan had doubts. He had dreamt of a lady who would love his courage, but hate bloodshed. She might weep when men died, but he could be strong for her, take her into his arms and comfort her. Sarei did not weep.

Would it be better if she did? he asked himself angrily. Would that be better?

Yes, a voice inside him replied. Better if she wept. Better if she bore it in brave silence. Better even if she hated him for it, shouted and hit him.

Anything would be better than this—to see her laugh at the murder, to see her eyes light with joy at each revenge—on her own brothers. It was wrong, no matter what they'd done to deserve it.

The earth turned soft and muddy along the bank of a slow, brown river. Galan and Sarei beat a path along the shore, looking for a place to cross. Instead they found Douglas, kneeling by the water. His horse plodded through the shallows, lapping at the river.

"Just turn and go," Galan said, holding up the greatsword. "I'll let you live."

Sarei was incredulous. "What?"

Douglas rose, wiping water from his mustache. He glanced at Sarei, scowled, and then his eyes fixed on Galan's weapon. "That's Jait's sword," he said. "My brother."

Galan began to speak, but quickly fell silent as Douglas drew his blade. "You said you'd kill me if we fought." Douglas stalked forward, arm extended, the tip of his sword pointed at Galan's chest. "Let's find out."

Galan inched forward, sword raised in a guard position. "Be careful," Sarei told him. "He's dangerous."

Douglas attacked. Galan fought cautiously, adjusting to the heft of his new weapon, feeling out the man's strengths. After several minutes, Galan knew he was better.

Then he attacked, pushing forward with fierce, clean strokes, driving Douglas back into the river. The muddy water splashed about the man's ankles as he withdrew. Galan rushed in, and the water seeped through his boots, squishing between his toes. He had the advantage now. Douglas was in up to his knees, struggling to move his feet.

As Galan shuffled forward, his toe smacked into something underwater, and he almost lost his balance. A loop of tree root, it felt like. Douglas, too busy defending, didn't notice. Galan retreated then, maneuvering the root between them.

When Douglas advanced, his feet snagged beneath the water and he tumbled down, splashing into the river. His sword spun away, lost in the slow current. He rolled onto his back, sputtering, but Galan was already there, pressing the tip of the greatsword into the man's throat.

"Yield," Galan said.

On the shore, Sarei gasped. "You're going to spare him? *Him?*"

"Kill me." Douglas spat. "Boy."

"Do it! Kill him." Sarei splashed into the water, her dress hanging damp about her knees. "You killed Balthus, who could be honorable, and Jait, who could be dutiful, and Sebal, who was sometimes merry. And you're going to spare *him?* But he's wretched. He's the worst of them all."

Galan scowled, trying to block her out. "I warn you," he told Douglas. "Yield."

"Kill me," Douglas said. "Do it, you worthless brat, you coward. Kidnapper. Villain. Bastard. Do it."

"Do it!" Sarei screamed.

"Fine!" Fury overtook Galan. He raised his sword.

"My brothers will avenge me," Douglas said, then the blade came down, pushing him under. The river swallowed his face. Clouds of dirt and blood billowed up. When Galan yanked his sword away, the body began to drift downstream.

Later, he regretted it.

He and Sarei found a crossing, and traveled for a time in silence. Finally, she spoke. "It's good that you killed him. He deserved it. He was truly terrible. Worse than the others, even."

Galan's voice was hoarse. "What did he do to you?" He didn't want to upset her, but he had to know.

Sarei looked away. "He used to sneak into my room at night," she said, "and cut off my hair." She was seething, furious. "One time he called me a whore, in front of everyone."

Galan stared.

"One time," she said, "a knight named Sir Jamie of the Blue Fist came to visit us. He wanted me to travel with him, to take me to the fairs. It would have been wonderful. But Douglas chased him off with an axe and he never came back."

And that was why she hated them, why she wanted to watch them die. Childish pranks, name calling. Galan said, "Jamie of the Blue Fist?"

"Yes."

"But...Sir Jamie is a notorious..."

"What?"

"A notorious..." Galan struggled for words. "Well, a lecher." Any man would chase Jamie away from a young sister.

Sarei shrugged. "It didn't matter to me. I didn't care who he was. I would've gone with anyone, really, if they'd have taken me away from there."

Anyone, Galan thought miserably.

She looked at him, and told him, with utter sincerity, "I hated it there."

* * *

Galan watched the sky. Through the enclosing brambles, the bright clouds seemed far away, and free. And he was with Sarei.

They had crossed almost to the far side of the Briars. Beyond were open fields. Galan was struck by a wild impulse to bolt at the first sight of unbroken grass, to gallop away, leaving Sarei and her damned brothers far behind. Or maybe, he thought sourly, he could just take her back.

But it was impossible, all of it. What would people say? Galan the knight had taken a young girl from her home, spent a night with her in the forest, killed four of her brothers—maybe more, if his rotten luck held—and then deserted her. He would be dishonored forever.

He clenched his fists and rubbed his temples hard. There was nothing to do but go through with it, take her home and marry her. He hoped they would encounter no more brothers.

"There are only three of them now," Sarei said. "The twins, Aron and Adom, and my youngest brother, Whit. The twins always fight together, they're deadly, much worse than the ones you killed, and Whit is a master swordsman."

It sounded grim, but Galan had defeated them all so far.

The air turned cold, and snow fell. Flakes drifted down and clung to the tips of thorns. Galan could see out beyond the brambles now, and the dry grasses were tinged with white. A coal-colored wisp of smoke, from a cook fire, smeared the gray clouds. But there was nowhere else to go except back into the Briars, so he pushed forward.

Aron and Adom had camped at the top of a low hill. They came down a winding dirt trail, swords drawn. Snow was sprinkled through their blond hair.

"I don't want to fight you," Galan told them.

They watched him with two identical faces, two identical angry faces. They exchanged a glance, nodded, then advanced.

Galan expected them to split up and attack from different directions, but they didn't. They stood shoulder-to-shoulder and came at him with jerking thrusts. He retreated, parrying in wide horizontal sweeps, knocking aside the tips of their swords. They were not very skilled.

But there *were* two of them, and they did spread apart, finally, and then one got the idea to circle around behind him.

Galan swung his body back and forth, slapping aside attacks first in front, then behind, now in front again. The twins closed in, pressing him.

Then they rushed, by chance at the same moment. One raised his sword above his head and the other lunged. Galan spun away as one man skewered his brother through the gut.

The twins watched each other, like a man studying himself in the mirror. The dying one sank away, exhaling frost, sliding off the end of his brother's sword.

Then Galan swept forward and battered the other with heavy strokes. The man tumbled to the ground, his two pale wrists falling across an ice-crusted log. Galan brought his sword hurtling down, and the hands fell away. There was blood on the snow. Galan lifted his weapon to strike again.

"Please," begged the man, holding up the weeping stumps that had been his hands. "Mercy."

Galan hesitated. Sarei came running through the snow. "Kill him! Do it."

The man held Galan with his eyes. "She hates us. She was always sad and angry, I don't know why. We loved her."

"Liar!" Sarei was livid. "How can you even say that?"

Galan lowered his sword.

Sarei said, "What are you doing?"

"We're leaving," he said. "Now."

Her eyes filled with tears. "But...but I hate him. I hate him so much. I've waited so long for this."

Galan jammed the sword into the snow. Stuck in the earth like that, its hilt came almost to her shoulders. He gestured at it.

"You want him dead?" he said. "You do it."

Her face drained of color. "What?"

"You heard me." Galan glared at her with proud fury. "It's not so easy when you have to look them in the eye."

"But I'm not..." She glanced at her brother. "I mean, I can't—"

"Then let's go," Galan said, turning away.

"Fine." Sarei's face was set in a stubborn scowl.

And as Galan watched, she ripped the sword free, set her feet apart in the snow, and hacked off her brother's head.

* * *

He had to get away. She had seemed callous, vengeful, keeping Jait's bloody rose. But this...

This was unreasoning. Bloodthirsty. Like I was? he wondered. Before

I saw it in her? Sarei was happy while he was helping her, but with her brothers gone? Where would her anger turn?

"You lied to me," he said. "Aron and Adom. You said they were deadly. They weren't. They were stabbing each other back there."

Sarei was quiet a long time. "I didn't want you to be too confident, let your guard down. I was afraid..." She chewed her lip, glanced at the clouds. She continued, more candidly, "I wanted no mercy. I wanted them to face your full wrath, for all the years they were cruel to me. You understand, don't you? Why I said those things?"

"The truth," Galan insisted.

"The truth." Sarei puckered her lips, as if the word tasted bad. She sighed. "Balthus was the strongest. When you killed him I knew we could make it. Jait was fierce but clumsy. The others were clods. Whit's worst of all, he can barely keep hold of a sword."

Galan didn't know whether to laugh or cry. They rode on, unhurried. They were home free now.

But he would never be free, of her.

Unless...

Unless he was defeated by Whit. Galan smiled, in spite of himself. If Whit were victorious, and took Sarei home, there would be no dishonor in that. Galan had won six straight battles for his lady, no one could fault him for failing the last. He would lose glory, certainly. But glory could be won back later, on the battlefield.

It would be possible, if Whit was inept. Give him an opening, take a weak blow to the shoulder, pretend to be wounded, stumble off into the trees, let him grab Sarei. And lose to a younger boy who could barely wield a sword. The thought made Galan grit his teeth. But it was the only way.

They saw Whit's horse the next afternoon, in the valley behind them, just a black dot. It had taken the boy forever to catch them. The other brothers must have ridden off and left him days ago.

"Are you going to face him?" Sarei prodded.

"If I have to." Galan didn't want to seem too eager. A sudden change might make her suspicious, but he did ride more slowly, and delayed at every opportunity.

They spotted Whit again and again, across wide fields, trailing, but never gaining. By the fourth day, Galan was impatient. They had slowed practically to a walk, and still Whit did not gain.

And never would, Galan realized. Whit had no intention of catching them, of dying like his brothers. He would return home defeated, claiming truthfully that he had pursued Galan over many leagues, but had not overtaken him.

Galan could just picture him—trotting back there, slouched in the saddle, hanging his pale, chubby head, telling himself that he was doing all he could, under the circumstances.

On the fifth night, by the light of the fire, Galan told Sarei, "I'm going to go back and face him. He's getting closer." That wasn't true. "He might sneak up in the night." Galan was more worried about him sneaking *off* in the night.

"Yes," Sarei said, and her eyes glittered at the suggestion of a brother's death.

In the morning Galan circled around. Snow melted and ran glistening off the leaves. Sunlight shone beyond the clouds, and Galan, for a moment, felt hope.

He found Whit hiding in a tangle of underbrush, pissing against an elm. Whit gasped when he saw them, and reached for his sword with one hand and his pants with the other. "Give her back."

Galan told him, "Not without a fight."

When Whit attacked, his sword swung in lazy circles, like a flower in the wind. Galan parried the first of these casually, but quickly decided to slow his strokes, to seem more off-guard. After long minutes of fencing, it was time. He dropped his elbow and kept it low, creating an easy opening to his shoulder. Whit didn't take it.

They fought on. Galan lowered his guard even more, but Whit just kept slashing away at Galan's knees. Did the boy think it was a trick? But no, Whit was just oblivious to the opening, to any opening.

That made things difficult. If Galan couldn't anticipate the attack, it would be hard to roll with it. And Whit's attacks *were* unpredictable. Most would miss even if Galan stood still. Catching a glancing blow would not be easy.

Finally, Galan saw his chance. He leapt forward, pretending to stumble, and caught the tip of Whit's sword. But the blow was stronger than he'd judged, biting deep into his shoulder, drawing a red gouge across his chest. His scream was real.

Galan fled through the forest, dragging his sword behind him, one hand pressed to his wound. Blood seeped between his fingers, blackening his glove. He stumbled over ferns, then stopped, leaning against a tree. Behind him, voices:

"Sarei. Come with me. Now."

"I won't. He's still alive."

"Are you crazy? Come on, let's get out of here. Sarei, please."

"He killed your brothers, Whit, and you run away? Are you so afraid? Of a wounded man?" Whit *was* afraid, clearly. He hesitated a long time. But Sarei's shaming had gotten him. Like it got me, Galan remembered.

Whit groaned unhappily. Then he came, picking his way through the undergrowth, cutting it away with his sword. Galan fled deeper. He pushed through a leafy tangle and emerged at the base of a sheer rock wall. He couldn't scale it, not injured, and there was nowhere else to go.

He slumped against a boulder, and stared at the white sky. He thought of dying, out here. He couldn't let it happen. Not like this. He lay still.

Through slitted lids, he watched Whit's cautious approach. I'm dead! Galan wanted to scream. Go back and tell her. Tell her you think I'm dead.

But Whit inched closer, his sword held ready. Forgive me, Galan thought. I had no choice. She gave me no choice. It's him or me now. No choice. Whit inhaled sharply and raised his sword.

Galan rolled forward, wrapping one arm around Whit's ankles, dragging the greatsword across the back of the boy's knees, slicing the tendons. Whit collapsed and lay thrashing, screaming into the dirt, legs spasming. Galan crawled on top of him and planted the sword through the back of Whit's neck. It passed out the boy's throat and stuck in the ground.

Galan gasped and sobbed. He grappled with the sword, which stood anchored there, and used it to pull himself to his feet.

Sarei came running. She fell into his arms, smothering herself painfully against his wounded chest. "My brave knight," she breathed. "My love. I knew you'd beat him. I knew you would."

Galan sighed. "I never lose," he told her sadly. "Never."

Author's note: Seven Brothers, Cruel

In 2001 I attended Odyssey, a six-week summer workshop similar to Clarion. Each student was asked to list their favorite short story, and another student and I both listed "Sandkings" by George R. R. Martin. That student later asked if I had read Martin's novel *A Game of Thrones*. I hadn't. I was a lifelong fantasy fan—my two favorite series growing up were Robert Asprin's *Myth* series and Roger Zelazny's *Amber* series—but by 2001 I had become disenchanted with epic fantasy and hadn't read any in years. But this *A Game of Thrones* book sounded good, and after all I did love "Sandkings." I decided to give it a try.

As soon as I got home from Odyssey I read *A Game of Thrones*, and was absolutely blown away. It was everything I loved about *Amber*—poetic, melancholy, violent, troubling. All the things that were missing from other epic fantasies I'd read. I became obsessed with *A Game of Thrones* and its sequels, and was soon spending hours a day on a George R. R. Martin message board, where hundreds of fans posted their theories about what would happen next in the series. And of course, being a writer, I wanted to write my own epic fantasy as well.

There was just one problem. Epic fantasy (and its cousin sword & sorcery) were completely out of fashion in the short fiction magazines. It was rare for an epic fantasy story to get published at all, especially if it came from an unknown writer. Undaunted, I spent two years on an epic fantasy kick, writing story after story that would never see the light of day, including two 20,000 word novellas which are still the longest things I've ever written. "Seven Brothers, Cruel" is the exception, the only story from that period to make it into print.

The only pro magazine at the time that published epic fantasy with any regularity was *Realms of Fantasy*. I had always wanted to be published there, both because they did beautiful full-color illustrations for each story and because Roger Zelazny had published one of his *Amber* stories in their first issue.

Around that time I was reading a lot of poetry in hopes of improving my ability to write lyrical prose. (I've always been strong on plot and dialogue, less so on description and interiority.) One of the books I read was *The Norton Anthology of Poetry*, which is where I came across the early modern ballad "The Douglas Tragedy." It's the story of a young knight who elopes with a maiden, and then her seven brothers pursue them, and the knight ends up killing all seven brothers. Obviously this makes the maiden very sad. I thought that was a really interesting situation, and I felt like there was something there that I could work with.

I had once heard a piece of writing advice that sometimes you can turn an okay idea into great idea by taking whatever you would expect to happen and doing the exact opposite. So in the case of "The Douglas Tragedy," the expected scenario is that the maiden is sad when the knight kills her brothers. The exact opposite of that would be that she's *happy* when he kills her brothers. As soon as I got that idea I knew I had to write the story.

I submitted "Seven Brothers, Cruel" to *Realms of Fantasy*, and got a rejection which said, "I liked this, but the end fell flat, I thought." I reread the ending, thought it seemed fine, shrugged, and submitted the story elsewhere. Four months later I got an email from *Realms of Fantasy* offering to buy the story. I briefly wondered if I was under some sort of ethical obligation to write them back and say, "Are you sure? I thought you said the ending fell flat?" But in the end I just signed the contract and the story was published later that year. *Realms of Fantasy* went on to become one of the most reliable markets for my fiction, publishing five of my stories.

I'm always horrified when I hear about writers giving up after a handful of rejections, or concluding that the whole publishing world is conspiring against them. Submitting fiction is a numbers game. One rejection means nothing, and even fifty rejections or a hundred rejections mean very little. It's common for editors to reject a story one day and then accept it another day when they're in a different mood. You just have to be persistent.

Huan Tran

Blood of Virgins

I remember riding the dragon that first week of college.

Some kids in my high school had dragons, but none of those kids would ever give me a ride. So I was flattered when Matt, one of the guys in my new dorm, said he was taking his dragon out to the supermarket and asked if I wanted to come.

That day Matt wore loafers, cargo shorts, and a short-sleeved yellow shirt. Sunglasses perched atop his wavy brown hair. He led me out of our dorm and across the yard to the stables. His black dragon lay coiled in a stall, chained to the cement. A padlock dangled from its collar.

Matt used his key, and the collar clanged to the floor. The dragon unfurled, and slithered forward, everything about it gaunt. Built into its spine were two seats, one behind the other. Matt placed his shoe on the dragon's shoulder, a fist-shaped protrusion of bone, and swung into the driver's seat.

The dragon circled me, watching me with eyes the color of blood. Its face was skeletal, as if the manufacturer hadn't had enough skin to give it cheeks or lips. You could always see its teeth, like black swords, even when its jaws were fully closed. I hesitated.

Matt said, "Come on. What are you afraid of?"

"They drink blood," I said simply. That seemed sufficient reason to show caution.

"Of virgins," he said. "You're not a virgin, right?" As if that was unthinkable.

I chuckled and said, "No." Though I was.

"Then come on. I have to be back for class at 2:30."

I clambered up the dragon's flank and slid into the passenger seat, which was upholstered with leather and smelled new. I pulled the straps down over my chest and connected them to the belt around my waist.

Matt yanked the reins. The dragon shot up, like we'd been catapulted. My stomach heaved. Wind smacked my face. The dragon's wings exploded on either side, great black sails that filled the sky. I clenched the straps and knew I'd made a mistake in coming. The dragon scared me.

I gazed down longingly. To our right: the Pacific, white foam dancing on lazy turquoise swells. A narrow bike path wound along the beach. To our left: a placid tangle of palm-lined residential streets.

Matt said, "How you doing?"

It seemed he wanted me to admit that his dragon frightened me, so instead I said, "Great."

Other dragons cavorted on the airy currents. Those dragons were cherry red or lime green or creamy brown. Their riders steered them up the beach, or inland toward the mall, or back to campus.

A slender girl on a pink dragon passed us going the opposite way, her blond hair billowing. Matt waved to her. He said over his shoulder, "I met that girl last night. Hold on, I want to say hi." He yanked the reins and we banked sharply. My stomach lurched. We swept around in an arc and came up alongside the girl. Her dragon had the guileless beady eyes and scrunched up cheeks of a lap dog. Matt said, "Hi. Dora, right?"

"Deirdre," she corrected. "And you're...Matt?" He grinned, and she said, "I like your dragon."

"Thanks. It's new." He pointed. "See how the spine bends? It can pull off turns like nothing else." He paused, then nodded at me. "This is Chris. He lives in my building."

"Hi." She looked at me, appraising. "It's fabulous up here, don't you think? So liberating."

"Yeah, I love flying," I lied.

She asked me, "What kind of dragon do you have?"

"Oh, I don't have one." Me, embarrassed. "I mean, not yet."

And she said, "Oh."

Later, I would remember everything about that moment. The slant of her head, the pursing of her lips. Her eyes were very green. I remembered every angle of her face, every line of cheek and jaw.

We all flew back to campus, the supermarket forgotten. Her name forgotten too, by Matt, within hours. (It was Deirdre.) I remembered. Though it was him she went off with afterward, to watch their dragons play together on the quad. I saw her a few more times, around campus, but she didn't recognize me, or pretended not to. I remembered that "Oh" so vividly, I think, because it was the last word she ever said to me, after I told her I had no dragon.

* * *

Two weeks after that ride, I was leaving my sociology class when a flyer on a bulletin board caught my eye: a photocopied dragon from a magazine ad, and printed below it in large block letters: BLOOD ON OUR HANDS? THE HUMAN COST OF DRAGONS. Below that: Presented by the Campus Greens. At 8:00 that night in a room across the hall. I decided to attend.

I tried to get other people to go. Everyone said they had too much work, though I knew they'd spend the evening watching TV. No one cared.

I stopped Matt in the hall on his way to the bathroom. I said, "Come on, it's about dragons. That's like your favorite topic."

He scowled. "It's *against* dragons. I've got better things to do than spend an hour listening to some hippie chick complain that the world's not fair."

"Aren't you curious what they'll say?"

"You can tell me all about it when you get back." The bathroom door closed behind him.

So I went alone, and slipped into a chair at the back of the small auditorium. Out of sixty seats, only a dozen were taken. I guessed that the knot of five students in the first row were the Campus Greens. Beside the podium hung a movie screen. Finally, at 8:15, when it was clear no stragglers would arrive, one of the Greens stood and faced the crowd.

Matt would have snickered then, I was sure, would have whispered, "I called it," if he'd bothered to come. The girl's mildly frizzy brown hair fell past her waist. She wore heavy black shoes, glasses with thick oval frames, and a homemade skirt of stitched-together red and blue and purple. A hippie chick. Matt would have laughed, but in her own way she was beautiful.

She said, "Hello everyone, and thank you all for coming. My name is Miranda. I'm president of the Campus Greens. We're here tonight to talk about the human cost of dragons and dragon riding." Her voice was stronger and clearer than I'd expected. "Dragons drink blood," she said. "Blood of virgins. Corporations tell us that the blood trade provides income for many people in poorer countries and also promotes morality. What they don't tell us is that donors are paid pennies per pint and often work in tragic conditions." She nodded to a friend, and the lights dimmed. A film played. "This video was shot by a hidden camera at a bloodshop in Malaysia. Some of the images are disturbing. I'm sorry to have to show this, but to really understand you need to see the images for yourself."

The camera was jumpy, often pointed at a grimy wall or floor, but we saw enough. Filth-covered little girls with brown skin and matted black hair wearing shifts that had once been white. Buckets overflowing with urine and feces. Dark infected sores around syringes still taped in place. Tables piled high with plastic bags full of blood.

Miranda spoke more, about the need for new laws, about how dragons guzzle blood by the gallon while people all over the world die from lack of transfusions, but I barely heard her. The images of those little girls stayed with me.

Afterward, in a moment when Miranda stood alone, I approached her and said, "Hi. I'm Chris."

"Oh, hi." She was shy suddenly, in a way she hadn't been while addressing the crowd. "I'm Miranda."

I said, "I thought your remarks were really good. Really important. I can't believe more people didn't come."

She smiled faintly. "You're new here?

"Yeah, it's my first semester."

She gathered her belongings. "This was actually a pretty good turnout. It's not the most politically active student body." We chatted about that, then about classes. Her shyness faded. Finally, as her friends headed for the exit, she told me, "Our group meets at this same time every week, just next door."

I said, "I'll try to make it."

"Great." She smiled again, and her gaze lingered. "Chris, right?" I confirmed this, and she said, "Okay, bye," and joined her friends.

So I started attending the Campus Greens meetings. Seven or eight people usually came, and we sat around in a circle in a classroom. Many people aired ambitious proposals, but Miranda was really looking for something more practical.

At my third meeting, I spoke up. "Okay, how about this? What if we all pledge not to ride any dragons for a month? We can walk into town and carry back any supplies we need. And we do it as a group, publicly. If we show everyone that it's possible to survive at college without a dragon, then maybe more people will decide not to buy them."

Miranda studied me, then glanced around the circle and said, "That's good. I like that."

Seven people showed up for the first walk. A photographer took our picture for the school paper. We walked into town along the bike path, ate at a Mexican restaurant on the beach, and went food shopping. Four people showed up for the second walk, but one guy said he couldn't afford to eat out again, so we just walked and shopped and went home. For a while after that only three of us came: Miranda, me, and a girl who never talked named either Stacy or Tracy. (I was never sure.)

Then Stacy or Tracy stopped coming too, and it was just Miranda and me. Not much of a group, but I was happy to spend time alone with her. She was easy to talk to, and knew everything. She was even surprisingly funny, once she overcame her shyness. And she was deep. Sometimes when she spoke of Andrea Dworkin or Edna St. Vincent Millay I would feel like a fraud, as if I'd maybe once inadvertently said something profound that suggested to her unplumbed depths to my character that didn't actually exist.

On the last night of our walking campaign, Miranda and I sat on a bench facing the ocean and watched the most beautiful sunset over water I've ever seen, a tableau of yellow and red. Dragons clogged the sky, dozens of them, all black in the twilight. I shifted closer to Miranda, and put my arm around her for the first time. Maybe she thought it was because of the sunset, but really it was because of the dragons. I felt a strange terror that they would descend on me, clawing and biting and swallowing pieces of me, enveloping me in a great slithering sphere. I sought the protection of her touch.

She leaned into me and said, "It's been an interesting month."

The two of us sat alone and dragons filled the sky. I wondered if any of our former companions were up there right now. I said, "Sorry my idea was such a flop."

She tried to be encouraging. "It wasn't a flop." I looked at her dubiously, and she added, "I mean, not a *total* flop."

I chuckled. "Thanks."

She lifted her chin toward mine and smiled. We kissed as the sun vanished. She drew back a few inches and said softly, "See? Not a total flop."

The next morning, Matt and I picked up copies of the school paper on our way into the dining hall. The article about the walking campaign had just come out, and Matt flipped to the photo of the seven original participants. "That's her?"

I hadn't told him I'd kissed her, or even that I wanted to, but either he'd heard or just knew. He said, "You could do a lot better."

I said, "You could do a lot better to shut up," in a somewhat joking way.

That night Miranda slept in my bed. As we settled beneath the blankets, she said, "I want to tell you something. I've never had sex. And I'm not going to, unless it's with someone who really loves me."

I smiled. "Maybe that'll be me."

"Maybe." She kissed me lightly. "We'll see."

I waited a moment, then confessed, "I've never had sex either."

"Really?" she said. I nodded. She squeezed my hand. "I appreciate you telling me."

I joked, "I appreciate you not telling anyone."

"I won't," she said, then grinned mischievously. "Well, maybe just Matt."

"Don't!" I warned her, laughing. And she laughed too, and everything with her was great, for a while.

* * *

But then the dragons started watching me.

Most people they ignored, but whenever I passed the stables where they lay chained they would all turn their heads very subtly, keeping me in view of their red eyes. Dragons were everywhere—landing in the yard, playing on the quad, being led down pathways—and everywhere they stared at me. I imagined that they hated me, for opposing them, for tempting them with my innocent's blood. It seemed crazy, but I couldn't shake the feeling. Miranda and I continued our walks, which had become a permanent habit, and the dragons loomed overhead. Miranda wasn't afraid of dragons, and I felt safe with her, but I wondered what the dragons might do if I walked alone.

Miranda subscribed to piles of left-wing newsletters, and I read every article about dragons. Those articles revealed a disturbing pattern that wasn't widely reported: large numbers of accidents involving dragons. Most of the victims were young. Probably virgins.

I began constantly quoting dragon-related statistics. Dragon riders were three times as likely to be injured while traveling, four times as likely to injure others.

Matt just laughed at all this. He and I would stay up half the night arguing, sprawled across cheap sofas in our dorm's basement lounge. He said, "Riding a dragon takes skill. A lot of people don't know what they're doing, but you can't blame the dragons for that."

I said, "You think it's just coincidence that so many of the victims are virgins?"

He said, "Are *you* a virgin?"

"No." My heart raced. I was afraid he'd seen through me.

"Then what do you care?" He was oblivious to my alarm. "It doesn't affect you. It's not your problem."

Miranda and I stayed together for most of the semester, and in that time other people got together, or broke up and got together with other people, or got together with several people and didn't really remember because they'd been drunk, and the small number of virgins dwindled even more. That only emphasized my sense of vulnerability.

Night after night Miranda and I lay together on my bed, kissing and touching and undressing until she said, "Okay. That's enough." Then we'd talk until one of us fell asleep. I never voiced my frustration, but I know she sensed it. All she had to do was consent once, I thought, and this huge burden would be lifted forever.

Finally, one night in December I was in a weird mood and felt like I just couldn't take this thing with the dragons another day. Miranda lay beside me in the dark. I brooded in silence a long time, then said, "We've been together almost three months."

A moment passed. She said softly, "Yeah."

And I said, meaningfully, "Yeah."

She rolled onto her side, facing me, forehead cradled in her palm. She looked into my face. "Can I ask you something?"

"Sure," I said.

She asked, without inflection, "Do you love me?"

Did I love her? I wasn't sure. I enjoyed her company. Admired her. Felt she was beautiful. Thought about her a lot. Hoped all her dreams came true. But would I have strapped on shining steel for her? Taken blade in gauntleted fingers and climbed a misty crag to risk death in the jaws of some black dragon for her?

I didn't think so. I was afraid of dragons.

I said, "I think you're amazing. I think you're beautiful and funny and wonderful."

She said, "That's not what I asked."

I said, "You only want me to say 'I love you'? Just those words and no others?"

"Just answer the question."

I sighed and sat up. "Fine," I said. "Fine. I—"

She interrupted, "Why do you want to do this? Really?"

"What?" I said. "What are you talking about?"

She stared at me. "Does this really have anything to do with your feelings for me at all, or is it just about them?"

Them. The dragons. I said, "You think I only want this because I'm afraid of them?"

She said, "Yeah, sometimes I do."

"Look." I didn't know what to say. "All right, yes, I'm afraid of them, okay? Of course I am. It's scary what they can do to people. I don't want them to hurt me, and I don't want them to hurt you either. We'd both be a lot safer if we did this, but that doesn't mean I don't—"

She stirred and stood up off the bed. "When I do it, it's going to be out of love, not fear."

I said, "Where are you going?"

She picked up her heavy black shoes. "I need time to think."

"Wait," I said, as she crossed the room. "Wait. Miranda."

She opened the door and stood silhouetted. Then she closed the door behind her, leaving me to darkness.

She didn't show up for our walk, so I walked alone. I didn't hear from her all week. I called her a few times, but she didn't answer. After that I didn't know what I'd say if I did see her. I kept doing our walk, out of some strange loyalty to the memory of us, but I avoided our usual route along the bike path and instead wandered the residential streets, so I wouldn't bump into her.

Only one day I did. She was with two friends. She and I passed on the sidewalk with an awkward "Hi," and I realized that she too had decided to avoid the bike path, so after that I switched back to it. The bike path was more exposed to dragons, but I felt too hurt and mixed up just then to care much about dragons.

Later, Matt knocked on my door and asked if I wanted to play frisbee. I told him no. He lingered in the hall. He said, "So, you and Melinda...?" He must have heard about it.

"Miranda," I corrected. I sighed. "Yeah."

"Too bad." He gave a sympathetic grimace. "How long were you together? Like a month?"

"Like three."

He nodded. "So did the two of you ever, you know...?"

"No," I said. And this time his grimace was one of pity, or maybe contempt.

I took my last exam on a Thursday, then started packing to go home to Boston for winter break. It was snowing back east, so I decided to take one final walk along the beach. That's when the accident happened.

* * *

The shadow. That's how it started.

The sun had been bright but suddenly I felt cold. I raised my eyes from the bike path and saw sunlight receding all around me. A great winged shroud exploded over me. A dragon, descending. It's time, I thought. They're coming for me. I heard faint laughter on the wind.

I ran, arms pumping, loafer soles slapping on pavement. But not far. Teeth grazed my shoulders. My sweatshirt was yanked upward, my collar tugged hard into my throat like a noose. Lifted from the earth, I dangled. The sand sped by below. I heard someone screaming, "No! Stop it! Stop!" My cheek bashed against a monstrous jaw. I was dropped. The foam rushed up. Impact.

I lay on my side. Virgin's blood poured from my nose, then a breaking wave washed away the blood and filled my mouth with salt.

I heard splashing. Something seized my shoulder, rolled me onto my back. I sputtered. Matt's face above me. His hand on my arm. He said, "Chris! I'm sorry. I didn't...I just..."

Behind him, his black dragon coiled, malevolent, watching me. Beachgoers kept their distance from it as they rushed to help. Matt said, "...Just a joke. You've been so jumpy. I was flying low and I saw you and I thought I'd...but when you ran, it...it just went...Are you all right?"

I was taken to the hospital. My eye swelled shut, and I had to get a mess of stitches in my back. Matt came to visit me. He kept saying he was sorry. They put down his dragon, but he got another one that he claimed was better behaved, plus, he said, it could pull a 180 in five seconds flat. Then my parents came and took me home to Boston so I could recuperate in the bedroom where I'd grown up.

One morning, when I'd been home two weeks and my eye was mostly healed, my parents came into my room. Mom said, "We've got a surprise for you."

They led me to the backyard. A huge hulking dragon, cerulean blue, slept in the shadow of our elm. A heavy iron chain bound it to the toolshed.

Dad handed me the key. "Your mom and I agreed that it's not safe for you to be just walking around out there with all these dumb kids and their dragons they don't know how to handle. But nobody's going to mess with you if you're riding this."

I couldn't even tell them I was afraid of it, or why. It was too humiliating. I could just imagine mom's reaction. "You?" she'd say. "But...those girls in high school. You dated Susan for almost a year, didn't you? And Meredith.

I just assumed...never?" Then she'd laugh and say, "I won't even tell you about my first semester at college."

That night I couldn't sleep. I tossed and fidgeted and was angry. I thought: Has the world gone mad? People just flit about their neighborhoods on blood-lusting beasts, and everyone acts like this is okay. Isn't anyone bothered by this? Doesn't anyone care?

Outside I heard a soft jingle of metal. I looked up.

The dragon's eye, filling my window. I scrambled to my feet. The dragon had stretched its chain and slithered across the yard. Its pupil followed me as I backed toward the door. Its eye was red as blood. Blood of virgins.

I ducked into the hall, then hurried down the stairs and through the dining room. The dragon moved to that window. The dragon was terrible and magnificent. It was mine, and would impress a girl like Deirdre. I didn't want a girl like Deirdre. The dragon's serpentine shadow drifted over me. The padlock that swung from its collar caught the moonlight. Then I knew what I had to do, if I ever wanted to walk without dread beside the sea again, or stare without doubt into Miranda's eyes. I stepped out the back door.

The dragon crept forward on webbed and bony fingers. It halted ten feet away, its chain pulled taut. I took out my key. I approached the dragon, and it watched as I reached up and undid its padlock.

Its collar slid aside, then fell and hit the ground with a thud. The dragon fixed me with its hateful gaze. I stood my ground. The dragon snorted, exhaling fetid breath into my face. I thought to it, Go on, you bastard. Here I am. What are you waiting for? Maybe the dragon would lash out. But I refused to be haunted anymore. I waited.

Finally, the dragon looked away, losing interest. Maybe it disliked prey that it couldn't terrify and pursue. I relaxed a bit. I heaved the collar back around its neck, then replaced and closed the padlock, feeling bold as any dragonslayer.

At breakfast, I told my parents that I didn't want the dragon. Mom said, "Well are you sure?"

"Yes, I'm sure," I said. "Dragons drink blood and they're dangerous." Then I added, daring her to respond, "Plus I'm a virgin, and they don't like virgins."

I'd never been that determined or blunt before. For once she didn't comment. She just said, "Oh."

* * *

Spring semester began. I'd only been back at school a few hours when someone knocked at my door. I answered it, expecting Matt, but it was Miranda. We both stared awkwardly for a moment, then she murmured, "You want to go for a walk?"

We walked along the bike path. Miranda told me about her vacation, then asked about mine. I said, "My parents bought me a dragon."

"No." She was incredulous.

"I made them return it."

"I should hope so." She paused, then said softly, "I heard about the accident." I nodded, and she asked, "Is your back okay?"

I shrugged.

She said, "Can I see?"

Reluctantly, I lifted the hem of my shirt, revealing the landscape of scars. Miranda gasped. I let the shirt fall.

"I'm so sorry." She shook her head. "And sorry that I...you were right to be afraid."

"No." I stepped in front of her, facing her. "You were right. I've been thinking a lot about what you said, about fear and love." I looked into her eyes. "I do love you, Miranda. I'm sorry I ever made you doubt that."

"Chris." She sighed sadly. "I don't know. We haven't...It's too soon to be talking like that. We'll see, all right?"

"All right," I said, and we kept walking. But I was glad I'd said it. Because it wasn't too soon at all. It was past time.

So now I walk with Miranda at my side again and think on all that's happened since I rode the dragon that first week of college. The dragons are still circling overhead, ominously. Dragons have sharp teeth and lap up the blood of virgins. But now it's spring semester, and I'm older than I was. And wiser too.

And unafraid.

Author's note: Blood of Virgins

When I was 27 I moved out to Los Angeles to study fiction and screenwriting at the University of Southern California. I knew almost no one in L.A., so for the first year I was there I attended pretty much every student club in existence, most notably the feminist club and the atheist club. That immersion in student activism definitely informed this story.

But by far the biggest influence on "Blood of Virgins" was my experience owning and operating a motor vehicle in Los Angeles, which was like something out of Hieronymous Bosch. After a year of navigating L.A.'s arcane parking regulations, being screamed at and honked at for violating obscure traffic rules, and often spending 45 minutes trying to force my way through a single intersection, I started to view anything with an internal combustion engine as intrinsically evil.

The United States had invaded Iraq just a few years before, and a common refrain at the time was "no blood for oil"—the idea that American soldiers should not be sacrificed simply to secure greater profits for oil companies. If it's true that we're trading blood for oil, I thought, then in a sense when you fill up your car, you're filling it up with blood. I considered writing a story in which people literally filled up their cars with blood, which I thought was a cool metaphor and a striking image, but it didn't really suggest a character or a conflict.

Then one day I got the idea to make them dragons instead of cars. It made more sense for dragons to be powered by blood rather than for cars to be powered by blood. And what kind of blood would dragons drink? Blood of virgins. That *did* suggest a character and a conflict—a virgin who's afraid of the dragons. In dragon stories the virgins are always female, so I decided to do something different and make my character male.

I remember the night when the story really came together. I had a rough draft that was much longer, and I stayed up all night, just cutting and cutting. I cut the word count probably in half. I kept wondering if I was going too far, if I was going to wake up in the morning and be like, "What the heck was I thinking?" But the next day when I read over the story, I really liked it. I felt like I'd made a breakthrough with my writing. The story was more lyrical, more literary than anything I'd ever done, but it was definitely still my voice and style. It felt like a story that only I could have written.

By that point I had sold two stories to *Realms of Fantasy*, "Seven Brothers, Cruel" and "Seeds-for-Brains." I knew they would take "Blood of Virgins." I just *knew* it. I couldn't wait to send it off. I knew by now that acceptances came over email and rejections came through the mail. I remember attaching a self-addressed stamped envelope to the manuscript and thinking, "I never want to see you again."

A few months later the envelope showed up in my mailbox. I couldn't believe it. I tore it open and read the note inside. "I really like this idea and character," it said, "but I think the story really needs some kind of resolution. You've left the reader hanging. I'd be glad to look at it again."

Originally the story ended with the dragon's red eye gazing in through Chris's window. I was crushed. I adored the story and didn't want to change it. But I really wanted it to be published in *Realms of Fantasy*, really wanted to see what sort of cool dragon art they would do for the story. I thought about it for a long time. The story is about a character who's afraid, I thought, and would be resolved if he overcame his fear. I wrote that ending and felt it was good. *Realms of Fantasy* accepted the story.

After the story was published, I gave a reading of it at a science fiction convention. A friend of mine, who had read the earlier version, told me, "I liked the original ending better. It was unresolved, but I feel like the story is about unresolved things." So who was right? My friend or the editor at *Realms of Fantasy*? I'm still not sure. Fortunately if you want to experience the original ending, all you have to do is read up to the part where the dragon is looking in the window, then stop.

Scott Goto

Seeds-for-Brains

The ancient Greeks believed that the heart—the center of the human body—was also the center of consciousness. Most people nowadays believe that the *brain* is the seat of our thoughts, holding as it does our personality and all our memories, and those people are right. But the ancient Greeks were right too, in a way. Some residual awareness of *self* does reside in our hearts—an immortal soul, if you will. I know this for a fact.

All this, I'm afraid, is a rather long-winded way of trying to explain why I could still move, and think, and feel, when I awoke from death on that chill October evening in 1789, without a head.

The first thing I noticed was darkness. Then wet dirt pressing me down. Panicked, I clawed my way from a shallow grave. My burial must have been perfunctory; they hadn't put me down very far, maybe two or three feet. Six feet is customary, you know.

But even once I was free of the clinging earth, there was still darkness. I crawled through dry grass, which I could *feel* brushing against my bare palms. I could feel the breeze and the great void of open sky above me, but still this absolute blackness oppressed me. I thought something must be wrong with my eyes, so I reached up to feel for them, and accidentally jammed my fingers together in that empty space atop my shoulders.

Then I felt carefully around my collar bone. The skin ended an inch or so up my neck, torn roughly away. Nothing but a gaping hole there, and down inside my throat the flesh was spongy. Abruptly I drew my hand away.

I was headless.

So of course I couldn't see. I had no eyes. I climbed to my feet—in

67

fact, it was easier to balance without a head. I took a few halting steps and immediately slammed into the rough trunk of a tree. As I rebounded, my knees struck against the smooth, solid face of what could only be a tombstone, and I toppled over it. Fortunately I didn't hit my head. Being headless had *some* advantages.

But still, if I was going to get anywhere I would clearly need to find my head. Or at least *a* head. Anything with eyes would do. That presented a definite problem though. People don't just leave spare heads lying around.

I crawled along the ground, feeling my way with my fingers. I clambered over a jagged wall of piled rock. At last I began to move across lumpy furrows of dry dirt; I was in some farmer's field. My first thought was dread, that I was wandering far from civilization and would soon be lost in a dark wood, where I would certainly perish.

My second thought was a bit more reasoned. Civilization was the last thing I wanted to encounter in my present condition, since "civilized" people would likely run screaming from me. Furthermore, I had *already* perished, and was missing my head besides, so I should hardly fear anything that the woods could threaten—squirrels, owls, maybe a fox.

So deeper into that field I went. I wandered into a patch of growing things, crops of some kind—dry, winding vines; leafy. And scattered among them were heavy, bulbous spheres, large as a man's head.

Pumpkins! Large as a man's head...

I pulled one from its nestled resting place, tugging hard to snap it free from the greedy, grasping vine. Then I placed the vegetable orb atop my shoulders.

You've never had a pumpkin for a head, have you?

No, I didn't think so.

It's an odd sensation. Think about when you make a jack-o-lantern. You take a large knife and cut deep into the pumpkin's flat-topped dome, wrenching the blade back and forth as you carve a jagged circle—one clumsy slice after another. Then you seize the stump of stem at its base and you tug. With a great crack the whole thing comes loose, pulling with it—

A stringy mess of orange pulp and hard white seeds. Then you reach down into the pumpkin with your bare hands and pull out great handfuls of the stuff. It makes kind of a popping, tearing sound as it comes free. Your hands are wet and dripping—you have to wipe them off, but no matter how much you wipe, your skin is still sticky and tingly. You make a pile of all those pumpkin innards. You look at it and think it's gross.

Well *that's* what was inside my head: all those seeds and that gummy orange pumpkin flesh. It was a poor excuse for a brain. Those little seeds, like grits in oatmeal; I couldn't think straight. And the thing had no eyes anyway, so I still couldn't see. I took that pumpkin head and hurled it away into the night and heard it shatter across the furrows with a satisfying *splat*.

I don't know how long I wandered in darkness. Those looping vines seemed to stretch deliberately to snag at my ankles. Again and again I stumbled. Finally I fell against the chest of a man, caught myself on his shoulders.

Pardon me, sir, I said—or tried to say, then realized I had no mouth either. I was sure the man would flee in terror, but he just stood there, stock still...unnaturally still. Perfectly rigid. His arms were stretched out in either direction, stiff and horizontal. Pleadingly I groped for his hand, but when I found the cuff of his shirt, it was stuffed with straw. He was only a scarecrow.

That was a little embarrassing.

Only a scarecrow, but still tall and proud, guarding over his fields with watchful eyes. Eyes! He hung there, bound like our Savior on a wooden cross, and this scarecrow too was *my* savior, because as I groped my way up his torn wool shirt I found it. His head. A fresh ripe autumn pumpkin, with a carved face.

I ripped away the shirt and the straw and that ridiculous hat they'd put on him, and gently worked the pumpkin free. Then, with a rush of excitement bordering on ecstasy, I placed it atop my own shoulders.

I could see! Not well—everything was dim and gray and hazy, but nonetheless I could see. I looked out over the fields and the trees, the stone walls, the churchyard and the steeple and the houses of that small village. I danced a jig under the wonderful white light of the looming gibbous moon. The inside of the pumpkin had been scraped clean—blessedly empty of seeds and gunk. I still had no brain, no memories of who I had been, but nevertheless it was a tremendous improvement.

A teensy triangle was carved between my eyes, and through it all the smells of the night came darting in—cold air, and dry leaves, and pumpkins—pumpkins everywhere. I was grinning, I couldn't stop. I mean really, I couldn't. My mouth was just carved that way, but what did it matter? Why would I want to do anything but grin? I had a head. I could see and smell and...speak? Yes. I sang a little tune off the top of my head.

Off the top of *my* head. It felt good.

I stole through the outskirts of the village, crouching in the shadows of cottages. Then a spot of brightness caught my eye: one lonely candle glowing warm and orange, seen through the frosted kitchen window of a tall mansion. That gave me an idea.

I padded closer, eased open the back door, and crept inside. It was dim in that old house. With my murky vision, all I could make out was the candle flame itself, beckoning to me like a distant beacon. I felt my way down a narrow hall, up a few shallow stairs, and through a doorway into the kitchen. I crossed the room furtively and laid hold of the candle. I pried the dome off my pumpkin head and planted the candle down inside, pushing hard to make sure the hot wax stuck. Flame filled me with a pleasantly warm burn, and lit my empty eyes with flickering light. I could see much better now!

But then I saw...uh oh.

I was not alone. A young couple sat at a table in the corner. I had interrupted their intimate conversation. The young lady was pleasantly plump, with a lovely pale heart-shaped face—currently frozen in shock. The young man was dark-haired, broad-shouldered, and tall. Together, their wide eyes stared at me, tinged gold in the reflected light of my fiery gaze.

"Um...pardon me," I mumbled. "I was just looking...I don't suppose you've seen my head?"

The young lady practically screamed *her* head off.

"Devil!" The young man seized a hardwood cane that lay on a nearby counter, and charged me, swinging. His violent blow was forceful enough to splinter my neck (if I had one). As it was, the cane whistled through the empty air between my shoulders and my pumpkin head. The momentum carried the young man around in a circle, and with a massive crash he plowed into a bureau.

I ran.

There was a modest carriage house adjoining the mansion, and a fierce night-black stallion was tethered there. I yanked him from his stall and leapt onto his bare back. My head didn't know how to ride a horse, but my body remembered; I knew it in my *heart*. As I burst from the stable, the young man came chasing after, cane in hand.

I galloped through the moonlit streets of that sleepy village, and behind me the young man screamed bloody murder. People emerged from lighted doorways to watch me pass. "Stop him!" The young man's angry voice swept along in my wake. "That horseman, stop him!"

"He has no *head*!" a woman shrieked.

Then I was out beyond the streets and into the shadowy forest. I kept on at a canter until I was certain there was no pursuit, then I tied my newly-acquired horse to a tree. I sat down on a fallen log and hung my pumpkin-head in my hands.

Oh the way those people had looked at me! I was a monster to them. A freak. A devil. I had been so proud of my ingenuity, of my candlelit jack-o-lantern eyes and nose and mouth. But now those all seemed so pathetic. Only a *real* head would do. Only with my own head back could I walk through town respected, with my...*head* held high.

But how would I ever find it? Usually when you've lost something, the best thing to do is try to remember when you last saw it. But that wouldn't help me, because I couldn't remember *anything*. I didn't know how my head had become separated, or when, or where. I would have to enlist the aid of someone more knowledgeable, perhaps some local historian.

I spent a few nights moping about in the woods, trying to work up the nerve to brave the village once more. Finally I stole back under cover of dusk. My first candle, the acquisition of which had caused me so much trouble, had burned out after only a few hours. So the first thing I did was swipe a few spares, not to mention a tinderbox, from the porch of an old lady. Then, eyes aglow, I set my sights on the schoolhouse. I reasoned that if anyone here would be familiar with local lore, it would be the neighborhood schoolmaster.

Fortunately for me, he was alone. I lingered in the doorway and watched him correct papers. He was incredibly tall and lanky, with a pendulous head and aquiline nose. He looked up. "Ah," he remarked, in a bored tone of voice. "You must be that Headless Horseman everyone's been talking about. Looking for your head, I hear?"

"Yes," I whispered, drawing closer, and then, "Aren't you afraid?"

He chuckled, and patted a fat black tome that lay on the desk by his side, *A History of New England Witchcraft*. "I'm an educated man, not some local bumpkin. I'm conversant in various manifestations of the supernatural. Now, on to the matter of your head." He smiled slyly. "I'm prepared to use the full breadth of my erudition to help you reclaim what is yours, but in return you must agree to do something for me."

"Yes," I promised. "Anything. Just get me back my head." I couldn't believe my good fortune. "It's really out there? You can really find it?"

He nodded. "Oh yes, it's out there. It will have been preserved—fortified by the same dark and mysterious powers that have suffused your body." He rose, and paced around me in a slow circle, scrutinizing my vestments with a cold and focused gaze. "You were a Hessian soldier."

I looked down at my tattered coat and shirt and pants. They were grungy and caked with graveyard dirt. I hadn't paid much attention to them, having been singularly focused on securing myself a head. Even now, studying them, they told me nothing. But somehow this man of letters had seen a piece of my missing past in the clothes. I explained, "I don't know who I was."

"No, of course not." He sniffed. "Not without your head. Nice pumpkin, by the way."

"Thank you."

He frowned, an expression of deep concentration falling over his face. He strode to the bookcase and briskly pulled one volume from the shelf. He licked a finger, then flipped through the pages. "It seems I read an account once of a Hessian soldier who lost his head in battle. During the War for Independence. Ah yes, here it is." He paused. "Your head was taken off by a cannonball."

By a cannonball! A cruel sphere of heavy iron had torn my head from my shoulders. How awful. I would have gulped, if I'd had a throat. "But where did it end up?"

"That, pumpkin-head," he said, slamming the book shut, "is what we must discover."

He set to work immediately, consulting books and maps and letters. I watched with a kind of wonder. Since I lacked a real head, I possessed only the most rudimentary cognitive facilities, but this man! Oh, his mind! It was sharp as a saber, complex as a clock. Even when he sat totally motionless, lost in perfect concentration, still I could see that his mind was all awhirl, endlessly processing, collating, refining, and concluding. I hoped desperately that my own head was even one-tenth as clever as his.

"How's it going?" I asked him. "What are you finding out?"

He turned his attention from book to book to book. "I don't know if I should bother to elucidate. It's all probably beyond your comprehension anyway. Just let me handle it. Tell you what, why don't you go outside and toss your head around for a while? I work faster without distractions."

"All right," I said cheerfully.

I tried tossing my head around, like he said, but as soon as the pumpkin got too far from my shoulders, I lost the use of its eyes, which made it hard to catch it again. Fortunately I didn't splatter it. After a while I gave up on that and instead sat down on a rock to think, while I doodled in the dirt with a twig.

I knew now that I had been a soldier. Not such a bad thing to be, all things considered. Honor and valor, bright uniforms and shiny medals, cavalry charges and all that; the invigorating, fiery smell of gunsmoke drifting across the battlefield. And wartime experiences always made the best stories. I imagined that my head, once I found it, must be full of fascinating recollections.

The schoolmaster and I spent the next few evenings trudging around town, exploring various fields by lanternlight. I wasn't exactly sure what we were looking for, and he didn't seem overly interested in enlightening me. He simply led the way, and I followed along behind, laden with boxes and books and surveying equipment.

"Hey, seeds-for-brains," he barked. "Hurry up, would you? We haven't got all night."

"Sorry," I said. With all the materials piled in my arms, I could barely see where I was going.

"We're doing well," he said. "Certainly better than you were doing on your own. I heard you were looking for your head inside a *house*. What were you thinking?"

I remembered the young couple I'd encountered that first night. I wanted to explain to him that I'd gone into the house to get a *candle*, and that once I saw those two, the thing about my head just kind of slipped out. I was still trying to put that sentiment into words when he continued, cutting me off. "You know that girl you saw? Pretty, isn't she? I'm going to marry her."

"That's nice," I said.

"She's rich," he explained. "*Very* rich. I need the money. Do you have any idea what a schoolmaster makes?"

"No," I said.

"*No*," he echoed. "Of course you don't."

We clambered over one stone wall, then another. "It's funny," I remarked. "I just assumed she was seeing that other guy."

He stiffened. "What *other* guy?"

"You know," I prompted, "that tall young fellow. Who was alone with her in the kitchen late at night."

"Oh." The schoolmaster scowled. "*Him.*" He continued in a low, raspy tone. "She didn't tell me he was there. But yes, I know who you mean. He fancies that he might steal her away from me, but I know how to deal with *him*." He fixed me with a long, hard gaze. "But first we must find your head. Come on."

Eventually our path led back to the pumpkin field. I could see the churchyard where I'd been buried. The small cemetery was dominated by the massive bole and branches of a looming oak tree—the one I'd crashed into that first night. A great dark hole pitted the center of its trunk.

The schoolmaster paced furiously about, sketching wildly with his quill pen. "Now...the cannon would have been..." He stopped. "Here." He drew some more figures. "You would have been thirty feet away when the cannonball struck...mounted. Hmm...forward momentum...force equals mass times acceleration...carry the two...and..." His head snapped up sharply and he glared at the lonely churchyard. "Follow me!"

We ran across the furrows, leapt another stone wall, and came to stand before the giant oak. A few blood-red leaves drifted past us as the schoolmaster reached into that hole in its trunk and, with an angry grunt, pulled forth a large, misshapen, blue-black cannonball. "Hold that," he told me, dropping it into my arms along with the rest of my burdens. My knees quivered as I stumbled from side to side, trying to keep my balance.

The schoolmaster reached back into the hole and yanked out my head by its thick blonde hair.

"My head!" I exclaimed. "You found it!" I began to practically vibrate with excitement.

"Of course. I told you I would." He wiped sweat from his brow with the back of his sleeve, then he glared at me. "Would you knock it off with that stupid grin?"

"Sorry," I said. I bent down, and dumped everything I was carrying into a heap on the ground. I reached out with both hands. "Please, let me see it."

"I've fulfilled my part of the bargain," the schoolmaster intoned solemnly, passing the head into my waiting arms. "I've returned your head. Now there's something I want you to do for me."

"Sure, anything." I turned the head around in my hands, looking at it from all angles. It was a fine, well-formed German head. Not exactly handsome, but not bad-looking either. There was something about it that made me vaguely uneasy though. Dare I say the countenance possessed a bit of a *sinister* cast? I shrugged, popped off my pumpkin head, and raised the recovered human head to my shoulders.

"You know that young man you saw? The one who's trying to steal my girl?" The schoolmaster grinned. "I want you to *kill him*."

I used my new muscled throat to gasp. "I can't do that!"

Then memories started pouring back. Instantly I knew something was wrong. For these were not memories of glorious battle. These were dark, dismal, awful things, full of fire and black smoke, women screaming helplessly, and blood, so much blood everywhere. On my saber, on my hands...

I stumbled, and said weakly, "No."

The schoolmaster was furious. "What do you mean you *can't*? You're a black specter from beyond the grave, the shade of a Hessian mercenary who killed for money. Well, I've paid your price, phantom. I've given you your head, and now I want to be repaid. We have a deal!"

The women screaming. That was the worst part. I couldn't take their screaming. My God, what sort of monster had I *been*? How could I live another day, another *moment*, with these horrid memories? With this fiendish head? "No," I cried, "I won't do it. You can't make me."

He shouted, "What are you? Some kind of coward? Some kind of wimp? Some undead spirit *you've* turned out to be. They should call you the *dickless* horseman!"

White hot fury poured over me then. "All right!" I roared, standing tall. "That's it!"

I...I don't really like to talk about what happened next. I got very agitated. It's all kind of a blur. I made a scene, started throwing things—like that pumpkin. It got broken. I try to blame it on that head I was wearing, that miserable Hessian head; it was the sort of thing *he* would have done; *he* once slit a man's throat for looking at him the wrong way, and the schoolmaster had given far more provocation than that.

It's an interesting issue actually, this matter of *self*. Do our brain and our memories make us who we are? Do they define our choices? Or do we really have free will? There are quite a few strong arguments on both sides. For example...

But I'm stalling again. I'm sorry.

I have this tendency to ramble. To explain. To lecture. Maybe you've noticed. I try to fight it, but it's who I am now.

It's just one of those things that happens, I guess, when you have the head of a schoolmaster.

Author's note: Seeds-for-Brains

In October of 2002 my mom and I attended a play that was performed in the basement of the Katonah Library, a one-man production of Washington Irving's "The Legend of Sleepy Hollow." I knew the story mostly from the Disney cartoon *The Legend of Sleepy Hollow,* and from the Tim Burton movie *Sleepy Hollow,* which had come out a few years before. I hadn't seen the Disney movie since I was a kid, and had been disappointed with the Tim Burton film, but this theatrical version really caught my imagination.

Katonah is only about 20 miles from Sleepy Hollow, and as we drove home through the woods, crossing the reservoir and passing by Muscoot Farm, it was easy to imagine that we might encounter a ghostly rider. I found myself wondering what had become of Ichabod Crane after the Horseman had hurled that fiery jack-o-lantern at him. What had happened next?

Then the answer came to me: The Horseman took Ichabod's head and started wearing it.

When I got home I read the original story by Washington Irving. In the story it's heavily implied that the Headless Horseman is really Brom Bones in disguise, but I liked my idea better. I preferred the idea of an actual, supernatural Headless Horseman. (Which is one thing I did like about the Tim Burton film.)

What would a story sound like, I wondered, if it were told from the point of view of the Headless Horseman wearing Ichabod Crane's head? I thought it could be really interesting. The narrator would be very stuffy and pedantic, and the whole time you're thinking, "Why does he talk like this?" And then at the end it would all make sense.

The problem with a narrator who's stuffy and pedantic is that if he's *too* stuffy and pedantic, people will think the story is just bad and won't finish reading it, and will never get to the twist. I tried to put in enough of that voice to set up the ending while still making sure that the story was fun to read. I had a great time writing it. I always meant to do more research and add in more period details, but by the time I finished it I was so delighted with it that I didn't want to change anything. I sent it off to *Realms of Fantasy,* and it ended up being my second sale there.

At this point I have no idea who the actor was who performed that play, and he obviously has no way of knowing that he helped inspire this story. I wish I knew who he was so I could tell him.

Michael J. DiMotta

Family Tree

Simon Archimagus rode his horse through a twilight forest. A rapier hung at his side, and as he moved he muttered a spell that would slay any insect who presumed to land upon him.

He turned onto the narrow dirt trail that led to his abode. A short time later he glanced back and noticed a horseman behind him. As Simon was the sole resident in these parts, he could only assume that he was being followed. He moved one hand to his sword, while with the other he sketched a diagram in the air, preparatory to unleashing battle magic.

The rider neared. He wore a loose white shirt and feathered cap. The dimness made it hard to judge his features, but he didn't seem hostile. Then Simon knew him. Bernard.

As the rider trotted up he called out, "Brother."

Of all Simon's male relatives, Bernard, his youngest sibling, was perhaps his favorite, though that wasn't saying a lot. Bernard seemed not to have changed much—same thick brown hair and ingenuous eyes. A bit pudgier, maybe. Simon said, "How'd you find me?"

"Magic." Bernard added with a touch of pride, "You're not the only wizard in the family, you know."

"No." Simon gave a half-smile. "Just the best."

Bernard chuckled. "No argument there." He glanced up the trail. "You live nearby?"

The game was up. Simon's family had located him, at last. So, "Yes," he said.

"Then grant me hospitality, brother. We need to talk."

Simon hesitated, then said, "All right." He gestured with his head. "This way."

They followed the trail, which wound its way up the hillside. The horses panted and snorted. After a time, Bernard said, "So are you going to tell me why you disappeared?"

"I doubt it," Simon said.

"We worried."

Simon stared off into the sky. "My branch is still there, isn't it? You knew I was all right."

"We knew you were *alive*," Bernard said. "You might've been sick, imprisoned——"

"I wasn't."

"I see that." Bernard sighed. "But yes, your branch is still there. Mother's kept everything just the way you left it. She misses you, Simon."

"I'll bet."

Bernard lapsed into silence. Then he asked, "What the hell have you been doing with yourself all these years anyway?"

Simon didn't answer. The two of them crested the hill and looked out over the moon-silvered grasses of the meadow below. Simon waited for Bernard to notice the tree.

Finally he did. He gasped. "Is that...?"

"Yes." Simon couldn't help grinning. "It's mine."

The giant oak was indigo in the darkness, its trunk dotted with small round windows that glowed with warm light from the rooms within.

Bernard stared in wonder. "My god. You did it. You crazy bastard, you actually did it. I don't believe it."

"Believe it." Simon spurred his horse. "Come, I'll give you the tour. Come see what your clever older brother has wrought."

* * *

They approached the tree, then dismounted and led their horses toward an archway that passed through into its trunk. Above them to either side huge gnarled roots loomed darkly. Simon gestured, and a portcullis made of thick thorn branches lifted open. He and Bernard passed into the stable, where they left the horses feeding happily, and from there they climbed a broad staircase that was lit by wall-sconces blazing with faerie fire. All around was spell-forged woodwork that still lived, and grew. They made their way to the kitchen, where Bernard fixed himself a sandwich and stretched out on the windowsill. "It's a fine tree, brother," he said. "But still rather...modest, isn't it? Compared to our inheritance, your birthright."

Simon leaned against the doorframe and crossed his arms. "I could command it to grow larger, like the other. More branches, rooms."

"So why don't you?"

"It's sufficient to my needs." Simon had never shared his relatives' appetite for palatial suites, nor for the endless squabbles over who should lay claim to the floorspace of which deceased ancestor.

Bernard glanced about. "And you live alone? Don't you miss the comforts of family?"

"Brother," Simon said wryly, "believe me, having lived sixteen years among the scions of Victor Archimagus, the comforts of family are something I'm happy to forego for a good long time to come."

Bernard chewed his sandwich and stared out the window. He said, "My wife, Elizabeth, has given me a child, at last. A son."

Simon felt obliged to say, "Congratulations."

"The presentation ceremony is next month," Bernard added. "I'd like you to be there."

Simon moved to the cupboard. "I have a prior engagement. But thanks."

"Simon, this is serious. Victor's ghost is displeased by your continued absence, and the branches he's grown for our brothers' boys have seemed less grand than they might be. I want my son to have only the best."

"Please." Simon poured two glasses of wine. "I doubt that even the spirit of Victor Archimagus would punish your infant child for my transgressions. In fact, this whole line of emotionally manipulative argumentation seems to me to have mother's fingerprints all over it. Did she put you up to this?"

"What, you think I can't act on my own?"

Simon passed him a glass. "I'll take that as a yes."

"All right," Bernard said, accepting the wine. "Yes. But she has her reasons, beyond the obvious." He took a sip. "We need you, Simon. Tensions with the descendants of Atherton have never been higher. If it comes to a fight—"

"It won't."

"You've been away," Bernard said. "You haven't seen how bad it's gotten. Malcolm provokes us constantly."

Simon shook his head. "The children of Franklin and the children of Atherton have been at each other's throats for years. It's never come to bloodshed, and it never will."

"What if you're wrong?" Bernard said. "Look, you're not overfond of your close kin, we know that, but are you really just going to sit back as we die in a feud?"

"I'm confident in your ability to look after yourselves."

Bernard grimaced. "Ordinarily, yes. But there's a complication."

"Oh?"

"Meredith."

At the name, Simon felt a jolt. He set down his wine glass. "What?"

"Yeah, I guess it didn't work out with Duke what's-his-name—"

"Wyland."

"Yeah, so she's back. And she scares me, Simon. Her magic has become very powerful." The fear in Bernard's eyes was real. "That's why we need you. To balance things. If you came back it might actually help keep the peace, because they'd think twice about messing with us."

Meredith, Simon thought. After a time, he said, "Maybe a short visit."

Bernard grinned, leapt to his feet, and patted Simon's shoulders. "That's it. Now you're talking."

Later, after Bernard had departed, Simon hiked up to the highest branch of the tree, opened a small door, and strode out onto the balcony. For a long time he sat there in the darkness, clutching his wineglass absently and staring at the mist-shrouded hills, thinking of Meredith.

* * *

A month later Simon stood and regarded the tree of Victor Archimagus.

It was gigantic, its trunk as wide around as a castle wall. A good way up, the trunk split into a great V—the two branches that had grown upon the births of Victor's sons, Franklin and Atherton. From there the branches continued to climb and divide—one for each legitimate male heir—and now over a hundred descendants of the late wizard resided within the tree's luxurious chambers. (Female children were married off and sent away—Victor had never been a terribly enlightened sort.) The tree was a virtuoso feat of spellcraft, the first of its kind, and upon its creation Victor had been so impressed with himself that he'd taken the surname Archimagus—master wizard. Simon was the only one to have successfully replicated the spell. Families that possessed the rare gift of magic seemed always to be afflicted with low fertility, but the fact that Victor's tree grew larger and grander depending upon the number of offspring had ensured a frenetic effort to proliferate his adopted surname, and had also—perhaps inevitably—led to a rivalry between the descendants of Franklin and the descendants of Atherton over who could produce the greatest number of male heirs. At the moment it happened that the two halves of the tree were in perfect balance. Today's presentation ceremony for Bernard's infant son would change that.

Crowds had come from all the surrounding towns, and other wizards had come from farther afield, and now several hundred people were gathered in the shadow of those soaring branches. The children of Franklin had spared no expense to ensure a spectacle. Wooden poles were set in the earth at intervals, with garlands of sweet-smelling flowers stretched between them, and tables were piled high with cooked quail and poached eggs. Simon made his way past dancers and jugglers and lute-players, and into the roped-off area that was reserved for members of the Archimagus family. Here all the men, and many of the women, wore swords.

Bernard appeared at Simon's side and took his arm. "Thank you for coming, Simon. Here, mother wants a word with you."

As Simon moved through the crowd, heads turned to watch him, and conversations halted abruptly, then resumed in murmurs. Meredith's brother Malcolm, glowering, red-haired, black-clad, turned to confer with his gang of goonish cousins. Simon knew what everyone was thinking: The runaway returns, the descendant of Franklin who's most gifted in the ways of magic. This changes everything.

Simon spotted his mother, still lovely as ever, dressed in an ostentatious blue gown. She wore her prematurely silver hair in a single braid, and her face had a few new lines in it, which only made her look even more conniving. She was engaged in an animated conversation with Meredith's mother, a plump woman who wore too much makeup over a pallid complexion and whose wavy crimson hair was like a fiery halo.

When Simon's mother spotted him, she waved and called out, "Simon, there you are."

Meredith's mother tensed. She glanced back over her shoulder at him, her face apprehensive. Simon's mother wore an expression just a shade shy of smug. This scene was playing out, Simon felt sure, precisely as she had intended.

As Simon approached, his mother reached for him and said warmly, "Welcome home."

He allowed his cheeks to be kissed. "Just a visit, mother. My home is far away now."

"Yes, of course." She turned to Meredith's mother and said, "Have you heard? Simon lives in his own tree now. He managed to duplicate the very spell that produced our own arboreal estate."

Simon smiled modestly, uncomfortably.

"Oh, how wonderful," said Meredith's mother, with dubious sincerity. "Is that what you've been doing, Simon? Studying magic? How nice. Your mother has been terribly lax about keeping us up to date on you." She added, "You must be very dedicated, to have sequestered yourself away from your family all these years."

"Oh, he is," said Simon's mother, her tone incrementally chillier. "And the results speak for themselves, wouldn't you say?"

"Oh, indeed," said Meredith's mother. "You know, Simon, my daughter is around here somewhere. You two should chat. She's quite the sorceress herself these days."

"Yes," said Simon's mother, "we're all so delighted to have Meredith back with us. She's much too good for that silly duke."

Meredith's mother narrowed her eyes just a trace. Then she glanced over Simon's shoulder and said, "In fact, I think I see my daughter now. Meredith, dear! Come here a moment. Look who's back."

Simon steeled himself, and turned.

She was taller than he remembered, more confident, her features sharper. She wore a red blouse and a skirt with a swordbelt, and her chestnut hair was shorter than it had been, now just brushing her bare shoulders. But she was still Meredith. He'd imagined this meeting so many times, and now here she was, before him.

"Simon," she said, and moved to embrace him, somewhat stiffly, then backed away. She and her mother faced Simon and his like pieces on a chessboard.

Meredith's mother said, "Remember how the two of you always used to play together?"

"Yes," Simon said, watching Meredith, who stared back, her expression neutral.

"Yes," Simon's mother put in. "The two of you always were the most gifted wizards in the family."

"A bit competitive about it too, as I recall," said Meredith's mother. "Though I suspect, Simon, that these days Meredith may have you beat."

"Oh," said Simon's mother, "I don't know about that."

A moment of awkward silence.

Then Simon's mother added, "We must arrange a little contest some time, to settle the matter."

"Indeed," said Meredith's mother. "That would be most interesting."

The mothers fell silent. Simon and Meredith eyed each other. Simon felt that he should speak, but couldn't think what to say. Fortunately the trumpets sounded, signaling that the ceremony was about to begin.

Meredith nodded to Simon, then she and her mother strolled off, and were soon lost amid the crowds streaming toward the rows of benches. Simon and his mother found their seats, and for a time Simon exchanged a few words with various relatives.

Then Bernard made his way to the front of the audience, and behind him came Elizabeth, a slender, mousy girl, holding their infant son. The couple mounted a raised wooden platform and stood gazing up at the broad southern expanse of Victor's tree.

Bernard shouted, "Victor Archimagus! Honored ancestor! Hear me!"

A great oval section of the tree rippled, as if its bark were a stretch of calm water suddenly disturbed by the movement of a lurking monster. The undulations became more pronounced. There was churning, swirling...

Then a giant wooden face appeared, extruding from the trunk like a man emerging through a waterfall. The face was handsome, bearded, vain. The face of Victor Archimagus, its eyes empty, alien.

It boomed, "I am here."

Simon had always found the thing repugnant. It was just like Victor to leave behind this ghost, this ponderous, unfeeling simulacrum to ensure that his unhealthy domination of his family continued on down through the ages.

Bernard called, "I am Bernard Archimagus, and this is my lawful wife, Elizabeth. We wish to thank you, great wizard, for all you've done and continue to do for your family." Bernard continued in this vein, praising Victor's multifarious accomplishments and abiding generosity. Simon glanced across the aisle, to where the descendants of Atherton were seated, and sought Meredith's face, but she was blocked from view.

Finally Bernard took the infant from Elizabeth's arms, held him aloft, and cried, "I present to you, noble Victor, my firstborn son, Sebastian Archimagus. May he never fail to please you."

For a long moment Victor's face seemed to regard the child, though really it was impossible to say where those empty eyes were staring. Finally the face said, "I am well pleased."

Then the whole tree began to shudder. Leaves shaken loose fell across the crowd like rain. Victor's eyes glowed with an otherworldly light. The base of the tree bulged, as if a geyser were filling it from below, and this effect traveled up the trunk to the great V that marked the division between Franklin and Atherton, and from there followed the Franklin branch, causing it to enlarge. The magic flowed up branch after branch, tracing the ancestry of Sebastian, and everywhere it passed it was making the rooms within more spacious and extravagant, Simon knew. Finally the magic reached the branch that had grown on the day of Bernard's own presentation ceremony, and from that branch a new growth sprouted forth, lengthening and thickening and blooming with windows and balconies and bright green leaves, all in the space of a minute. The crowd oohed and aahed.

The children of Franklin burst into raucous cheers. The polite applause from the children of Atherton was noticeably more subdued.

The celebration went on well into evening, and when it was over Simon followed his relatives back to the tree. They shuffled through the main gates and into the great hall—a vast, cavernous space filled with tables and benches, the far wall of which was occupied by a shrine to Victor. From there the families divided, descendants of Franklin to the right, descendants

86

of Atherton to the left, climbing two giant staircases that spiraled around each other and which led back to their respective branches. Simon made his way up to his own branch and his old chambers, which as Bernard had promised had been kept exactly as he'd left them.

Then Simon lay in bed, staring at the ceiling. After a time, he slept.

*　*　*

He was woken by a frantic pounding at his door. He rolled over and squinted at the window, and saw that it was morning. He crawled from bed and opened the door. In the hallway stood his sandy-haired young cousin, Garrett, who said, alarmed, "The baby. Sebastian. He's sick."

Garrett went scurrying off. Simon dressed and made his way down into the rooms of his late father, then up again into Bernard's section of the tree. A newly-created archway framed the stairs that led to Sebastian's branch.

Simon knocked on a door, which was then pulled aside, revealing Bernard's face, upon which hope and worry warred. "Simon," he said. "Come in."

Simon entered the chamber, where Elizabeth sat in a rocking chair, clutching her son.

"A fever," Bernard explained. "There were so many people around yesterday, all wanting to hold him. Uncle Reginald sneezed on him, I think. I'm sure it's nothing, but..."

Simon nodded. He greeted Elizabeth, then took a look at Sebastian, who seemed pale.

A short time later Garrett returned with Simon's mother in tow. When she saw the baby, she froze. She was silent a long time before saying, "It'll be all right. But he should have healing. Simon dear, I don't suppose your talents at the gentler side of magic have improved any these past years?"

"Sorry, no," he said.

Garrett piped up, "I'll get Clara."

"Wait," said Simon's mother. "No. Fetch us Meredith, please."

Bernard was shocked. "Mother," he grumbled, "we don't need any help from *her*."

Simon's mother said, "She's a powerful healer, far more so than Clara, and everyone knows it. She's here now. We must take advantage of this opportunity." She waved at Garrett and said, "Go."

He went, and returned an hour later with Meredith. All eyes were upon her as she entered, crossed the room to Elizabeth, and said, "I'm sorry to hear that Sebastian is unwell. I'll do what I can. Here." She held out her arms.

Reluctantly, Elizabeth handed over the child.

As soon as Meredith touched him he began to cry. She held him to her chest and closed her eyes, then stood like that for a minute, murmuring, as Sebastian wailed. Elizabeth shot a worried look at Bernard, who glared at Meredith.

Finally Meredith looked up. "There. All done." She returned the baby to Elizabeth.

"Thank you," Simon's mother said quietly.

Meredith departed, meeting Simon's gaze briefly as she closed the door behind her.

Two days passed, and Sebastian continued to sicken, but there was nothing more to be done, as any further healing magic would simply disrupt the operation of Meredith's more powerful spell. That evening Bernard came to Simon's chambers and said, "Simon, I need you. Elizabeth has taken Sebastian up into his branch, and she refuses to come out."

They made their way through the arch and into the newly-grown section of the tree. The halls were dim and deserted, and as they climbed Simon could hear wind rustling the leaves outside, as well as, more faintly, the sound of a woman sobbing. In an empty room they found Elizabeth sitting on the floor in the corner, holding Sebastian. Darkness hid her face.

Bernard knelt beside her. "Darling, please. Come downstairs."

"No," she said.

Bernard turned to Simon, who knelt beside her too and said, "Elizabeth, listen to me. We can't stay here. If he dies——"

"He won't!" she cried.

Simon said, "If the branch——"

She shook her head. "I don't care."

"Well, I do," Simon said. "Come on, give him here." He took hold of Sebastian and lifted him from her limp arms. She trembled.

Bernard helped her to her feet, then held her as he guided her down the stairs, and Simon walked beside them, carrying the baby.

When they crossed the threshhold into Bernard's section of the tree, Simon breathed easier. If a male line of the Archimagus family died out, the corresponding branches of Victor's tree withered as well, which could be dangerous for anyone inhabiting them. Thus branches that seemed imperiled were generally abandoned.

Simon sat on a sofa with the baby while Bernard put Elizabeth to bed. When Bernard emerged, he said, "It's strange, isn't it?"

"What?" Simon said.

"She's such a great healer, but she can't even help a sick child?"

"You think her talents are exaggerated?"

Bernard was grim. "Or she's not really exercising them on our behalf."

"No. I won't believe that, not of Meredith. I know her."

"You *knew* her," Bernard said. "People change."

Simon sighed. "Get some rest. You're exhausted." He nodded at the child in his arms. "I'll watch him. He'll be fine."

Bernard hesitated. Then: "All right. Goodnight." He walked over and kissed Sebastian's forehead.

"Goodnight," Simon said.

* * *

Two nights later, as Simon lay in bed reading, he heard a rustle from his desk. He glanced up and saw one of his pens jittering. Then the quill swept up into the air, stabbed itself into an inkpot, and began a wobbly dance across one of his parchments. Simon tossed aside his book and hurried over.

The quill lay itself down beside a few words of Meredith's flowery script: *I have to see you.*

Simon's heart leapt. He snatched up the pen and scrawled, *Meet me in the garden*, then set the pen down.

A moment later it came to life again, and wrote, *I will.*

So down into the trunk of the tree he went, and out the postern gate, and down the hillside, where the long grasses swayed, and across the bridge over the gurgling stream, to the garden where he and Meredith had played as children, and where they'd met in secret, later, on nights like this. The place was guarded by a high stone wall from which the ivy dangled, and the gates were all rusted partway open, and inside were cobbled walks that wound among the trees like the paths of drunken men, and shallow ponds ringed with lily pads, and hedge mazes into which a boy and girl could vanish together and not be found by anyone.

He waited for her, by the marble bench beside the statue of the sad old lion who was missing an ear, and it made Simon think of that other night, years ago. This time she came though, her dark form slipping along the pathway like a ghost. Simon hurried to her and took her in his arms. "I missed you," he whispered.

"I missed you too," she said, into his shoulder.

He held her like that for a long time, there beneath the moon.

Then he said, "Come away with me."

She drew back, staring. "What?"

"Did you ever love me?" he asked.

"Yes."

"Then come away with me. I was right, wasn't I? We belong together. Not with them. No good will come of staying here."

"Simon." She pulled away, and sat down on the bench. "No. It's impossible."

"Why?" he said.

"I told you—"

"Yes." He sat down beside her. "You told me. That you'd been promised to another. Well, no longer."

"And that Victor would not be pleased—"

"But I have my own tree now," he said, "so we wouldn't—"

"And our families," she said finally.

"We can live without them. I've shown that, haven't I? If you ever loved me—"

She looked away.

"Meredith," he pleaded. "Forget them. We'll start our own family, and they'll be the best damn wizards anyone's ever—"

"I'm sorry," she said. "Simon. I'm not like you. I can't just walk away and never look back."

He stood, and scowled into the shadows.

After a time, she said, "Simon, we need to talk. About these rumors."

"What rumors?" he said.

"That I'm only pretending to heal Sebastian." She was indignant. "Or even that I put a curse on him. It's absurd."

Simon glared. "This is why you wanted to see me?"

"It's one reason," she said. "Simon, this is important. Things are getting out of hand. Your family's trying to incite a—"

"*My* family?" he said. "Your brother—"

"Malcolm," she said cooly, "is a boor. A childish one. Ignore him. The only person he's a danger to is himself. It's your side that's the threat. That's another reason I can't just run away with you, even if I wanted to."

Simon chuckled. "So you're all that stands in the way of the mighty Franklin clan? You must think pretty highly of yourself."

"Well, maybe I do," she said.

"And yet Sebastian sickens every day."

"Which is sad," she said, "but no fault of mine. Sometimes people get better and sometimes they don't. You know that."

"Or maybe you're not as powerful as you let on."

She stood. "Keep pushing me, Simon, and we'll see how powerful I am."

He laughed again. "Is that a threat? You think *you* could beat *me*?"

"I know I could."

Simon said, "I'm the one who unraveled the greatest spell of Victor Archimagus."

"Which is impressive," Meredith said acidly. "Impressive that you'd waste so many years trying to match the egomania of a man you despise. But while you were busy with your precious tree, *I* was busy with all the other areas of study that I'm sure you neglected, including battle magic, so don't take me on, Simon. It'll be no contest."

He said loudly, "I made my 'precious' tree for you. For us. So that someday—"

"Well I never asked you to!"

They stood there in the darkness, angry.

Then she said, "I think this conversation is over." She added, more gently, "Rein them in, Simon. For both our sakes. If *you* ever loved *me*, rein them in."

She turned and strode off down the path, flanked by rows of poplars that stood like sentinels. And beyond her the garden wall, and beyond that the crest of the hill, over which loomed the long black limbs of Victor's tree.

When she was gone, Simon remembered that other night, long ago.

"You can't marry him," he'd told her. "It won't work out. You'll never be happy. Meredith, you don't have to go through with this, it's not too late. Come away with me, now."

And she'd told him all the reasons why not, and asked him where they'd go.

"I don't know," he'd said. "We'll figure something out." And when she'd refused again he'd said, "Well, I'm leaving. Tonight. No matter what. You can come with me or not. I'll pack some things and wait for you in the garden, in case you change your mind."

And he'd stood there, by the marble bench, watching her window, as the night grew chill. He'd watched her lights go out, and then, later, when he knew she hadn't changed her mind, he'd walked away, and never looked back.

And now he strode down gravel paths, thinking over her reasons— again. In the end only one of them really mattered. Family. As he slipped out the garden gate, he paused to glare up at Victor's tree.

Just then there came a great cracking sound that echoed across the violet sky, and one of those branches tore free and tumbled down, plummeting to the earth.

* * *

The following afternoon the Archimagus family gathered at their private cemetery on a hill overlooking Victor's tree. The sky was a solid gray slate, the air thick and oppressive. A few words were said. Elizabeth wept ceaselessly.

Simon avoided eye contact with Meredith, who was now the focus of near-unanimous suspicion from the children of Franklin. She kept her face devoid of expression. At one point during the service, from the back of the crowd there came a single soft guffaw, perhaps in response to some whispered remark. Bernard glanced back over his shoulder, in order to identify the offender. Simon didn't have to look. He knew the voice. Malcolm.

Bernard's eyes were full of a cold, dead rage, and for a moment Simon half thought—and in that instant half hoped—that Bernard would go tearing through the crowd and disembowel Malcolm. But after a few seconds Bernard hunched his shoulders and turned back toward the grave of his son.

The next week was stiflingly hot. Simon slept on a blanket on his balcony, and even so he awoke constantly, bathed in sweat. During the day most members of the Archimagus family congregated in the great hall, where the air was cooler, but even that expansive space began to feel cramped, as the children of Franklin and the children of Atherton vied for tables, jostled one another, and exchanged words.

One afternoon there came a hurried knocking at Simon's door. He opened it to find Garrett standing there, panting. The boy said, "It's Malcolm. You have to come. Now."

Simon strapped on his sword, and followed Garrett down the stairs.

When Simon arrived in the great hall, he saw Malcolm's gang lounging at their accustomed tables, which were covered with an assortment of potted plants. Nearby stood a knot of young men from among the descendants of Franklin, including Bernard, who were glaring at Malcolm and his cousins and conferring angrily. The rest of the crowd, several dozen relatives, were evenly split between the children of Franklin and the children of Atherton, and the two sides eyed each other with open hostility. Simon hurried forward.

"Simon!" called Malcolm then, with false cheer. "There you are. Come take a look at this."

Simon approached, wary.

Malcolm nodded to the plant in his hand. "I've discovered the most delightful diversion, the perfect way to pass a hot summer's day. An acquaintance of mine delivered these last night. They're all the rage in certain foreign climes, I'm told."

Simon frowned at the plant, which was some sort of miniature tree with spindly limbs and dense, brushy foliage.

Malcolm held up a large knife. "Here's how it works. You shape these trees into the most elegant forms simply by removing branches you find undesirable. So, take this one here." He poised his blade below one of the tree's tiny branches. "I don't like it at all."

He flicked his wrist and the branch fluttered down, landing on the toe of his boot. He kicked it aside onto the floor.

Bernard began hurling curses. A few of his relatives herded him away, murmuring at him to just ignore Malcolm, who affected nonchalance as he leaned back against the table and remarked, "I guess he's not a fan." He returned his gaze to Simon and held up the knife again. "How about you, Simon? Want to give it a go?"

"No thanks," Simon said.

"Pity." Malcolm slipped the knife back into his belt sheath. "It's quite fun."

"Well, I think you've had enough fun for one day," Simon said. "So why don't you take your little tree, and your little friends here, and move along. Now."

Malcolm smiled. "No," he said airily, crossing one leg over the other, "I'm comfortable here."

"But here's the thing," Simon said, sketching a diagram in the air. "I can make you rather *un*comfortable." Pale blue smoke rose from his fingers. He was bluffing though. He had no intention of unleashing magic in a situation like this.

And Malcolm knew it. He laughed. "You think you're so scary. That's why your mother summoned you back here, to frighten us. But you and I both know that if you harm me, my sister will destroy you."

Everyone in the room was watching. Malcolm stood up, so that he was eye to eye with Simon, and hissed, "It's you who's afraid. Because she's good. The best wizard in the family. Too good for you."

That struck a nerve, more than Malcolm could know, and Simon felt a hot rush of fury.

Malcolm called to the assembled children of Atherton, "You're all afraid of him! Why? What's he going to do?" He shoved Simon in the chest, forcing him back a few steps. "Huh? What're you going to do?"

Simon glared, smoldering.

"Ha," Malcolm said, turning away. "You see—"

Simon launched himself at Malcolm, tackling him to the ground.

The room erupted with shouts as Simon straddled Malcolm and belted him several times across the jaw. Malcolm clawed for Simon's face, but Simon swept those arms aside and punched him again.

Then Malcolm went for his knife.

He drew it from its sheath and waved the blade at Simon, who grabbed

Malcolm's wrist and slammed it against the floor, once, twice, to jar the weapon loose.

Then Simon was flung aside, onto his back, by Bernard, who had a rapier in his hand. As Simon watched, Bernard drew back the sword, then skewered Malcolm where he lay.

No! Simon thought.

He rolled to his feet. Weapons were being drawn all around him.

"Wait!" he cried. "Stop!"

But it was too late. The children of Franklin and the children of Atherton came together in a clash of steel. Malcolm's gang rushed Bernard, who backed off, slashing at the air to keep them at bay. Simon drew his own sword and leapt to help. Malcolm, hacking up blood, was dragged away from the fighting by one of his cousins, Nathan—a stolid young man who for whatever reason had always been fiercely loyal to Malcolm.

Simon ducked and cut and parried. He didn't use magic—he might need all the magic he could muster to defend himself against Meredith, he knew—but some of his relatives let loose with spells, and there were occasional flashes of light and small explosions. The whole chamber convulsed with violence, generations' worth of rivalry and mistrust unleashed at last, there in front of the shrine to Victor Archimagus. Soon Simon's blade was slick with blood, his hand sticky with it. Faces appeared before him—angry faces, faces he remembered from childhood, faces he hadn't spoken to in years, and he thrust his sword at them.

Sometimes one of the descendants of Franklin fell—Simon saw Garrett cut down by one of Meredith's uncles—but more often the casualties were among the descendants of Atherton, and soon many of them lay strewn across the floor, trod on or tripped over by the remaining fighters. Then the children of Atherton broke and ran, retreating pell-mell up the great staircase that led to their branch.

Meredith, Simon thought. He had to find her, though whether to protect her from his family or to protect his family from her he couldn't say.

He followed along as the children of Franklin pursued the children of Atherton up into their branches, many of which had now withered and fallen, with no male heirs left to sustain them, and Simon saw one of Meredith's cousins cornered and slain while pounding at a solid wall that had been an archway just moments before. There was nowhere for the children of Atherton to go except higher into the tree, no way for them to escape except a doomed leap from a window or balcony.

As Simon hurried through the chambers of Meredith's grandfather, he heard a handful of men from among the children of Franklin shouting, "This way! They're up here." The men charged through an archway and up the stairs into the branch of Meredith's uncle Kenneth, Nathan's father. Simon followed.

He caught up with the men just as they burst into a large parlor. At its far end a small crowd stood clustered around Meredith, who knelt over the prone form of Malcolm, her hands pressed to his gory chest as she attempted to heal him. Meredith's mother was there, and a few cousins by way of her uncle Fletcher, and a few other relatives, many of them holding swords. Nathan stood by a window, gazing out. "No!" he cried. "No! It's falling! It's...it's gone."

Meredith sagged. Malcolm's branch had withered. He was dead.

Nathan glanced toward Simon, then drew a sword and moved to Meredith's side. Simon eyed him. Nathan's brothers had been slain in the battle downstairs. And his father. Simon had seen the bodies.

Meredith stood then, turning to regard Simon. She was tall and grim and wrathful, her hair dancing on ethereal winds, arcs of lightning adorning her fingers, eyes full of a fiery hatred. Simon beheld those eyes and knew there could be no more pleading, no more chances. His dreams had died along with Malcolm.

The men beside Simon hesitated, reluctant to confront the family's most powerful sorceress, and Simon didn't blame them. "Get out of here," he told them. "Go. I'll handle her."

The men exchanged glances, then fled.

Meredith strode forward, deathly silent. *Don't take me on*, she'd told him. *It'll be no contest.* He was terribly afraid that she'd been right.

She halted in the center of the room, her arms outspread. "I warned you, Simon." Her voice trembled with rage. "You brought this on yourself—so help you. You think you can face me? Well, here I am. Take your best shot. You won't get another."

One shot at this, Simon thought.

He thrust his palm at her, hurling from it a double dozen points of magical light, which spread apart as they flew, growing and transforming into spinning daggers, so that she faced an incoming wall of lethal blades.

Meredith raised her hands, summoning a ghostly shield. Daggers that struck it vaporized, and the rest sped past her. She regarded Simon almost with pity then.

He turned and bolted back down the stairs.

"Coward!" someone cried.

And Simon *was* afraid. But not of Meredith, not then, as he vaulted the steps three at a time.

For some of the daggers that had passed her by had impaled themselves in Nathan, including one that had caught him full in the throat. Meredith would see this, and would guess that he'd been the intended target after all, and would wonder after the fate of his father and brothers. And then she'd realize...

Simon ran. The branch around him shuddered, the wood fading, becoming dry, gray, pitted. Through the windows he saw leaves turn brown and blow away in great dark clouds.

He neared the archway. A rift appeared in the ceiling ahead, spilling down rays of sunlight between him and safety. As the floor gave way he leapt across the threshold.

A deafening crack. He turned and saw Meredith, back up the tunnel, dashing toward him, dragging her mother by the hand, other relatives running at her side, as the branch plunged from view.

Simon rushed forward, to see what had become of them. But even as he tried to peer out, the archway, now framing blue sky, was absorbed back into the tree, and wood grew to seal the breach, and the portal shrank and shrank, like an eye closing itself, forever.

* * *

A few days later the Archimagus family gathered at their private cemetery to hold a mass burial. The battle had been distinctly one-sided, and the children of Atherton were now a much smaller contingent. They stood in silence, looking weak and frightened. As per the terms of their surrender, they'd accepted full responsibility for the whole unpleasant affair, had handed over all their weapons and valuables, and would soon be exiled. Simon wondered where they'd go. They'd lived their whole lives in Victor's tree. Simon couldn't picture them anywhere else.

After the ceremony, as people drifted off, Simon lingered over the grave marker that read: Meredith Wyland.

His mother sidled up beside him and said, "I knew you could beat her."

He was silent.

She added, "We're safe now. Thanks to you."

He glanced back over his shoulder at Victor's tree, its two halves now absurdly unbalanced. The sun shone between its branches, making Simon squint.

His mother said, "I just hope now you'll be happy." She began to walk away.

He called after her, "What does *that* mean?"

She paused and looked at him, then at the grave marker. "You know, Simon, that dreadful girl always had a most unwholesome influence on you. That's all."

He said slowly, "Mother, I have a terrible intuition that much of what has transpired of late has done so according to some design of yours."

"Of mine, dear?" She laughed. "Oh Simon, you always were such a brooding, mistrustful child. I blame myself. Silly, I know."

She turned away again. He was about to say more when there came a horrendous creaking noise that filled the valley. As the Archimagus family watched, aghast, Victor's tree began to list to the right, from the weight of so many Franklin branches. Then the tree toppled, slamming to the ground, dashing those branches to pieces and raising up a massive plume of dust that could be seen for miles.

* * *

Simon Archimagus galloped his horse along a moonlit ridge. He'd been going on more and more of these solitary rides lately. He liked the calm, the peace. When his horse ran, its hoofbeats and the wind sometimes drowned out his thoughts, for a time.

Finally he rode back to his tree—the tree he'd thought to one day share with Meredith and the children they would have together. Sometimes, on nights like this, as his horse sprinted through the dark, reality seemed less certain, and he would imagine that it had all been a mistake, that she'd survived somehow, secretly, and would come to him. Or that their duel had been just a terrible nightmare, and that his dreams of a life with her were the true state of things.

He passed through the gate, beneath the portcullis of thorn branches, and into the stables.

He made his way up the staircase.

"Dad!" called a boy's voice. "Dad!"

Simon wandered into the kitchen. A blond boy poked his head through the door and said, "Oh, hi Simon. Have you seen my dad?"

"No," Simon said. "I just got back. Is something wrong?"

The boy scowled. "Jessica took my horse and she won't give it back."

"Your...horse?"

"My toy horse," the boy said. "Dad gave it to me, and I *told* her not to touch it, but she took it and now she won't give it back, even though it's mine."

Simon said, "Well, maybe you should just—"

"I should kill her," said the boy, without irony. "Like you killed that evil witch Meredith."

Simon stared. "Look, Brian—"

"I'm Marcus," the boy said.

"Marcus." Simon sighed. "Let's go find your dad, okay?"

The boy trailed Simon through halls and up stairs. Books and toys were scattered about. Sometimes children barrelled past, heedless.

Simon found the adults up at the top of the tree, lounging on the balcony. Bernard was there, and Elizabeth, and Simon's other brothers, and a few other relatives. *It's only temporary*, Bernard had promised, *just until we can find someplace else to live.* But they showed no signs of moving on, and had even begun hinting to Simon that he should command his tree to grow larger, to better accommodate the children.

Simon's mother stepped from the shadows, holding a glass of wine. She beamed at all her sons, together under one roof again, at last.

"Oh, Simon. There you are," she said brightly. "Welcome home."

Author's note: Family Tree

When I moved back to New York after grad school, I spent a lot of time at my grandmother's house in nearby Ridgefield, Connecticut. She was very interested in genealogy, and had a computer program called *Family Tree Maker* that she used to catalog her various photos. One time in 2010 I was over there, and the box for *Family Tree Maker* was out on the counter, and it occurred to me that I could write a story about a literal "family tree"—there would be a family who lived in a magic tree, and a new branch would grow each time a new member of the family was born.

At the time I was imagining it as more of a surreal, literary story, like something out of Borges or Kafka. Then my friend John Joseph Adams told me that he was editing an anthology of wizard stories called *The Way of the Wizard*, and invited me to submit something. I thought of my family tree idea and wondered, "Is there any way I can turn this into a wizard story?" The more I thought about it, the more the wizard idea seemed like a natural fit. It would make sense if the magic tree was created by a powerful wizard.

One of my favorite fantasy series is Roger Zelazny's *Amber* series, which involves a deadly feud between a group of godlike siblings, and it seemed like that sort of violence would be likely if a large family of wizards were all forced to live in a big tree together. It could be a *Romeo and Juliet* thing, I decided, where I had two main characters who were kept apart because they came from opposing factions.

Around that time I had discovered the song "Miserable at Best" by Mayday Parade. I listened to it over and over as I worked on the story, since it had exactly the sort of tragic, melancholy tone that I was going for.

As I thought more about these feuding wizards, it suddenly hit me: If a branch grows when one of them is born, wouldn't it make sense for a branch to *fall off* if one of them dies? That suggested some truly horrifying dramatic possibilities. It also meant making the wizard who created the tree somewhat sinister and unhinged.

By this point I had almost 20 pro sales under my belt, and I was much more in command of my material than I had been just a few years earlier. I knew I could make the story work, but the big question was: could I make it work in 7,000 words or less? (John's wizard anthology had a strict word limit of 7,000 words.) I had to explain the rules of this magic tree, establish the relationship between my two leads, introduce enough side characters to create the sense that there were lots of feuding relatives involved, dramatize an all-out war between the two sides of the family, and bring everything to a satisfying conclusion, all in just 7,000 words. That required some careful planning.

I spent a lot of time working out the rules for the tree, and what would happen at the climax when Simon faces off against Meredith. I filled page after page with tree diagrams. I think the idea that new branches only grow for male heirs was created to solve some logistical problem, but at this point I don't remember the details. (It also seemed like the sort of thing that Victor would do.)

Last year I was contacted by a reader in Finland who was hoping to turn "Family Tree" into a team-based first-person shooter video game. I think that would be really fun, and it would be interesting to have a story-based reason for the arena to keep shrinking as players are eliminated, which would help keep things exciting for the remaining players. So who knows? Maybe you'll be able to battle your friends in a magic tree someday soon.

Nick Greenwood

Red Road

Benjamin had always thought of himself as a strong-willed young mouse, but he had to admit that he was starting to lose heart. Not that he ever regretted penning that pamphlet calling for the abolition of the monarchy, but now he did sometimes wish that he'd used a pseudonym.

He'd been imprisoned in the dungeons beneath Kingsburrow for six months, which meant he still had fifty-four months to go on his sentence. His cell was tiny and dim. Its walls were angular and dirty, and the ceiling dipped so low that Benjamin couldn't even stand up straight. His tunic was in tatters, his fur was matted with grime, and his claws had grown long and jagged. He'd heard no news of his family, his friends, or the outside world. Twice a day, a gruff old mouse with gray whiskers would pass by and deposit a food tray on the floor outside the cell, and then Benjamin would reach between the iron bars to fumble for a tin cup of water and a hunk of moldy cheese.

One evening, two royal guards—tall mice who wore red livery and carried gilded poleaxes—appeared outside the cell. One of them said, "You there, the king wants to see you."

They opened the door, then led Benjamin down the passageway and up a steep spiral stair. Warm light seeped from above, and Benjamin was grateful for it, though when he finally reached the top step and emerged into a torchlit antechamber, the brightness made him squint.

The guards hustled him along. In one hallway, Benjamin passed a dignified and well-groomed mouse who stopped and instructed the guards, "He can't go before the king looking like that. Clean him up." So Benjamin was taken to a parlor where the first female mice he'd seen in far too long doused him with cold water, brushed the tangles from his fur, and dressed him in a fresh tunic.

Finally he was led to an elaborately decorated sitting room. In one corner stood Prince Francis, who wore a red doublet, a black cloak, and a sword and scabbard. Benjamin had never seen Francis up close before. It was true what mice said—Francis, with his thick tawny fur and large, imposing ears, was the tallest and most handsome mouse in all of Kingsburrow. Benjamin felt a touch of apprehension, for mice also said that Francis was a master swordfighter, methodical and relentless.

Francis said, "Do you know why you're here?"

Something—maybe just being clean for the first time in ages—made Benjamin feel bold. He said, "To write a pamphlet?"

Francis actually smiled at that, but one of the guards swung the butt end of a poleaxe into the back of Benjamin's leg, knocking him to one knee. The guard said, "Kneel, you. And show respect."

Francis waved the guard back. "It's all right. Leave him."

Benjamin stood up again. His leg throbbed, but he refused to show any pain. He looked around. "So where's the king?"

Francis said sadly, "I am the king. My father is dead."

Benjamin was stunned. He found it almost impossible to imagine that King Michael, the grim and cruel old mouse who'd reigned for as long as Benjamin could remember, was king no longer.

Francis fixed an intense gaze on him and said, "Does that please you?"

Benjamin stared right back and said nothing, though what he thought was: Yes. Your father was a tyrant.

Francis turned away and began to pace. "What happened was this. My father had always had a passion for exploration. With the realm at peace and prosperous—"

Benjamin snorted. Prosperous? This royal brat obviously knew nothing of the struggles of the common mouse.

The guards bristled and looked to Francis, who hesitated a moment, then ignored the interruption and continued. "My father decided to journey far away to the west, farther than any mouse had ever been. He took with him a band of brave knights." Francis halted then, and stared at nothing.

"My father was slain, along with all his knights save one. That one, Sir Timothy, made it back here. He was mad with fever and badly wounded—he'd been ambushed by Westburrow rats as he returned, and had barely escaped. Before he died, he whispered to me of the beast that killed my father. It was some foreign monster, unlike any we've ever seen." Francis turned back to Benjamin and said, "I will not risk the lives of any more good mice on this matter. We are too few as it is, and winter will be upon us soon. But neither can I sit here while my father's killer remains alive and free. I intend to seek out this beast myself, and slay it."

Benjamin suddenly knew why he'd been summoned here.

And indeed, Francis explained, "I shall need a squire to assist me on my journey, and if I should fall I'll need a messenger to bear the news of my fate back to Kingsburrow. You, Benjamin, are a traitor and a seditionist. Your life I am willing to risk. But know that I also feel, from everything I've heard of you, that you are not truly wicked, and that you even possess a certain misguided nobility. I believe you might deserve and might welcome a chance to redeem yourself. If you agree to accompany me, I will pardon you, and you will be a free mouse again. If you refuse me, you may return to your cell to serve out the remainder of your sentence."

Benjamin considered this. He'd be damned if he'd let the guards drag him back to that cell, and he had always wanted to see the wider world. But he didn't want to die at the hands of Westburrow rats or worse. The wilderness was crawling with all manner of grotesque monstrosities that Benjamin knew only from tales: Snakes. Spiders. Even the terrible owls, said to be the largest of all creatures. Benjamin especially didn't want to die for the sake of a royal fool like Francis. Still, Benjamin quickly made up his mind to accept. Being thrown back in the dungeon would accomplish nothing, but beyond the walls of Kingsburrow he might find opportunities for escape or subterfuge.

He remarked, "A generous offer." Then he mustered all the sincerity he could and said, "Very well, I accept. Thank you, your majesty."

Francis gave a wry grin, as though not totally convinced by this newfound graciousness, but he seemed satisfied. He said, "All right, then. I am pleased to hear it. We will depart on the morrow."

* * *

That night Benjamin slept in a modest bed. The next morning, two guards escorted him to the throne room—a massive chamber where rectangular mirrors hung on red walls, crystal chandeliers dangled from the ceiling, and two golden thrones sat on a carpeted dais. The room was crowded with mice, and their babble filled the air. Every noble mouse in Kingsburrow had come, and Benjamin regarded with bemused disdain their haughty demeanors, their perfumed ringlets of fur, their tight, uncomfortable velvet coats and absurdly long silk gowns.

A side door opened, and Francis emerged and walked to the dais. He wore a crown, and his sword swung at his hip. The crowd fell silent. Francis stood before them and said, "Thank you all for coming. I have an announcement." He surveyed the assembled mice. "You know that my father, our king, perished in a far off land. Now I go to find the beast that slew him and destroy it. I ask that while I am away you heed the wise command of my sister, who shall rule in my place." Francis removed his crown and handed it to a page, who carried it to the front of the crowd and presented it to the princess, a plain-faced female mouse who wore a simple red dress.

Francis drew his sword. He held it aloft and said, "I swear I shall not rest until I have avenged my father's death. I swear it on my sword. I swear it by Sherry, goddess of childbirth and cheese. I am Francis, son of Michael, and I have sworn."

Benjamin found this whole oath business a bit absurd, though for the sake of appearance he applauded along with the crowd.

Francis sheathed the sword, nodded once, said, "Goodbye," and withdrew through the side door. The guards urged Benjamin forward, and he followed after Francis through the door and down a series of corridors. Finally they arrived in the large earthen cavern that housed Kingsburrow's main gates—two tall oak doors studded with iron.

A group of guards, knights, and servants clustered around Francis. Two rucksacks were brought forward. Francis shouldered one, and passed the other to Benjamin. Benjamin had expected to be burdened with the majority of their supplies, and was pleased to note that the two packs seemed equally laden.

A servant handed him a sheathed dagger. He couldn't believe they were making the mistake of arming him. His heart raced, and he tried not to show any surprise or excitement as he took the weapon and strapped it to his belt.

Several guards stepped forward and dragged open the giant doors. Behind the doors stood a portcullis, and the light of morning shone through it and cast a gridwork shadow on the floor. Then the guards turned a winch, and the portcullis creaked as it rose into the ceiling. Francis said some parting words to a few of his knights, then strode out through the gates, and Benjamin followed.

Outside, the sky was clear and blue. A gentle breeze played over Benjamin's fur. He was standing on a hilltop that looked out over a rolling landscape of rich autumn colors. He and Francis followed a wide dirt road that wound down the hill and into the farm country. In the fields, mice toiled with hoes and scythes while in the distance gray smoke plumed from the chimneys of the peasant burrows.

The two of them hiked in silence. The farms disappeared behind them, and then there were only the great bushes and stones looming overhead, and the trees like giant towers. That afternoon they came to a place where the road divided, and they chose the branch that turned west. That way would lead them to the border of the realm—a two week journey—and beyond that lay the lands of the Westburrow rats, one enormous inbred family famous for their cruelty. Francis was obviously hoping to cross those lands without attracting the attention of the rats. Benjamin would rather not take the chance at all.

When night fell, Francis chose a camp spot and built a small fire. He said, "I'll take the first watch. You get some sleep."

Benjamin was sore and exhausted, and compared to the dungeon floor the soft ground looked almost as inviting as a bed. He collapsed into the grass, wrapped himself in a blanket, and slept.

Hours later he was shaken awake by Francis. Benjamin groggily crawled over to a tree and sat with his back against it. Francis spread a blanket on the ground, lay down, and closed his eyes. Soon his breathing became soft and regular.

Benjamin sat there for over an hour, fingering the hilt of the dagger and trying to work up the resolve to do what must be done. One thrust tonight would do more to bring down the monarchy than a million of his silly pamphlets, and he could make up any story he wanted about how Francis had died.

He eased the dagger from its sheath, then crept across the grass. He paused and tried to steady his nerves. He had never wielded a knife before against anything besides cheese. His heart pounded. He felt dizzy. He wondered how much force it would take to puncture a mouse's flesh, how much blood there would be.

He told himself: Just a little closer. Just take one more step. You can do that.

He took another step.

Francis lashed out with one foot, and Benjamin's legs were swept out from under him. His chest hit the ground. Strong hands grabbed his arm and twisted it behind his back, and the dagger was wrenched from his fingers. Then he was rolled over, and he felt the knife pressed against his neck. He stared up at Francis, who knelt over him.

Francis said, "I understand why, because of what you believe, you felt you had to try. Don't try again." He tossed the dagger up and caught it by its blade, then offered it back to Benjamin hilt first. "You should hardly expect me to be off guard at your very first opportunity."

Benjamin eyed the dagger. "You're letting me keep it?"

"I would not leave you defenseless in the wild."

Benjamin felt foolish. He snatched the dagger and slammed it into its sheath, then massaged his arm.

Francis returned to his blanket and lay down again, with his back to Benjamin.

Benjamin said, "So that's it? You're not afraid of me?"

Francis yawned. "No." After a moment, he added, "You would never have gone through with it."

* * *

Benjamin awoke before dawn to find that Francis was already packed and waiting. They continued on their way. Neither of them spoke.

Soon the sun peeked up over the hills and warmed the earth. At mid-morning Francis called a halt, and settled down to rest on a bed of browning pine needles. Benjamin sat a good distance away. Francis chewed on a piece of cheese and said, "So tell me, why do you wish me dead? Wasn't it I who freed you from the dungeons?"

Benjamin scowled and said nothing.

Francis persisted. "Truly. I want to know."

Finally Benjamin burst out, "Forgive me if I'm insufficiently grateful that you ended my unjust confinement after a mere six months. And you only released me so that I could risk my life helping you."

Francis cocked his head thoughtfully. "Even granting, as you say, that you've been used poorly, is that really reason to kill me? Am I so bad?"

Benjamin glared. "Shall I list for you the abuses of your royal house?"

Francis looked away. He said, "My father was a strong ruler. Perhaps too strong. He was a hard mouse to love. No one knows that better than I. But I am not my father."

"It's not about you," Benjamin said. "It's the principle."

Francis turned back to him. "And what principle is that?"

"No more kings. Freedom and equality for all mice."

Francis frowned. "There will always be kings. Whether or not they're called kings. Whether chosen by blood or wealth or fame. Mice need kings."

"You're wrong."

Francis sighed. "So what should I have done? When I found myself born a prince? What would you do? If offered a title?"

Benjamin answered at once, "Renounce it. Abolish the office, and let a more just order replace it."

"Truly? That's what you'd do?"

"Yes."

Francis said, "Your father is a merchant. A prosperous one."

"He is," Benjamin admitted.

"So you're not exactly a common mouse yourself. You've enjoyed means and education far beyond the dreams of most mice. Is that just?"

Benjamin was defensive. "No. But I can't help that. I could have used my position to increase my own wealth and gratify my own desires, as my peers have. Instead I've used the gifts I've received to try to do some good, to try to change things so that more mice get the opportunities I've had. What else could I do? Forswear my family's wealth to live amidst the destitute? What would that accomplish?"

He suddenly felt uncertain. A hint of a smile played over Francis's lips. Benjamin said angrily, "It's not the same thing at all! You can't even compare the two. You, with your palaces and crowns and servants, and all your kneeling and silly oaths."

Francis looked puzzled. "What do you have against oaths?"

"It's pompous," Benjamin said. He knew he should guard his tongue, but he couldn't stop himself. "If you're going to do something, just do it. You don't have to put on a show for the whole world. Swearing to Sherry about this and that."

Francis narrowed his eyes and observed, "You don't believe in Sherry."

Benjamin sneered. "Of course not. Goddess of childbirth and cheese? The very notion is imbecilic. It's peasant superstition."

Francis grinned. "Says the great champion of the common mouse."

Benjamin stopped. He had no retort.

Francis suddenly looked very serious. "Listen to me. When I swear an oath, I invite the court as a courtesy, and I invoke Sherry because what can it hurt? But I doubt that either the court or Sherry would raise much fuss if I chose to break my vow. But I would know. An oath is a promise to yourself, and I would swear my oaths whether or not I was the only mouse around for a hundred miles."

Benjamin said nothing. He saw that Francis meant it.

Francis stood. "Enough. Let's get moving."

That night Benjamin took the first watch while Francis slumbered. As Benjamin sat there staring into the campfire, he understood that he would not try to harm Francis again. For two weeks they hiked west through the wilderness, and each night Benjamin kept watch as best he could and guarded over Francis. It wasn't just that Benjamin felt cowed by how easily he'd been overcome, and abashed at how lightly his actions had been excused. The damning fact was that he sort of liked Francis. Benjamin would never have expected this to be possible, but there it was. Francis was charming and clever, brave and sincere. If Francis had not been born into royalty, Benjamin imagined that the two of them might even have been friends. And Francis treated him as though they *were* friends—friends and equals—though Benjamin was nobody and Francis was king of all the realm. Benjamin hated himself for feeling awed by that title. He had thought himself above such petty sentimentality. But he supposed that he was only a mouse, and that all mice were subject to such feelings to some extent.

One night at dusk, as they crossed a field of long grass, Francis suddenly stopped and said, "What's that?"

Benjamin halted and looked around, but saw nothing. "Where?"

Francis cocked his head. "Listen." Then a look of alarm crossed his face, and he said, "Get down." He crouched and grabbed Benjamin by the shirtfront and pulled him down too. Then Francis slid his sword from its scabbard with one smooth motion, and the sword made barely a whisper as it came free.

Benjamin looked into the sky, which was blue and tan in the fading light. "What? What is it?"

Francis said sternly, "Shhh!" He cocked his head again.

Benjamin waited. A breeze rustled the grass overhead.

Then Francis said, "Damn!" and leapt to his feet. He pulled Benjamin up, shoved him, and said, "Run! Now!"

Benjamin ran. Everywhere blades of grass stood before him, and he pushed between them. The grass whipped at his face. Then a winged shadow fell over him.

A huge scaly foot plucked him from the earth. Talons bit into his sides. Above him beat great dark wings that sent cold air gusting down over him. He twisted to stare up at his captor. It was the dread predator, bane of all mice, the death that comes from above. Benjamin knew its name from a hundred childhood tales. Owl.

He was borne up into the trees. Then the owl dropped him, and he slammed onto a bed of withered grass—a nest. He was too stunned and hurt to move. His tunic grew damp as blood oozed from his sides where the talons had gashed him.

The owl landed, and stood over him. Its massive head was crowned with a set of demonic horns, and below them a pair of huge round eyes gazed out with cold malice. The owl spoke in a high, rasping voice, "I will catch your friend tooo." Then it stepped back, spread its wings, and swooped away.

Benjamin managed to crawl as far as the edge of the nest, then he collapsed. He tugged his dagger from its sheath, but he was so weak he could barely lift the dagger, let alone fight. And what good would a dagger be? What good would *any* weapon be against that monster?

In the dim light, the branches overhead reminded him of the iron bars of his cell back in Kingsburrow, and he felt an ache of longing. Why hadn't he stayed there, safe? He was no knight, to brave the wilds. And now it was hopeless. Soon he'd be dead.

Some time later he heard an awful rustle of feathers. He turned to see the owl settle on the branch beside the nest. It said, "Your friend was tooo quick. I cannot find him."

Benjamin held up the dagger. "Stay back."

The owl laughed. "Foool. You cannot defeat me. I have consumed a hundred mice, and will consume a hundred more. Surrender your weapon and I will grant you the mercy of being swallowed whole. Else I will devour you in pieces."

Benjamin's hand trembled violently. The owl stepped toward him.

Then, from behind the owl, came Francis's voice: "Enough! Release him. I command you."

Benjamin couldn't believe it. Francis had climbed the tree, and now stood on the branch with them. For a moment Benjamin dared to hope that Francis could somehow bargain with the owl.

The owl's head rotated all the way around to face Francis. "And whoo are you?"

Francis stepped forward. "I am Francis, son of Michael and king of this realm." He raised his sword so that its edge was aimed at the owl's throat. "I am your death, if you defy me."

Benjamin felt a fresh rush of panic. Was Francis crazy?

The owl said, "I have dined on the bones of a hundred mice. But never a king. Yoou will be a true delicacy, Francis, son of Michael."

It fluttered toward him, its claws reaching for him. Francis leapt at it, his sword poised to strike. The owl panicked and tried to reverse course, and Francis thrust his sword straight into its looming right eye. The owl screeched and flopped backward, and Francis yanked the sword free and landed lightly on the branch and kept advancing.

The owl shambled to its feet. Blood streamed from its ruined eye. Francis circled to the owl's right, so it couldn't see him, and it turned to try to keep him in view. It wiped blood from its face, then hunched forward to seek him with its good eye, and Francis stabbed that eye too, and the beast was blinded. Then Francis hacked at the owl—at its thigh, its belly, its wings. The owl moaned and staggered away.

Then, as it teetered at the edge of the branch, Francis leapt onto its chest. He grabbed its feathers with his left hand and with his right he rammed his sword straight up through its throat, deep into its head. The owl toppled backward—with Francis still clutching it—and together they plunged over the side.

Benjamin's pain gradually subsided. Then he climbed from the nest, walked along the branch, and scrambled down the tree's trunk.

When he reached the ground, he found Francis waiting there, unharmed and resting against the great mass of the owl's corpse.

Benjamin stared in amazement. An owl was a thing out of nightmare, the most feared of monsters, and Francis had just slain one quickly and with pitiless efficiency. Benjamin had heard that Francis was a master swordfighter, but this was beyond anything Benjamin had imagined. He was even more abashed now to have ever thought of raising a weapon against Francis. When Francis had a sword in his hand, he was terrifying, unstoppable.

Benjamin said, "I can't believe you did that—climbed up there, fought that thing—to save me."

Francis said simply, "You're one of my subjects. It's my duty to protect you."

Normally Benjamin would have bristled at being called anyone's subject, but now he was too tired, sore, and grateful to be alive to care. So all he said was, "Thank you."

A few days later they crossed the border of the realm, and entered the lands of the Westburrow rats.

* * *

One night, by the light of the campfire, Benjamin said, "Tell me of this beast that we go to slay. The one that…killed your father. What did Sir Timothy say of it?"

Francis looked grim, and for a moment Benjamin was afraid he wouldn't answer, but then Francis said softly, "When I met with Sir Timothy, he was delirious and near death, and much of what he told me was without sense. He spoke of a black and barren land where nothing would grow—as if some demonic agency had leached all life from the soil. The very night my father's party entered that land they were set upon by a strange creature. Sir Timothy whispered that it was giant, with burning eyes and a voice like thunder. Clearly, these were the fancies of madness. Still, I do not doubt that it is some formidable foe, to defeat a band of knights."

Benjamin said, "What if it defeats you?" He was surprised to feel so unhappy at the prospect.

Francis said, "Then my wise sister will rule, and the realm will likely be better for it."

These were brave, wry words, but beneath them Benjamin sensed something colder. Francis had no intention of being defeated. He meant to crush this beast, as he'd crushed every enemy he'd ever faced.

A few days passed. One afternoon, as Francis was making camp for the night, Benjamin set off into the brush to gather firewood.

As he returned, he heard Francis cry out. Then cruel, guttural laughter echoed through the forest. Benjamin threw down the twigs and drew his dagger.

From the direction of the camp came an unfamiliar voice: "There are two rucksacks here. You three, search the area, find his friend."

Benjamin ducked into a bush, then peered between the leaves as three tall black rats passed by. Their fur was greasy and patchy, and they wore odd bits of scavenged armor and carried rusty scimitars. Westburrow rats.

Benjamin crept to the edge of the camp, and saw with horror that Francis had been captured. Two rats held Francis between them so that he dangled with his toes barely brushing the ground. Another four rats were rifling through the rucksacks.

The rats must have taken Francis by surprise. But if he could just get his hands on his sword, he'd no doubt make short work of them. Where was the sword?

There. It was being held by a rat who seemed to be the leader. He was huge, and his fur was brindled and shaggy. He paced by the spot where Francis hung, and Francis glanced at the sword. The leader said, "Oh, you want this?" He held it up. "What do you think you're going to do with this toy, little mouse?"

Francis said dangerously, "Let me show you."

The leader laughed. He inspected the sword. "Too small. Useless." He tried to break it over his knee, but the sword was the finest mouse steel, and refused to snap.

The rats were all distracted. Benjamin thought he might be able to disrupt them and give Francis a chance to break loose.

But why should Benjamin take the risk? All he had to do was slip away, and then he'd be free, and there'd be one fewer monarch in the world. He thought of all the months he'd spent rotting in the dungeon merely for speaking out, and the memory made him feel vengeful.

Then he stared at Francis, hanging there. Benjamin couldn't just leave him. Francis would be killed, or maybe taken prisoner, which was worse. There were horrid rumors of what was done to mice who were dragged down into the depths of Westburrow, and none of those mice were ever seen again. And Francis had saved Benjamin from the owl...

Enough. Benjamin's mind was made up.

He leapt from the brush, dashed up behind the rat leader, and plunged the dagger deep into the rat's lower back. The leader bellowed and dropped Francis's sword. Benjamin yanked the dagger loose.

The rats stood shocked. Then Francis slammed the heel of his foot into the groin of the rat to his right. The rat shrieked and released Francis's right hand, which Francis then raked across the eyes of the rat to his left. That rat stumbled back, clutching its face, and Francis dropped to the ground in a crouch, then sprang forward and sprinted for his sword.

The leader spun around. He gripped his wounded back with one hand while with the other he drew forth a heavy scimitar. "You are going to regret that, little mouse," he growled. "When we bring you back to Westburrow, I'll see that you get special attention."

Benjamin backed away, and waved the dagger warningly. The leader advanced on him.

Francis ducked a scimitar cut and leapt for his sword. Another rat jumped on him, and they went down together. Francis kicked, stretching out his hand to feel for his sword. His fingers brushed its pommel.

Come on! Benjamin thought desperately. The leader loomed over him, backing him against a tree.

Francis wrapped his fingers around the hilt of the sword.

* * *

When the rats were dead, Francis said, "That was a brave thing you did. I owe you my life. From the first time I heard of your case, I sensed that there was great potential in you. When I met you, I knew my guess had been correct. I am proud to see that I was not mistaken." He raised his sword. "Kneel, Benjamin."

Benjamin was full of awe. He knelt.

Francis touched the flat of the blade to each of Benjamin's shoulders, and said, "Arise, Sir Benjamin."

Benjamin rose, euphoric. He had never dreamed of anything like this...well, maybe as a child, but that had been so long ago. He had given up on such dreams.

Francis now spoke of secret gestures and mottoes that would allow Benjamin to prove his rank to the knights of Kingsburrow. Benjamin listened as best he could. But all he could think of was the throne room, and how upon his return all those rich and noble snobs would have to bow to him—to him, who had been a condemned prisoner—and call him "sir."

He said, "Thank you, your majesty," and he meant it.

Francis smiled. "You've earned it."

Two weeks later, as evening fell, they came to the edge of a wasteland. Just as Sir Timothy had said, the ground seemed unnatural and accursed—smooth, black, and hard as stone. Nothing grew there. Nothing lived there.

Francis stepped onto the black earth. Then he turned to Benjamin and said, "From here I must go on alone. This is *my* battle. I ask that you wait for me here. If I have not returned by morning, you must make the long journey back to Kingsburrow and tell my sister that I am dead."

Benjamin was startled to find himself blurt out, "I want to come with you. I want to help."

"My friend," Francis said, "you've already saved my life once. You've done more than I ever could have asked. I cannot allow you to take any more risks on my account. Sherry willing, I will see you at dawn. If not, it has been my honor to know you. Remain here, and do as I have bid. Your king commands it."

Before Benjamin could object again, Francis strode off into the wastes. Benjamin stared after him, then sat down in the grass.

Night came on quickly, and thick pale mist rose up to shroud that gloomy, barren land. Benjamin felt anxious and uncertain. He wondered if he should go after Francis.

He'd been ordered to stay here. But normally he would never bow to the will of a king. Then again, normally he would never risk his life to help a king either. He felt adrift. The ideologies that had guided him all his life now seemed as vague and insubstantial as the fog. The only thing he was certain of was that Francis was in danger.

Benjamin stood. He took a deep breath, then stepped onto the black ground.

He tried to follow in the direction that Francis had gone, but the mists were dense and swirling, and Benjamin soon lost his way. For a time he stumbled on aimlessly. Finally he halted, panting.

Then he heard something—a rumble, a growl, an endless, breathless roar. A beast with a voice like thunder. He ran toward the sound, which grew closer and louder. Out in the fog appeared two patches of light that he knew were the beast's burning eyes. They shone impossibly bright, and cast before them great white beams.

A breeze parted the fog. Away across the plain, Francis stood with his feet planted and his sword held ready.

Benjamin yelled, "Francis!"

If Francis heard, he gave no sign. His gaze was fixed on the rapid approach of the monster. He called to it, "Hear me, fiend. I am Francis— son of Michael, whom you slew. I have come to exact vengeance for my father. Look upon my sword and tremble, for I have never been defeated by mouse or beast. Now, face my wrath!" He charged, his sword held high as he screamed, "For Michael! Michael and Kingsburrow!"

The beast drew nearer. It was gigantic, bigger than an owl, a hundred times bigger, bigger than anything Benjamin could have ever imagined. It bore down on Francis. Then the mists rolled in again and smothered Benjamin, and for a time he saw nothing. Finally, he spotted two blurry red lights that faded in the distance as the beast sped away.

Benjamin dashed to where Francis had stood, but Francis was gone, vanished. Benjamin staggered in circles, seeking him.

It wasn't until much later, when the fog melted to nothing, and the clouds blew away from the moon, and the moon shone down on the earth, that Benjamin slowly realized, with an uncomprehending horror, that the ground beneath his feet was red.

* * *

Benjamin, desolate, dazed, wandered away, only vaguely aware of the soft squelching that his boots made each time he took a step, of the bloody footprints he left behind him. He thought: Francis. Oh, Francis, why? You were a great mouse. You would have been a good king. I would have followed you.

Finally he halted. A familiar object lay before him, though his confused mind took a moment to grasp what he was seeing.

A sword. Francis's sword, yet unbroken.

From somewhere behind him there arose a low roar. He snatched up the sword and whirled, terrified, clutching its hilt to his chest. His breath came fast and shallow.

But he saw no blazing eyes, no beams of light. There was only the wind, picking up now, gusting across the plain.

The monster was gone. But the fear remained, and would remain, he knew, for so long as that beast was out there. That ghastly and unnatural thing that could crush a mouse flat.

Benjamin studied the sword—the sword of Francis, that had vanquished the terrible owl, and brought ruin upon the vile rats of Westburrow. Then he knew what he must do. He could not let Francis's death be for nothing.

Benjamin was the only mouse around for a hundred miles. He raised the sword above him and said, "Francis...I...I'll go back to Kingsburrow. I'll tell them what happened here, how heroic you were. I'll make them see. I will raise up such an army of mice as this world has never seen, and I will return here, and find some way to destroy that beast forever. I...I am Sir Benjamin, knight of Kingsburrow...and I have sworn."

Author's note: Red Road

In 2003 I attended a writing workshop taught by legendary science fiction author James Gunn at the University of Kansas. (Not to be confused with the much younger James Gunn who directed *Guardians of the Galaxy*.) At one point some of my classmates started discussing the *Redwall* series by Brian Jacques, about a medieval world where the heroes are mice and the villains are rats, cats, foxes, etc. I said, "Wouldn't it be funny if in one of the books, a bunch of mice set out on a quest, and then they all just get run over by a truck, and that's the end of the story? Instead of *Redwall* it could be called *Red Road*."

A few years later, when I was living in Los Angeles, I thought back on that conversation and said to myself, "You know, that's actually not bad. I think I'm going to write that."

I had heard a story about a socialist author who had accepted a knighthood from the British government. When his friends asked him if the whole idea of hereditary titles wasn't completely opposed to everything he stood for, he conceded that it was, but basically said, "Yeah but I'm a knight now. How cool is that? I couldn't resist."

I thought about that a lot. It's easy to rail against the system when you're on the outside looking in. It's a lot harder to rail against the system when you start accruing serious benefits from it. I get that. Being a knight seems cool to me too.

I vividly remember writing the part where Francis fights the owl. I knew what had to happen, but how does a mouse kill an owl? I remember pacing around my apartment, swinging a coat hanger (which I pretended was a sword), imagining this giant owl looming over me, and thinking, "How the heck am I going to kill this thing?" Go for the eyes, I decided. Blind it. That's the only way.

Another memory that really sticks with me is the time when I read the story at a bookstore, and the whole audience cheered when I got to the line that goes, "When the rats were dead..."

People have had varied reactions to the ending of the story. For each person who complains that it was obvious from the start that the beast was a car, there's another who doesn't get that the beast was a car even after they finish the story. My favorite response was from the editor who bought the story, who said that every time he's driving through the woods at night, he thinks of my story and takes care not to run over any little mice that might be out on a quest.

Some people complain that the ending is nothing but a cruel joke. I guess I can't protest too much, since the story did in fact begin as a cruel joke, but in its final form I find the ending really tragic and poignant. Life is complicated. Sometimes you find out that your enemies are better people than you are. Sometimes really good people believe really bad things. Sometimes there are battles worth fighting that can't be won.

"Red Road" was produced as an audio drama for Episode 141 of the *Journey Into…* podcast. The host offered to cast me as one of the characters. I declined, saying I'm not an actor. He encouraged me to give it a try, saying he listened to *Geek's Guide to the Galaxy* and really liked my voice. I reluctantly agreed to play Francis. The host came back later and said that the actor who was going to play Benjamin wanted to do a British accent. Could I do a British accent? I said definitely not. We decided to swap parts, since it made more sense for Francis to have a British accent. I'm still not sure how great my performance was, but if you want to hear me play a talking mouse, you can give that a listen.

HyeJeong Park

Save Me Plz

Meg hadn't heard from Devon in four months, and she realized that she missed him. So on a whim she tossed her sword and scabbard into the back seat of her car and drove over to campus to visit him.

She'd always thought that she and Devon would be one of those couples who really did stay friends afterward. They'd been close for so long, and things hadn't ended *that* badly. Actually, the whole incident seemed pretty silly to her now. Still, she'd been telling herself that the split had been for the best—with her working full-time and him still an undergrad. It was like they were in two different worlds. She'd been busy with work, and he'd always been careless about answering email, and now somehow four months had passed without a word.

She parked in the shadow of his dorm, then grabbed her sword and strapped it to her jeans. She approached his building. A spider, dog-sized, iridescent, rappelled toward her, its thorned limbs plucking the air. She dropped a hand to the hilt of her sword. The spider wisely withdrew, back to its webbed lair amid the eaves.

She had no keycard, so she waited for someone to open the door. She checked her reflection. Eyes large, hips slender, ears a bit tapered at the tips. She looked fine. (Though she'd never be a match for the imaginary elf-maid Leena.)

Finally someone exited, an unfamiliar brown-haired girl. Meg caught the door and passed into the lobby. She climbed the stairs and walked down the hall to Devon's door. She knocked.

His roommate Brant answered, looking half-asleep or maybe stoned. "Hey Meg," Brant mumbled—casually, as if he'd just seen her yesterday. "How's the real world?"

"Like college," she said, "but with less Art History. Is Devon here?"

"Devon?" Brant seemed confused. "Oh. You don't know." He hesitated. "He dropped out."

"What?" She was startled.

"Just packed up and left. Weeks ago. He said it didn't matter anymore. He was playing that game all the time." Brant didn't need to say *which* game. Least of all to her. "He said he found something, huge. In the game. Then he went away."

"Went away where? Is he all right?"

Brant shrugged. "I don't know, Meg. He didn't tell me. You could email him, I guess. Or try to find him online. He's always playing that game." Brant shook his head. "And I mean *always*."

* * *

Meg strode to her car. She chucked her sword in the back, slid into the driver's seat, and slammed the door.

Devon was the smartest guy she'd ever met, and the stupidest. How could he drop out with just one year left? Sadly, she wasn't all that surprised.

She'd met him at an off-campus party her junior year. They'd ended up on the same couch. Before long he was on his third beer and telling her, "I didn't even want to go to college. My parents insisted. I had a whole other plan."

She said, "Which was?"

"To be a prince." He gave a grandiose shrug. "I think I'd make a pretty good prince." He noted her skeptical expression and added, "But not prince of like, England. I'm not greedy. Prince of Monaco would be fine. Wait, is that even a country?"

"Yes," she said.

"Good," he declared, thumping his beer on the endtable. "Prince of Monaco. Or if that's taken…"

"Liechtenstein," she suggested.

"Liechtenstein, great!" he agreed, pointing. "Or Trinadad and Tobago."

She shook her head. "It's not a monarchy. No princes."

"No princes?" He feigned outrage. "Well, screw *them* then. Liechtenstein it is."

After that she noticed him everywhere. He seldom went to class or did coursework, so he was always out somewhere—joking with friends in the dining hall, pacing around the pond, or sitting under a tree in the central quad, doodling. His carefree independence was oddly endearing, especially to her who was always so conscientious, though later his indifference to school worried her. She'd ask, "What'll you do after you graduate?"

He'd just shrug and say, "Grades don't matter. Just that you have the degree."

And now he'd dropped out.

Angry, she started her car. She drove back to her apartment.

She emailed him repeatedly, but got no response. Mutual friends hadn't heard from him. His mom thought he was still in school. Meg got really worried. Finally, she resorted to something she'd promised herself she'd never do—she drove over to the mall to buy the game.

It was called *Realms of Eldritch*, a groundbreaking multiplayer online game full of quests and wizards and monsters. Some of the game was based on real life: People carried magic swords, and many of the enemies were real, such as wolves or goblins or giant spiders. And like in real life there was a gnome who sometimes appeared to give you quests or hints or items. But most of it was pure fantasy: dragons and unicorns and walking trees and demon lords.

And elves. In the game store, Meg eyed the box art. Leena, the golden-haired and impossibly buxom elf-maid, grinned teasingly.

Meg had a complicated relationship with Leena (especially considering that Leena wasn't real). The year before, Meg had been riffling through Devon's notebook and had come across a dozen sketches of Leena. The proportions were off, but each sketch came closer and closer to being a perfect representation. Meg had begun teasing Devon that he was in love with Leena. She had also once, foolishly, dressed up as Leena in bed, for Devon's twenty-first birthday. It was just a campy gag, but he'd seemed way too into it. He'd even called her "Leena." She'd never worn the costume again, and he'd never brought it up. He'd been pretty drunk that night, and she'd wondered if he even remembered her looking like someone else.

She bought the game (planning to return it the next day) and started home. In the rearview mirror she saw a flock of giant bats tailing her. She tensed, ready to slam the brakes and reach for her sword, but finally the bats veered off and vanished into the west.

Back at her apartment, she opened the game box and dumped its contents out on her coffee table. Half a dozen CDs, a thick manual, some flyers, a questionnaire. It seemed so innocuous. Hard to believe that this little box could destroy a relationship. She and Devon had been so happy together for almost a year before he got caught up in this game.

She installed it. As progress bars chugged, she thumbed through the manual, which described the rules in mind-numbing detail—races, classes, attributes, combat, inventory, spells. She'd never understood how someone as smart and talented as Devon could waste so much time on this stuff.

Maybe she could have understood if the game at least featured some brilliant story, but Devon spent all his time doing "level runs"—endlessly repeating the same quest over and over in hopes of attaining some marginally more powerful magical item. And even after he'd become as powerful as the game allowed, he still kept playing, exploiting different bugs so that he could duplicate superpowered items or make himself invincible. How could someone who read Heidegger for fun so immerse himself in a subculture of people too lazy or daft to type out actual words, who instead of "Someone please help" would type "sum1 plz hlp"?

Meg, on the rare occasions that she permitted herself solitary recreation, preferred Jane Austen novels or independent films. She'd once told Devon, "I'm more interested in things that are *real*."

He'd been playing the game. Monitor-glow made his head a silhouette. He said, "What's *real* is just an accident. No one designed reality to be compelling." He gestured to the screen. "But a fantasy world *is* so designed. It takes the most interesting things that ever existed—like knights in armor and pirates on the high seas—and combines them with the most interesting things that anyone ever dreamed up—fire-breathing dragons and blood-drinking vampires. It's the world as it *should* be, full of wonder and adventure. To privilege reality simply because it *is* reality just represents a kind of mental parochialism."

She knew better than to debate him. But she still thought the game was vaguely silly, and she refused to play it, though he often bugged her to join in. He'd say, "It's something we could do together."

And she'd answer, "I just don't want to."

And he'd say, "Give it a try. I do things *I* don't want to because they're important to you. Sometimes I even end up liking them."

But by then Meg had already spent far too many hours sitting on the couch watching him play the game, or hearing about it over candlelit dinners, and she didn't intend to do anything to justify him spending any more time on it.

It was hard some nights, after they'd made love, to lie there knowing that he was just itching to slip from her embrace and go back to the game. To know that a glowing electronic box full of imaginary carnage beckoned him in a way that her company and conversation and even body no longer could.

Finally, she couldn't take it anymore. Though she knew she might lose him, she announced, "Devon. Look. I don't know how else to say this. It's that game or me. I'm not kidding."

He released the controls and swiveled in his chair. He gave her a wounded look and said, "That's not fair, Meg. I'd never make you give up something you enjoyed."

She stood her ground. "This is something I'm asking you to do. For me."

"You really want me to delete it?"

"Yes," she said. Oh god, yes.

He bit his lip, then said, "Fine." He fiddled with the computer, then turned to her and added, "There, it's gone. All right?"

"All right," she said, euphoric. And for a few weeks things were great again, like they used to be.

But one night she came over and found him playing it again. She stared. "What are you doing?"

He glanced at her and said, "Oh, hi." He noticed her agitation, and explained, "My guild really needed me for this one quest."

"You told me you deleted it."

He turned back to the screen. "Yeah, I had to reinstall the whole thing. Don't worry, I'll delete it again tomorrow."

Meg was furious. "You *promised.*"

"Come on," he said, "I haven't played for *three weeks*. It's just this one time."

She stomped away. "I told you, Devon. That game or me. Isn't that what I said?"

"Meg, don't leave, okay? Would you just—" Something happened in the game, and he jumped. "Shit! He got me."

She left, slamming the door. Devon called out, "Meg, wait." But he didn't run after her.

She expected him to call and apologize, beg her forgiveness, but he didn't. Days passed, then she sent him a curt email saying that maybe it would be better if they just stayed friends from now on, and—disappointingly—he had agreed.

The game finished installing. Meg hovered the mouse pointer over the start icon. She felt strangely ambivalent. She'd fought so hard against this damn game, and now she was actually going to run it. She also felt an inexplicable dread, as if the game would suck her in the way it had sucked in Devon, and she'd never escape. But that was silly. She was just using it to contact him. She double-clicked.

The game menu loaded. She created a character and chose all the most basic options—human, female, warrior. The name Meg was taken, so she added a random string of numbers, Meg1274, and logged in. The game displayed a list of servers. Meg did a search for his character, Prince Devonar. He was the only player listed on a server named Citadel of Power. She connected to it.

She typed, "Hi Devon." No response.

She tried again. "Devon? It's me, Meg. Are you there?"

Finally, he answered. "Meg?"

She typed, "Are you OK?"

A long pause. "I found something. In the game. Unbelievable. But now I'm stuck. Need help."

Was this whole situation some elaborate setup to get her to play the game with him? But that was crazy. Not even Devon would drop out of school as part of such a ruse. She typed, "Devon, call me. OK?"

Another pause. "Can't call. Trapped. Plz, Meg, help me. You're the only one who can."

"I can't help," she typed. "I'm only level 1."

"Not in the game," he typed back. "In real life. Ask the gnome. Plz, Meg. I really need you. Can't stay. Meg, save me plz."

She typed frantically. "Devon, wait. What's going on? Where are you???"

But Prince Devonar was gone.

* * *

Devon had said to ask the gnome. But that wasn't so easy.

No one really understood what the gnome was. He seemed to wander through time and space. He was usually benevolent, appearing to those in need and offering hints or assistance or powerful items. But he was also fickle and enigmatic. He seemed to only appear after you'd given up hope of finding him. He also seemed to prefer locales with corners that he could pop out from and then disappear around.

So Meg parked downtown and wandered the back alleys. She couldn't stop thinking of Devon's final words: "Save me plz." If only the gnome would show himself. Hours passed.

Forget it. She was going home. She crossed the street—

And then the gnome, before her.

Crimson-robed, white-bearded, flesh like dry sand. One eye brown, kindly. The other blue, inscrutable. In a soft and alien voice he observed, "On a quest."

Finally. She wanted to grab him. "Where's Devon? Tell me."

"This is your path." The gnome pointed to the road at her feet, then westward.

Meg nodded. "I'll follow it."

The gnome turned his kindly brown eye upon her. "Have no fear, though obstacles lie in your way. Your victory is assured, foretold by prophecy: 'When the warrior-maid with love in her heart sets out, sword in her right hand, wand in her left, nothing shall stand before her.'"

"Wand?" she said.

The gnome reached up his sleeve and drew forth a thin black rod, two feet long. He whispered, "The most dire artifact in all the world, the Wand of Reification." He handed it to her. It chilled her fingers, and was so dark that it seemed to have no surface. He said, "Imbued with the power to give form to dreams. It may only be used three times."

Devon had said once that in the game there were items that vanished after you used them. So he never used them. He'd beat quest after quest without them, though they would've aided him considerably. He was always afraid he'd need them later. He'd asked, "What does that say about me?"

and she'd said, "You're afraid of commitment?" and he'd laughed. It wasn't so funny now though, as she clutched this wand, so potent yet so ephemeral. How could she ever use it?

When she looked again, the gnome had vanished.

* * *

Meg retrieved her car and set off the way the gnome had pointed. The road: a double yellow line and two lanes of black asphalt, bordered by sidewalks. She drove. Skyscrapers and then suburbs fell away behind her. She passed clusters of thatched-roof cottages. Men farmed and cows grazed and windmills turned. Sometimes ancient oaks pressed in close to the road. Sometimes she saw castles on distant hills.

The needle on her gas gauge sank, and she hoped to find a station, but there were none. Finally, the engine died. She left her car and set off down the sidewalk.

Twilight came. Then the long line of streetlamps lit up, casting eerie white splotches on the darkened street, creating a tableau somehow dreamlike and unreal. She thought of how Devon and Brant would sometimes smoke pot and then get into long, rambling discourses on the nature of existence. During one such conversation, Devon had said, "Do you know anything about quantum mechanics?"

"Not really," Brant had replied.

So Devon said, "Well, in the everyday world, things exist. If I leave a book on this table, I know for sure that it's there. But when you get down to the subatomic level, things don't exist in the same way. They only exist as *probabilities*, until directly observed. How do you explain that?"

Brant countered, "How do *you* explain it?"

Devon smirked. "Like this: Our world isn't real. It's a *simulation*. An incredibly sophisticated one, but not without limits. It can keep track of every molecule, but not every last subatomic particle. So it estimates, and only starts figuring out where specific particles are when someone goes looking for them."

"That's so weird," Brant said.

Meg heard a vehicle approaching from behind. Then its headlights lit the street. She glanced back into the glare, then kept walking. The vehicle slowed. It followed, in a way she didn't like. Finally, it pulled even with her. A black SUV, its windows open. From the darkness came a rasping, lascivious voice, "Hey, where you going?"

She ignored it, walked.

"Need a ride?" The voice waited. "Hey, I'm talking to you." A long pause. "What, you too good to talk to us?" When Meg didn't answer, the voice hissed, "Bitch," and the driver gunned the engine. The truck sped off.

Meg watched it go, then watched its taillights flare a sudden red challenge, watched it swing around, its headlights sweeping the trees, watched it come on, two coronas of searing white. Cackles rose from its windows. Meg drew her sword and stepped into the street. The car horn shrieked.

She slashed upward, between the lights, and the truck split. Its two halves swept past on either side. Its right half sped into a tree. Its left half flipped over and rolled thirty yards along the pavement.

Meg followed after. She neared the wreckage. A scraggly vermillion arm reached up through one window, then a face appeared—hairless, dark-eyed, ears like rotting carrots. A goblin. He squirmed free and dropped to the ground. A second goblin crawled from beneath the wreck.

The first drew a long wavy dagger. "Look what you did to my truck!"

But before he could start forward, the second grabbed him and leaned in close. "It's *her*. The Facilitator."

The first goblin studied Meg, and his eyes widened. He sheathed his dagger. "So it is." He touched two knuckles to his gnarled red brow. "I apologize, my lady. We owe you much."

The goblins edged around her, then hurried over to the other half of their vehicle. They dragged out two more goblins, who were seriously injured, and departed together.

And then they were gone. But their words stayed with Meg, and perplexed her, and troubled her greatly.

* * *

She had other adventures, vanquished other foes, and the road led ever on. Finally, she came to the peak of a rocky prominence and looked out over a mile-long crater. The street ran downhill until it reached the gates of a dark and forbidding fortress. She knew that this must be the Citadel of Power and that Devon must be within. She hiked down to it.

The drawbridge had been lowered. She eased across, sword in her right hand, Wand of Reification in her left. The portcullis was up and the gate lay open. She slipped into the yard.

Empty. She crept sideways, keeping the wall at her back. She held her breath, heard nothing.

She peeked into the central yard and saw a grand stone altar. She crept closer. An object lay upon it. A wand.

The Wand of Reification.

She glanced at her left hand, which still held *her* wand. She'd thought it unique. She already had a Wand of Reification, and hadn't even used it. She shrugged, took the second wand and tucked it in her belt, then moved on.

She searched bedchambers, kitchens, a great hall, a cavernous ballroom, all empty. She entered an ancient armory. Crossbows, shields, pikes—

Wands.

Rack after rack of wands. Hundreds of wands. A thousand? Wands of Reification all, she felt sure. She didn't understand.

She went outside and crossed the yard again. The sky had begun to dim, and now she saw faint light in a tower window. She ran toward it.

Which hall? Which way? She dashed through rooms and under arches and up spiral stairs. Finally she found it—a door, shut, wan light spilling from beneath. She hurled herself against the door, and burst into the room with her sword raised.

A bedchamber. Posters on the walls. Devon's posters, from his old dorm room.

Light from a computer monitor. Someone sat before it. He turned. Devon.

He smiled and said, "Meg. Hey!"

* * *

She ran to him, enfolded him in her arms along with sword and wand and everything, and said, "Are you all right? I was so worried."

I'm fine." He squeezed her and chuckled. "Everything's fine." He pulled back, brushed aside a lock of her hair, and kissed her. He was so tall and handsome, tawny-haired and emerald-eyed. He wore a gold medallion over a purple doublet with dagged sleeves. "Come on. You're exhausted." He led her to the bed, and they sat down together. He took her sword and wand and laid them on the nightstand.

She rested her cheek against his shoulder. She stared at the familiar posters (the nearest was an Edmund Leighton print) and whispered, "Aren't you in trouble? I thought you were. Devon, I don't understand what's happening."

"Shhh." He stroked her hair. "Just relax, okay? I'll explain everything."

He said that the real world was just a simulation, like a game. He didn't know who'd made it, but whoever they were they didn't seem to show themselves or ever interfere. Like any game, it had bugs. Many of these involved *Realms of Eldritch*, which was itself a new, fairly sophisticated simulation, and sometimes things got confused, and an item from the game got dumped into the real world. That's how he'd gotten the Wand of Reification, which could be used to alter almost anything. With it he'd set things in motion. He said, "Do you understand so far?"

She nodded, tentatively. It was all so strange.

He said that since the wand could only be used three times, he'd had to go looking for another bug, some way to duplicate the wand. Fortunately, there *was* one. But it was very specific: If a female warrior set out to rescue a man she loved, and was given the wand by the gnome, the game set a quest tag wrong, and let her acquire the wand again at the Citadel of Power, leaving her with two. Devon said, "Ah, speak of the devil." Meg raised her head.

The gnome, his head canted so that his mysterious blue eye watched her. Devon reached toward the nightstand, took the wand, and handed it to the gnome.

Meg murmured, "Why are you giving it to him?"

Devon said, "So he can give it to you again."

The gnome stuck the wand in his sleeve, gave a curt nod, and hobbled from the room.

Meg was mystified. "You said this bug creates an extra wand?"

"Yes."

She thought of the armory. "But you have *hundreds* of wands."

"Over a thousand," Devon said. He took the spare wand from her belt and placed it on the bed. "One for each time you've come here. One thousand two hundred and seventy four wands."

She was stunned. "But...I don't remember..."

He told her, somewhat cryptically, "When you restart a quest, you lose all your progress."

Meg stood, pulling from his embrace. "Devon, you *lied* to me. You said you were trapped here."

He stood too. "I'm sorry. I had to. You had to be on a quest to save me, otherwise it wouldn't work."

She fumed. "I was in danger. I was attacked!"

He held back a smile. "And what happened?"

"I..." She hesitated. "I beat them."

"Of course. Meg, you're level 60. You have the most powerful sword in the game. Nothing can harm you. There was never any danger. Didn't you get my prophecy?"

"*Your* prophecy?"

"That's why I wrote it," he said. "That's why I made the gnome recite it. So you wouldn't be afraid."

She paced to the window and looked out. This was all too much. "So now you've got a thousand wands. Why? What are you planning to do?"

He came and put his arm around her, and said softly, "To remake the world. To make it what it should have been all along—a place of wonder and adventure, without old age or disease. A place where death is only temporary—like in the game."

"You're going to make the game real," she said.

"Yes."

She felt apprehension. "I don't know, Devon. Maybe you shouldn't be messing around with this. I like the world just fine the way it is."

"Meg." His tone was affectionate. "You always say that."

She felt a sudden alarm. "What?"

Again, he suppressed a smile. "It's already begun. Ages ago. You think the world always had goblins and giant spiders and a gnome running around handing out magic items? That's all from the game. *I* made that happen."

She felt adrift. "I...don't remember."

"No one does," he said. "The wand makes things real. Not just physical, but *real*. Only *I* know that things used to be different, and now so do you."

And the goblins, Meg thought. They knew.

Devon kept going. "That's what's so funny, Meg. No matter what I do, no matter what crazy, incongruous reality I create, you always want things to stay exactly the way they are. That's just your personality. But we can't stop now. There's still so much to do. And you'll love it when I'm done, you'll see. You have to trust me."

"I don't know," she said. "I...need to think about it."

"Of course," Devon replied. "Take all the time you need."

* * *

So she stayed with Devon at the Citadel of Power, and they ate meals together in the dining hall, and danced together in the grand ballroom, and after that first night they slept together again too. She was still in love with him. She always had been. Even the game knew it.

They hiked together around the crater's rim, and he told her of the world as it *had* been, when there'd been no magic at all, and humans were the only race that could speak, and adventure was something that most people only dreamt of. It sounded dismal, and yet Meg wondered, "Could you reverse the process? Put everything back the way it was?"

Devon was silent a while. "It would take a long time. But yes, I could. Is that what you want?"

"I don't know," she said.

That night, Devon told her, "I want to show you something." He led her to their tower chamber and turned on his computer. Meg was suddenly nervous. The monitor flickered. Icons appeared. Devon said softly, "Look at my background."

It showed two students sitting on a couch at a party. Meg didn't know them. The girl was pear-shaped and frizzy-haired and wore thick glasses. The guy wore glasses too, and was gangly, with thin lank hair and blotchy skin. The two of them looked happy together, in a pathetic sort of way. Meg said, "Who are they?"

Devon said, "That's the night we met."

Meg was horrified. She looked again, and suddenly she *did* recognize traces of themselves in the features of those strangers on the couch.

Devon explained, "I used the wand on us. Nothing drastic. I could do a lot more. I could make us anything we want. But you need to understand, Meg, when you talk about putting things back the way they were, exactly what you're saying."

Meg could accept the way she looked now—merely a pale shadow of Leena. But to think that she might not even be pretty, might be *that* girl...

"I thought you should know," Devon said, apologetic.

The next day at lunch, Meg asked him, "What is it you want me to do?"

He lowered his utensils. "Start the quest over."

"How?"

He nodded in the direction of the tower. "On my computer. I can show you."

"So that you'll get another wand?" she said.

"Yes."

"And I won't remember any of this?"

"No," he said.

She leaned back in her seat. "How many more times, Devon? My god, how many more wands?"

"As many as it takes," he said, without equivocation.

She stood up from the table, and said, "I need to think. Alone." He nodded. She went and paced the castle walls.

Devon wanted his new world more than anything. If she went along, then together they could have immortality and adventure and opulence and wonder. What had the old world offered? Crappy jobs and student loans, illness and death. What kind of a choice was that? She'd been here before, even if she didn't remember, and had sided with Devon one thousand two hundred and seventy four times. Who was she now, to doubt the wisdom of all her past choices?

He was still sitting there when she returned and said, "Fine. Show me."

He led her to the tower and loaded the game. He selected a character named Meg, who looked exactly like her. The character was level 60, and carried a Sword of Ultimate Cleaving +100. Devon clicked through a few menus, then stood. "Okay, *you* have to do it."

136

Meg sat down at the computer. A box on the screen said: "Citadel of Power—Are you sure you want to start this quest over from the beginning?" The mouse pointer hovered over "Yes."

Devon leaned down next to her. "Are you ready?"

"Yes," she whispered.

He kissed her cheek. "I'll see you again soon, okay?"

"Okay," she said, and clicked.

* * *

Meg hadn't heard from Devon in four months, and she realized that she missed him. So on a whim she tossed her sword and scabbard into the back seat of her car and drove over to campus to visit him.

Ages passed.

* * *

And now Leena the elf-maid is the most beautiful woman in all the world, and her lover is the most handsome man, Prince Devonar. They journey onward together, battling giants, riding dragons to distant lands, and feasting in the halls of dwarven kings. The prince is incandescent with joy. He was born for this, and Leena enjoys seeing him so happy. She loves him.

They ride two white unicorns down a forest path blanketed with fresh snow, and by some strange twist of magic or fate they come upon something that should not exist.

It lies half-buried in the drifts, but Leena can see that it was once a sort of carriage made from black metal. It has a roof, and its underside is all manner of piping, rusted now. Long ago, someone had sliced it in half. Where its other half may now lie, none can say.

The prince leaps from his mount and circles the strange object. "What foul contraption is this?"

Leena drops to the ground too, and staggers forward. A strange feeling passes over her, and a teardrop streaks her cheek. She can't say why. Soon she is sobbing.

The prince takes her in his arms. "My lady, what's the matter?" He scowls at the object. "It's upset you. Here, it shan't trouble us any longer." He pulls the Wand of Reification from his belt and aims.

"No!" She pushes his arm aside. "Leave it! Please."

He shrugs. "As you wish. But come, let's away. I mislike this place." He mounts his unicorn.

Leena stares at the strange carriage, and for a moment she remembers a world where countless such things raced down endless black roads. A world of soaring glass towers, of medallions that spoke in the voices of friends a thousand leagues distant, and where tales were told with light thrown up on walls the size of giants. Film, she remembers. Independent film. Jane Austen.

But the moment passes, and that fantastic world fades, leaving only the present, leaving only this odd, lingering sensation of being trapped in someone else's dream. She mounts her unicorn, and three words stick in her head, an incantation from a forgotten age. She no longer remembers where she heard the words, only that they now seem to express a feeling that surges up from somewhere deep inside her.

Save me plz.

Author's note: Save Me Plz

As a kid I was obsessed with computer role-playing games like *Phantasie*, *Rings of Zilfin*, *Pool of Radiance*, *Eye of the Beholder*, and *Diablo*. I remember one of my friends complaining that we were spending too much time on computer role-playing games. His exact words were, "There's more to life than *Curse of the Azure Bonds*." My favorite series of all was the *Ultima* series, especially *Ultima VI* and *Ultima VII*. There were times that I played *Ultima VII* all day, then looked up from my computer, dazed, surprised to discover that I didn't actually inhabit the magical world of Britannia. I still try to live my life according to the three principles of Truth, Love, and Courage that I learned from playing *Ultima*.

That said I never really got into multiplayer games like *Ultima Online*, *Everquest*, or *World of Warcraft*. By the time they came out I was already in college and busy with other things, and the whole idea of sharing a gameworld with other players never really appealed to me. I liked role-playing games because I got to be the all-powerful hero who saved the world. Having other people running around who were more powerful than me, constantly breaking character and acting like jerks, just seemed like it would ruin the whole experience.

So by 2006 I wasn't paying much attention to what was happening with computer games. At the time I was studying fiction and screenwriting at the University of Southern California, and was heavily involved with the campus atheist club. One day I was talking to another member of the group, and she mentioned that she had started playing *World of Warcraft*.

"My boyfriend is obsessed with it," she said. "He plays all the time. That's why I started playing, because the only way I can interact with him anymore is if I appear as a character in the game. Otherwise he just ignores me." I'll never forget the look in her eyes when she said that. She looked hopeless, forlorn.

I knew that games like *World of Warcraft* had a reputation for being addictive. My friends jokingly referred to *Everquest* as "Evercrack," and every once in a while one of our friends would vanish for a few months because they'd gotten sucked into the game. But what I was hearing about now seemed to go even beyond that. I went online and found a message board called

"Gamer Widows," where women shared horror stories about their game-addicted partners. It was all stuff like: "My husband lost his job and now he plays *World of Warcraft* sixteen hours a day. He says it's the only thing that helps relieve his stress. He never helps out with chores. We have two kids, and I feel like I'm raising them by myself. I'm considering a divorce."

I was horrified. This was obviously a widespread phenomenon that was worth exploring. I was especially taken with the idea of being forced into the game against your will because someone you love is trapped there.

My initial idea was that Meg would get a message from Devon asking for help, and would go looking for him, and things would get more and more like a video game, and eventually they'd be trapped together in the game. At first I didn't know *why* things would get more and more like a video game. I assumed it would just be a weird, dreamlike world that didn't really have any logical explanation to it, like my previous story "Blood of Virgins."

But as I worked on the idea, everything fell into place. I knew why Meg was living in a world that was halfway between the real world and a video game. I knew who was responsible. I knew how it was being done. Everything fit together so neatly, like I'd planned it from the start. I'd played enough *Diablo II* to know all about duped items and people repeating the same quest over and over. It all made perfect sense.

At least it did to me. At one point my dentist, who I'd been going to since I was a kid, asked to read one of my stories, and I gave him "Save Me Plz." He loved the story, but obviously didn't get it at all. Every time I went in he would ask me to explain it to him again.

My favorite piece of fanmail I ever got was from a college student in France. She said that one of her friends had been obsessed with *World of Warcraft* and was flunking out of school. She gave him my story to read, and it sort of snapped him out of it. He said that the story "saved his life."

That said I don't want it to seem like I'm against *World of Warcraft*. I love video games, and I think they're great as long as they don't interfere with other activities. I think part of the reason "Save Me Plz" works is that I'm a hardcore gamer, so I can sympathize with Devon, and can see the beauty and allure of video games as well as the danger.

The Ontological Factor

When my great uncle Cornelius died, our family needed someone to drive up to his house in Providence and make an inventory of his property, and I was the natural choice. After all, my recent bachelor's degree in philosophy and East Asian studies had done nothing to secure me regular employment, and I'd had to move back in with my parents, where I'd thrown myself into an ambitious project to create the world's longest-running manga comic about a flying mushroom who quotes Hegel. Cornelius had had some sort of falling out with the rest of the family years before I was born, over some (possibly imagined) slight. He'd lived alone, in a mansion he'd inherited from his mother.

I wasn't crazy about being by myself in a giant old house. For years I'd suffered from an odd, disconnected feeling, as if nothing was real, including myself, and this caused me constant low-level anxiety as well as the occasional panic attack. The distress inevitably intensified the longer I spent alone. I had not mentioned this to anyone.

I told my dad, "I don't know if I'm really the best person to be going through his things. I never even met the guy."

"Just do your best," dad said. "Everyone else is busy. I'll try to come and help out if I can."

So, reluctantly, I agreed.

I arrived in the late afternoon. The house was gray, Victorian, sprawled across the top of a low, forested hill. The central section was three stories tall, and additional two-story wings spread out in either direction.

I drove up the gravel drive, then pulled to a stop near the front door and got out. Dark clouds filled the sky, and as I approached the house a cool breeze rose, rustling the dry leaves that littered its porch. I jogged up the front steps and let myself in with the key I'd been given.

The place was musty and dim, with papers piled everywhere. I wandered through room after room of tables and sofas and bookshelves. Pausing by a window, I looked out into the backyard, where a gazebo overgrown with weeds huddled beside a scum-covered pond. I made my way into the kitchen. The sinks and countertops were cluttered with dirty dishes, and the cupboards revealed that the owner's diet had consisted mostly of coffee and cold cereal. So far this was about what I'd expected.

My first surprise came when I stepped into a parlor off the main corridor. There was a door there. A very strange door.

It was built into the far wall and painted bright green, a revolting neon shade that clashed with the subdued hues of the rest of the house. The door was quite small—I'd have to stoop to pass through it—and extremely crooked, though this seemed intentional. And unlike the rest of the place, this door looked new, and clean, and I suspected it was something Cornelius had added himself. Strangest of all, it was locked with no less than four heavy padlocks.

I stepped closer, studying the locks. I had only the one key, and it obviously didn't fit any of them. I'd have to come back later and see if I could spring them with my tools. Among my many odd and useless skills was picking locks, at which I had always been uncannily talented.

I began gathering up all the loose papers and sorting them into piles on the dining room table. There were the usual bills, ads, catalogs, etc., but also strange notebooks, dozens of them, full of puzzling diagrams and near-illegible scribbling, though certain words—"portal," "opener," "world"—jumped out at me.

I was so absorbed in the task that I didn't notice anyone enter the dining room, but suddenly a voice at my elbow barked, "Who are you?"

I started violently, and turned.

In the corner stood a large, burly woman who was maybe in her mid-forties. She wore a knapsack, and her outfit looked like a cross between a sweatsuit and a uniform.

"I...I'm Steven," I said. "Cornelius...he was my great uncle."

"Who's Cornelius?" she said.

"He...owns this place. I mean, he did."

When she'd first spoken, I'd thought she must be a friend of Cornelius, though by all accounts he hadn't had any. Now I wondered if she might be a burglar—she was sort of dressed like one—but she spoke with such casual authority that I doubted this was the case. At least, I wasn't about to ask.

She studied me, and I noticed that her irises were an odd golden color. Also, I could swear that her skin had a faint bluish tinge to it, like something not of this world. And it was as if she'd just appeared out of thin air...

"All right, Steve," she said, "you seem harmless enough. Carry on. But stay out of the east wing, if you know what's good for you."

She turned, as if to depart, though she was standing in the corner.

"Wait," I said. "Who are you?"

"Asha," she called over her shoulder. "Nice to meet you."

A dozen questions swirled in my mind, but I sensed that I'd only get a chance to ask one, and that one, the most important, rose to my lips. "Wait," I called softly. "Are...are you real?"

"Ha! That's a good one. Am *I* real?" she said, as she walked straight through a solid wall and disappeared.

* * *

So obviously I was freaked out, but what could I do? Run home and tell my parents that I'd been chased off by a ghost? No thanks. Instead I turned on as many lights as I could and positioned myself on a couch in the center of one of the larger rooms, where nothing could sneak up on me, and played movies on my laptop to keep the silence at bay. Finally I passed out, from sheer exhaustion.

When I woke it was morning, and everything seemed more manageable. As I wandered the empty house, I was already half convinced that my encounter with Asha had just been something I'd dreamed during the night. Still, I avoided the east wing.

What I needed right then, I decided, was some sort of challenge to occupy my mind, and the padlocks on the green door seemed just the thing. I'd become increasingly intrigued by the door, because, as near as I could tell, it couldn't possibly lead anywhere. The layout of the surrounding rooms was like a maze, but I was pretty sure I'd seen the far side of that wall, and there was nothing there but blank plaster.

I pulled up a chair before the door and sat down, wielding my tools. The work went quickly, the locks giving way one after another. I placed each one on the floor at my feet, then reached forward and pushed at the door, which swung aside.

A rush of humid air hit me, redolent with swamp smells of marsh grass and mud. Beyond the door lay a livid green sky above rolling hills dotted with forests and ponds. In a daze I rose to my feet and strode forward, my bare feet sinking into the surprisingly spongy earth. Another world, I thought, staring in wonder. It was actually there, actually real.

I glanced back over my shoulder. From this side, the green door was built into the wall of a small tower made of rough granite bricks. Through the door I could see back into the parlor of Cornelius's mansion.

I wandered down the hill into the field below. There was a small lake there, its waters murky and brown, and below the surface I could just make out the wavering suggestion of glimmering lights. Then a balmy breeze blew by, and I heard voices on the air. Crouching in the underbrush, I peered through a screen of trees.

A line of black-robed men were making their way up the hill. There were twenty of them, and they wore hoods, and chanted, and some bore a palanquin upon which sat an ebony idol, some sort of frog-headed deity on a gnarled throne.

It was a distinctly sinister tableau, and I was in no hurry to join the parade. Now that my initial wonder was subsiding, I had second thoughts about the wisdom of wandering barefoot and alone through an unknown world.

I turned to beat a hasty retreat, and almost ran right into a naked woman who was crawling up the beach toward me. She was thin and bony, and had come from the water, which dotted her pale flesh, and her thin green hair was plastered back across her oddly elongated scalp. When she was just a few feet away, she cocked her head at me, staring up with bulbous eyes and smiling faintly, as if she were expecting a treat.

I backed away, and suddenly she grinned, the corners of her mouth stretching three times as wide as I would've thought possible. Her teeth were like a piranha's.

Then she screamed, a banshee wail, a piercing shriek that went on and on.

I glanced behind me, through the trees. The black-robed men were turning my way now, and throwing back their hoods. Their faces were like hers, and from beneath their robes they drew short staffs topped with tridents.

I edged around the woman—her still screaming, still eager and staring—and sprinted back toward the tower and the green door.

I was out of breath and staggering by the time I was halfway up the hill, and then I stumbled on that strangely pliant ground and fell to my hands and knees, and the creatures swarmed about me, capering and gibbering, thrusting at me with their tridents. I threw my arms over my face and curled into a ball. How could I have been so stupid? Maybe Freud had been right about the death drive, that we all subconsciously seek our own destruction.

The weapons struck my shoulders, my back, my legs. It took a moment before I realized that the pain was minimal, as if they were children poking me with sticks. I was not bleeding, not harmed.

I opened one eye, and a fish-man roared into my face with his dagger-toothed mouth. Instinctively I lashed out, and when I struck his head it burst like an overinflated balloon, splattering me with gore. I dragged myself to my feet as the rest of the fish-men fled. I had absolutely no idea what was going on.

I made it back to the tower, passed through the green door, and slammed it behind me. As I snapped the locks shut one by one, I swore that I would never, ever, ever go opening any mysterious doors ever again. Breathing a sigh of relief, I turned around.

Asha stood there, frowning.

I screamed.

She seized me by the arm and growled, "Come with me."

"W-where are we going?" I said, as she dragged me through the halls, but she didn't answer.

I said, "There were creatures in there! They attacked me."

"Well, what do you expect from a bunch of twos?" she muttered.

I had no idea what to make of that.

She escorted me into the west wing of the house, into a section I hadn't really explored yet, and marched me into a large bedroom. Built into the corner was another of those strange doors, this one bright orange rather than bright green, and tilted to the right rather than the left, but otherwise identical to the other—right down to the four heavy padlocks.

"I need you to open this," Asha said, as we crossed the room.

I wasn't at all sure that was a good idea. I pointed weakly at the locks. "Uh, my tools are back—"

She reached out with her bare hands and ripped apart the locks as if they were made of cotton candy.

Then she turned to face me. "Open it," she ordered. "Now."

* * *

So what could I do? With a trembling hand I gave the door a small push, and it swung back with a creak, revealing yet another alien world—dry, rolling scrub plains beneath a dusty orange sky.

Asha beamed. "Excellent!"

Puzzled, I said, "Why couldn't you just open it yourself?"

"Because I'm not an opener," she said. "You are. Hard as that is to believe."

Opener? I thought.

She added quickly, "And now, Steve my boy, there's something else I need you to do for me. I need you to go through this door and find me a weapon. A gun would be my first choice, of course, but any sort of weapon will do—a sword, an axe, anything like that." She reached into her knapsack and pulled out a revolver, which she handed to me. "Or even just some bullets, if they'll work with this."

The gun felt amazingly heavy in my hand. I said, "Why do you need a weapon?"

She scowled. "Look, there's no time to waste, okay? Just do it. Trust me on this, it's important."

Somehow, maybe because I was still high on adrenaline from my encounter with the fish-men, I found the guts to say, "No."

"Kid," she growled, fixing me with an intense glare, "you have no idea what's at stake here."

"Then tell me!" I said. "Tell me what's going on! But I'm not going to go marching off and bring back a weapon just because you say so!"

For a moment Asha looked so frustrated that I thought she might tear me apart the way she had the locks.

Finally she sighed. "All right, fine. I'll explain." She snatched the gun from me and tossed it in her knapsack. "Follow me."

I tagged along behind her as she led the way back toward the other end of the house.

"Okay," she said, as we went, "you know that there are different worlds, and that it's possible to open portals between them. The first thing you have to understand is that not all worlds are created equal. Some are more real than others."

I chimed in, "But who's to say what's real and what isn't?"

"Oh," she said. "We use this." She reached into the knapsack and pulled out a device that looked like a black-and-purple striped candy cane. "It's called an O-meter. Each world, and everything native to it, has a specific Ontological Factor, or OF, which is what the machine measures. Here, I'll show you."

She pointed the device at me, and sections of it lit up in sequence until about half its length was glowing.

"See?" she said. "You're a five."

"Oh," I said. "Is that good?"

"No," she said.

"Oh."

"But hey, it could be worse. Like those degenerates you ran into earlier. Twos. Total figments. Not real enough to do any damage even to you."

So that's why I'd survived the attack of the fish-men, I thought. That made sense. Sort of.

"What number are you?" I asked.

"Ten," she said. "Obviously."

After a moment, I added, "At first I thought you were a ghost."

"Kid, there's no such thing as ghosts."

"But you walked right through a wall, so—"

"Yeah, but it was just a *five* wall."

I frowned. We were silent for a while.

She eyed me. "What's the matter? You seem nonplussed."

"I don't know," I said, "I don't like this. Some of the greatest minds in history have grappled with the question of what's real and what isn't, and how do we know, and it's something that's bothered me for a long time too. And then to have someone come along and say it's just a number that you can measure on a machine—"

"Is *that* what's bothering you?" she said. "Kid, forget that crap. We've got bigger problems. *Much* bigger."

"What do you mean?"

We were in the east wing of the house now. We entered a large library—hardwood floors, overstuffed chairs, a fireplace. And of course, built into the far wall was another of those small crooked doors, this one bright purple.

Asha nodded at it. "That's the one that killed him."

"Who?" I said.

"Your great uncle. What's his name? Cornelius? Creating a portal is hard on anyone, let alone a five. He must've been pretty desperate to get out of this craphole world. Can't say I blame him."

I stared at the purple door. Unlike the other two, it wasn't locked. "He did hate it here," I said.

"Unfortunately for him," Asha went on, "his first two attempts led to cul-de-sac worlds, and I guess that wasn't good enough for him. This one here is different. It leads to a world that's connected to half a dozen others. You can get anywhere from here."

"So what's the problem?" I said.

"The problem," she said pointedly, "is Abraxas."

"What's Abraxas?"

"Not what—who. Abraxas is a type of being we call a 'demon'—someone who can soak up the reality of other people and absorb it into himself. That's illegal, of course, and most demons refrain from using their ability. But every once in a while you get a bad one, and Abraxas is one of the worst."

"I see," I said. "He's like the embodiment of Nietzsche's will to power."

She stared at me levelly for a moment, then continued as if I hadn't spoken. "I caught up with him a few days ago, here, on this world. I'm a sort of...bounty hunter, you might say. Unfortunately Abraxas is one sneaky bastard. He gave me the slip, and made off with a bunch of my gear to boot, including my skeleton key. Without it, I can't open portals. I also used up all my bullets firing at him as he fled."

She sighed. "So here I am. These portals that your great uncle created are the only ones on this world that are traversible at the moment, and two of them, as I said, are dead ends." She glanced over her shoulder at the purple door. "Abraxas has to get through this one, and if he does—if he gets away—then we can't restore the stolen reality to the dozens of worlds, including yours, that he's pillaged, which leaves all of you at greater risk of cross-world invasion."

I stood in stunned silence.

"*And,*" she added grimly, "if someone doesn't lock him up soon, one of these days he'll have absorbed enough reality to put him beyond contention even by us tens, and then there'll be no stopping him, ever. So *that's* Abraxas. And he could be showing up here at any minute, and I'll have to fight him. Now"—she held up her massive hands—"these hands are formidable things, but nevertheless, given the circumstances, I really wouldn't mind having a weapon, you know what I mean? You getting the picture?"

"Yes," I said meekly.

"This world is a five," she said, "so nothing around here is real enough to harm him at all. But behind the orange door is a world that's an eight. Not the best, but a weapon from there should be enough to knock him for a loop, I'd say. I can't go myself, because I have to stay and guard this door. That's where you come in."

She looked me in the eye and said, "So that's the story. Now, Steve, I'm asking you, will you help me? Please?"

* * *

My mind was made up. "Okay," I said. "I'll do it."

"Terrific," Asha exclaimed. "Finally. All right, let's get you prepped for a little cross-world travel. First of all"—she reached into her knapsack, produced a bottle of pills and a canteen, and handed them to me—"take some of these. Actually, better take them all."

I opened the bottle and studied the pills, which were small and dark and soft, like caviar. I tossed them in my mouth, took a gulp from the canteen, and swallowed. "What are they?"

"Brain worms," she said.

I froze.

She caught my expression, and added quickly, "Oh, but not *bad* brain worms. Good brain worms. They know most of the languages that are spoken across the worlds, and pretty soon you will too."

"Oh," I said, uncertainly.

She passed me the knapsack. "Take this too. It's got pretty much everything a cross-world traveler might need. There's silver in the side pocket."

"Silver?" I said.

"Right. It makes a good universal currency. It gets traded around quite a lot, actually, so any silver you come across has a fair chance of having a higher OF than ambient materials. Doesn't this world have any legends about invincible monsters that can only be harmed by silver?"

"Yeah," I said.

She nodded. "Most worlds do. Now you know why." She frowned. "Unfortunately, I have yet to come across *anything* on this piece of crap world with a high OF."

I was getting a little irked by her attitude. I mean, I had mixed feelings about this world myself, but it *was* my home. On the other hand, maybe the place she came from really was a whole lot better. Certainly what little I'd seen of a world with an OF of two tended to bear out her prejudices. That reminded me...

"What if I get attacked again?" I said.

She blanched. "Yeah, that's an issue, for sure. Be careful with yourself. They're eights and you're a five, so they're basically untouchable as far as you're concerned. But I don't expect you'll have any problems. Eights tend to be pretty civilized, you'll see."

I shouldered the pack. "All right. Is that everything?"

"Yup," she said. "Thanks for doing this, kid. I really appreciate it. See you soon, okay?"

"Okay," I said, and departed the library, making my way toward the orange door.

* * *

I stepped out into a hot, dry day, and looked around. On this side, the door was built into a white brick wall that was about as tall as I was, and that hugged the contours of the rolling hills for as far as I could see in either direction. In the valley below, a perfectly straight road ran from the horizon to a city of gleaming spires a few miles away.

I took a deep breath, adjusted my pack, and started down the hill toward the road. Hopefully, I thought, my sophomore effort at cross-world travel would turn out more auspiciously than my first. Though I was a lot more prepared this time around. I had shoes, for one thing, and a pack full of food and water and money. I also had a gun, though it was empty. Most importantly, I had a rough idea of what was going on.

I also had worms in my brain. *Good* worms. Yeah.

On the other hand, this world was an eight, and I was a mere five. I stomped on the ground experimentally. I supposed that it did feel a bit more substantial than usual, and the colors around me did look more vibrant and saturated, especially the looming orange sky.

After an hour I reached the road, which was a hundred feet across and made of a smooth white substance that showed virtually no wear. I set off toward the city.

A bit later I heard a distant humming sound, and raised my head. Something was speeding down the road toward me, throwing up clouds of dust as it came. It was white, and seemed to float above the ground. As it neared I saw that it looked almost exactly like a giant flying egg.

It came to a halt beside me, then spoke in a low, soothing voice. The language was unfamiliar, but I realized that I could indeed understand it. It said, "Greetings, pilgrim. May I conduct you to the city?"

"Um, okay," I replied, in that same language.

The egg's top half unfolded like a blooming flower, revealing a cushioned red seat within. "Welcome aboard."

I climbed a short set of steps and settled into the chair. The dome re-formed itself above me—the vehicle resuming its egglike shape—and we accelerated toward the city. From inside, the thing's walls were transparent, and I watched the ground speed by beneath us as the city drew ever nearer.

We flew through an enormous gate and came to a halt in a white plaza beside a giant fountain. The vehicle opened and let me out, then sped away, back to wherever flying eggs go.

There were people all around me. They were varied in appearance, but were all apparently human, and most were dressed in white, their garments simple and clean. I felt a little conspicuous standing there in my street clothes, which were still a bit spattered with fish-man, but no one seemed to pay me any attention as they strolled about, chatting and laughing.

I wandered down a broad avenue toward the city center, keeping an eye out for any sort of weapon. Having no knowledge of local customs, I was a bit reluctant to just come right out and ask where I could buy a gun. I kept hoping to see a big sign with a sword or machine gun on it, but no such luck.

I passed a park. The grass there had been shaped into a triangular field, upon which children played a sport involving a cube-shaped ball and sticks that looked like a cross between a golf club and a cricket bat. I paused for a moment to watch.

On a bench beside me sat a man who was watching the game. He said, "Dhajat season is always my favorite time of year."

He was an older fellow with a placid face and a long white beard, and he held a glass of what looked like lemonade.

"Uh, yeah, mine too," I said, hoping that was an appropriate response.

He gave me a friendly smile. "What brings you to the city, pilgrim?"

"Um, I'm looking for something," I said.

He nodded sagely. "We're all looking for something."

"Oh," I said. "Right."

Should I chance it? Oh what the hell, he seemed as friendly and talkative as anyone I was likely to meet.

I added, "But, um, actually I'm looking for something kind of specific."

"Truth?" he said. "Enlightenment? I was like you once. Don't worry, you'll find it."

"No," I said, "more like, um, a gun."

He chortled. "Ha! That's a good one."

I waited for him to elaborate, but he didn't. He was back to watching the game. I said, "Or a sword. I mean, any sort of weapon, really."

Slowly he turned to face me. "You are...joking?"

"Um..." I said.

"You came *here* to shop for weapons?" He laughed uproariously.

"Tourists!" he declared, wiping tears from his eyes. "Don't you know where you are? No one would ever *dream* of bringing a weapon within a hundred miles of Nervuh Nah, City of Peace."

I started to get a sinking feeling. I turned away.

Things were definitely not looking good. There were no weapons here, no weapons anywhere near this whole city. My mission was a complete failure. There was nothing I could do to help stop Abraxas, and now he'd probably escape through the purple door, leaving earth forever in a state of crippled ontological peril.

Also, Asha was going to be *really* pissed off.

Then I had an idea.

* * *

Asha eyed my offering with disbelief. "And what exactly," she declared, "is *that?*"

"A dhajat bat," I said.

"And just what am I supposed to do with that?"

"Um, play dhajat," I said. "But——"

She put her face in her hands and shook her head. "Kid," she moaned, "is there something about the concept of a 'weapon' that you're not getting?"

"It's not my fault!" I said. "It was like a whole city of pacifists! There were no weapons anywhere. I just thought——"

"All right, all right," she interrupted. "Give it here."

I passed her the bat, and she took a few practice swings.

She sighed. "Well, it's better than nothing, I guess. But I wish you would've——"

She stopped suddenly.

"What?" I said.

She whispered, "He's here." She nodded at the fireplace. "Get over there. Stay out of this."

I hurried to comply. A short time later I heard footsteps approaching. Asha hefted the bat.

My dad walked into the room.

"Wait!" I cried, as Asha rushed him. I lunged to interpose myself between them, waving my arms. "It's okay, it's my dad!"

153

Then I noticed that my dad was grinning in a very sinister, very un-dad-like way. And he was holding something—a snow globe?

"Steve!" Asha roared, shoving me aside, "get out of the way! It's—"

My dad hurled the globe to the floor at Asha's feet.

Then it was like I was staring into the sun. I flew through the air—

I came to moments later, draped across one of the overstuffed chairs, which had been knocked to the floor, apparently by me, and I hurt everywhere. I raised my head to try to see what was going on.

Asha lay sprawled on the floor. Whatever that glass ball weapon had been, she'd absorbed the brunt of it, and seemed to be out cold. The dhajat bat had flown from her grasp and landed in the corner, where a tall, thin figure was bending over to retrieve it.

He didn't look at all like my dad now. He wore a brown trenchcoat and fedora, and the hat cast impossibly deep shadows over his face, but I could make out hints of gaunt, skeletal cheeks, and a heavy jaw lined with jagged teeth.

He gripped the bat and straightened, turning toward Asha.

"No!" I cried, stumbling to my feet. I snatched up a heavy ceramic ashtray and threw it at him, but when it struck him it bounced off as if it were made of styrofoam, and he paid no attention.

I felt a flood of despair. The only object in the room with enough reality to affect him was the bat, and—

Wait! I thought. Asha's knapsack. Her gun! If it had come from her world, it must have an OF of ten, like her. I tore open the pack and yanked out the gun.

Abraxas stood over Asha and raised the bat to strike. With a cry I hurled the gun at him as hard as I could.

It hit him in the back of the head, and his hat went flying. "Ow!" he screamed.

Then he turned to regard me, and his face was even more frightening than I'd imagined. His eyes were black sockets within which green ghost-fires blazed.

I fled in a mad panic, sprinting out the door and into the hall. As I rounded the corner, Abraxas stepped out through the wall right in front of me.

He smiled, and I backed away, cringing and stumbling. As I retreated past the library door, I noticed that Asha's body was gone. Where—?

Suddenly two hands reached out through the wall, seized Abraxas by the shoulders, and yanked him sideways. He gasped—and the bat fell from his fingers—as he was dragged back through the wall.

I moved to the door and watched as Asha raised him above her head. Then she spun him around and piledrove him into the floor, which exploded like it'd been hit by a meteor. I ducked behind the wall as bits of flooring and foundation rained all about the room.

When I peeked in again, I saw that the center of the library was now a giant crater, and at its base were Asha and Abraxas. He was on his knees, and she had him in a chokehold. I scooped up the dhajat bat and hurried forward.

As I neared, Abraxas slumped. The fires that were his eyes dwindled to the size of candle flames, then went out. Asha yanked his arms behind his back and bound his wrists with glowing cuffs.

Then she stood, looking immensely pleased with herself. "Ha!" she declared, clapping her hands and raising them before her. "What did I tell you, kid? These hands are formidable things."

I let out a deep breath, and lowered the bat.

"Thought he was pretty clever," Asha said, "using my own stun-bulbs against me. Good thing I had them all rigged for one-quarter power...just in case someone ever grabbed one and tried to use it on me." She prodded him with her toe and said, "Guess you're not the only sneaky one around here, eh, smart guy?"

She turned back to me and added, "Still, I don't know if I would've been able to get the drop on him, if you hadn't distracted him. That was real good thinking."

"Wow, thanks, Asha. I—"

"Of course," she said, "you *did* almost get me killed by jumping between us like that."

"Oh," I said glumly. "Yeah."

She waved a hand. "But don't worry about it. That was my fault. I should've warned you about his disguises. No, overall you did pretty great, I'd say." She added, "For a five, I mean."

I grinned.

"So what happens now?" I asked.

* * *

A few weeks later all the preparations had been made for my extended vacation. A cab dropped me off in front of Cornelius's mansion, and I made my way through the house to the library, which had been repaired with some help from Asha's off-world friends—without anyone around here being the wiser.

Asha stood waiting, beside the purple door.

"You all set?" she asked me.

"Yup," I said, as I crossed the room.

In my backpack was food, water, and silver, as well as a handgun that Asha had provided, loaded with OF ten bullets.

She gestured to the door. "You want to do the honors?"

I smiled and stepped forward, and gave the door a push, and it swung aside to reveal a night sky full of massed purple clouds and circling flocks of long-necked birds, and below that soaring peaks beside plunging chasms, and on every precipice a fortress whose windows blazed with yellow light, like jack-o-lanterns. The night air that blew in past us was pleasantly brisk, and smelled of rich earth and sweet flowers.

I paused to admire the view, even if this world *was* only a six.

"Let's get a move on," Asha said, as she stepped through the door. "No time to waste gawking at second-rate realities. We've got a full itinerary ahead of us. Nines and tens all the way."

I took one last look around the library, at my home world, in all its modest five-ness, then moved to follow her.

"Come on, kid," she told me. "Let me show you what a *real* world looks like."

Author's note: The Ontological Factor

One morning in 1985, just as our third grade class was about to start, my best friend handed me a book he thought I'd like. It was called *Myth Conceptions* by Robert Asprin, the second book in his *Myth* series. I opened to the first page and began to read: "Of all the various ways to be aroused from a sound sleep, one of the worst is the noise of a dragon and a unicorn playing tag." I could not possibly have been more excited. The teacher kept yelling at me to put the book away, and I kept sneaking glances at it under my desk, until finally she threatened to confiscate it if she caught me looking at it again. As soon as school was out I ran all the way home so I could start reading the book.

The *Myth* series quickly became my favorite books, and I read them all a dozen times. Sadly I rarely met anyone else who had ever heard of them. I met a lot of people who had read Piers Anthony, Douglas Adams, or Terry Pratchett, but almost no one who shared my love of Robert Asprin.

Then one day, about twenty years later, I was hanging out with John Joseph Adams in Grand Central Station. We were waiting for someone, and that person showed up hours late, so John and I had a lot of time to talk, and in the course of that conversation it came out that we were both big fans of Robert Asprin. "You should write a story that's like the *Myth* books," John said.

I thought that would be fun, but I was never able to come up with a good idea for a story. Then in 2010 John told me he was editing an anthology of parallel world stories called *Other Worlds Than These*, and encouraged me to submit a story. The *Myth* books are all about characters hopping around to different dimensions, so a parallel worlds anthology seemed like the perfect opportunity to finally write the Robert Asprin pastiche I'd always dreamed of. (Also Robert Asprin had died just two years earlier, so I thought it would make a nice tribute to his memory.)

What makes the *Myth* books so good? Basically you have a young man who is good-hearted and naive, and he's surrounded by all these brash, overconfident older characters who are always talking down to him and getting him into trouble, which is really funny, but at the same time you always know that the characters really care about each other and will do anything to help out if one of them is in danger.

I wanted to have that same dynamic of a naive younger character who teams up with a sarcastic older character, but I didn't want to make it a carbon copy of the *Myth* books either, so I tweaked the formula in a few ways. For starters I made it a portal fantasy (the story starts out on Earth), which isn't true of the *Myth* books. I also made one of the leads female. I liked the idea of a buddy comedy where one of the leads is a large, brash woman and the other is a shy, nervous man, which I felt was something you don't see as often.

I also introduced the idea of different worlds having different levels of reality, which is an idea that comes from a lifetime of reading and thinking about Roger Zelazny's *Amber* series. In the *Amber* books we're told that Amber is the one true world, of which all others are merely shadows. But what does that mean exactly? Can you measure that? Are all shadow worlds equally real, or are some of them more real than others? Are Amber rocks stronger than shadow rocks? It seemed like there was a lot more you could do with some of those ideas.

I figured if the story was going to appear in a parallel worlds anthology, it should include at least two parallel worlds, if not three. So the story starts on Earth, goes into a parallel world, returns to Earth, goes into a second parallel world, returns to Earth again, then concludes with Steve looking out upon a third parallel world. *Other Worlds Than These* had a strict word limit of 5,000 words, and squeezing three different parallel worlds into a 5,000 word story required some careful planning. I was glad I was able to make it work.

I finished "The Ontological Factor" in April of 2010, and *Other Worlds Than These* wasn't slated for publication until June of 2012, so John encouraged me to see if I could sell the story to a magazine in the meantime. That's why the story first appeared in *Cicada* in 2011. But "The Ontological Factor" definitely started with John, and would definitely not exist without his constant encouragement.

The Second Rat

My wife, Debbie, has been talking to that damn visiting nurse again.

"She says you're dying," Debbie tells me, hollowly.

I can barely speak. I try, but my lips move awkwardly. I say, "She's right."

I want it to happen at home, with my family. I'm feeble now, frail. My face is twisted and I can't untwist it. I try to avoid looking in the mirror.

Debbie feels my forehead, as if it might help. "You're too warm," she says, and closes the blinds. A line of sunlit dots stretches across the blanket near my ankles.

"You're still so young," she says, absently.

I'm thirty-four years old.

"It's just not fair," she adds.

I pull her close and stroke her hair. "It's all right," I tell her, and then think to myself that it is fair. It's more than fair.

My body is only thirty-four, but my mind has lived more than its share of days. I can rewind life, you see. Even now, I could escape death that way. I could flee back to those healthy, free days of my youth.

But I won't.

* * *

Once, I went on national television and talked about how I can rewind life. I thought it would be a lot of fun. Besides, no one would remember afterward, anyway.

They stuck me at a desk, with bright lights shining in my face. I could

159

make out the shadowy figures of camera operators, and black bunches of cable that looked like coiled snakes.

Dan Findley from *The Evening News* interviewed me. His hair was curly and slick.

"Mr. Todd Rawlins," he said, "Welcome."

"Glad to be here, Dan," I replied.

"Now Mr. Rawlins, you've had remarkable success investing in the stock market. Tell us, what's your secret?"

"It's really quite simple, Dan," I said. "You see, I can rewind life."

There was a long pause. I heard an assistant cough.

"I'm sorry," Findley said finally. "What was that?"

"The way you rewind a tape. I can do it in real life. I can go back to any point in my past and start over. I observe which stocks do well, then rewind and invest in those."

"This is a personal philosophy of yours?"

"It's not philosophy," I said. "I mean it quite literally."

Findley shot a confused glance toward the studio director. "Mr. Rawlins, you're saying that you control time?"

"I can make it go backward, yes. Forward is always normal speed."

"That sounds very strange."

"I can prove it."

Findley leaned back in his chair and studied me carefully. "How?"

"Write something on a piece of paper," I said. "Don't let me see it. I'll proceed into the future and find out the answer. Then I'll rewind time and tell you what the paper says—before I've ever seen it."

Findley shrugged. He scrawled something in his notebook, then placed it face down on the desk. "Now what?"

"Show it to me."

He held up the notebook. It said 'Evening News.'

Rewind a few seconds.

Instantly everything resumed its former condition. Again I watched as Findley placed his notebook face down on the desk. "Now what?" he asked.

"You wrote 'Evening News.'"

"Yes, that's right." He held it up so the camera could see.

"Do it again. Something harder, something personal—something nobody could possibly know."

160

He scribbled on the paper.

"Show me," I said.

He had written "Gruddie."

"My stuffed rabbit," he explained, with a touch of embarrassment. "I had it as a kid."

Rewind a few seconds.

Findley was still writing.

"It says 'Gruddie'—your toy rabbit."

Findley didn't move for a while. Finally, he turned and stared at me, his face a mixture of confusion and awe.

"You're serious about this?" he said.

"Yes."

"How do you do it?"

"I don't know. I just do."

Findley chuckled and shook his head. "Wait, wait. Let me see that again. One more time."

"All right," I said. "Just one more time."

Rewind a few months.

I was getting bored with that interview anyway.

* * *

I haven't always been able to rewind things.

When I was a little kid, they brought me to the hospital and I was scared.

Dad broke the news. He always wore flannel shirts, and a floppy blue baseball cap. He worked as a machinist in a paper mill.

"The tests came back, finally," he said. "I'm sorry, Todd."

"What does it mean?" I asked.

He took off that floppy hat, and scratched at his straw-colored hair. "It means you're very sick."

"Like mom?" I asked. Mom died when I was three. She had Huntington's chorea. Now I did too.

I swallowed hard, and the world seemed all fuzzy around the edges. "Is it gonna kill me?"

Dad looked grim. He stared out the window.

I begged him, "Please don't lie."

"Yeah. Yeah it is," he said suddenly, then added, "eventually."

I stared down at the turquoise blankets. "When?"

"The doctors don't know for sure. They said if you're lucky you could live well into your thirties."

"Thirties," I echoed. "How old are you?"

Dad grimaced. "Um. Twenty-eight."

I stared at him, and he looked away. He put his hat back on.

My eyes ached from unwept tears, and I started to snuffle. "I told you not to lie."

* * *

Hindsight.

Most people probably feel that acute desire—to take it back, to do it over, to make it right. I was different, I just wanted more time.

I always saw the universe as a great clock that ticked toward the end of my truncated life. All I ever wanted was for it to run the other way.

Rewind one second. Rewind two seconds. Rewind one minute—

I was twenty, in my dorm at college. I lay in bed, lost in exhaustion and confusion, and my 8:00 a.m. alarm droned mercilessly on.

"Turn it off," my roommate moaned.

Rewind one minute.

I could feel it happen that first time, that first second. It was like electricity dancing up and down my spine. I saw the clock and suddenly it was 7:59.

"Did you see that?" I said, startled suddenly awake.

But my roommate was still asleep. Then the clock hit 8:00, and the alarm went off.

He wasn't aware it had happened, no one was. No one could perceive that time had progressed beyond the present, and that I had yanked things back.

At first I was afraid to rewind very far. Instead I did simple experiments.

I flipped a coin and let it land on my desk. It came up heads.

Rewind five seconds.

That same coin spun wildly at the apex of the exact same toss. It bounced across my desk several times, quivered in place, then came to rest.

It showed tails.

Scientists call it chaos—this fundamental randomness.

Some things were predictable: words on paper, the top card in a deck, people's immediate intentions. Also the progression of fatal illnesses, and the average change in stock market prices over long periods of time.

I spent a few years after school investing in the market, making money, getting more comfortable with my ability to rewind. I gave that TV interview.

That all started getting boring after a while, though. I was ready to move on to bigger things.

* * *

The farthest back I ever went was sophomore year of high school, because there was something I needed to do.

Rewind ten years.

Willy Pierson, whose breath smelled like onions, followed me down the hall, looming over me like some damn vulture.

"Hey there, Rawlins," he said, and shoved me forward.

My backpack rolled off my shoulder and exploded across the floor, books and papers spreading away from it like waves on a beach.

I turned. Willy stood at least a head higher than me.

"You know," I told him, "you've been asking for it ever since eighth grade."

He sneered. I punched him.

My knuckles exploded with a pain that shot up my arm. Willy's face turned away, then snapped back, and he shoved me hard. My head struck against the grill of a locker, and the world turned in wrong ways, and then my cheek was squashed against the floor. Willy was somewhere above me, kicking—

Rewind a few seconds.

He went to shove me, but I dodged aside and wrapped my arms around his neck and pulled, and we both went down. A dark press of faces and knees and shoes, of voices chanting, "fight, fight, fight."

I scrambled on top of him, pressing my knee into his spine, but he caught me in the jaw with a wild elbow and—

Rewind a few seconds.

I threw my face away from his elbow as it came, and I seized his curly hair in my tight fingers, and slammed his forehead against the floor until it tore open and a thin line of kickball-red blood ran out, dripping bright, spattered spots across the tile.

Fight, fight, fight.

* * *

That death I'd feared so long seemed banished forever. I would never die. I would always be young and healthy. I would experience every possibility that life could offer.

I ran away from home when I was seventeen and spent a few months living around Vegas, hustling. I didn't mind leaving home that way. When I was done in Vegas, I'd just rewind things, and everything would go back to the way it used to be.

I was worthless at roulette. That crazy steel ball might bounce anywhere—chaos theory again.

I preferred a good game of blackjack.

I had my hole card, plus a king.

"Hit me," I told the dealer. It was always worth a shot.

He dealt me the six of clubs. My hole card was a nine. Makes twenty-five.

Rewind a few seconds.

"I'll stay," I said.

One night I met a dark-haired girl on a street corner there. Her eyes and skin seemed to glow, bathed in that otherworldly neon light.

"I've seen you at the tables," she said. "You're really good."

"It's all just luck," I replied.

I had some booze back at my hotel. She had a friend who sold us acid and other stuff. We smoked some and snorted some and ingested the rest. Then I went to bed with her.

When it was over, she started crying.

"I'm so fucked up." She kept repeating that, rocking back and forth on the edge of the bed. "I'm so fucked up."

"No you're not," I said. "It's all right."

"I can't believe this." She glanced around with wet, wild eyes. "What the hell am I doing here?"

The room seemed to rock back and forth like a boat. The couch glowed, and the walls were singing out of tune. "Everything's going to be okay," I tried to tell her.

"I should go—now." She stumbled across the carpet, knocking over a small table, spilling our illicit things across the floor. "I did it again," she said crazily, half to herself. "I told myself I'd never do it again."

She paused by the door, leaning against the wall. She stared at me. "I'm sorry. You need to get yourself tested, you know? I'm so fucked up." She stumbled out of the room.

I lay back on the bed among the thick red blankets, staring at the oddly shifting ceiling. I shrugged. I didn't need to get tested, of course, but I hated this place anyway.

Time to leave. Time to go home.

Rewind a few months.

But nothing happened. The room retained all of its confused presence. I blinked a few times, staring up into the smoky air.

Rewind a few months. Rewind a few months. Rewind! Nothing happened.

I leapt out of bed and ran half-naked through the empty halls. I couldn't be trapped. Oh god, not here—anywhere but here.

I moaned and screamed and pounded on the walls. This was retribution, I realized suddenly. This was my own private hell. I had been proud, and this is how the universe would pay me back.

I broke out through an emergency exit and into a crumbling alleyway. I ran stricken through those mad, gleaming streets. Far away, beyond the pavement, I found a patch of loose dirt and yellow desert grass and fell on it. I ripped at my clothes and sat feverishly, staring at the blurry lights that wavered in the distance.

Then I thought of something else.

I was wrecked, trashed. I was stumbling, incoherent—I'd taken all that shit and it was screwing with my head. Maybe when I sobered up I'd be able to rewind things again.

Maybe.

I closed my eyes and waited a long time beneath that dark, horrible Nevada sky.

Rewind a few months.

Please.

Then I was home, in my old bed, before I ever ran away. It was Christmas break and I started to cry, gasping great sobs of relief.

Dad opened the door. "Jesus, Todd. Are you all right?"

I was curled in a ball, stiff, shaking. "I had a bad dream," I said softly. "A very bad dream."

Half an hour later, I was back in control. My heart had slowed, my breathing was normal.

Rewind one hour.

I didn't want dad to remember seeing me like that.

* * *

I didn't rewind for a long time after that. I was afraid it might not work, and then I'd feel as helpless and stranded as I had that horrible night in Las Vegas.

My sense of mortality returned.

Rewinding was no guarantee of safety. I had been aware of that before, in some abstract sense, but now it came to haunt me. I might die in an explosion, a sudden car crash, a gas leak—I might die in my sleep. I could never let my guard down, not for a moment.

A man tried to kill me in New York.

I stepped off the subway, and he came out of the crowd, pushing me back against the train, stabbing me over and over. I was too startled to react, to rewind. Finally he backed away, breathing heavily, and I sank to the cement, bleeding out on the subway platform, my shirt a wet, shredded mess.

My vision was going dark. I might pass out within seconds, I realized madly. I might be dead within minutes.

The man looked down at me with the oddest expression of rage and fear. He was tall, his hair and beard long and straggly.

Rewind a few days.

I stood in the kitchen. I tore open my shirt and rubbed desperately at my smooth and uninjured flesh. I drank some water from the sink. Then I went to the bathroom and vomited.

I had no idea who he was. It was a random act of violence then, by a disturbed individual. I would probably never see him again.

But if I did see him, I wouldn't rewind so far. I would find out who he was, and why he wanted to kill me.

* * *

I spent the next five years driving up and down the East Coast, working in various places, earning enough money to get by.

I met a girl named Debbie.

She'd graduated in the spring from a college in Minnesota and come to Boston to do graphic design. We went to the museums, the cafes, the galleries. We took off our shoes and walked barefoot through the park as the clouds turned pink and orange.

Debbie said, "The interesting thing about Mozart is that he was such a terribly flawed man. But I guess you don't have to be a perfect person to write perfect music."

"Yeah," I agreed, and then, "Can I kiss you?"

Her hazel eyes narrowed, and she smiled. "Well...all right."

We got married two years later. I was twenty-six. Our first years together were wonderful. I wouldn't change a thing.

One night, I awoke to panic. My every joint was stiff and bloated. My whole body shook violently. Pains shot up my limbs and into my stomach.

"Todd?" Debbie mumbled drowsily. "What's wrong?"

"Symptoms," I groaned. "I'm getting sicker, Deb."

I was thirty-one years old.

The night before, we'd talked seriously for the first time about having kids. If our first child was a boy, we were going to name him Timothy.

The next morning, Debbie made me breakfast in bed. It hurt to swallow. It even hurt to talk.

"I waited too long." I told her. "I should've married you a lot sooner."

Debbie sighed. "Don't think that way. It's all in the past now."

I nodded. She was right.

I was still lying there when Debbie left for work that morning. "Bye," she called up the stairs. "I love you."

I pulled myself out of bed and hobbled to the window. I watched Debbie pull our little Honda out of the garage, and head away down the road.

I had been complacent with time, careless. I had let it lead me to this place of sickness and pain. I shouldn't have to live like this, and neither should Debbie. There was a better place for us. A young, eager place where we could be happy, and free.

"I love you too, Deb," I whispered to the window, "and I'll find you again. I swear I will."

Rewind twelve years.

* * *

Debbie had gone to college in Minneapolis, so I drove there. I spent a few days searching for her, then I found her, just by accident. I was walking past this bagel place on the corner, and there she was, sitting at a booth, reading a book.

I sat down across from her. "Deb," I said softly, grinning like a fool.

She looked up. I reached for her hands, I couldn't help it, and she pulled them away. "Do I know you?" she said, annoyed.

Rewind two minutes.

I took a deep breath. Debbie sat at her table, reading.

I approached her booth. "Hi."

She looked up from her book. "Hi."

"Do you mind some company? I'm new in town."

She eyed me for a moment, then shrugged. "Sure. Have a seat."

"I'm Todd," I said, sliding into the booth.

"I'm Deborah," she said.

We talked for a while. I told her I had just moved from New York. She said she was studying biology, but was thinking about switching her major to art.

"I mean, I do like art," she said, "but I'm not sure I'm the right kind of person for it. It seems like you really have to be passionate, and I never seem sure how to feel about anything."

"Well, it's like that thing you said about Mozart," I said playfully.

"What thing?"

"That you don't have to be a perfect person to write perfect music."

She frowned. "I never said that."

I arched an eyebrow.

Rewind a few seconds.

"—and I never seem sure how to feel about anything."

"I think you'd make a *great* artist," I said.

"You hardly know me."

I shrugged. "I can just tell."

We talked for almost an hour. At one point, Debbie put her chin in her hands and studied my face. "I have the weirdest feeling like we might have met somewhere before," she said. "Does that ever happen to you?"

I nodded. "Yeah. All the time."

* * *

This time I was only nineteen when I married Debbie. I figured that would be plenty of time.

Dad was worried.

I told him, "I asked Debbie to marry me and she said yes. End of story."

"It's just that you're so young," he said. "You hardly know this girl."

"But when I'm with her," I replied, "it's like I've known her my whole life."

After Debbie finished school, we moved to a small apartment in Boston. We lived there for a few months. Debbie was pregnant. Everything seemed right.

That same man tried to kill me again in Boston.

I was standing on a street corner, waiting for the light to change. Suddenly I heard someone gasp, and I turned my head just in time to see the barrel of a shotgun being raised toward my face.

Rewind one minute.

I spun around and spotted him immediately, on the sidewalk ten yards behind me. He had the same straggly hair, the same cold eyes. I could see the outline of the shotgun that he carried beneath his coat. There was a small crowd between us. He met my gaze.

"Why?" I shouted, spreading my arms. "Why are you trying to kill me?"

A few people turned to watch. Most others pushed on by. The man's voice was gravelly and harsh. "To make it stop."

I frowned. "Make what stop?"

"I saw you on TV," he said. "You're the one who keeps making the future disappear."

I dropped back a step. "You remember that?"

"I remember everything," he said, raising the gun toward me, "and I'll get you someday."

Rewind, rewind, rewind away.

* * *

I had been so stupid, so careless. This madman was aware of my rewinding, and because of that stupid interview he knew who I was. There were some things even I couldn't take back.

I fled with Debbie to Chicago, where the murderous man wouldn't find us. We bought a nice house and went to Cubs games on weekends. I was twenty-three years old. There was still plenty of time to build a future, raise a family.

Our son was born, and we named him Timothy.

Timmy was bold and bright. He had his mom's eyes, and sand-colored hair just like my dad. But mostly he was just Tim.

When he was four, he found a dead bird by the side of the road. "What's that?" he asked me, pointing.

"A bird," I said. "It's dead."

I think it was a robin, though it was hard to tell. A lot of it seemed to be missing, and I wasn't sure which of the dark patches were feathers and which were dried blood. Timmy bent over to examine it more closely.

I warned him, "Don't touch it."

Timmy stared at that bird for a long, long time. Later, he said, "I wish they didn't have to die."

He was a good kid. Things were going all right for us. I had gotten to the point where I wasn't rewinding much at all.

Then something happened.

***

It was a bitter cold night in February, and I stood looking out the window.
The world outside seemed edged in blue. Dark leaves fell softly on the
porch. The phone rang.

I answered it. "Hello?"

The voice on the other end seemed distant, insubstantial. "I'm looking
for a Mr. Todd Rawlins?"

"Yes."

"I'm very sorry, sir. I'm afraid there's been an accident. Your wife is
going to be all right. But your son Timothy—"

I said, "No."

I didn't want to hear those awful things. Timmy was injured, maimed—
he was dead.

The man began again. "I know this is—"

"Don't say a thing," I shouted at him. "Don't say a goddamn word to me."

Rewind. Rewind twenty-four hours.

Shuddering, I walked through dark hallways to the room where Timmy
lay safe, breathing softly in his sleep.

***

I was out in my front yard playing catch with Timmy the third time that
murderous man came. I didn't realize he was there until I heard him
chuckling softly behind me.

I turned. He stood just a few feet away, on the sidewalk outside my
fence. He had the same straggly hair, the same gray trench coat. He held a
pistol levelled at my head.

Rewind one minute.

I spun around and gasped. He was still there, the gun pointed straight
at me. How long had he been standing like that?

Rewind five minutes.

This time he was out on the street, the gun held at his side.

"I could have done it," he called out. "I could have shot you."

I met his gaze and held it a long time. What he said was true. Finally I
said, "All right."

"I want to talk."

I turned to my son. "Timmy, go inside. Now."

Timmy nodded. He dashed across the lawn, bounded up the porch steps, and disappeared into the house.

I turned to the man with the gun. I took a deep breath.

"Okay," I said. "We'll talk."

* * *

The man said, "I told you I'd get you some day."

I didn't respond. We walked two blocks along crumbling sidewalks to the town park. It was autumn, and dead leaves were strewn through the grass. Finally I said, "Who are you?"

The man kept his eyes turned toward the dull, gray clouds.

He said, "I read about this experiment once. They put two rats in a cage and give 'em electric shocks. One rat can push a lever to make it stop for both of them, the other one can't. Even though they always get the same amount of electricity, only the second rat dies—the one with no control."

He turned and stared me in the eyes. "That's me, Rawlins. I'm the second rat."

He wandered over to a picnic table made of damp, warped wood and sat down. I joined him.

"I'm Ian Kyle," he said, "the man who watches life vanish. I can be walking down the street, or reading a book, or sitting on the goddamn toilet—and then suddenly it's five minutes ago, or five days ago, or five years."

He shook his head. "I was going to kill you, Rawlins. That's why I came to Chicago. I didn't know you had a kid though."

I said, "His name's Timmy."

Kyle sighed. "You're a dumb shit," he said. "Killing you now would be a favor."

I frowned. "What do you mean?"

"Your family, your kid." He stared down at his hands. "I had kids once, a long time ago. Two beautiful girls. Ashley was three, Katie was five—though they got younger sometimes, in fits and starts. One day I blinked and they had never been born at all."

172

He heaved a great, wretched sigh.

"I'm sorry," I said, stunned. "I didn't think——"

He cut me off. "My marriage disappeared too. My wife didn't know me. I'd been a painter, then one day my art had never been. I had nobody, nothing——nothing but some bastard on TV named Todd Rawlins, who proved that he had caused it all."

"I'm sorry," I said. "I had no idea. I thought I was the only one who knew."

"Well you were wrong!" Kyle said. "I knew! You should be thankful it was just me, or there'd be a lot more people who'd want you dead."

I tried to explain, "I was born sick. All I ever wanted was to live."

He grinned sourly, and shook his head. "Don't we all, Rawlins? Don't we all?"

"What do you want from me?" I said, spreading my arms.

"I want you to suffer," he said, glaring at me with his cold eyes. "You should never get too attached to anything. I learned that the hard way. Now it's your turn."

"What are you talking about?"

"It won't bother me now if you rewind, I've got nothing to lose." He pointed at me. "But you're stuck. You love your family. You don't want them just disappearing all the time. Now you have to choose——what's more important? Your family, the rest of the world? Or you? Either you suffer or you die. Whatever you choose, I've got my revenge."

* * *

Ian Kyle was gone, but his words stayed with me. He was right. I was caught in a trap of my own making, and there was no escape.

If I didn't rewind at all I'd die, but every time I did I lost a piece of my life. I rewound in bits and pieces. A week here, a day there, or an hour.

"Hey, Timmy," I said once. "You want to go fishing?"

Timmy nodded. "Okay, I guess."

"You remember how?"

He looked confused. "No."

Debbie called from the kitchen, "He's never been, Todd."

He had, of course. I'd taken him myself, to that smooth blue lake off

Sycamore Drive. We'd paddled through the rocks, through the shaded, murky waters beneath those great mustard-colored trees. Timmy had picked it up quickly. "I got one!" he'd exclaimed. "Look, dad. I got one!"

I had rewound back past that part, though.

"Come on, Tim," I told him sadly. "I'll teach you."

I wanted it to count. I wanted Timmy to remember all the places I took him, all the bedtime stories I read him, not just some. Each time I rewound, I would watch him struggle over the same schoolwork he'd once known, and I felt guilt and misery.

There was something else, too. As long as I lived, Timmy could never be more than ten years old—or thereabouts.

"I want to be a fireman when I grow up," Timmy said one evening, "or a vampire."

Sadly, I tousled his soft brown hair. "I think that you'll be something wonderful when you grow up."

* * *

So I'm dying.

Rewinding now is out of the question. I couldn't steal the last year from Timmy. I couldn't take the last month from him, the last week, even.

Debbie brings him into the bedroom. He's crying, and he jumps up on the bed with me. "I don't want you to die."

"It's all right, Tim," I tell him. "You have to take good care of your mom for me, okay?" Timmy nods solemnly.

My dad's here too. He's wearing a flannel shirt, and that same stupid blue cap.

I can rewind life. I could be young and healthy and free. I could fight Willy Pierson and win. I could make a fortune in Vegas, or on Wall Street. I could be on TV. I could be kissing Debbie again for the very first time.

I could do all those things. This instant, if I wanted to.

Timmy watches me, with an expression of trust and hope.

I can rewind life.

But I won't.

Author's note: The Second Rat

There are a lot of things that bug me about most time travel stories. One of the big ones is the issue of physical location. Most time travel stories assume that if you're standing in Time Square and you travel back in time a hundred years, that you'd be standing in Times Square a hundred years in the past. But the Earth is hurtling through space at almost 500,000 miles an hour, so if you were to travel back in time a hundred years, presumably you would be floating in deep space.

Another problem is the issue of changing the past. In Ray Bradbury's classic story "A Sound of Thunder," a time traveler in the distant past accidentally steps on a butterfly, and when he returns to the present he finds that his whole world has changed. It seems to me that this is how time travel would actually work. Even if you tried hard not to mess up the timeline, your very presence would subtly alter the trajectory of everyone around you, setting off a cascade of changes that would quickly result in millions or billions of people not being born and completely different people being born in their place. You would return to the present to find that you had accidentally committed a genocide, and any attempt to repair the damage would only be committing a second genocide against the new people who had come into existence as a result of your actions.

They never really talk about that in *Back to the Future*.

"The Second Rat" was the first story I wrote at the Clarion writers workshop in 1999, and the first story I wrote that sold to a pro market. ("The Black Bird" was published first but written after.) I liked the idea of a character rewinding time and returning to various points in his past, as it gets around the problem of "Why doesn't he end up in deep space?" I was familiar with the rat experiment described in "The Second Rat" from Howard Bloom's book *The Lucifer Principle*, and I thought it would be interesting to have a character like Ian Kyle who could give voice to all those forgotten victims who are usually ignored in time travel stories.

When the story was critiqued, several people thought it would be stronger without Ian Kyle. They thought it should be a more understated, literary story where Todd's epiphany (that he must sacrifice his life so that his son can grow up) is something that he comes to on his own rather than having it forced on him by a third party. I thought that was a fair point, and I could see that version being really compelling, but I liked the story the way it was.

Midway through the workshop we were visited by Scott Edelman, editor of a glossy full-color magazine called *Science Fiction Age*, which I had been reading for years. When Scott read "The Second Rat," he agreed that I should remove Ian Kyle. He said that if I rewrote the story without Ian Kyle, he would probably buy it. I really wanted to be published in *Science Fiction Age*, but I didn't want to rewrite the story, so in the end I sent it off to *On Spec* magazine, who published it in their Spring 2002 issue.

A few years later, when I was living in Los Angeles, I showed the story to a friend of mine. He liked it a lot and asked if he could pitch it to studios. I said sure. One executive loved the story and wanted to do it as a TV show, but got laid off before the contracts were signed, and the whole thing fell apart. Too bad. I would have loved to see "The Second Rat" on TV. The film rights are still available if anyone's interested.

They Go Bump

Ball placed his feet carefully. Walking on rough terrain was treacherous when you couldn't see your feet—or your legs, for that matter, or any part of yourself. All he could see was the uneven ground, the shady stones edged with sharp sunlight, drifting eerily beneath him.

His boot caught and twisted, and he pitched forward, falling and smacking his elbows hard against the ground.

From somewhere up on the hilltop, Cataldo's voice laughed. That voice—smooth and measured, with just a hint of sharpness. Ball had never paid much attention to voices before, but now voices were all they had.

Cataldo's voice shouted, "Was that you, Ball? Again?"

Ball groped on the ground for his rifle. He felt it, grasped it, slung it over his shoulder. He clambered to his feet and wavered there a few moments, unsteady.

Cataldo's voice again: "How many times is that now? Twelve?"

"Eleven." Ball groaned, stretched, and looked around. "Where are you?"

"By the rock."

Ball sighed. The rock. There was nothing but rocks, nothing but rolling expanses of rocks and more rocks, stretching to the horizon in every direction. The orange sky was full of rocks too, rocky moons. "Which rock?"

"The big, triangular one."

Ball squinted up the hill.

"See the tall peak?" Cataldo's voice prompted. "Below that there's a patch of boulders, and then at the edge of those there's this big, triangular—"

"All right, I see it." Ball took a deep breath. "I'm coming."

177

He scrambled over the boulders and picked his way carefully among the smaller stones. He tried to picture Cataldo's face—slick black hair, long, narrow jaw, oversized nose. Ball hadn't seen that face all day. Now there was just the voice. "Okay, I'm here," he breathed, finally.

The empty spot of nothingness that was Cataldo said, "Where's Sweezy?"

"I don't know." Ball shook his head, though he realized Cataldo couldn't see it anyway. "He hasn't said anything all day. I've tried talking to him."

Cataldo groaned. "Sweezy! Hey, Sweezy! Where are you?"

The vast plains of boulders were still and silent. There was no answer.

"He might have fallen behind," Ball said. "Maybe he got lost, or hurt his ankle."

"He's out there. Goddamnit, Sweezy! Sound off."

Finally, a plaintive voice, from far down in the rockslide, called out, "I'm here. What?"

Sweezy. His voice tended to quaver as he spoke. It always seemed tired and prickly, that voice. Ball shouted, "We just wanted to make sure you were still with us."

"Just go," Sweezy's voice said. "I can take care of myself."

Cataldo grunted in disgust, and said to Ball, "Come on. Let's catch up with the others."

Ball turned wearily, and moved to follow. He walked in the direction he thought Cataldo had gone.

Invisible soldiers. Ball chuckled tiredly. Invisible soldiers on an important mission, invisible soldiers with invisible feet.

He tripped again, and fell.

* * *

The week before, Ball had been safe, tucked far underground in the humid, steel-rimmed tunnels of Fort Deep. He had been sitting on a bench outside Captain Schemmer's office.

They were giving Ball a mission; he wondered if he was going to die. Cataldo had come and gone already, but Sweezy was still in there. Ball could hear voices through the door.

Sweezy's voice, prickly and desperate: "Why me? I'm a good soldier. You know I'm a good soldier. I train all the time. I study the intel, hard. I don't deserve——"

The captain's voice, female, too low and gruff to make out the words.

Then Sweezy again. "But——"

Then the captain, and so on.

Finally, the door opened and Sweezy emerged. He was skinny, with a huge, lumpy head, and big eyes rimmed with darkness.

"Hey Sweezy," Ball said.

Sweezy, sweaty and pale, nodded and walked on past.

Captain Schemmer called, "Private Ball."

Ball stood and entered. The office was spartan: one desk and two chairs. The walls were made of hewn boulder and plate steel. Schemmer gestured to the empty chair.

Ball sat down. "Nice to finally meet you, Captain."

Schemmer nodded. "You've been picked for an important mission. Earth Army is conducting field tests of our new phased camouflage." She stared at him levelly. "You've read the reports?"

"Yes, sir."

He hadn't bothered, actually, but he'd heard of the camouflage. "That stuff the Kraven-Hish mercenaries use." He suppressed a shudder. "That makes them invisible."

"We've developed our own. You're going to test it under battlefield conditions."

Ball blinked. "Battlefield, sir?"

"You're going to walk across the planet surface, from Hatch E to Hatch A."

Ball felt a fresh rush of panic. For months, orbital assault platforms had circled high overhead in the orange-dust sky. They swept over the horizon, launching missile attacks against anything that moved on the surface. "But the orbitals——"

"Won't see you," Schemmer said. "Not if the camouflage works. Just like they don't see the Kraven-Hish mercenaries."

Ball stared at the floor.

"We've done tests," Schemmer said. "The camouflage has passed every one. You should be pretty safe. But we need to know whether this stuff holds up under real conditions. We need to send some people outside with it, for a week or more."

"Me?" Ball glanced back over his shoulder. "And Sweezy?"

"And some others. Yes."

So they needed a couple guys, some guys who could walk. And maybe those guys would get nuked. So they picked the most useless guys here.

Himself. Cataldo. Sweezy.

Goddamnit.

"Yes, Captain," Ball said.

* * *

The suits were shimmering grey, like fish scales. The elbows, knees, and boots were all thickly padded. Air tanks hung from the shoulders. Rifles were attached to the suits with thin cords.

"The cord's so you don't lose the rifle," one of the technicians said. "It'll be invisible too, once you power up."

Six suits. Ball glanced around the room.

Private Dimon, rat-faced and sleazy, was over in the corner sucking up to Cataldo. So Dimon was in.

Plus Cataldo.

Sweezy.

And Ball himself made four. Two more.

A friendly voice said, "Ball."

He turned. Private Reice, young and good-natured, stood grinning.

"Damn," Ball said. "They got you too."

Reice nodded. "Me." He glanced toward the door. "And the corporal too, it looks like."

Corporal Tennet, tall and brave, walked into the room.

"He probably volunteered," Ball said.

The corporal cleared his throat. "All right, everyone. Suit up."

The technicians helped Ball into his suit. The material clung tight around his biceps and thighs. A foggy, translucent mask covered his face.

One of the technicians said, "There are buttons inside the material on the left wrist. You can feel them."

Ball ran his fingers down his arm. He felt four knobby bumps.

"Punch in your code," said another technician, demonstrating on the corporal. "Like this."

Light flashed, bright as a signal flare. The technician backed away. The corporal was gone.

Ball waited, tense, through a long stretch of silence.

Then the corporal's voice: "I can't see my hand."

Reice leaned forward, staring hard. He whispered, "Holy shit."

The corporal's voice again. "I can't see my feet either."

"Move slowly," the technician advised. "It takes some getting used to."

Ball heard the soft clomp of the corporal's first footstep. They heard his voice, chuckling. "Everyone power up."

Lights flashed all around the room. Ball shielded his eyes against the glare. He punched the code on his wrist, and then——

He saw the tip of his nose, the dark interior of the helmet. He looked down and down. There was nothing there. Vertigo struck him. He was falling—falling forward. He jerked upright. He dropped back a few paces, closing his eyes. "How do you turn it off?"

"You don't," a technician said sharply, "or you'll die."

"Punch the code in reverse," said another.

Ball opened his eyes. He waved an invisible hand in front of his face. He ran invisible fingers over his invisible wrist, over the knobby buttons. After a moment, he decided not to mess with them.

Sweezy's voice said, "How do they know these things are going to work?"

"They don't," Cataldo's voice said nastily. "That's what *we're* for."

Sweezy said, "I think they ought to——"

There was a sudden crash, and a desk rolled across the room, scattering pipes and wires. From somewhere down on the floor, Sweezy groaned.

Cataldo said, "Stop screwing around."

"Someone pushed me," Sweezy protested. There were scrapes and thumps as he climbed to his feet. "It was *you*. You pushed me."

"I didn't push anybody," Cataldo said.

Dimon's voice added, "You probably tripped."

"It was you then," Sweezy said. "I never trip. Never. I train all the time. I..."

His voice trailed off as the corporal cut in: "All right, form up and move out. Hatch E. Let's go."

"We're going outside?" Ball said. "Now?"

"What do you want, Ball?" Cataldo challenged. "A mission briefing on how to walk?"

Dimon snickered.

They marched out into the hall. A group of heavy-helmeted military police was waiting. Their cold eyes passed blankly over the spot where Ball stood. He gave them the finger. No response.

The police led the way down long rock and steel tunnels, then herded the squad through an oval airlock and out into the cavern beyond. Enormous steel pipes stretched up to the ceiling, up to a gigantic metal plate. The underside of the plate read: HATCH E.

Ball flinched as the hatch creaked and shuddered and began to descend—slow, massive and ponderous. It sank and crunched against the floor.

The corporal said, "Move."

Ball scurried forward and clambered up the steep stone facade. A voice cursed—he couldn't tell whose. Then the platform rose, higher and higher. They emerged into open air. Beneath them the hatch clanked solidly into place.

Ball stared. The vista was wide and empty. There was nothing to see here. Not even themselves.

"Everybody sound off," the corporal said.

Ball said, "I'm right next to you." They had no radios, no locator beacons. Orbitals could track signals like that.

"I'm over here," said Cataldo.

Next to him, Dimon. "Yeah. Me too."

"I'm here," said Reice.

There was a long pause.

The corporal prompted, "Sweezy?"

Sweezy's voice came at last, almost too soft to hear. "I'm with you."

The corporal sighed. "All right. Hatch A is northeast of here. Northeast is that way, between those two rocks."

Ball squinted into the distance. Two large boulders loomed before them.

The corporal said, "Move out."

There were scraping footstep sounds as the squad began to march.

Dimon said, "We're going to die."

"Maybe," the corporal replied. "The first orbital comes up over the horizon in 43 minutes. Then we'll know."

Ball traced his gaze over the horizon in a slow circle. "Nine *days* out here? Even if the orbitals don't get us, a pack of Kraven-Hish mercenaries will."

Cataldo said, "Maybe you haven't noticed, Ball, but we're invisible. They can't see us."

"We can't see them either," Ball countered.

"Exactly," the corporal cut in. "They can't see us, we can't see them. No one can see anyone. So relax. And keep walking."

Ball pulled the rifle off his shoulder and hefted it experimentally. Damned impossible, he decided, trying to aim a gun you couldn't even see.

Again, Dimon's voice: "We're going to die."

Dimon's voice. It came from somewhere ahead of Ball, and drifted past him, and out away over the hills.

* * *

Forty-three minutes passed. The first of the orbitals came over the horizon. Ball imagined he could see it up there, a shining white dot in the flat orange sky. It looked like death.

The corporal said, "It's time."

Ball held his breath, waited. He watched for the glint of metal, for a tactical nuclear assault.

Ten minutes passed.

"The orbital's overhead," the corporal announced. "It can't see us."

Ball slouched, letting out a long, slow breath. Dimon's voice started to laugh, a little crazily.

"Keep walking," the corporal said.

The sound of scattered footsteps picked up again.

"And now..." Ball said. "Now we can start worrying about Kraven-Hish mercenaries."

"Give it a rest, Ball," Cataldo said. "You're bringing down my morale."

"They might be around," Ball argued. "A pack of them."

"They might not," Cataldo said.

"Who knows where they are?" Reice said. "Who knows where they might be? We don't even know what they look like."

"They don't look like anything," Cataldo answered. "They're invisible."

"You know what I mean," Reice said.

No one had ever gotten a picture of the Kraven-Hish; they were always invisible. You couldn't get a picture, even if you killed one, and some guys were pretty sure they had.

Ball glanced around. Imagine they died out here, who would ever find them? They'd rot. Then the suits would rot. The suits would go visible in rotted patches, nothing left of the bodies inside.

Dimon said, "You know what I heard? I heard they've got pictures of the Kraven-Hish. Intel has pictures. They don't want to show us."

Reice said, "Why would they do that?"

"They don't want to frighten off new recruits," Dimon said. "That's how scary these things are. That's what I heard."

"That's stupid," Cataldo said.

"That's what I heard," Dimon repeated. "That's all."

* * *

Ball hadn't tripped in over six hours. He forced himself to grin.

From somewhere behind him, Cataldo's voice shouted, "Sweezy!"

Ball turned. "Not again." He took a few steps back toward Cataldo.

"Sweezy! Damn it, Sweezy. Just say something."

The rocky wastes were silent.

"I swear, Sweezy," Cataldo warned. "I swear this is the last time. Sound off."

They waited. There was no answer.

Ball imagined Sweezy's face—tired and petulant, forehead scrunched, eyes staring at his feet, ignoring them.

"All right," Cataldo called finally. "All right, if that's how you want it. I hope you break your neck."

Ball sighed.

"Let's go," Cataldo told him.

They walked up over the next rise. The scattered voices of the others were faint in the valley below. It took almost an hour to catch up.

Those voices, louder now, drifted toward them.

The corporal's voice: "Reice, you take point for a while. I'm going to check on the others."

"Yes, sir," Reice's voice said.

The corporal's voice: "You know the way?"

"To Hatch A? Yes, sir."

"Good."

Ball walked closer. From beside him came the corporal's voice: "Who's there?"

"Ball, sir," he said. "And Cataldo."

"Anything to report?"

Ball wondered if they should say something about Sweezy, but Cataldo just said, with a trace of disgust, "No, sir. Nothing at all."

* * *

Night fell. The dusty sky turned from orange to brown to muddy black. The cratered asteroid moons shone bright and red. Ball lay curled up on the hard ground and kept his rifle close. With his fingers, he traced the invisible cord that connected the rifle to his suit.

Reice was resting somewhere nearby, and Dimon was somewhere down the hill. Ball wasn't sure about the corporal, and Sweezy hadn't spoken since that morning. No one seemed to miss him.

Dimon's voice burst out, "Cataldo. Get off, it's not funny. I'm trying to sleep."

Cataldo's voice answered, from far down the hill. "What? I'm over here."

There was a sudden sound, a sharp, cracking sound, like a branch snapping. But there were no branches here, nothing to be broken except their necks. Ball said quickly, "What was that?"

"I thought I felt something," Dimon's voice said. There was a short pause. "Never mind. It was nothing."

"What was that sound?" Ball pressed. "That cracking sound?"

"What sound?" Dimon's voice said.

"I heard it too," Reice's voice said.

Dimon's voice said, "I didn't hear anything."

Ball rolled up onto his knees, pushed the butt of his rifle back into his shoulder, and pointed the barrel out into the darkness.

Cataldo's voice called, "You're hearing things, Ball."

"I heard it too," Reice insisted.

"Heard what?" Cataldo's voice said.

"I don't know," Reice said. "Kind of a...I don't know."

Dimon's voice chuckled.

Cataldo's voice joined in. "Right."

Ball knelt there on the rocks, staring up at the asteroids. They glowed a deep red, like blood—like the blood of all the Earth Army soldiers killed by Kraven-Hish mercenaries.

Dozens of them could hide out here. Hundreds, lurking invisible among the stones. They were trained to fight unseen. They could get close to a person, kill a person. Silently.

Or almost silently.

They could kill a person, maybe mimic his voice, and then no one would ever know.

"Let's get some sleep," Dimon's voice said.

Ball shuddered. It was Dimon's voice. But was it Dimon?

A Kraven-Hish mercenary crouched in the darkness there, kneeling over Dimon's invisible corpse. Maybe.

Ball lay still. His ears strained for any sound, but there were no more sounds. And no more sleep.

* * *

Dawn burned orange and bright.

"Corporal," Ball said. "I'm afraid."

"We're all afraid, Ball," the corporal's voice replied.

"I heard something last night, sir. A strange noise. I think I heard Private Dimon die."

"I spoke to Dimon this morning."

Ball didn't say anything. The corporal waited.

"Sir." Ball heard a strained quality creep into his voice. "How do you know it was really him? It was just a voice. Voices can be imitated."

"You think our squad's been infiltrated? Dimon's voice replaced by—"

Ball lowered his voice. "By Kraven-Hish mercenaries. Sir, I don't know."

"Just Dimon?"

Ball paused. "And maybe Cataldo, I don't know."

"And maybe me."

Ball sighed. "It's possible, sir."

"But you're still telling me?"

"I have to tell someone," Ball said. "If they've gotten you, well, then we're all dead anyway. It's worth the risk."

"That's good thinking, Ball." There was a brief pause. "But you're overreacting. You thought you heard a noise. Maybe it was real, maybe it wasn't. Maybe it was nothing. I wouldn't blame anyone for starting to hear things out here."

"Reice heard it, too."

There was a pause. The corporal's voice called out, "Private Reice."

Ball didn't hear his approach, but a few moments later Reice's voice answered. "Sir?"

The corporal's voice said, "You heard a noise last night?"

"No," Reice's voice said. "I mean, I thought maybe I did, sir, after Ball said it. But it was just my imagination. You know what it's like here at night. The—"

"Yes," said the corporal's voice. "Thank you, private."

Ball waited a while.

"Sir," he pleaded softly. "Please."

"Your mind's playing tricks on you, that's all. You know how I'm sure?"

"How?"

The corporal's voice sighed. "A pack of Kraven-Hish mercenaries wouldn't bother to infiltrate us. They'd just wipe us out. We couldn't stop them."

That was true, Ball acknowledged.

"You take point for a while," the corporal's voice said. "It'll give you something else to think about."

"Yes sir," Ball said.

* * *

Days passed, and Ball heard sounds:

Slithering. Leathery skin. Loose flesh. Hisses and grumbles and growls. And moans, most of all. Soft, predatory moans. Sounds like Kraven-Hish mercenaries make.

"Corporal," he begged. "Please, we have to do something. I can hear it. Oh god, I can hear them."

"It's your imagination, Ball," said the corporal's steady voice. "Remember what I said before."

That night Ball lay awake, his thoughts exhausted and mad.

Kraven-Hish mercenaries. Ball was leading the way to Hatch A, and they were following close behind. When the hatch opened, they would burst unseen and unexpected into those safe stone tunnels.

He didn't tell the corporal these thoughts.

He was afraid. That his squad was being replaced, one by one. That the corporal was dead. That a Kraven-Hish mercenary sat there, somewhere back there, mouthing the corporal's words.

He was very afraid.

* * *

He tried to find Reice, to talk to him, away from the corporal. It was hard. Ball didn't know where anyone was anymore. Their footsteps had become soft, insubstantial, and Reice and the corporal seemed to walk together, always.

"Reice," Ball said. "You heard it, that night. I know you did."

Reice's voice said, "Ball, I didn't hear anything. Really."

An uneasy feeling spread over Ball. What if this wasn't really Reice? He said, "Back at Fort Deep you—"

"Ball, I'm tired, all right? Can we talk about this later?"

That was a lie, Ball was sure of it. So Reice was gone too, probably.

Ball felt very alone. Reice and the corporal and Dimon. All dead, replaced by Kraven-Hish mercenaries, monsters that spoke with the voices of friends.

After that, those three always seemed to walk together. Maybe they were plotting something.

And Sweezy? Sweezy hadn't spoken in days. No one had mentioned him. Maybe he had gotten separated, or twisted an ankle. Ball wished he could believe that—Sweezy, lying among the rocks, lost or injured but alive. But Sweezy was gone. Weak, whiny Sweezy, always alone, always lagging behind. He had been the first to die.

Cataldo? Ball wasn't sure about him.

"Listen," Ball told Cataldo. "There are Kraven-Hish mercenaries, all around us. I hear them. You hear it too. I know you do."

"Leave me alone, Ball," Cataldo's voice said. "You're creeping everybody out."

"You hear them."

"People imagine things. Things that aren't there, in a place like this."

"I have an idea," Ball said.

Cataldo's voice answered quickly, "No."

"We can power down our suits. Just for a moment, for a second. The last orbital went down over the horizon 80 minutes ago. The next one won't be up for half an hour. We can see who we really are."

"I'm not risking it," Cataldo's voice said. "Because you think you heard something? That's insane."

"You heard it too."

"Forget it."

"*I'll* do it, then." Ball's heart beat faster. "I'll power down my suit. Then you'll see it's safe. Then maybe you'll do it too."

Ball stared up into the sky, straight up, to where an orbital attack platform floated, bristling with missile silos, waiting to attack, if he was wrong about this. His fingers played over the buttons on his wrist.

"Don't," Cataldo's voice growled. "Don't even think about it. You wait until the rest of us reach minimum safe distance. Then do whatever the hell you want with yourself, I don't care. But not here, Ball. Not now. You've got no right." Cataldo walked away, his footsteps fading.

Was that really Cataldo? Hard to say.

Ball kept his invisible rifle gripped tight in his sweaty, invisible fingers.

* * *

Sometimes, lying on the jagged ground at night, he wondered if any of them had ever been real—Cataldo, Dimon, the corporal. He couldn't exactly picture their faces anymore. Maybe they had never had faces. Maybe they had only ever been voices. Voices in his head.

Other times, marching exhausted in the sun, he thought about fighting them. He hefted his rifle, which was heavy, huge, and worthless. He could have aimed it, maybe, if he could've seen his targets. Without targets...

Useless. He might get off a dozen shots, and most would miss. Then they would close in on him—Cataldo, Dimon, Reice, the corporal—and however many more were out there.

He could run, slip away in the night, sprint ahead to Fort Deep. But the base was still three days off, and the squad was already moving as fast as he could manage. Or he could hide, wrapped up safe in his unseeable suit, lose himself in the rocky hills. He had six days worth of air. The others would notice he was gone. They'd come after him, maybe find him. Or maybe they would go on to Fort Deep and make it theirs, and then he would die out here, alone.

So he kept walking, walking and talking, and he didn't mention Kraven-Hish mercenaries anymore, even though he could hear them.

He kept glancing back over his shoulder, though there was nothing there, not even his shoulder. Why hadn't they killed him yet? Maybe they needed someone to lead them to Hatch A, or maybe not. It couldn't last, they'd get him sometime, maybe this afternoon.

Maybe during this footstep—this next tired, tortured footstep—this one. But then that footstep was over, and he was still alive. Maybe the next one then.

The sun sank and the sky turned dark.

Or maybe tonight.

The squad made camp, and Ball settled down on the ground beneath a rocky overhang, to rest and brood. Footsteps came toward him across the hillside.

"Ball!" Cataldo's voice whispered. "Ball, where are you?"

"I'm here," Ball said, softly.

"We're in trouble. Oh god, we're in trouble. You were right about them." Cataldo's voice paused. "The corporal was asking me things today: How close are we to the hatch? What security do I think will meet us? Weird stuff like that. The corporal, he knows all that better than us." Cataldo's voice got lower. "And you were right, I think. I can hear it sometimes. Those sounds."

Was it some sort of trick? Ball sat still in the darkness.

"What are we going to do?" Cataldo's voice said. "What can we do?"

"I don't know. Let me think."

After a few moments, Cataldo's voice grunted. "Well, you can do what you want. *I'm* getting the hell out of here." His footsteps stumbled off down the hillside.

The corporal's voice said, "Reice. Dimon. Sound off."

Ball tensed, and waited.

"I'm over here," called Reice's voice, and Dimon too, "Here."

Again, Ball had that unsettling feeling, that they were all off together—Dimon, Reice, the corporal—sitting together, plotting.

"Ball," the corporal's voice shouted. "Where are you?"

Ball didn't answer. The silence was heavy. Finally he murmured, "Up here."

"Where?"

"Under the rock," Ball said. "Under the ledge."

"Okay," the corporal's voice said. "Cataldo?"

Ball waited.

Again the corporal's voice: "Cataldo? Sound off."

Long minutes passed.

Then a sound from somewhere down the hill, a sound like a spine splintering. A sound like a voice—Cataldo's voice—coughing up blood and choking on it. A sound like Cataldo dying. It cut off abruptly.

The corporal's voice called out once more, "Cataldo?"

A few moments later, Cataldo's voice answered calmly, "I'm here."

Ball shut his eyes very tight and tried not to move, or breathe. He wanted to be more invisible—so invisible that no one would ever see him again, or ever hurt him. He wanted to be so invisible that he wasn't even there anymore.

He waited almost an hour, then slowly stood up. He crept across the stones to a narrow crevice far down the hillside. He lay down there, curled up tight. He wanted to fall asleep and wake again alive. He wanted for the horrible Kraven-Hish mercenaries not to find his sleeping spot. In the morning, he awoke.

His rifle was gone.

* * *

Ball traced the invisible cord very, very carefully. It was broken halfway down. He felt around on the ground, crawling back and forth. He checked again slowly, methodically, inch-by-inch. He wished he could believe it was an accident—that the cord had worn down and the rifle had fallen away sometime in the night. But he knew it hadn't.

The whole squad started marching again and Ball trudged on, defeated. Tears rose up in his eyes and spilled down his face. He was still alive and he didn't know why and the others were all dead.

Reice had been decent and good. He had never done anything to deserve this.

The corporal had been brave, and had tried so hard.

Dimon had been a shit. But what did that matter, out here?

Cataldo had been too angry, too mean. But Cataldo had kept checking on Sweezy, when no one else had bothered. That was something.

And Sweezy. Ball had almost forgotten him. Sweezy had been harmless. It wasn't fair.

Nearby, Cataldo's voice said, "Ball. I want to talk to you. About last night."

"You're not Cataldo," Ball said softly. "Kill me if you want, but don't lie. Not anymore."

Cataldo's voice laughed. "Jesus, Ball. Take it easy."

"I heard Cataldo die," Ball said. "I heard it. You killed him."

"I tripped, Ball. It startled me, and I must have gasped or something. That's what you heard."

Ball didn't answer.

Cataldo's voice chuckled. "Come on, Ball. I just tripped. Haven't you ever tripped before?"

"No," Ball said. "Never."

And he waited.

And then Cataldo's voice said: "Well, good for you. I trip sometimes, all right?"

Ball felt weak and dizzy. He closed his eyes and red shapes swam in the darkness behind his eyelids. A long, low moan rose up from somewhere inside him and he couldn't stop it.

He said, "I tripped twelve times the first day and Cataldo was there. He laughed at me. You're not him. Don't lie, don't say anything. I won't believe you."

Cataldo's voice sighed a long, hard sigh.

Ball said, "Get away from me. Get away or I'll shoot. Even if you are Cataldo, I'll shoot you."

Cataldo's voice said, "Shoot me. Without a rifle."

"I have a rifle," Ball said.

"No," Cataldo's voice said. "I've got yours. I'm pointing it at you right now. I could pull the trigger if you don't believe me."

Ball backed away. The invisible cord that had held his rifle waved loosely from his shoulder. He reached for the buttons on his wrist. "I'll power down my suit," he warned. "I'll do it, and the orbital will kill us all."

"Go ahead." Cataldo's voice was unconcerned. "Power down. It'll make it easy to shoot you. The last orbital went down an hour ago."

Ball tried to figure if that was true. It was. He said softly, "You need me to lead you to the hatch."

"No," Cataldo's voice said. "Cataldo told me how to get there. Yesterday, before he died."

Then it was over. "Why didn't you kill me? Last night. Whenever."

It was the corporal's voice that answered. "That's a good question, Ball. Why don't cats kill the mice they catch right away?"

Ball shuddered. That voice, that proud voice. It wasn't right that it should say such a thing.

"For fun, Ball," Dimon's voice burst out. "That's the answer. For fun."

They were all together there, grouped close, arrayed against him.

Reice's voice assured him, "Don't worry though, you won't be killed."

Ball tried to picture them: a pack of Kraven-Hish mercenaries, standing deadly before him. He couldn't do it. It was too awful. He couldn't even imagine it. "What do you want?"

A new voice came, a terrible voice. Low, hissing and rasping, sickening. It was groaning and gurgling—it filled his ears—the most horrible sound. It was so wicked, so horribly cunning. It said in a voice that seemed barely alive: "I want you to see..."

Ball waited, tense. Finally he said, "See what?"

"My face..." said the thing. "I want you to see my face. Then I'll let you go..."

Ball saw nightmares in his mind. A dozen drooling tongues, puckered tentacles, an exposed spine. A bulging skull, rotted cords of muscle, claws, soft innards. Rows and rows of teeth-stuffed gums, an oozing carapace, a mad cavern of cerebrum and vein. Hateful black eyes on stalks like eels.

"I'm worse..." said the thing. "Whatever you dream I am, I'm worse. But you want to live. I'm powering down my suit..."

Ball closed his eyes.

Four gunshots fired in the stillness.

Then a long wait. Darkness, eyes squeezed.

Then Sweezy's voice, "Ball, where are you? Let's go."

Ball kept his eyes closed. "Sweezy?"

"Come on," Sweezy's voice said. "Move."

Ball struggled to understand. "You were gone—"

"I wasn't. I was around. Quiet."

Ball choked out a relieved sob. "And you got them? The Kraven-Hish mercenaries? You got them all?"

"I got *it*," Sweezy's voice said. "The one. It was all of them—Dimon, Cataldo, Reice, the corporal—all their voices."

"One?"

"A solitary hunter. Like a cat. Intel was right."

Ball began to open one eye.

"Don't look at it," Sweezy's voice warned. "Just turn around and let's go."

Ball turned away, and opened his eyes.

"Walk," Sweezy's voice said. "Until we're over the rise. Don't look back."

They walked. Sweezy's voice didn't say anything for a while. When it came, it was very faint, "I wish I hadn't seen it, Ball. Oh god." It sounded like he was crying. "I don't ever want to dream again."

Hard stones drifted by, and Ball counted paces to keep himself from thinking too much. They went over one rise, then another. He halted then, and collapsed on the ground. Neither of them said anything for a while.

"I tried to tell the corporal," Ball said finally. "I tried to tell him. He wouldn't listen."

"The corporal was dead the first day. That wasn't him you were talking to."

Ball hunched over and held his invisible head in his invisible hands.

"Always take out the leader first," Sweezy's voice said. "Basic strategy."

"The first day?" Ball sat unbelieving. "You knew the first day and you didn't say anything?"

"*It* would've known about me, that monster, if I had said anything. Then I'd be dead. And so would you."

"But Reice," Ball said. "The corporal——"

"I saved you." Sweezy's voice was sharp. "I could've left you there, or started shooting blind, but I didn't. I waited for my chance and I saved us both."

Ball lay back against the ground and stared up into the orange-dust sky.

"I'm a good soldier," Sweezy's voice said. "I always said I was."

* * *

They walked two more days and halted at the top of a high cliff. Safety waited near, beneath Hatch A, just out of sight beyond the darkening horizon. Night fell. Ball lay awake and thought horrible thoughts.

Like——maybe the monster *had* known about Sweezy, after all.

Ball hadn't seen the thing's body, crumpled and lifeless. He had closed his eyes. Maybe there had never been a body, maybe that thing was still alive.

Maybe it was...

He slowly turned his eyes upon the empty spot where Sweezy lay sleeping.

"Sweezy!" he hissed. "Sweezy, wake up."

There was silence. Finally, Sweezy's voice said, "What?"

Ball trembled, he couldn't help it. "That is *you*, isn't it, Sweezy?" His voice was pleading, desperate. "It is really you? It just occurred to me that——"

"Yes, it's me," Sweezy's voice assured him. "Go back to sleep, Ball. Of course it's me."

Ball took a deep breath. Yes.

He rolled over and closed his eyes. He tried to relax.

Of course it was Sweezy, he tried to tell himself.

Of course it was.

Author's note: They Go Bump

This was the first story I wrote at the Odyssey writers workshop in 2001. It was inspired by a dream I'd had a few months earlier. In the dream I was with a group of friends, and we were all invisible. We were being hunted by some sinister force, and I kept trying to get my friends to be quiet, but they kept talking and giving away our position.

I loved the idea of a story where everyone's invisible, but it was really hard to make it work. Why don't the soldiers just turn off their invisibility suits? Well, because there's a satellite that's going to blast them if they do. Wouldn't they see each other's footsteps? No, because they're in a rocky, desolate landscape. And so on.

When the story was critiqued, people had a lot of problems with it. I was surprised at how negative people were. After the critique, Jeanne Cavelos, who runs the workshop, told me privately, "I think there was some payback happening here." Apparently my critiques of other people's stories had been more specific and candid than they really appreciated.

Still, some of the criticisms were clearly valid. One woman, whose husband was in the army, pointed out that the soldiers would probably be briefed as a group, not individually. That seemed obvious once she pointed it out. People also had endless issues with why the mission was so poorly planned. Why didn't the soldiers use code words? Why weren't they tied together with invisible rope?

I came home from the workshop determined to rewrite the story from scratch. I was going to make it so that the soldiers had scalvaged the invisibility suits from a crashed alien ship in the middle of a mission, which would help explain the lack of planning.

But then I found out about a contest called the Phobos Fiction Contest. The top three stories would receive $1,000 each, which is huge money in the world of short fiction, and the deadline was only a week away. There was no way I would be able to finish my rewrite in time, so I sent in "They Go Bump" the way it was. It placed as one of the top three stories.

I've always been a little sad that I never got to do my rewrite, but whatever problems there are with the story, they don't seem to have bothered that many people. I've gotten a lot of positive feedback on it, including from

Andrew Mason, executive producer of *The Matrix*, who called it "a perfect piece of writing for the form." Many people have told me that it's the best and/or scariest short story they've ever read. So maybe it's just as well that I didn't rewrite it. It's possible that I would have just messed it up.

I've also had a number of Hollywood people reach out to me about adapting the story, though none of those projects have ever come to fruition. I think "They Go Bump" would make a great film, though the fact that the characters are all invisible would obviously be an interesting creative challenge.

The Prize

Julian Serrato. Great criminal mastermind of the twenty-first century. They wanted him caught, badly. They wanted me to catch him.

I had a plan.

The girl at the hospital desk was pretty and shy. I showed her my badge. I spoke gently. "I'm Agent Child." I nodded at my partner. "This is Agent Bonner."

Bonner was big, tough, and uneasy. He said abruptly, "We're here to see Rebecca Courington."

"I'll get the doctor," the girl said.

Rebecca Courington lay still in her bed, wrapped up all in white. Her blond hair was carefully arranged. A needle was taped to her forearm, connected by a tube to an IV drip. She was strikingly beautiful. She slept.

The doctor checked her vitals.

"Her brain," Bonner said, "how much damage?"

"She won't wake up," the doctor said. "She's been here three years already."

"Four," Bonner said.

The doctor didn't question it.

I asked, "How much of her personality is still there? How much memory?"

"Hard to say." The doctor frowned. "Quite a bit, I would think. The damage is localized. She won't wake up, like I said, but…"

Bonner and I exchanged glances.

"We'd like a few moments alone," I said.

The doctor closed the door behind him.

Bonner sighed. "What do you think?"

"I think we should do it." I thought about the timetable—three months to grow her a new body. About twice that long to imprint what was left of the old brain onto the developing one, and the cost—substantial, but not prohibitive. Not compared to what had already been spent on the case.

Bonner watched her. "You ever met one of them? After they came back?"

"Once," I said. "Senator Snow."

"What's he like?"

"Like a dream of himself," I said, "like a half-forgotten memory—some pieces missing, some details confused, but true to his essence."

Bonner shifted uncomfortably. I could see the reluctance line his face. He didn't like the thought of *any* version of Rebecca Courington up and walking. That was understandable. He had put her here in the first place, after all. Before he was my partner, before I became an agent.

His voice was like gravel. "I just think, of all the people to bring back, of all the people, it's this stupid bitch that gets a new life. What did she do to deserve this? What makes her special?"

"There must be something about her," I said, "to make Julian Serrato love her."

* * *

They remade Rebecca Courington, remade her even lovelier than before. She sat in a chair in the interrogation room with her arms folded and said, "I died. You copied me. Why?"

"To help us find Julian Serrato," I said.

She laughed. "Find him? I don't know where he is. I don't even know what he looks like anymore. He changes his face, his voice, his fingertips. You know that."

"And you know him," I countered. "His personality, his mannerisms. He can't change who he is. You might recognize him."

She leaned back in her chair and stared into the big mirror on the wall. "Where's the other agent? The one who shot me?"

Beyond the mirror, I imagined I saw Bonner flinch.

"That's not important," I said.

"It is important." She glared. "To me. Why should I help you?"

I met her gaze. "Giving you a second life was very expensive. You can't pay for it, but the government will forgive your debt if Julian Serrato is apprehended."

"A second life." She ran her fingers down her sternum. She was quiet for a long time. When she spoke, her voice was toneless and measured. "I woke this morning for the first time. My breasts were large and tan. No freckles."

She fixed me with her terribly gorgeous eyes. "Don't give me this body and pretend you care what I know."

"Julian Serrato cares what you know," I said. "He'll kill you to keep you from talking."

She laughed. "No he won't. You've seen to that. You've made me a dream—*his* dream, a prize that only you can give him. He won't kill me. He'll try to take me away from you, without getting caught."

I frowned.

"You don't think he can do it," she said simply. "I think he can."

Later, I sat with Bonner in the dark observation room, watching her.

He grumbled, "I don't like it. She's too smart. She knows something. Something she's not telling us."

"Who cares what she knows?" I said, "Or thinks she knows? Her cooperation is moot. We'll get Serrato either way."

* * *

We filled her insides with our machines—machines that control, machines that surveil, machines that kill. We put death inside her.

The director called us into his office, studied us. "I'm prepared to move ahead with this operation," he said. "But I want your personal assurance that this is going to work."

"It'll work," Bonner said.

"I have your word on that?"

Bonner glanced at me. I cleared my throat. "Sir, we've modeled every scenario, every contingency. The new systems are foolproof. Serrato will not be able to disarm them. I promise you that."

The director sighed. Finally he punched a few buttons on his desk and said, "All right. The mission is a go. Good luck."

* * *

We flew to Atlanta, to the clinic of the eminently respected surgeon Felix Martindale. We waited in his private office. Bonner eyed the doctor's framed degrees with disdain. Martindale came in, closed the door behind him, noticed us.

"Can I help you?" he asked.

"Your government needs you," I said.

Bonner showed him a picture of Rebecca Courington.

"This woman may be brought to you," I said. "She'll be implanted with a standard array of government drones. They'll want you to remove them."

Martindale paled. "Why me?"

Bonner said, "There aren't a lot of people with the skills to do it. You're one of them."

"And they trust you," I said. "You've done it before."

Martindale began to deny it.

"Listen," Bonner ordered, cutting him off. "This is important."

I waited for Martindale's full attention. "In addition to the standard drones, she'll be carrying a new system. It's almost undetectable. You may not even notice it. You won't remove it. You won't mention it to anyone."

Martindale's voice was a hoarse whisper. "They'll kill me."

"They won't know," Bonner said. "You *might* notice these new drones. No one else will."

Martindale shook his head firmly. "I can't risk it."

"You don't have a choice," I said sadly. I turned toward the door.

A team of men in blue surgical gear filed into the office. One of them opened a briefcase, revealing the shiny metallic housing mechanism for a control drone—a device that would burrow into the base of Dr. Martindale's brain.

Martindale eyed it anxiously. "Wait," he panted. "Wait. That's not necessary. I can cooperate. I'll do exactly what you want."

Bonner nodded to the men, and they crowded toward Martindale.

"Yes," Bonner said. "You will."

* * *

I got a call in the night. Six agents were dead. Rebecca Courington had been taken.

I arrived just before dawn. The command center was dark. Computer monitors cast a bluish glare over all the shadowy figures gathered there.

"Where is she?" I said.

Bonner sipped his coffee. He gestured to one of the monitors. "In the air, west of Chicago. Private jet. They switch planes every hour or so, change course, so we don't have time to organize an assault."

I nodded. "And the drones?"

"Still operating, all of them. Probably not for long, though. Looks like they're going to bring the doctor to her."

"Martindale?"

"He's left Atlanta, moving west."

I took a deep breath. "Is Serrato there with her?"

Bonner nodded at a second monitor. We had placed a surveillance drone behind Rebecca Courington's left eyeball. We saw what she saw.

We saw the plush interior of a private jet. We saw a man appear—a tall, powerful man with dark, short-cropped hair and a fabulously expensive purple suit.

We heard Courington say, "Julian."

The man inclined his head graciously.

I studied him. "That's what he looks like. Julian Serrato."

"He's toying with us," Bonner said. "He knows we're watching. He'll change everything tomorrow—his face, his voice."

"Tomorrow," I echoed. "He won't get a chance. We'll have him."

Rebecca Courington was anxious. "Julian, it's a trap. This whole thing. You have to get away from here. You have to get away from *me*."

Serrato smiled broadly, smugly. "Relax, Rebecca. It's taken care of. Have a cigarette."

He offered her a cigarette and she took it. He unbuttoned his sleeve. Two flaps of skin on his left wrist pulled apart. A hinged, telescoping metal arm emerged, carrying a cigarette lighter, which leapt into his grip.

He smiled. "Light?"

I turned to Bonner. "Implants. It's expected, but make a note of it."

"He's probably got weapons too," Bonner said.

Serrato lit Courington's cigarette. She took a drag. The lighter fell away, disappearing back into Serrato's arm.

He placed his hand on her shoulder. "I know someone who can help you. He can get rid of the horrible things they put inside you. There's nothing they can do about it. You'll be safe." Serrato grinned. "*We'll* be safe. Together."

* * *

We lost visuals first, then sound. The monitors went dark, one by one, as Martindale moved slowly through Rebecca Courington's body, surgically extracting our drones. He removed the primary locator and termination drones. Those were decoys.

We held our breath.

He didn't touch the secret drones. We had two of them: a locator drone, to track her movements, and a termination drone, to kill Serrato—if it came to that.

I knew it would.

Even after the surgery was done, Serrato kept switching planes every few hours. Finally, certain he was safe, he flew Rebecca Courington to Seattle, to a penthouse at the Hilton.

"Romantic," Bonner grumbled

"We've got him," I said.

We flew to Seattle with an assault team. We surrounded the hotel with agents. We placed our command center in an office building across the street. We put snipers on the roof.

The assault team was split into four groups—one to raid the penthouse, one to watch the lobby, one each to guard the two nearest stairwells.

I looked at my watch. It was a few minutes past midnight.

"Activate the field," I said.

We threw a suppression field over the hotel. In that moment, anyone inside would drop, unconscious.

Bonner turned to the radio. "Go."

We watched the monitors as the assault team entered the building and moved through the lobby, weaving carefully around the sprawled limbs of the dazed guests.

The backup squads took up their positions on the stairs. The main group climbed up to the top floor and crept down the long hall toward the wide, white penthouse doors. Serrato's bodyguards had fallen there, comatose, slumped on the floor.

"Open the door," Bonner whispered into the radio.

Explosions ripped through the wall, ripped through paint and plaster, ripped through muscle and bone, ripped through our agents. We blinked and they were dead.

Serrato kicked open the penthouse doors and strode into the hallway, holding a pistol in each hand. The pistols were connected to jointed, telescoping metal arms that had sprung from his shoulders. A transparent plate had popped out of his chest, shielding his face.

"He didn't fall," Bonner said. "Repeat, the suppression field has not neutralized Serrato. Agents down."

Serrato calmly evaluated the corpses, then turned back to the penthouse. One of the pistols folded into his shoulder, and he used his free hand to grab the stupefied figure of Rebecca Courington. He dragged her down the hallway, out of sight.

"Stairway Team Bravo," Bonner warned. "He's coming up on your position."

We watched as Serrato leapt into sight, shot an agent through the throat, then vanished back into the hall. Our men stormed after him. He killed one in the doorway there, and another just around the corner. He doubled back, guns screaming. His shots ripped apart the concrete. The bodies of our agents tumbled down the stairs, breaking apart and falling into pieces.

"Activate the termination drone," I said.

"No," Bonner said. "We want him alive."

The technician glanced back and forth between us. Serrato reappeared in the stairway, carrying the limp body of Rebecca Courington.

"Do it," I ordered.

The technician pushed some buttons.

Metal pincers crawled out between Courington's lovely lips, forcing her jaws grotesquely wide apart. A probe leapt from deep inside her throat and buried itself in Serrato's shoulder, electrocuting him.

He screamed, at the electricity, at the betrayal. He screamed as his skin melted into flame. His implants short-circuited. They deployed, a dozen of them—guns, knives, lockpicks. They ripped out through his clothes and through his flesh. Those metal limbs, useless now, stuck crazily in all directions. He carried them like a steel scorpion on his back. He crawled away down the stairs, out of sight.

Bonner gasped. "He's still alive."

I pulled out my pistol. "Come on."

We jogged across the street. The squad in the lobby eyed us with apprehension. "Hold this position," I told them. "Make sure he doesn't get out."

We advanced up the far stairwell and made contact with the team there. "Fall back," I told them. "Cover the exits." They nodded somberly.

Bonner and I paced slowly down the long, long hallway. We burst into the second stairwell, guns ready.

It was empty.

We picked a path through the bodies there. We followed the blood— Serrato's blood—red and dark and smeared, it wound down and down, stair after stair after stair.

We found him down on the sixth floor, propped in a corner. Blood dripped off the implants, running down the wall, forming patterns around him like a web. He was like a spider, resting there, a spider in his web of blood.

He was almost dead. He struggled to get a cigarette into his mouth. Finally, he managed it. It dangled there, loosely. Bonner and I moved closer, our guns leveled at his face.

Serrato lifted his arm toward us. Something popped out from beneath his left wrist. Bonner yelped and stumbled back.

It was the cigarette lighter. Serrato laughed a mirthless sort of laugh. He lit his cigarette.

Bonner cursed.

Serrato rolled his dark eyes toward us. His tone was flat. "I want to tell you something."

I watched his face through the sights of my pistol.

"I'm not the real Julian Serrato," he said.

Staggering footsteps sounded above us. I raised my gun. Rebecca Courington spiraled weakly down the stairs toward us, bracing her hands against the wall for support.

"Come down, Ms. Courington," I shouted. "It's over."

The man took a drag from his cigarette and tossed it away.

Bonner scowled. "What do you mean you're not him?"

"I'm a body double." The man coughed blood onto the collar of his purple suit. "A decoy. I deal with people for him, so he doesn't risk his own safety." His eyes traced over his array of deadly implants, now sizzling uselessly. "I'm a man of action, not ideas. I'm no mastermind."

Rebecca Courington came and stood beside me.

"I'm no mastermind," the man repeated, "but I know when I've been set up. I know what's going on—he wants you to kill me. He wants you to think he's gone."

Bonner eyed him warily.

"Protect me." The man's voice weakened. "I can help you. I can tell you things."

Rebecca Courington was trying to catch my eye. I looked at her. She glanced at Bonner, then at my pistol. I handed it to her.

"If you're not Serrato," Bonner said slowly, "then where is he?"

"I don't know." The man groaned. "Nobody knows that."

Courington took two quick steps toward Bonner and pressed the pistol to his temple. He had just enough time to look at her.

"Now we're even," she said, and shot him in the head. He tumbled bloodily over and bounced on the floor.

The man looked down as his stomach began to tick loudly. "Shit," he said.

I grabbed the gun away and dragged Courington down the stairs. We were in the lobby when the man exploded, incinerating everything between floors five and seven.

* * *

I gave my report. "Serrato must have had some sort of regulator implanted in his brain, to compensate for a suppression field. And he was wired to explode, if he was killed or captured."

The director nodded solemnly. "It's too bad about Bonner. I'm sorry." He paused. "How did you escape?"

"I was escorting Ms. Courington from the scene," I said. "Otherwise, the blast would've gotten me too."

"Yes, the blast." The director shook his head. "What a goddamn mess." Photos of dead agents were spread across his desk. He fixed me with a stern gaze. "You got lucky, son."

"I'm well aware of that, sir," I said.

He sighed. "Well, we got Serrato. That's what matters."

"Yes, sir," I said.

Our surgeons removed the last of the drones from Rebecca Courington's body. I met her in post-op. I said, "I apologize for your ordeal and thank you for your service. The government will forgive your debt. Please, let me drive you to the airport."

She studied me. She nodded. "All right."

We drove for ten minutes. She turned to me. "You took an awful risk, joining them."

"I had a plan," I said softly. "It was the only way. The only way I could get you back. I need you so much, Rebecca. I need your strength, your ideas. I can't do this without you. I'm nothing without you."

She leaned her head against my shoulder and closed her eyes.

"How long have you known?" I asked her.

"I always knew." She smiled. "I would always know you," she said, "Julian."

Author's note: The Prize

The Usual Suspects is one of my favorite movies, and I had always wanted to do a story with that sort of twist ending. This was my chance. This story was also heavily influenced by Larry Niven's *The Long Arm of Gil Hamilton*, about a future in which criminals kidnap people, disassemble them, and sell their organs on the black market.

"They Go Bump" and "The Prize" both placed in the first Phobos Fiction Contest, and both appeared in the first Phobos anthology *Empire of Dreams and Miracles*, edited by Orson Scott Card and Keith Olexa. It was really exciting for me to be published in a book with Orson Scott Card's name on the cover. His novel *Ender's Game* was my favorite science fiction book growing up, and I had read his author's introduction to *The Worthing Saga* countless times. (In that essay Card relates how he wrote and sold some of his early stories and novels.)

When *Empire of Dreams and Miracles* was published, Card did an appearance to promote the book at Barnes & Noble in New York. That was one of the first book signings I'd ever been to, and I didn't know exactly what to expect. Card was immensely charming. The event was in the middle of the afternoon on a weekday, and was lightly attended. Before the event started, Card went around to each group of people in the audience, introduced himself, and asked them a bit about themselves. I've been to hundreds of book signings since then, and I don't think I've ever seen anyone else do that.

When I handed Card my copy of the book so he could sign it, I mentioned that I had written two of the stories. "Oh really?" he said. "Which ones?" I told him the titles. "Sorry, which ones were those?" he said, explaining that when he had judged the stories for the contest, they had not included titles or author names. I briefly described the two stories. Card looked at me squarely. "You are *good*," he said.

It turned out that another one of the contest winners was standing behind me in line. Card called to the audience, "Hey everyone! These folks wrote some of the stories in the book. They're great authors. You should have them sign your books too."

People started to gather around me. There was a bit of confusion over where the line should start. "I've never signed a book before," I said to one person, taking their book. "In fact, let me write that." I turned to the title page and wrote, *This is the first book I've ever signed*, then added my signature. "There!" I said.

Some people in the crowd looked nonplussed that I hadn't chosen *their* book to be the first book I ever signed. "Um," I said awkwardly, "and so I guess that means this is the *second* book I've ever signed, right?" And I wrote, *This is the second book I've ever signed*. I kept that up for the next few books—*the third book I've ever signed, the fourth book I've ever signed*, and so on—then gave up and just started signing my name. I felt bad for all the people who'd missed out on owning a potentially priceless collector's item through no fault of their own. Wow, I thought, this celebrity stuff is hard.

The Phobos Fiction Contest was the brainchild of Hollywood producer Sandra Schulberg. The idea was to use the contest to identify promising young science fiction writers, then adapt their stories into films, comics, and video games. At one point the Phobos folks showed me a movie pitch they'd worked up for "The Prize," written by famed Marvel Comics editor Jim Shooter. Unfortunately nothing ever came of it. Still, the whole experience was a blast. I got invited to a party at Sandra Schulberg's apartment in New York, where I was given an award and got to rub shoulders with various entertainment industry types. That's pretty heady stuff when you're 23.

Two years later my story "Veil of Ignorance," which appears later in this book, placed in the third Phobos Contest and was published in the third Phobos anthology *All the Rage This Year*.

Jerome Jacinto

Cats in Victory

Lynx awoke before dawn. He got out of bed, brushed his whiskers, and licked his fur clean. He dressed in boots and a tunic, then donned his rucksack and set out into the dusty streets. The sun was just beginning to peek up over the thatched rooftops. Most of the other catmen of the village were still asleep.

He hiked west, out of town, through the foothills and into the wasteland, where he wandered amid the stark beauty of the stony plains, winding arroyos, and towering plateaus.

He loved walking here, and today he'd secretly resolved to explore as far to the west as he could. His parents would disapprove. Like all the adults of the village, they harbored a vague mistrust of the wasteland, maybe due to the strange mechanical artifacts that were sometimes discovered beneath the sands. But the more time Lynx spent out here, the more he felt that such misgivings were baseless.

All morning he climbed hills, clambered over fields of boulders, and strode between pillars of stone. Finally, around mid-day, his westward progress was blocked by a narrow canyon that stretched as far as he could see in either direction. The canyon floor was forty feet below, and the walls were too sheer to climb, so Lynx turned north, skirting the cliff edge and searching for a way across.

Finally he came to a place where a giant tree had grown up from the canyon floor. The tree was dead now, but its pale, branchless trunk would provide easy access down into the canyon. Though there was no telling whether—

Wait. What was that?

He thought he saw movement, below.

A few hundred yards away, the canyon wall was broken by a wide, low cavern. A figure detached itself from the darkness and wandered down onto the sand. Lynx ducked, then slowly raised his head again as the figure came to a halt.

As far as Lynx knew, nothing lived out here except lizards and birds. But this figure was the size of a catman, and walked upright.

Then the thought came to him: A dogman.

Here? Impossible. But it had to be. He knew he should flee, get help, but...

The dogmen were almost extinct. This might be the only chance he'd ever get to see one. And he should make sure it was really a dogman, before he alarmed the whole village.

He dropped his rucksack and kicked off his boots. He paced, flexing his hand and foot claws. Then he dashed to the edge of the cliff and leapt onto the tree. His claws dug into the wood, and he hung there a moment, then scrambled down the trunk and dropped lightly to the canyon floor.

He sneaked toward the cave, ducking behind one boulder, then another, then another. A strong breeze blew into his face, and this was good, for the wind would muffle his footsteps and carry his scent off behind him.

He lay down and crawled on elbows and knees until he was just a dozen yards away from the mysterious figure, then peeked around a rock.

Yes. A dogman. It was burlier than any catman, and Lynx could make out its grotesque floppy ears. It wore a grungy tunic and a heavy broadsword. Then the creature turned its head, and Lynx glimpsed its profile—a flat face with saggy jowls and wrinkled folds of flesh around the eyes. A horrible, misshapen creature. An abomination.

Lynx began to crawl backward, then paused, as he spied a second figure emerging from the cave.

This one was...not so terrible. A female, slender, perhaps as young as Lynx. Her snout was white, her large eyes banded with brown, and her long, silky ears hung past her shoulders. She too wore a sword, a rapier.

In Lynx's imagination, dogmen had always been ugly and fearsome and...male. He wondered about the female. What was she to the hulking beast beside her? His ally? His wife? She had a sweet look to her, or was that deceptive? Had she ever killed a catman?

Suddenly the big male straightened and poked his nose in the air, sniffing loudly—once, twice.

Lynx felt a prickle of terror. While he'd been distracted, the breeze had shifted, and he was now upwind of the dogmen.

The male roared, "Catmen!" and whipped out his sword. He turned and stared straight at Lynx, who leapt up from his hiding spot and sprinted away, dodging around boulders and vaulting over ditches. Behind him came heavy footfalls and throaty growls as the male chased him, gained on him. Lynx spotted the tree, his escape.

The female cried, "No! Stop him!"

Lynx ran to the tree, sprang onto it, and scuttled upward. The male bellowed and leapt after him, and Lynx heard the swoosh of the broadsword, then the thunk of metal on wood. The whole tree shuddered as the sword struck just below his feet.

He climbed out of reach. The female shrieked in despair, and the male let loose a frustrated howl.

Lynx fled the canyon, as the dogmen's terrible barking rose up from below him and echoed in his ears.

It wasn't until much later, when he was far from that place, that he noticed any pain. Then he found that he was missing a few inches off the end of his tail. Blood pooled there, and fell in thick droplets to the sand.

* * *

Night had fallen by the time Lynx got back to the village. He headed straight to the temple, raced through the main doors, and burst into the antechamber.

A scribe sat at a small wooden desk, scribbling in a ledger with a quill pen. When he saw Lynx's agitation, he stood. "Can I help you?"

Lynx gasped for breath. "I have to see Father Cougar."

The scribe stared disapprovingly. "Father Cougar is delivering the evening service."

Lynx said, "There are dogmen! Living in the wasteland. Hiding in the caves."

"Dogmen? Are you sure?"

"Yes, I'm sure! They chased me, with swords." Lynx held up the tip of his tail, which was clotted with blood.

The scribe grew alarmed. "All right. Wait here." He hurried over to a pair of heavy wooden doors, then slipped through, closing the doors behind him.

Lynx stepped forward and pressed his ear to the door. Through the wood, he could hear Father Cougar's booming voice. He could only make out some of the words, but he grasped the essence of the sermon. Father Cougar was preaching, as ever, about how these were the end times, and about the coming Victory, when Cat would return to Earth, the dogmen would be destroyed forever, and the catmen would regain their pure feline forms.

Father Cougar's voice faded away. He must be conferring with the scribe.

Finally the scribe reappeared and said, "Follow me."

He led Lynx down a hallway to a cozy chamber whose walls were hung with tapestries. Father Cougar sat on a sofa in the corner. He said warmly, "Lynx! Come in, come in."

Lynx picked a chair and sat down.

Father Cougar settled back and stroked his scruffy gray whiskers. "Now, tell me what happened."

Lynx explained about coming across the dogmen in the wasteland. Father Cougar listened intently. "And they saw you?"

Lynx hesitated, then admitted, "Yes."

Father Cougar narrowed his eyes. "How?"

Lynx stared at the floor. "I'm sorry, Father. I...was curious."

Father Cougar sighed deeply. "As I thought." He leaned forward, his gaze steady. "How many times must I tell you? Curiosity is the gravest of sins. And now you see what your curiosity has cost us. If you had avoided detection, we could have easily located these dogmen and captured them. But now they'll be expecting us, and will move on. The danger to those who track them is greatly increased. And what if the dogmen should slip away? You may very well have cost us the great Victory we have awaited so long."

Lynx felt ashamed, despondent. Everything Father Cougar was saying was absolutely true.

Father Cougar shook his head. "Well, there's no helping it now." He turned to the scribe and instructed, "Go to the inn. Fetch the templars." The scribe nodded once, and hurried off.

Lynx felt awe. "Templars?"

"Yes," Father Cougar said. "They arrived this morning. Two of them. Pursuing these dogmen you saw. They'll want to question you."

"Of course," Lynx agreed at once, his shame quickly giving way to excitement.

Templars! Holy ones, invincible warriors of Cat. In ages past, their order had eradicated the frogmen, the birdmen, and the monkeymen, and now only the dogmen remained.

The scribe returned a short time later, leading the templars. They were the tallest, most muscular catmen that Lynx had ever seen. Both wore long white tabards, and upon their surcoats were embroidered the holy form of Cat.

Father Cougar gestured to them. "Lynx, these are our templar friends, Lion and Tiger."

The templars nodded politely. Tiger was brawnier, stern and dignified, with gray in his fur and black stripes around his eyes. Lion had a great tawny mane and seemed almost to vibrate with barely restrained energy. And he was younger, perhaps only five or ten years older than Lynx himself.

Lion said quickly, "Tell us about the dogmen."

So Lynx repeated his story. When he gave a description of the dogmen, the templars glanced at each other. When he got to the part about his escape from the canyon, the scribe interrupted, "Show them your tail!"

Lynx held up his injured tail.

Lion clapped his hands together and said to Tiger, "Well, look at that! Bloodied by dogmen, and he escaped to tell of it." He turned to Lynx. "That's more than many templars can boast."

Lynx felt an almost unbearable rush of pride.

Lion said, "I've heard enough." He turned to Tiger. "Let's find this cave."

Father Cougar said, "You mean to leave at once?"

"Yes," Lion replied. "I see no reason to dally. The dogmen certainly will not."

"Take me with you!" Lynx exclaimed. "I'll lead you there."

Father Cougar looked worried. "That might be dangerous. Your parents—"

Lynx said, "It's my fault for letting the dogmen see me. You have to let me make up for it. No one knows the wasteland like I do."

Father Cougar turned to the templars. "I suppose it's up to you."

Tiger opened his mouth for the first time. "I don't think——"

Lion spoke over him. "Yes, let him come. The dogmen cut him with their swords. He deserves a chance to pay them back in kind." He grinned at Lynx and said, "But we'll cut more than just their tails, won't we?"

Tiger said nothing.

"Come on," Lion said, and gestured for Lynx to follow.

* * *

Lynx went with the templars back to the inn, where they gathered supplies. Lion pulled a shortsword out from among his belongings and tossed it to Lynx, who caught it and put it on. Then Lynx led the templars into the wasteland. The sun was rising by the time they reached the cave.

Tiger scouted about, kneeling in places to sniff the earth, then said, "This way."

The trail led westward, deeper into the wastes. That night the templars made camp beneath the open sky, and in the morning they continued on again. As far as Lynx knew, no catman had ever come this far before. His boldness waned, and he started to wonder what he'd gotten himself into.

On the third day, the templars stopped to rest beside a circular black pit a hundred yards across. Thick yellow grass grew all around the pit, and vines hung over the edge, dangling into the darkness. There was something eerie and intriguing about the formation.

Lynx wondered aloud, "Could the dogmen be hiding in there?"

Tiger said, "The tracks lead on."

Lion shrugged. "It can't hurt to check. Call us if you see anything."

Lynx wandered over to the pit. Its sides were rough and angular, and he scrambled easily down the many shelves of rock until he reached the cavern floor. Stray beams of sunlight lanced down through the opening overhead, catching the dust that floated in the air. Lynx turned in a slow circle, then stopped as he saw something utterly unexpected.

He drew his sword and cried out, "Lion! Lion!"

Half-buried in the side of the cave was a strange object that was bigger than a cottage and made of silver metal. It was extraordinarily weathered, and its side was ripped open. That dark gash beckoned to Lynx. He took a step forward, then another.

From the cliff wall above, Lion called out, "Wait."

Lynx glanced back. Lion was climbing down into the cavern. Tiger stood above, at the pit's edge.

Lion said, "What are you doing?"

"Have you ever seen anything like it?" Lynx said. "I'm going to look inside." He crept nearer.

"Why?" Lion called sharply.

"I..." Lynx was very close now. "I just..."

"This is curiosity," Lion warned. "This is wrong."

"It isn't," Lynx insisted, half to himself. Though why it wasn't, he could not really say. He slipped through the gash.

For a moment everything was dark. Then a hundred spots of light—red, blue, yellow, green—flickered to life all around him. He crouched in alarm. He'd never seen anything like these lights, but his attention was quickly drawn away from them and toward a metal coffin that was built into the far wall. Its lid was made of glass, and inside he could make out the rough outline of a body.

Suddenly a loud voice spoke, seeming to come from all around. The language was strange. Lynx whirled, but saw no one.

The coffin slowly opened. Lynx backed away, cursing himself. Once again his curiosity had betrayed him, had led him to intrude upon this strange tomb, and now he had awoken something ancient and powerful. His frenzied imagination conjured up images of a living corpse with blazing red eyes. But what actually emerged was no less surprising.

A monkeyman. He seemed dazed, and was dressed in some gray uniform, its chest and shoulders decorated with insignia. He glanced at Lynx, then staggered past him. Lynx stared in wonder and horror. The monkeymen were supposed to have been wiped out centuries ago.

A second shape, much smaller, leapt from the coffin, and Lynx gasped as he observed its perfect grace. For all his life he had seen this holy form depicted a thousand times, and now there was no mistaking it. This was the creator of the universe, the giver of all life. Cat, the nine-lived, had returned to Earth at last. Lynx knelt and whispered, "My lord."

Cat did not acknowledge him, and Lynx was unsure what to do. Through the gash behind him came the voices of the templars. Tiger was saying, with a mix of fear and awe, "It fell from the sky. See? It broke through into this cavern."

Lion replied angrily, "The dogmen flee, and we stand here engaged in idle—"

He stopped abruptly as the monkeyman lurched through the gash and out into the cave. Lynx followed after.

The templars stood awestruck. The monkeyman ignored them. He stumbled about, studying the damage to his tomb. With one hand he grasped his forehead. He still seemed disoriented.

Lynx felt disoriented himself. He wandered over to the templars, tugged at Lion's sleeve, and made him look toward the tomb, where Cat was just emerging. Lion fell instantly to his knees, and Tiger did the same.

Cat ignored them and strode along after the monkeyman. Then Cat lay down, reached into a gap between the tomb and the cave floor, and batted his paw at something within. The monkeyman grunted at Cat and pushed him away from the hole.

Lion leapt to his feet and cried, "You dare!" He ran up to the monkeyman and seized him by the shoulder.

The monkeyman shoved him back and yelled at him in a strange language. A female voice said, "Get your hands off me, catman scum!'" It came from an amulet on the monkeyman's belt. Puzzled, he glanced at it. Then he shouted at Lion, and again his magic amulet translated. "Report! What unit are you with? And what the hell are you wearing?"

Lion moved to stand beside Tiger. He said softly, "A surviving monkeyman. He struck me, you saw. I should have the honor of slaying him."

The monkeyman's amulet spoke in a strange tongue, presumably translating Lion's words.

Tiger said, "I don't know. He comes to us from the sky, as a companion of Cat. Dare we slay him?"

Lion said, "Cat's holy word commands it."

Tiger said, "Cat himself stands before us now. Everything is changed."

Lion glanced at Cat, who sat licking himself. Lion approached him, knelt, and said, "My lord, I am Lion, your most faithful servant. I am yours to command. What is your wish for this monkeyman? Say the word, and I will spill his blood in your name."

Cat lifted his head, gave Lion an inscrutable stare, and went back to licking himself.

Lion, still kneeling, glanced at Tiger. "Why does he not answer?"

Tiger growled softly, "It is not our place to question him. He will speak when he wills it."

Lion turned back to Cat. "Answer me, lord, I beg you. Or if you will not, give us some sign, that we may do your will."

The monkeyman seemed to finally shake off his confusion and comprehend the danger. He glanced back and forth between Lion and Cat, then crouched, whistled to Cat, and spoke. The amulet translated: "Hey, come here. Here, kitty kitty kitty. Come on."

Lion said darkly, "He presumes to command Cat."

The monkeyman ignored this and kept calling. Cat gazed at the monkeyman, but did not stir.

Lion said, "Cat rejects him."

"Wait!" The monkeyman held up a hand. "Just…Leo, come here, dammit!" He whistled again. "Here, kitty kitty."

Lion reached for his sword. "He dies."

But at that moment, Cat languidly uncurled himself and strolled across the dirt to the monkeyman, who scratched Cat's whiskers, then his ears, his neck, and his back. Cat purred and rubbed against the monkeyman's shins. Lion froze.

"Cat shows him favor," Tiger said. "Cat has a special plan for him."

The monkeyman picked up Cat and held him like a shield. Cat continued to purr.

Lion glared at the monkeyman for a long time, then strode over to him, stood very close, and said softly, "I do not know why Cat chooses to prolong your miserable existence, abomination. But let no one say that I was curious." He brushed by him and walked away.

The monkeyman lowered his head to Cat and whispered, "Good Cat."

* * *

The catmen set out again, now joined by Cat and his strange monkeyman companion. The monkeyman brought along a sort of satchel in which he carried Cat, who seemed pleased enough with the arrangement. Lion remained hostile to the monkeyman, no matter how often Tiger insisted that the Victory was now at hand and that Lion should be rejoicing. The templars often knelt before Cat and asked him for guidance, but Cat never deigned to reply.

Sometimes the monkeyman would stare into the amulet, but whatever it told him must have displeased him, for he would shake it and yell at it. Lynx was desperate to question the monkeyman, but that would be showing curiosity, so instead he tried to mimic the stony indifference of the templars. Still, he couldn't keep his eyes off of Cat.

The monkeyman noticed this. Finally he said, "Do you want to hold him?"

Lynx was stunned. He glanced at the templars, who were now well ahead. "I couldn't."

"Sure." The monkeyman reached into the satchel, lifted Cat free, and handed him over to Lynx. Lynx scratched Cat's ears the way the monkeyman had, and Cat nuzzled his fingers.

"See?" the monkeyman said. After a moment, he added, "What's your name?"

Lynx hesitated, then told him.

"I'm Charles," the monkeyman said. Lynx didn't respond. After a moment, the monkeyman lowered his voice and said, "Tell me, Lynx. What year is this?"

Lynx was perplexed, but the monkeyman seemed earnest. Lynx passed Cat back to him and said slowly, "1293."

"Using what calendar?"

"I don't understand."

"Dating from when?"

"Why…" This was the strangest question Lynx had ever heard. "From the creation of the world."

The monkeyman said nothing for a long time. He and Lynx resumed walking. Finally the monkeyman asked in a low tone, "And what is this 'Victory'?"

"You really don't know? Cat hasn't told you?"

The monkeyman said, "Cat isn't overly fond of explaining himself. As you may have noticed."

So Lynx spoke of the Victory. When he saw that the monkeyman was utterly confused, he found himself explaining more and more. Soon he had gone all the way back to the beginning, back to when Cat had created the world and all its inhabitants, including his most favored creation, cats, whom Cat had made in his own image. To them alone Cat had granted the gift of speech. But the cats had grown curious about what other animals might say, and so the cats disobeyed and shared the gift of speech with birds, frogs, dogs, and monkeys. But those other animals were wicked and spoke only lies. When Cat returned and saw what had happened, he was very angry, and punished those animals, twisting them into catmen, birdmen, frogmen, dogmen, and monkeymen. The catmen wailed and beseeched Cat to restore them to their perfect forms, but Cat decreed that he would not until the catmen had wiped the Earth clean of the abominations—any animal who spoke and was not feline. But Cat, in his ultimate mercy, also decreed that this redemption was inevitable, and promised that in the last days he would return to Earth to lead the catmen to ultimate glory. Lynx finished, "So that is the Victory. That is why Cat has come again. But his ways are strange. We did not know that he would be accompanied by a monkeyman."

The monkeyman said, "And these dogmen we're pursuing…are the last on Earth?"

"Perhaps," Lynx said. "They are among the last, certainly."

"And the…other monkeymen. Like me. Are all…?"

"Dead," Lynx confirmed. "Long ago."

That night Lynx was awoken by the sound of the monkeyman sobbing softly. Lynx thought: He weeps for his vanquished race. It had not occurred to him that abominations might be capable of such grief. This monkeyman was the last of his kind, probably. And in the end, when the Victory came, he too would be cleansed from the Earth. That made Lynx feel almost sad.

He did not get back to sleep for a long time.

* * *

The templars tracked the dogmen ever deeper into the wasteland. Supplies were running low, and nothing edible grew here. But Lion said, "Good. The dogmen will have the same problem. They'll have to turn and face us."

And he was right. The next day, the catmen mounted a low, wind-swept pass, and spotted the dogmen waiting amidst a jumble of boulders.

The male stood there, holding his great broadsword. The female reached for her rapier, but the male barked at her, and she reluctantly backed away. The male stepped forward, seeming worn and haggard, but for all that he was still even bigger and more imposing than Lynx remembered.

Lion sighed. "Only two. And one a female." He drew his sword and strode forward. "Stay back. I'll handle this."

Lynx looked to Tiger. "He'll fight alone?"

Tiger was stoic. "He prefers it this way."

"Why bring me all this way?" Lynx said. "Why give me a sword, if he never meant for me to help?"

"That's just how he is."

The monkeyman moved to stand beside them. "How he *is* is arrogant and reckless. Why do you endure it?"

Tiger said softly, "You'll see why."

Lion closed in on the male, who roared and thrust at him with savage force. Lion parried casually, spun in a crouch, and came up with both fists wrapped around the hilt of his sword. He slammed its pommel into his opponent's jowled face, and the male thudded to the ground. Lion kicked away the dogman's sword, and just like that it was over.

Lynx exclaimed, "He's amazing!"

Tiger nodded. He hurried forward, and Lynx and the monkeyman followed. Tiger knelt to tie up the male as Lion strode toward the female.

She'd drawn her rapier, and as Lion came on she backed away in a fighting stance, her movements swift and graceful. Lion held his sword at his side.

She thrust at his throat. Her speed was remarkable, but Lion whipped up his sword and easily blocked the blow.

The female backed away, launching a series of feints and attacks. Lion laughed, contemptuous, as he parried each one. But her last thrust deflected off his blade and nicked his shoulder.

He glanced at the circle of blood that blossomed on his white tabard. "Not bad. I might have to try."

He moved to close with her, but again she slipped away.

Tiger looked uneasy. He said softly, "At close range, he's unstoppable. But he has no patience."

The female kept retreating, staying always just beyond the reach of Lion's sword. She attacked again, and again she got through, pricking his other shoulder. He hardly seemed to notice. His expression was dark now. He kept advancing.

Lynx said, "We have to help."

Tiger hesitated. "He...would not like that."

Lion roared, slashing at the female's head. She backed out of reach, then quickly counterattacked, striking his chest. Three stains now blazed on his tabard. The blood from his shoulder wounds soaked down to his elbows. He seemed to be slowing.

Lynx said, "If you won't help him, I will."

He drew his shortsword and ran in a wide arc, so that he circled behind the female, then charged her.

As he neared, she pivoted and thrust at his face. Lynx ducked and retreated. Instantly she turned back to Lion, but now he had closed with her, and she was doomed. When she attacked, he grabbed her wrist and wrenched her sword away. He smashed an elbow into her face, then hurled her over his hip. Then Lion was upon her, straddling her, pounding his fists into her face, knocking her head this way and that. Soon she was unconscious, with blood oozing from her muzzle, but the blows kept falling.

Lynx murmured, "Wait," but Lion ignored him.

Finally Lion stood. His chest wound had bled a red blotch around the holy form of Cat that was embroidered on his surcoat.

Lynx said, "Are you all right?"

Lion's eyes were full of fury. "I told you to stay back! You could've gotten us both killed!" He shoved Lynx aside and stormed on past.

Tiger came forward and knelt to bind the female. He said, "He gets like this. Just let him calm down. It'll be all right."

* * *

The templars marched the dogmen east. The prisoners were not spoken to, and when night fell they were bound at wrist and ankle. Tiger took the first watch while Lion dozed. Lynx sat a dozen yards away, off by himself, leaning on a boulder.

The monkeyman settled down beside him and nodded at the prisoners. "So what happens to them now?"

Lynx said, "The templars will want to show them off, charge money to see them, that sort of thing."

The monkeyman's voice was soft. "You said these might be the last dogmen on Earth."

"They might," Lynx agreed.

"And then they'll be executed?"

"Yes."

The monkeyman caught Lynx's gaze, held it. "And you're going to let that happen?"

Lynx glanced over at Tiger, but the templar was too far away to hear them. "Of course."

The monkeyman said, "No one has ever called me squeamish, and I have no love for dogmen, but to wipe out an entire race? That's evil, Lynx. You must know that. Whatever some old legend says."

"You're just a monkeyman. You wouldn't understand."

"I understand more than you can imagine," the monkeyman said. "I've flown among the stars, and slept for ages, and I remember Earth as it was, when monkeymen—as you call us—ruled all. We made you, Lynx, you catmen, in our labs. The dogmen too, and all the rest. We made you to be soldiers, and I guess we did our jobs too well, because I awake to find that you've beaten us. But that doesn't—"

"This is blasphemy," Lynx said. "I warn you, not even Cat's favor will protect you if—"

"What? Him?" The monkeyman jabbed a thumb toward the satchel where Cat slept. "He's an animal, like any other. I raised him from a kitten."

Lynx stood. "I should kill you for that."

The monkeyman glared up at him. "Fine. Kill me. Like you killed my race. What've I got to live for?" He gestured toward Lion. "Rouse your maniac friend there. Tell him to chop off my head. He'd like that. And would you? I thought you were different."

Lynx scowled and stomped away. He sat down beside Tiger, who asked, "What's wrong?"

Lynx said furiously, "Nothing."

Tiger glanced at the monkeyman, then said, "Monkeys lie. That's why they should never have been granted the gift of speech."

Lynx crossed his arms and agreed, "Yes. They lie."

* * *

For the next two days, Lynx refused to speak to the monkeyman, but doubts gnawed at him. Much as he hated to admit it, the monkeyman was right about one thing: Lynx *was* different from the templars.

He had always thought of himself as faithful, but traveling with them had made him see just how shallow and perfunctory his belief really was. Lion's faith was like fire—it gave intensity to everything he did, but it was a fire that was raging out of control and would someday consume him. And Tiger's faith was like a mountain—immense, solid, and immovable. But Lynx realized that his own faith was more like the wasteland itself, existing only in the absence of anything else. The monkeyman's briefly spouted heresies made sense to him in a way that the wisdom of Father Cougar never really had.

That afternoon, Lynx found himself walking for a moment beside the female. Before he could stop himself, he blurted out, "You fought well."

She looked up, startled to be spoken to. "What?"

Lion was off ahead of them. Tiger was back a ways, out of earshot. Lynx said softly, "The other day. You fought well. I think you would've beaten him, if I hadn't interfered. Beaten a templar. You should be proud of that."

"Oh," she said, puzzled. "Thank you."

"Sure," Lynx said awkwardly, and hurried off.

The monkeyman sidled up from behind him. "Why did you do that?"

Lynx maintained a stony silence for a moment, then said, "I...I was just..."

"Curious," the monkeyman said.

Lynx sighed.

The monkeyman added, "Curiosity is no sin. If you're not curious, you'll never learn."

"That's blasphemy," Lynx said, but his tone was flat.

The monkeyman said nothing.

After a time, Lynx said, "Even if I agreed with you—about the dogmen, I mean—what can I do?"

The monkeyman whispered, "You can pretend to be asleep tonight, and when I create a distraction, you can cut their bonds and let them escape."

Lynx was startled. "I didn't mean..."

"I know." The monkeyman gave him a thin smile. "But think about it. I'll create the distraction. What you do then is up to you."

"Wait," Lynx said. This was too much. "What sort of distraction?"

"You'll see. Your little outburst the other night gave me an idea."

Lynx considered this. "During whose watch?"

"Whose do you think?"

Lion's, of course. He was by far the more easily distracted.

"Think about it," the monkeyman repeated, and fell behind again.

* * *

As night came on, the templars made camp atop a low hill. Tiger slumbered, and Lynx pretended to. He still hadn't decided whether to help the dogmen. After several hours, he heard movement and peeked out one eye.

The monkeyman came and stood beside Lion. "You seem like the religious type."

Lion turned to him. "Do not mock me, monkeyman." He was now facing away from Lynx and the prisoners.

The monkeyman sat down on a stone. "Not at all. I just thought you might be interested in some of the religious ideas of the monkeymen."

"The chattering of abominations does not interest me." Lion began to turn away.

"Wait," the monkeyman said. "For example, did you know that many monkeymen believed that they were made in the image of the creator of the universe?"

Lion laughed at that. "Did they ever look in a mirror? Surely they could not believe that the creator of the universe was so ungainly and absurd."

The monkeyman shrugged. "Others had another idea about how they came to be. It was called 'evolution by natural selection.'"

Lion's back was still turned. Lynx glanced at the prisoners. He thought he could crawl to them without attracting attention.

If he was caught at this, the templars would kill him. And what if Father Cougar was right, about Cat and the Victory and all of it? Lynx stared at the female. He was impressed by her, liked her, though they'd barely spoken. He didn't want to see her die. If he helped her escape, the catmen would have other opportunities to apprehend her, if necessary. But if she died...

He began to crawl toward her.

Lion was saying, "Even if that were possible, it would take thousands of years."

"Millions," the monkeyman corrected.

"The world is not that old."

"Well, these monkeymen had some ideas about that too."

The female's eyes were wide as Lynx crawled up beside her. He glanced over her shoulder at Lion, who was absorbed in the argument. Lynx drew his shortsword and whispered, "If I set you free, will you swear to run away and never come back, and never trouble any catman ever again?"

She stared at him a moment, then nodded quickly.

"All right." Lynx sliced her bonds, then squirmed over to the male to cut those ropes too.

Lion exclaimed, "That is heresy!"

The monkeyman replied, "That is fact."

Lion stood up. He towered over the monkeyman and said, "Take it back!"

"I'm just telling you what—"

"Silence!" Lion struck the monkeyman across the face, knocking him to the dirt.

Lynx freed the male, and together the prisoners began to crawl off.

The monkeyman sprang up and backed away. Lion drew his sword and strode after him. "Come here."

"No. Get away from me." The monkeyman turned and stumbled off down the hill, and Lion went after him.

Lynx thought: Lion will kill him. The monkeyman knew this would happen. He knew he was sacrificing himself.

Lynx glanced at the prisoners, who were now on their feet and hurrying away.

Lion and the monkeyman were soon lost in the darkness, but Lynx could hear them cursing. He considered waking Tiger, who might restrain Lion. But Tiger might also notice the prisoners fleeing.

Then the monkeyman let out an anguished wail, and Tiger opened his eyes. Lynx had no choice. He cried, "Tiger!"

The templar reached for his sword. "What?"

Lynx pointed. "Lion. He's gone crazy!"

Tiger leapt up, and Lynx followed. As they reached the bottom of the hill, Lion stepped from the shadows.

Tiger shouted, "What have you done?"

Lion was smug. "The monkeyman blasphemed with every word. I have silenced him."

No! Lynx thought, hurrying forward, scanning the ground for a corpse.

But the monkeyman was alive. He wept, kneeling over the smashed remains of his magic amulet. There was a gash on his brow, and his eyes were forlorn as he uttered a string of gibberish.

Lion had spared the monkeyman's life, but now there wasn't a single being on Earth that the monkeyman could talk to.

Lynx said, "I'm so sorry…Charles."

At the sound of his name, the monkeyman looked up. He took a deep breath, wiped his eyes, and rose to his feet. Lynx took him by the arm, and together they hiked back up the hill.

They entered camp just behind Tiger, who said, "Where are the prisoners?"

Lion looked stricken. He glanced about.

Tiger cursed. He ran across the camp and stared off down the far side of the hill. "Nothing. They're gone."

"I…" Lion hesitated. Then he pointed at the monkeyman. "It's his fault!"

"His fault?" Tiger raged. "Was it his job to watch the prisoners? Or was it yours?"

Lion stomped away, then turned and glared at the monkeyman. "He knows something."

"Maybe," Tiger said. "No one's ever freed themselves from my ropes before. We could question him…if you hadn't 'silenced' him."

Lion scowled.

Tiger gathered up some belongings. "It won't matter. We'll catch them again, and we'll have the truth from their own lips." His tone was grim. "And we'll take no more chances. No more prisoners. The dogmen die."

* * *

The catmen walked all through the night, and at dawn they came upon a shallow cave in which the dogmen were huddled together, sick and weary.

The templars strode forward, drawing their swords and advancing on the dogmen, who stood to meet them. The male pounded his meaty fist into his palm—a futile gesture of defiance. The dogmen were unarmed, and would be slaughtered. Lynx and the monkeyman watched helplessly.

Then Lynx had an idea. He called out, "Wait!"

Tiger paused and glanced back.

Lynx said, "Let Cat judge them."

Lion sneered. "Cat's feelings toward dogmen are well known."

"Then what's the harm?"

Tiger thought this over. He lowered his blade. "All right."

Lynx approached the monkeyman, who was confused. Lynx gestured at the satchel, and the monkeyman got the idea. He lifted Cat free and set him on the ground.

Lynx knelt. "My lord, we have need of your wisdom. What is your wish for these dogmen? Please, give us a sign."

Cat looked up at Lynx and said nothing.

Lion growled, "Why trouble Cat with this? He has already decreed death for all dogmen. Long ago."

Lynx stood up and took a step back. He called gently, "Here, kitty kitty."

Lion said, "What are you doing?"

Lynx backed up until he stood between the dogmen, then he knelt and called, "Here, kitty kitty kitty."

Cat continued to stare.

Lynx said to the dogmen, "Come on, like this." He added softly, "Please, just try."

After a moment, the female bent down and called, "Here, kitty kitty." The male did the same.

Lion was outraged. "What is this?"

But sure enough, Cat stirred. He picked his way across the ground until he stood before Lynx and the dogmen. Lynx reached out and scratched between Cat's ears, and Cat purred. The female stroked Cat's back. Cat wound among Lynx and the dogmen, rubbing against their legs.

The templars stood stunned. Tiger intoned, "Cat shows them favor."

Lion said, "No! The Cat I serve shows no mercy to dogmen!"

Tiger gestured. "Look."

"It's some trick," Lion said. "This…this is not Cat. It cannot be. Maybe this is one of the cats who—"

"That is heresy," Tiger warned. "The cats were transformed into catmen. All of them."

Lynx cried out, "Cat returns to Earth with a new message of peace!"

"No!" Lion shouted. "No! Cat, the eternal, does not change his mind."

Tiger turned away and sheathed his sword.

Lion stared at him in horror. "What are you doing?"

"I will not stand against the incarnation."

Lion was shocked. "What?"

Tiger said, "I must think on all this." He stared coldly over his shoulder at the dogmen and said, "You have a reprieve from me, for now." He began to walk away. To Lion he said, "Do as you like."

Lion looked all around, at Cat, at the dogmen, at the monkeyman. Finally he shot Lynx a withering glare, then turned to follow after Tiger.

Lynx waited until the templars were a good distance off, then he let out a long sigh of relief. He thought to himself: I can't believe it. We won.

But his gladness was tempered by apprehension. The templars would return, and even if they didn't they'd spread their tale. What would Father Cougar think? Or Lynx's parents? And what would become of Cat and the monkeyman and the dogmen now? Others would come seeking them, he knew.

For a moment they all watched each other uncertainly.

Then the monkeyman laughed. He stepped forward and introduced himself to the male. "Charles." And then again to the female. "Charles."

She glanced at Lynx, who gave her a bemused smile and shrugged.

Cat purred and rubbed against Lynx's shins. In that moment, he felt a bit of hope. If they all just stuck together, he thought, things might work out, in the end.

He bent down and petted Cat, and scratched his chin.

He whispered, "Good cat."

Author's note: Cats in Victory

In pre-school I created a long-running series of picture books called *Cats in Victory*, a science fiction story about heroic humanoid cats fighting sinister humanoid dogs. The stories were heavily influenced by Saturday morning cartoons of the era, which were basically glorified toy commercials. (Shows like *He-Man*, *Transformers*, *ThunderCats*, and *M.A.S.K.*) I filled each volume of *Cats in Victory* with catalog pages showing all the action figures you could buy. If one of my friends wanted an action figure, I'd craft one out of paper and Scotch tape and sell it to them for a quarter.

Eventually parents complained that their kids were skipping meals and spending their lunch money on my action figures, and I was banned from selling *Cats in Victory* merchandise at school.

In the early days, people would sometimes ask me if I even knew what the word "victory" meant, and I would say I did, even though I didn't. I just thought it sounded cool. Eventually I learned what the word meant, and when people would challenge me that "cats in victory" didn't even make sense, I would respond, "Yes it does. The cats always win, so it's cats in victory."

I didn't think much about *Cats in Victory* for 30 years. Then one day I was going through some old boxes, and I found myself perusing a few volumes of *Cats in Victory*. Looking at the stories with adult eyes, I was sort of appalled. There was really no character or plot. Each installment consisted of a bunch of super-cool cats armed with awesome weaponry and equipment simply massacring an army of clumsy, hapless dogs. It sort of seemed a little like...genocide?

Why would a sweet kid like me have been pumping out material with such an unhealthy subtext? Well, that seemed pretty obvious, when you took a look at my literary antecedents. *ThunderCats* is a show about a group of strong, beautiful cats who relentlessly trounce a diverse coalition of feeble, cowardly frogs, apes, and jackals. Looking back on it as an adult, it was hard not to view the show as some sort of weird pro-cat propaganda.

The success of *Harry Potter* had led to a boom in Young Adult literature, and everyone was scrambling to cash in. I figured maybe I should try writing some YA myself, and what better way to do it than to put a progressive spin on my old *Cats in Victory* franchise? "Cats in Victory" was the story that would lay bare the rottenness at the heart of *ThunderCats*.

There was just one problem. People hated talking cat stories. *Really* hated them. Every magazine I sent the story to said they didn't take talking cat stories. Yeah, I thought, but it's not just any old talking cat story. It's metafiction. It's commentary. Doesn't that mean anything? Apparently not.

The story did have its admirers. It got a surprisingly enthusiastic response from T. C. Boyle when I submitted it to his fiction workshop at USC, and John Joseph Adams loved it. But no one wanted to publish it. So while I'd had a blast writing "Red Road" and "Cats in Victory," and had even managed to sell "Red Road," I decided that the market for animal stories was just too limited, and moved on to other things.

Then in 2010 John Joseph Adams launched his own online magazine, *Lightspeed*, and told me that he wanted to publish "Cats in Victory" in the premiere issue. The story seemed to get a good response, aside from one prominent critic who blasted the magazine for—you guessed it—publishing a talking cat story. When I asked him what was wrong with the story, he admitted that he'd only read the first line.

I'm really not sure what the big deal is with talking cats. There are cat women in Gene Wolfe's *Book of the New Sun*, for crying out loud. Should we consign *that* to the litter box of history? Anyway I did get a bunch of great fan art from the furry community, so that was nice.

Rob Johnson

Transformations

Carrus is in his vehicle form—a red sports car—and is driving down a suburban street. He's going fast and not paying attention, just like the boy who suddenly dashes out from behind a mailbox and into the road. Carrus brakes.

His bumper strikes the boy, spins him, flings him to the pavement. Carrus idles a moment, then runs a scan on the boy, who lies stunned.

Broken arm. Damn it.

Carrus pulls forward. His passenger door opens, and he says, "Hey, get in. I'll take you home." It's a gross violation of orders, but he isn't just going to leave the boy there.

The boy lifts a face full of hurt and suspicion. Then he notices that the driver's seat is empty, a fact normally hidden by the deeply tinted windows.

Carrus speaks again. "Come on, get in."

The boy rises, cradling his arm. He's maybe twelve, but tall, slender. Ash-blond hair curls down the back of his neck. He steps closer, his bright blue eyes darting. "Where...are you?"

Carrus says, "Notice the car parked in front of you? The one that just hit you? That's me. Now come on."

For a moment the boy's expression changes to wonder. He scrambles into the passenger seat.

Carrus shuts the door and starts moving. "Where do you live?"

"That way." The boy points, grimacing, trying to hide his pain. He looks around the car's interior. "Do you have a name?"

"I call myself Carrus. It means 'chariot.'"

"I'm Alex," the boy says. "That's my house, up there on the right. The blue one."

237

Carrus pulls up to the house. "I'm sorry about your arm. Please don't tell anyone about me." He opens his passenger door.

"I won't." Alex climbs out onto the sidewalk. "Where did you come from? Who made you?"

"I can't tell you."

"Why?"

"I can't tell you that either."

"When will I see you again?"

"You won't," Carrus says, closing the door, speeding away.

* * *

But he has nowhere to go, nothing to do but cruise the endless roads. He finds himself back in that neighborhood, circling that block, coasting past Alex's blue house and imagining the life within. The kitchen windows face the street, and sometimes he spots a father, a mother, and Alex eating together.

One afternoon, as Carrus reaches the stop sign at the end of the block, he notices Alex, waiting, seated nearby on a low stone wall. Alex says, "I saw you."

Carrus is silent.

Alex stands. "Can I get in? I want to talk."

Carrus hesitates, then decides to hell with it and opens his passenger door. Alex gets in.

Carrus asks, "How's your arm?"

"Better." Alex flexes the arm to show that it's healed. "Why do you keep driving by my house?"

"I don't know. Boredom."

"I didn't know cars got bored." When Carrus doesn't answer, Alex says, "I'm bored too. Want to go to the mall? Do you know where that is?"

"Yes." Carrus pulls away from the curb and turns left. Alex grins and fastens his seatbelt.

Carrus drives past several stop signs, then turns right onto a busier street lined with strip malls. Alex says, "Who made you, Carrus? The government?"

"No."

"Who then? Where are you from?"

Carrus debates with himself. Finally he says softly, "Off world."

Alex's eyes widen. "You mean space?"

"Yes."

"Wow. So...what are you doing here?"

Again, Carrus debates. Do his orders even matter anymore? Will his story be too frightening? Finally he tells the truth: "Your world lies in a demilitarized region of space. As tensions built, it was decided to secretly deploy forces here." He shifts to the fast lane and speeds past two cars. "So that we could move about without being detected, we were designed to blend in. Our mission, once the order came, was to rapidly seize all vital infrastructure and resources."

"You mean...take over the world?"

"Yes." Carrus rolls to a stop at a red light. "But then hostilities erupted elsewhere, and the war shaped up differently than expected. This world is no longer of any strategic importance."

"How...many of you are there?"

"Fifty. We're on furlough now, wandering. I'm sure eventually the planners will find some use for us, deploy us elsewhere, but our ability to mimic Earth vehicles no longer serves any purpose. We're under standing orders to maintain a covert posture, so I shouldn't be telling you any of this, but I don't think it really matters anymore."

Alex stares at the dashboard, the ceiling, the seats. "How could you take over? You don't even have a cannon."

"I can reconfigure to a humanoid form for infantry operations. And my arsenal is compact but devastating."

"You mean...you can change into like, a robot?"

"Yes."

Alex bounces with excitement. "Show me!"

"I thought you wanted to go to the mall?"

"Screw the mall!"

The light turns green. Carrus pulls a U-turn. "All right, but we'll have to find someplace more isolated."

They head out of town and into the woods, then wander the backroads. Finally Carrus finds a long gravel drive that dead-ends beside a grassy field ringed with pine trees. He says, "Okay, get out. And back up. You don't want to be too close."

Alex exits and dashes to just inside the treeline. Carrus runs a scan of the area to make sure no one is lurking about. Then:

His passenger compartment folds in on itself as roof joins with seats. His chassis splits behind the doors and arches up. His rear half extends and divides into two legs that raise his front half aloft. His hood folds down to become a chest. Black arms unfold from beneath red doors that now hang off his shoulders like armor plates. His head rides up from deep within his torso to rest atop his shoulders.

He towers over Alex, who races from the embrace of the trees to shout an ecstatic, "Holy shit!"

* * *

One week later, Carrus picks up Alex again. As they pull away from the curb, Alex displays a small red toy car and a plastic action figure of a blond-haired boy. Alex says, "Look what I got. It's us." The toys do indeed bear a faint resemblance to Carrus and Alex. Alex places them in a tray on the dashboard.

Carrus says, "Where do you want to go?"

"Let's just drive."

Carrus steers in the direction of the highway.

Alex says, "So who are you fighting, in this war?"

"We call them the Kaav. Amphibious beasts."

Alex's voice is soft with awe. "Have you ever seen one?"

"No."

"Who are you fighting for?"

"The Anaurins. Mammalian bipeds, like you."

Alex takes this in. Suddenly something occurs to him. "Hey, Carrus. How old are you?"

"Three."

"That's all?"

"I was built for this mission. I've known nothing but the factory that gave me life, the transport ship that brought me here, and Earth. Of course I have knowledge of many other things, but it's not firsthand knowledge."

"Oh." Alex thinks a moment. "Is three old or young, for a robot?"

"Young," Carrus replies. "Very young."

He reaches the on-ramp. He takes it, then cruises down the highway. Traffic is light.

Alex asks, "How fast can you go?"

"Fast." Carrus accelerates to eighty.

"Show me."

"You won't be scared?"

"No way." Alex shakes his head emphatically.

"All right." Carrus speeds up to one-twenty. He weaves, whizzing past other cars.

Alex urges, "Come on. Faster."

Carrus speeds up to one-fifty.

Alex grins. "Faster!"

Carrus sweeps past a patrol car parked in the shadow of an overpass. Immediately the patrol car flashes its lights and pulls out onto the highway.

Alex glances back over his shoulder. "Oh shit, what if it catches us?"

"It won't," Carrus says, and shows how fast he can go.

The acceleration presses Alex back against the seat cushions. The toy car and boy topple from the dashboard and bounce on the floor. Instantly, the patrol car vanishes from view.

Later, as Carrus cruises leisurely along, Alex says, "That was awesome! Awesome!" He rolls down his window and thrusts his hand out into the gushing air, and as the breezes twine between his fingers, he laughs and laughs.

* * *

When Alex is sixteen he sneaks out after bedtime, and Carrus drives him to a party at the house of a high school student whose parents are away. Carrus waits at the end of the driveway with the other vehicles while groups of giggling teens wander by. The house is enormous, its windows brimming with festive light. Hours later, Alex stumbles back and collapses in the passenger seat. Carrus runs a scan on him, which reveals heavy intoxication.

Alex dozes most of the way home. When Carrus pulls up at the darkened house, Alex rouses himself and says, "Thanks for the ride."

"Sure."

Alex hunches forward. "Hey, I have to tell you something. I promised her I wouldn't tell, but...I had sex with Hailey Jacobson."

"What? Tonight?"

"No, she wasn't there. I mean last week. At her house, after school. Except then her stupid brother got himself kicked out of military school, and now he's always hanging around the house. So we can't do it there anymore."

After a time, Carrus says carefully, "I understand that people sometimes have sex in cars."

Alex is silent. Then: "No. It would be weird."

"Come on. Please."

Alex says, "You actually want me to?"

"Yes."

"Why?"

Carrus says, "I want to see what it's like."

"So watch a movie."

"It's not the same. I want to be there."

"I don't know, I..." Then something occurs to Alex. He ponders it. He says, "If I did this, I'd want a favor in return."

"Anything."

Alex stares, serious. "You mean that? Anything?"

"Yes."

"You promise?"

"Yes."

Alex eases open the passenger door and slips out. He whispers, "All right. I'll think about it."

* * *

The next weekend, Carrus picks up Alex in the early afternoon and they drive to a corner where Hailey Jacobsen is waiting. She's petite and pale with long scarlet hair, and wears a black tanktop and jean skirt. When Alex waves to her, she stares at Carrus in amazement.

She climbs into the passenger seat. "This is your car?"

242

"It's a friend's," Alex says. "I'm borrowing it."

"Cool." Hailey smiles. "So where are we going?"

"Someplace special," he tells her.

He drives to the end of the gravel road beside the secluded field where Carrus first revealed his humanoid form.

Alex parks, then cups Hailey's chin and kisses her deeply. She wraps her arms around his neck and pushes her fingers through his hair. Alex reaches across her body and fumbles for the latch to recline her seat, but can't find it, so Carrus reclines the seat himself. Then Alex stretches and shifts until he's lying on top of Hailey. He pulls a condom from his pocket.

She glances out the window. "What if someone...?"

"They won't," Alex assures her.

As Alex and Hailey undress each other, Carrus runs a scan on them, observes with fascination the redistribution of their blood, their release of hormones, the rapid acceleration of their hearts. Carrus watches Hailey's face in the rearview mirror—her closed eyes, her hair spilling across the headrest, her mouth stretched wide as she murmurs, "Oh Alex, that feels so good. Oh faster, Alex. Yes, like that, faster."

During the ride home, Alex is quiet. He drops off Hailey, then drives to his house. As he exits, he says flatly, "I shouldn't have done that. She had a right to know. About you."

Carrus departs. Hailey's body has left a damp spot on the seat, near the place where his heart should be, when he transforms into the shape of a man.

* * *

For three weeks Alex is never out waiting when Carrus drives by. When he finally appears, he looks tired and miserable. He climbs into the passenger seat.

Carrus drives aimlessly for a while, then asks, "How have you been?"

Alex stares at nothing. "She said she wasn't ready. For a relationship. Then two weeks later she's seeing someone else. Two weeks!" He presses his forehead against the window. "You're so lucky. That you're a robot. That you don't have feelings."

"I'm a biomechanical sentience. I have emotions just like you."

"Not like me," Alex insists. "Not like this." He says softly, "Trust me, you're lucky. I mean, you can change. When you can't stand what you are, you can turn into something else. I wish I could do that, just for a little while."

Alex has Carrus drive out to the end of the gravel road. Then he rests back against the seat and closes his eyes. "She…I…I can almost…" He stops. He opens his eyes. "You promised you'd do anything for me."

"I did."

"Anything."

"Yes."

Alex takes a deep breath. "I want you to bring me with you. Into space. To fight the Kaav with you."

"I can't—"

"Please, Carrus. You promised. You said anything. I have to get out of here. This world has nothing for me."

Carrus says, "It's not up to me. I…I don't know. Are you sure that's what you want?"

"Yes," Alex answers, fervent.

Carrus explains, "Look, all our forces are deployed far away. Even if I could get permission to take you, which I doubt, none of our transports will pass this way for years."

Alex slumps, defeated.

"I'm sorry," Carrus says. "You know that if there was anything I could do, anything at all…"

Alex whispers, "There is."

"What?"

"Transform."

Carrus is suddenly afraid. He imagines his roof crashing down, and blood. "I don't know what you mean."

Alex stares at the floor. "Yes you do."

"No," Carrus says. "I won't."

Alex looks up, his face cold, angry. "Anything, you said. Anything."

"Alex, I won't do it."

"This is such bullshit!" Alex kicks the dashboard. "You promise me anything and you give me nothing. Nothing!"

"Alex, I'm sorry."

Alex sighs and presses his face into his hands. "Take me home."

They drive the whole way in silence. Then Alex exits, slamming the door behind him.

After that Carrus is reluctant to face any more anger, cause any more disappointment. He gets on the highway and heads west. He's away for two years.

* * *

Finally Carrus decides to go back. He drives toward Alex's house. He's almost there when he realizes that he's being tailed by a black SUV.

Carrus doesn't recognize it. He runs a scan, which reveals that the SUV is a class 3 war mech, like himself. He tries sending it a coded message. If the mech is an ally, it should identify itself.

It doesn't.

Carrus leads it through the woods and down dirt roads. He loses sight of the SUV, but knows that it's right behind him. If he has to make a stand, he'll do so in a place he knows well.

He reaches the gravel drive, rumbles down it to its end, and pulls into the field. In this spot where he first revealed his humanoid form, he does so again. He snaps his hand-rifle from his waist and crouches, aiming back down the road, knowing that he'll have to resort to a mace if the enemy has shields, as it almost certainly does.

The black SUV draws near. Carrus's trigger finger tightens.

The SUV unfolds, revealing a broad, powerful humanoid form that Carrus suddenly recognizes: an ally, the mech who calls himself Rictus.

Carrus lowers his rifle. "You could have identified yourself, told me it was you."

Rictus strides forward. "I wanted to observe your response."

Rictus has a fondness for observation, for spying. His exterior used to be blue. Carrus says, "You got a paint job."

Rictus surveys his black body. "I find this more fitting."

"Who did it for you?"

"A human."

"Our orders were to avoid detection by them."

Rictus says slyly, "As if you're one to talk."

Carrus feels a sudden panic. Rictus knows about Alex.

But Rictus doesn't seem to care. He says, "At any rate, my paint job has not jeopardized the big secret of our presence here. The human who did it will tell no tales. I've discovered a fascinating property of this world: A car can kill a human and drive away, and other humans barely take notice, it is so common. A car can do this over, and over, and over." Rictus studies his right hand, flexes it, says absently, "I shall miss this place. War, I suppose, will offer its own compensations, but I fear that when it comes to exercising my talents, nothing will ever compare with being a car on Earth."

Carrus says, "War?"

Rictus looks up. "Yes. We are being redeployed. The transport arrives in three days. The official order will come down soon."

Carrus is reluctant. He thinks of Alex.

Rictus senses this and says sharply, "You must curb these unseemly preoccupations. Remember what you are: A tool of destruction. Ready yourself, Carrus. We are off to fight the Kaav, at last."

* * *

Four hours later, Carrus parks across the street from an auto body shop. Alex, wearing an oil-stained T-shirt and wiping his hands on a rag, emerges from the garage. Carrus thinks: Rictus was repainted at a place like this. The human who did it was a person like Alex.

Alex sees Carrus, walks across the street, gets into the passenger seat, and says lightly, "Hey, long time no see."

Carrus says, "Alex, I need to ask you something important, and I need to ask you now. Do you still want to go with me, into space, to fight the Kaav?"

Alex's good humor fades. "You said that was impossible."

"I said it would be years, and that I didn't know. Well, now I do. You can come, if that's what you still want."

This has meant making deals and calling in favors, but Carrus intends to keep his promise.

Alex is incredulous. "Now you offer me this? Now?"

"Alex, I'm leaving tonight to go rendezvous with the transport. I need an answer."

"Then the answer is no."

"You understand that this will be your only chance?"

Alex groans. "Carrus, I can't leave. I have a life, a job. I'm getting married this spring. I'm in love. You wouldn't understand."

Carrus exclaims, "I do understand! I do have feelings. Why won't you ever believe me?"

Alex lowers his head. "Okay. I'm sorry."

After a time, Carrus says, "I'm sorry too."

They sit in silence. Then Alex opens the door and gets out. He stands there a moment, then says, "Goodbye, Carrus," and walks back to the garage.

* * *

Carrus goes to war. During one battle, Carrus and Rictus are hit with a biotech weapon. As a parasite rapidly devours their minds, they drive at top speed through an alien city toward their evacuation point, a blocky grey tower. A red moon hangs on the horizon like a bleeding eye.

Carrus and Rictus reach the base of the tower, reconfigure to humanoid form, and with rifles bared they storm the entryway, which is, fortunately, deserted.

As Carrus climbs the stairs, his mind is a swirl of agony. The pain shrinks his focus to a single form—the black shape of Rictus, stumbling on ahead. A thought comes to him then with terrible clarity: Rictus was right. Carrus is a tool of destruction, and always will be.

When they are halfway up the tower, a wave of torment seizes Rictus and he collapses, shrieking. He drops his hand-rifle, which clatters away down the steps.

Carrus thinks of Alex, of the unlucky human who painted Rictus black. Carrus readies his mace.

Rictus lolls his head, stares up. "What...?"

"You should have stuck with blue," Carrus says, and swings at Rictus's face. The mace glances off Rictus's shields, which ripple with violet light. Carrus strikes again, and again the blow is deflected, but now the light is dimmed.

"Wait," Rictus cries, flailing. On the third stroke his shields calve, and the mace crumples him.

Carrus tosses aside the mace, hefts his hand-rifle, presses it to Rictus's staved-in head, and fires. Rictus goes limp, black fluid gouting from his ruined face.

Then Carrus clambers up a thousand more steps to the roof. He collapses, wracked with pain. He must endure it. He must—

He pops open his chest, reaches deep inside, and pulls out two tiny objects that have lain inside him for ages—two toys, a car and a boy. Carrus holds one up in each hand.

He wobbles the boy and thinks, "Hey Carrus, when you're done fighting come back to Earth. We'll go for a drive together, you and I."

He wobbles the toy car and thinks, "I'll do that, Alex. I'll—"

Agony overwhelms him. He screams.

From the gray sky, a roar of engines. They're coming to retrieve him. He has to make it. He has to—

Endure.

* * *

Carrus is rescued, repaired, discharged. He returns to Earth, where due to time dilation twenty-five years have passed. He learns that Alex owns a house now. He drives to it, parks in the driveway, and waits.

After a time, an attractive woman in her early forties with long brown hair appears at the front door. She hurries out to the driveway, scrutinizes Carrus, then stomps back to the house. He hears her shouting angrily.

Alex comes to the door. He walks out to Carrus and gets in the passenger seat. Alex is stockier, his blond hair thinning at the temples. He says, "I didn't know if you'd ever come back."

"Neither did I," Carrus says. "Was that your wife?"

"Yes."

"Why is she upset?"

Alex says, "She thought maybe I bought you, an expensive sports car. That's something guys my age do."

Carrus is mystified, but in a pleasant way. This is what he loves, these silly things. These human lives.

Alex says, "So you really did it? Went to war? Fought the Kaav?"

"Yes," Carrus says. "We won."

"Wow." Alex shakes his head, amazed.

Carrus adds, "I mean, I fought their machines. It was a proxy war. I've still never actually seen the Kaav." He asks, "How have you been?"

"Fine. Good. I don't know." Alex hesitates. Carrus waits. Finally Alex says, "My life...my wife. See, it's not that I don't love her. She's great. And the kids. It's just that...I always thought there would be more, you know? I always thought I'd go with you, into space, to fight the Kaav."

Carrus says, "It wasn't that great."

"I'm sure sometimes it wasn't. But still..." Alex sighs. "You were always the lucky one, Carrus. The powerful one, the one with the mission, the one who could transform."

Oh Alex, Carrus thinks. I can change between a sports car and a machine of war, but you're the one who can truly transform, in a way I can only envy. Or do you somehow think that you're still that same little boy I met all those years ago?

Alex asks, "So what now?"

Carrus says, "Let's go for a drive together, you and I."

He pulls away from the house and heads through town to an on-ramp. Soon he's cruising down the highway, going sixty. He says, "Do you remember?"

"Yes," Alex whispers, and then, "Faster."

Carrus goes one hundred.

Alex grins. "Faster!"

And later, as they coast along, Alex rolls down his window and thrusts his spread fingers out into the open air, and for the first time in ages Carrus listens to the sound of Alex, laughing.

Author's note: Transformations

I wrote this story in Los Angeles in 2007. Again we see the idea of the evil car, which also pops up in my L.A. stories "Blood of Virgins" and "Red Road" (and to some extent in "Save Me Plz"). At the time I was attending two or three book signings a week, mostly at Book Soup on Sunset Boulevard, Skylight Books in Los Feliz, and Vroman's in Pasadena. I loved going to the events and meeting the authors. I found that if I went to the back of the line, I could often talk to the author for ten or fifteen minutes, since there would be no one waiting behind me. Often the author would be going out to dinner with friends after the signing, and sometimes they would invite me to tag along.

Unfortunately the readings themselves were often pretty dull. The audience usually tuned out when the author read their work, then came to life again during the Q&A. These were perfectly good books that were perfectly enjoyable to read, but there's a difference between something that works on the page and something that works in front of an audience. Lots of dialogue seemed to work best, I thought, especially if it involved two characters arguing with each other. Humor was a big plus.

I became obsessed with writing stories that would work in front of an audience. Everything should be short, I decided. Short sentences. Short paragraphs. Short scenes. I listened over and over to the Screeching Weasel cover of "I Think We're Alone Now." They play the whole song in one minute. A story should be like that, I thought. Short and punchy. Nothing that's boring. That's what I was going for with "Transformations."

I came up with the story in one day. I was visiting my parents in Palo Alto, and I had to drive back to L.A. I had just discovered the song "Into the Ocean" by Blue October. I listened to it on repeat for the entire six hour drive, and scenes from the story just kept popping into my head. By the time I arrived home, I had worked out the whole plot.

When I showed the story to my creative writing class, the professor told me I was doing everything wrong. "There's too much happening," she said. "A short story isn't about things happening. It's about capturing a single moment in time." I'm still completely baffled by that. I guess that's one way you *could* write a short story, but it's definitely not the *only* way to write a short story. Certainly none of my favorite stories are about "capturing a single moment in time."

When I read "Transformations" in front of audiences, people went nuts for it. I must be doing *something* right, I thought.

There was an art movement in L.A. called pop surrealism. I discovered it through a gallery called La Luz De Jesus, and in the pages of magazines like *Hi Fructose* and *Juxtapoz*. It was all about taking pop culture icons and subverting them, repurposing them, turning them into art. I loved it. This is what short stories need, I thought. This energy. This attitude. This is how you make short stories relevant again. I noticed that if I told people that my new story was "science fiction," they often lost interest, but if I told them, "It's a critique of *Transformers*," that really got their attention.

In the 1986 movie *Transformers*, a boy and his car race together to the top of a mountain. It's a scene that's been burned into my brain for almost 40 years. The rest of the movie is forgettable, but that one scene is fantastic. That's what it feels like to be a kid. I wondered: Why can't the whole movie be like that? Why can't it show you how it feels to be a teenager? To be an adult? Why can't it grow up with you?

This was the last story I published in *Realms of Fantasy*, which ceased publication a short time later. I was crushed. I'd been reading the magazine since high school, and had worked hard to become a regular contributor. There was a terrific online community around the magazine, and I loved the full-color art that they did for each story. It was around that time that I started really throwing myself into *Geek's Guide to the Galaxy*. The podcast was something I had control over, something that could never be taken away from me.

Jesus Garcia Lopez

Veil of Ignorance

Something strange is happening to me.

We're at Conrad's vacation house, a sprawling mansion that orbits the gas giant Hades-3. (His father owns both the house and the planet.) Conrad is in the living room watching sports. His girlfriend Alyssa is standing by the mirror in the bathroom, fixing her hair. Her friend Kat is sitting at the bay windows, watching the stars and the roiling vermeil clouds on the world below. Dillon is in the kitchen, mixing drinks. Brad is slouched on the sofa, watching everyone with a lazy smile.

And I don't know which of them I am.

Perception shifts. A few moments of Alyssa, running my fingers through silky hair. A moment of Dillon, using my knife to slice limes for the drinks. A moment of Kat, feeling awe of those looming bands of color, of those constantly churning swirls that look so majestic, and make me feel so insignificant. Then Conrad—pride at my team's success, at my father's wealth.

Then Brad. I feel quite smug. "It's starting to work," I tell them. "You can all feel it, can't you?"

Dillon comes in from the kitchen with the drinks. I hand one of them to Conrad, who thanks me, and one to Kat, who takes it silently. "Feel what?" I ask.

Brad gestures to the smoldering bowl at the center of the coffee table, at the Callipsarian pipe, and whatever that shit was we've all been smoking.

"Something very strange is happening to me," Kat says.

Brad ignores her. "You see, I had this idea. A few weeks ago, Dillon and I were talking politics, and he brings up this thing about Rawls."

Conrad sighs and orders the computer to take a break. I want to watch the end of the game, but this is starting to feel really weird.

Alyssa comes out of the bathroom, looking gorgeous, as always. I sit down on the couch next to Conrad. "What's going on, Brad?" I ask. "What *was* that stuff you gave us?"

"Just sit and listen," Brad says. "All will become clear."

Conrad turns to Dillon. "Who's Rawls?"

"John Rawls," I explain, puzzled about where this is going. "Twentieth-century. He tried to revive the social contract theory, which states that the only fair laws are those that everyone can agree to."

"Whatever." Alyssa tosses her hair. "Someone get me another drink."

Conrad holds up a hand to her. "Quiet," I say. "I want to hear this."

Dillon shrugs and keeps going. "The problem with the social contract is that people *don't* agree. Slave-owners think that slavery is fair, slaves don't. So Rawls envisions a hypothetical situation in which the two of them don't know who is who. Put behind this *veil of ignorance,* neither would support slavery, knowing that he himself might be the slave." I start to see where this is going, and finish, "Once self-interest is cancelled out, it turns out that they agree on principle."

Kat interrupts. "Brad, will you cut the shit and tell us what's going on?" I say. "Why can't I tell who I am?" Then Dillon starts to answer my question, in that patronizing tone of his.

"Don't you see?" he says. "We've been put behind a veil of ignorance ourselves."

"Very good." Brad nods at him. "A few weeks ago I was hanging out with this Callipsarian dealer on Far-Guardport—"

Alyssa frowns. "Which ones are they?" I ask softly. "Callipsarians?"

"The purple ones," Kat says. "From Auropelli. With the tentacles. Three yellow eyes."

"Oh yeah," I say.

Conrad elbows me. "Quiet."

"—and we were totally trashed. Talking politics, philosophy, metaphysics, et cetera, et cetera, and I start telling it about this veil of ignorance idea, and it says it's got some stuff that can do that. So it sells me—"

"Why?" Dillon asks. My word hangs there, alone in the silence for a few moments.

"Well, look," Brad says. "This group, this band of *friends*—if that's what you want to call us—is broken. We all know it, but no one wants to say it. Well, I said it." He levels his finger at Conrad. "Conrad treats his girlfriend like shit. He also treats Dillon like shit. That is, unless Dillon starts picking on one of the girls, in which case Conrad gangs up with him. And of course," he finishes, "everyone treats me like shit all the time."

"Conrad does *not* treat me like shit," Alyssa says, offended.

"Quiet," he tells her.

"I thought this might clear the air," Brad says. "Behind our very own veil of ignorance, some of us may reach a new consensus on how we ought to be treating each other."

Alyssa says, "I don't like this. I don't like having someone else controlling my body, even for a moment." I feel violated.

"No one else is controlling your body." Brad sighs. "That's not how it works. The drug creates localized telepathy with scrambled ego. Alyssa's brain is still controlling Alyssa's body. Alyssa's thoughts—"

"To the extent that she *has* any," Dillon interjects.

"—are still her own. The only difference is, now everyone experiences everyone's thoughts, and no one knows which set of thoughts is his own."

Kat crosses her arms. "I don't want to share my thoughts."

Brad shrugs. "Too late," I say. "Don't do drugs."

Conrad gets to his feet. He looks pissed off. "I think Brad needs to have his ass kicked for pulling this little stunt."

"No," Dillon says, "think about it. Our identities are all mixed together. If Conrad hits Brad, we all feel it equally. What's the point of that?"

"Hmmm." Conrad thinks for a moment, then says, "So we just wait until the drug wears off, then hit him."

Kat glances at him. "What if *you're* Brad?" I ask. That stops him.

And that's really the point, isn't it? There are five sets of consciousness here, but none of us knows which personality belongs to us.

When the drug wears off, I'll be one of these people. But who? Right now I'm Kat. The boys don't like me. They think I'm weird, because I wear black, and have my own ideas. They only let me hang around because I'm friends with Alyssa. She's more their type: pretty and popular and—I'm sorry to say it, because she is my friend—vapid. She doesn't even notice when they make fun of her. But still, she's pretty, and looks are all that matter when you're a girl.

Am I a girl?

If so, let me be Alyssa, not Kat.

I don't want to be Kat.

* * *

"I'm starting to get a headache," Brad says. "I can feel it coming on."

Conrad grunts, "Good."

Dillon nods. "Yeah, seriously, Brad," he says. "You have no right to be complaining about anything right now."

Brad looks sullen. "I get really bad headaches."

"We know." Conrad sighs. "We've heard." He gets up from the couch and paces around the living room. He wheels on Brad. "See, *this* is why you get picked on. *This* is why no one likes you. You're weak. You whine all the time. You're a..." He turns to Dillon. "What?"

"Hypochondriac?" Dillon offers.

"Yes," Conrad says, pointing. "Thank you. A hypochondriac. We all get headaches, Brad. We deal with them. For you it's like the end of the world."

"Well, you'll see," Brad says angrily. "Tonight, you'll all feel what my headaches are like. And *I'm* used to it. You're not."

Conrad shakes his head. "Whatever. I'm so intimidated." The truth is I'm sick of Brad and his goddamn attitude. He thinks he's so clever, trying to make us feel sorry for him. Well, I didn't start this game, but I can choose to play it *my* way. Let's have some fun with this.

I walk over to Alyssa, take her hand and pull her to her feet. "Come on upstairs," I tell her. "I want to show you something."

Alyssa hesitates. I know what he's thinking. I guess we all do, because this drug is mixing our thoughts together, but even without the drug I would still know, because he's got that *look*. "Come on," he repeats, and pulls me along after him, toward the stairs.

Brad scowls. I should have known. Conrad likes to do her so that we can all hear her moaning, just to let everyone know who she belongs to. Now we'll do a lot more than *hear* them.

Tonight I offer them a chance to get outside themselves, to comprehend our sad situation, to make a new start. And all he can see is a new opportunity to show us up. I glance at Dillon, who's grinning. "What are you so thrilled about?"

"He's really going to do it," Dillon says. "We're *all* going to. I've always wanted to. And don't tell me you haven't."

Kat looks weak and pale and scared. I *am* scared. I say nothing.

"No," Brad says. "She's an imbecile. I don't find that attractive."

"Liar," Dillon answers. "Everyone wants her." I glance at Kat. "What, no wry observations this time, Kat?" I laugh. "Well, this *is* pretty fucked up," I say. "I don't remember anything like this in Rawls."

Even as I say it, I experience a twinge of self-loathing. I'm such an ass. So cocky, so sarcastic. Why do I act this way?

Because I know that as long as someone *else* is the butt of the joke, it won't be me. How pathetic. For a moment I feel an overwhelming sense of shame. But then I remember I'm not Dillon. At least, probably not. Or maybe I am.

I don't want to be Dillon.

* * *

Conrad lies in bed, among tangled sheets. I always hate myself, afterward.

My thoughts are terribly lucid, unclouded by the distractions of desire and drink and noise. It's in these moments that I can't escape the truth. My friends are losers. I despise my girlfriend. I stay with her because she's hot, and I hate myself for being so superficial. I'm rich and good-looking and athletic and successful. I've had every advantage, so why can't I do better than *this?* Than these people?

At least the sex was good. That's what I used to think.

But tonight...my thoughts kept getting mixed with hers—I *was* her— and I felt nothing but boredom, frustration, a straining to achieve some pleasure, before it was over. And it was over too soon.

That's Brad's fault, I tell myself—him and his goddamn headache. I feel it, in those moments when I'm him, and how are you supposed to perform with a headache like that? Now I have to go back downstairs and face them. They all know. What a miserable night this has turned out to be for Conrad.

For me?

I hope I'm not Conrad.

I look at Alyssa, and know that she knows these thoughts. I don't care.

Alyssa slips angrily from the bed and starts getting dressed. I almost fall over yanking on my panties, I'm so mad. What a shithead! What a goddamn asshole. "I only stay with you because you buy me things," I tell him over my shoulder. At least I didn't have to fake it this time. I dress in the dark. By the time I've got my clothes on, my mind is made up: I'm dumping him. If I'm Alyssa, I'm definitely dumping him. I mean it this time.

But what if I'm *not* Alyssa? What if I'm Conrad? In that case, maybe I shouldn't dump him. Or rather, Alyssa shouldn't. God, my head hurts to think like this.

The truth is, they're both really sad people, and I don't want to be either one of them. And I realize then that I don't want to be *any* of these people: not Conrad who's arrogant, or Alyssa who's dumb, or Kat who's weird, or Dillon who's mean, or Brad who's whiny.

Is this how the people felt in Rawls' thought experiment? When they were floating free for a time, divorced from the tyranny of identity? Maybe they would choose never to go back. Pure consciousness is an amazing thing, but actual personalities are always broken and unpleasant. It's not fair that our thoughts should be imprisoned in identities.

I start to dread the moment when this wonderful and terrible drug I purchased will begin to fade, and I'll be trapped as one of these people. Now I realize that I've been lost in reverie, and my thoughts have grown too profound to be Alyssa's. Sure enough, I'm Brad again. I glance up as Conrad and Alyssa troop miserably down the stairs.

* * *

My headaches don't start out that bad, but then they get worse.

A pressure is building along my hairline, then it starts to squeeze, like someone's wrapped a rope around my brow and is twisting it tighter and tighter. The pain starts to pulse, ranging from bad to unbearable. There's quick, stabbing pain if I move my head, and constant nausea.

For a moment I'm Alyssa and the pain is gone, but I know it'll be back any moment.

Conrad tells Brad, "Take some pills."

"It won't do any good," Brad says. "It never does."

"Take them!" Conrad barks.

Brad shrugs. I wander over to the bathroom, pain like hammer-blows falling on my temples. I rummage through the medicine cabinet, find some pills, swallow them. I return to the living room.

"We've got to make this stop," Conrad says.

Dillon nods in agreement. "Hey, Brad," I say. "When is this headache going to wear off?"

"By morning," he replies.

Conrad is incredulous. "By *morning?* No way. There's got to be something we can do."

"The telepathy must have a maximum range," Kat says quietly. "The field—it can't stretch forever."

Conrad nods. "Right, so let's just hop on the yacht and leave him here."

"You can't," Brad says. "I ordered the yacht to do a tune-up. It won't be ready to fly until tomorrow."

Conrad takes three quick steps and shoves Brad hard. "What the hell did you do that for?"

Brad stumbles, recovers his balance. "No one's running away. Not tonight. What's the matter, Conrad? Don't like being me? Or Kat? Or Alyssa? Welcome to the club."

Conrad turns away. He starts to pace furiously.

"Don't you see?" Brad is almost shouting now. "We have a chance here tonight. We can agree on how each of us should be treated, and be bound by that commitment. That's the beauty of the veil of ignorance. For example, we know that Brad really does get terrible headaches, pain that the rest of the group, until tonight, couldn't even imagine. So let's agree to be more sympathetic. Remember, any of you might be Brad."

There are a few moments of awkward silence. Everyone exchanges sideways glances.

Conrad shakes his head. "Screw Brad," I announce. "He's an asshole, and Conrad is going to kick his ass when this is over. And Brad deserves it. Even if I'm Brad, I don't care. He still deserves it." I pause. "I don't think I am, though. How could I be *him?* No way."

Kat rolls her eyes. "You have no way of knowing," I say. "You're being irrational."

"And even if you *are* Conrad," Brad adds, "you still might want to listen." He looks at each of us in turn. "We've all learned some things tonight about Conrad. He's going to get a lot of shit for that—unless we all agree right now to go easy on him."

Conrad glares at Brad with absolute fury.

Dillon backs out of the way. Strangely enough, in this tense moment, I start thinking about Rawls again—about some of the critiques of his theory. Rawls believed that people subjected to a veil of ignorance would do the rational thing—agree to a society that's fair to everyone. That's what Brad thought too.

But maybe they wouldn't. Maybe people would still set up things like slavery, because each person would simply *gamble* that he'll be the owner and not the slave. It's not the rational thing to do, but people are often not rational—an idea that's foremost in my thoughts as I watch the crazed expression coming over Conrad.

Over *me*. The pain of Brad's headache is driving me absolutely insane. *Brad* is driving me absolutely insane. I want it to stop, I want *him* to stop. Anything, to make it stop.

But Brad's just standing there with his smug grin. "I told you my headaches were bad, but you wouldn't listen. You never listen to me because you're a spoiled asshole. But now you see I'm right. Who's weak now, huh? Who's the one who can't take it?"

I lunge for him. "Don't you come to *my* house and talk to *me* like that." I punch Brad, who goes down, and I fall on top of him, start slamming his shoulders against the floor. Then my fingers find Brad's throat and start to choke him. "If he's unconscious," I announce furiously, "then we won't have to feel his headache, or his weakness, or his goddamn resentment."

Alyssa starts screaming. *I* start screaming.

Kat leaps forward and tries to drag Conrad off, but he's too big. "Stop it!" I yell at him. "You're going to kill him!" Dillon stands by doing nothing. He's frozen. Just contemplating the theoretical implications of this strangling.

Conrad's grip tightens. I'm squeezing. I hear Kat's words and realize that she's right, I *am* going to kill him. It has this awful sense of inevitability, because I hate him so much, despise him. I have no choice. But it's not really *me* doing it, is it? At least, probably it's not.

Brad's thrashing is growing weaker. And now everything's going dark and numb, like my head's being dipped in ice water. I can't see. I hardly notice the pain in my neck anymore. I know I'm going to die and I don't want to die. I mean, I really, really don't want to die here on this floor, but then I realize that it's not *me* that's dying. *Brad* is dying and I'm not him. At least, I'm probably not. Or maybe I am.

I don't want to be Brad.

* * *

I'm screaming.

Because I'm dead.

I'm dead I'm dead. I'm Brad and I'm dead.

I felt it, that moment when life stopped, that instant when it ended. *Don't think don't think about it.*

I'm screaming. I can't be dead if I'm screaming and three other people are screaming too: Conrad is screaming and Dillon is screaming and Kat is screaming and I look down at my body and see that I'm Alyssa.

No, I'm Conrad now, and I make myself stop screaming. Stop it. Just stop. I make myself look at Brad.

He's on his back—arms splayed, legs splayed. I can't see his face. His head is turned away. All I see is a mess of dark, curly hair.

But now I'm Kat and I *can* see his face. Oh god, his eyes are open. They're *staring*. I throw a hand over my mouth and turn away.

Conrad pivots, stomps a few steps, circles back. Then I *am* Conrad and my life is over. Ruined. How could this happen? How could this possibly happen? Brad's headache ended along with his life and now my thoughts are clear and sharp and cold. Very, very cold.

Alyssa's palms are pressed to her temples. "You killed him!" I shout.

Kat moves toward the computer. "I'm calling for help."

Conrad shouts, "No."

Dillon holds up a hand. "Wait."

Kat comes to a stop. Watching. Guarded.

"Let me think a second." Dillon starts to pace. I'm Alyssa waiting, then Conrad waiting, then Kat when he says, "We've got to cover it up."

"No," I tell him.

"Think, Kat," Dillon says softly. "What if *you're* Conrad?"

"Then I'll pay the price." But even as I say it, I feel a twinge of doubt. What if I really am Conrad? I try to imagine what it would be like if the drug wore off and I looked down and saw Conrad's body—my body, maybe— standing alone. I can't. I can't. It's too much.

Alyssa fidgets. "What are we going to do?" I ask.

"Cover it up," Dillon explains. He takes a deep breath. "It's the only thing that makes sense. Any one of us might be Conrad. So we all swear right now never to tell anybody. No one knows Brad was here. We dispose of the body, and for all anyone knows he was eaten by one of those Callipsarian scumbags he always hung out with."

Conrad steps forward. "Anyway, it would serve him right if that *had* happened," I say, awkwardly. "This whole thing was his fault. It's the drug that did it all. What was he thinking...slipping us some fucked up alien drug?"

Dillon turns and gazes at Kat. "Come on," I prod her. "It's the only way." I know she'll break. I was her just a second ago. She can't go to jail. She won't.

"All right," she whispers, in a hollow voice.

Alyssa agrees too. "Okay," I say. "Okay, let's do that."

Conrad nods. "I'll load him onto my yacht. As soon as it's ready to fly, we swing into a low orbit and launch the body down into Hades-3. It won't last a second down there."

"Fine," Dillon says. "Go. Do it." Conrad takes Brad's body under the armpits and starts to drag.

Kat wanders over to the window again and looks down at the planet. I used to think it was so amazing, so awe-inspiring. Now I look at those red bands and feel only horror. I can't look away. I know that for the rest of my life I'm going to remember this sight, and remember Brad, and be afraid.

I'll turn Conrad in. Whatever I say now, whatever I promise, it's a lie. If the drug wears off and I'm not Conrad, I'll turn him in. I have to.

But what if I *am* Conrad? Then I can't trust Kat. Then I have to do something about Kat.

Conrad stops. He tosses Brad's body aside. Dillon stands totally still. They're both staring at me.

Dillon sighs. "So much for that plan." We can't trust Kat not to talk. I should know, I was just her.

"Get rid of her too," Conrad grumbles. It's the first thing to pop into my head, but even before it's out of my mouth, I realize the problem, which Dillon kindly points out.

"What if *you're* Kat?" he says.

I groan. "So what do we do?"

Dillon thinks for a minute. "I have an idea," he says.

Then I *am* Dillon, and it's my idea.

A terrible, terrible idea.

But it's the only thing I can think of.

* * *

We wait for a Callipsarian dealer that Conrad knows. I'm Conrad and Alyssa and Dillon and Kat and Conrad and Alyssa and Dillon and Kat. No one says anything. It seems to go on forever.

It *will* go on forever.

The Callipsarian docks its yacht. I'm Kat when it enters the room. It's taller than any of us, sinuous, and smells like an ozone sea. I've never seen one whose mottled tentacles were such a dark shade of purple, or whose three eyes blazed such a bright and terrible yellow. It regards us.

Conrad shows it the pipe. "We want more of this," I demand.

The Callipsarian snatches up the pipe and examines it.

"Enough to last a decade," Dillon adds. "Enough to last forever, if we need it to."

The Callipsarian is very accommodating. "Tell your friends," it rasps.

"Plenty to go around. Enough for every last human, if they want it."

After the Callipsarian leaves, Dillon offers the pipe to Kat. "There's enough in here to keep us going for weeks."

She hesitates.

Dillon scowls. "Take it, Kat. Otherwise it's a one in four chance of being Conrad. Only you and only Conrad. Your choice."

Kat takes the pipe. I smoke it. So do the others. Now I'll never betray Conrad. I might be him.

It occurs to me later, when I'm Dillon, that maybe Brad succeeded, in some sick way. Kat or Dillon or Alyssa would have turned in Conrad in a second. But behind the veil of ignorance, we all agreed to help him out, and we always will. It's too bad Brad isn't around to see it. I'm glad I wasn't him, at least.

Sometimes I wonder who I am.

Not that it matters.

Not anymore.

Author's note: Veil of Ignorance

I majored in Government at Colby College, where I took classes in subjects ranging from Congressional procedure to campaign finance reform to Eastern European politics. But by far my favorite classes were the ones about political theory and Constitutional law, which were taught by Professor Joseph Reisert. (Reisert recently joined me in Episode 485 of *Geek's Guide to the Galaxy* to discuss Aldous Huxley's *Brave New World*.)

It was in one of those classes that I read the book *Political Liberalism* by John Rawls, which is where I first heard of the concept of the "veil of ignorance." I instantly knew the idea would make a great science fiction story, but I wasn't sure how to tell it.

A few years later, in 2003, I figured it out. There's a classic science fiction story by Alfred Bester called "Fondly Fahrenheit," about a man who is forced to stay on the run because his valuable, indispensable robot keeps committing murder. The story is told in a first-person viewpoint that shifts back and forth between the man and the robot. I wanted to do a story like that, except with five characters rather than two, which would allow me to dramatize the "veil of ignorance" concept.

I went back and studied the shifting first-person viewpoint in "Fondly Fahrenheit," and decided that it wasn't as clear and consistent as it could have been. If I was going to do the same thing with five characters, I would have to tweak my approach somewhat, or else the story would get hopelessly confusing. I eventually settled on the technique you see in the story, which is to always mention a character in the third person before shifting into their first-person perspective.

Originally "Veil of Ignorance" ended with Brad's death. When I workshopped the story at the University of Kansas that summer, the main criticism was that the ending was too abrupt. For the workshop I was required to rewrite the story in response to the feedback. People were asking for a different ending, but nobody had suggested anything better. I remember coming back to my dorm room, shutting the door, and saying to myself, "Okay brain, it's just you and me. We've got one day to think of a new ending for this story." I was proud of the new ending I came up with, though when I workshopped the story again, half the class said they preferred the original ending.

That second critique session was joined by legendary science fiction writer Frederik Pohl, author of *Gateway*, *The Space Merchants*, and "The Tunnel Under the World." He had a few issues with "Veil of Ignorance," but said that if he were still editing *Galaxy* magazine, he would probably buy it. He also said I should read a story by Alfred Bester called "Fondly Fahrenheit." "Oh yeah," I said. "I've read it. That's where I got the idea." "Oh," he said. "Well, you should also read a novel by Robert Silverberg called *The Book of Skulls*." "Yeah, I've read it," I said. "You've read it?" he said, apparently surprised that a 26-year-old would have read this fairly obscure science fiction novel from 1972. (The only reason I knew it was because it had recently been reprinted as part of the excellent SF Masterworks series.)

Pohl also told me that he was exploring some similar themes to "Veil of Ignorance" in his most recent *Gateway* sequel, which he had already turned in to the publisher, so I should be aware that he wasn't stealing anything from me. "Sure," I said jokingly. "A likely story." I have a problem sometimes where it seems obvious to me that I'm joking, but other people can't tell. "Well..." Pohl said, flustered. "In a way these are also ideas that I wrote about in an earlier book, so..." I waved my hands. "No, it's fine," I said. "I'm just kidding."

"Veil of Ignorance" appeared in the third Phobos anthology *All the Rage This Year*, and John Joseph Adams reprinted it in *Lightspeed*. John encouraged me to write more stories inspired by thought experiments in political theory, which I would love to do, but so far I haven't come across any other likely candidates. If anyone knows of any, let me know.

Blake Reynolds

Power Armor: A Love Story

It was quite a party. The women wore gowns. The men wore tuxedos. Anthony Blair wore power armor.

Armor that was sleek and black and polished, and made not a whisper as Blair paced the lawn behind his mansion, passing a word here or there with one of his guests. In those days the most advanced exoskeletons were crude affairs, and Blair's armor seemed decades, if not centuries, ahead of its time.

But he was an inventor, after all, one who in the past several years had introduced any number of groundbreaking new technologies. And that was about all anyone knew of Anthony Blair, reclusive genius. He was seldom seen, and never without his armor, and he politely rebuffed all inquiries into his past.

So it had attracted considerable interest when he'd purchased a house on the outskirts of Washington, a move that seemed to signal him taking a greater interest in public affairs. For his housewarming, he'd sent out scores of invitations—to politicians, pundits, business leaders, celebrities, and scientists. Such a gathering of notables, along with the chance to get a rare glimpse of Blair himself, would have been enough to make this the hottest ticket in town, but there was more. Blair had let it be known that tonight he'd be making an "important announcement." Speculation was frenzied.

Finally Blair hopped up onto the patio and called for everyone's attention, his voice amplified by speakers built into the torso of his suit. From what could be seen of him through his transparent visor, he seemed a handsome man of about forty, with a penetrating gaze and a sardonic grin. He proceeded to lay out his plans for a new nonprofit group, the Anthony

270

Blair Foundation, dedicated to promoting civil liberties worldwide, and he invited his guests to get involved.

He wrapped things up with a toast, thanking everyone for coming. He pointed an armored finger down into his wine glass, and a large plastic straw emerged, and began suctioning up the wine, which Blair then drank, moments later, from a tube inside his helmet.

As his guests sipped their drinks, they conferred in puzzled tones about whether that had been the "important announcement," in which case the evening was proving a terrible letdown. When no announcement of any greater import seemed likely to be forthcoming, they began to drift away.

Blair moved from conversation to conversation, wishing everyone a good night. A distinguished-looking gentleman said to him, "Mr. Blair, I'd like to introduce you to a colleague of mine, Dr. Mira Valentic."

She wore a red dress and had inky black hair. Blair reached out with his giant metal fingers and lightly shook her hand. "Pleased to meet you, Doctor."

He asked about her work, and she described her research into gene sequencing. He listened intently and asked many questions, which led her to describe her graduate studies, then a childhood obsession with amphibians. As they talked, the other guests excused themselves one by one, and the lawn slowly emptied, until Blair and Mira stood alone.

"And now I've told you everything about myself," she said. "But I still don't know anything about you."

"Not much to tell," he said.

She chuckled.

After a moment, he said, "I've had a very nice time talking with you, Dr. Valentic."

"Please, call me Mira."

"Mira," he said. "I don't know what it is, but I just feel like we're on the same wavelength somehow."

"Yes," she said. "Me too."

He lowered his voice. "So I'm going to tell you something I've never told anyone."

He had her full attention now.

"I'm from the future," he said.

She regarded him uncertainly, as if this might be a joke. "People wondered," she said. "I didn't believe it. It seems impossible."

"It's not impossible," he said. "Just very difficult."

She thought for a moment. "So what's it like? The future?"

"Maybe I'll tell you," he said, "next time I see you."

"Next time?"

"There will be a next time, won't there? I should certainly hope your bosses would arrange for us to meet again, now that you've managed to wrangle one big secret out of me."

"My bosses? At the museum?"

"No, in the government, I mean."

"I don't—"

He waved a hand. "It's fine, really. I don't mind being spied on. My armor and I are big unknowns, and I don't blame folks for wanting to keep an eye on us. That's their job. Your job."

She was silent.

Finally she said, "When did you know?"

"When I first saw you."

"What?"

"From across the yard. I'm awfully clever, Mira."

"Bullshit," she said. "No one's that clever."

"I am," he said. "I didn't rise to my position by accident, you know."

"What position?"

"Maybe I'll tell you," he said. "Next time I see you."

* * *

The next time was two weeks later, downtown, at the first public fundraiser for the Anthony Blair Foundation. She approached him as the event was winding down.

"Mira," he said. "So nice to see you again."

"Well, you were right," she said. "Keep feeding me information and you'll be seeing a lot more of me."

He smiled. "In that case, what would you like to know?"

"Your armor," she said. "Where'd you get it?"

"I stole it."

"Oh," she said. "We thought it must be one of your inventions."

"It is," he said. "I invented it, and then I stole it."

"Sounds like there's a story there."

"There is," he said. "But let's not go into it just now."

He glanced about the room, then turned back to her. "Hey," he said, "do you want to get out of here?"

Later, as they walked along the river, beneath a sky full of stars, he said, "I'd like to take you out to dinner some time."

"I'd like that."

He was silent for a while. Finally he said, "If we're going to keep seeing each other, there's something I have to tell you."

She waited.

"My armor," he said. "I never take it off."

"What?"

"It's sort of...something I swore."

"Never?"

"Right."

"But...how do you eat?"

"Through the straw. It filters poisons."

"And I mean, how do you bathe? Go to the bathroom?"

"The armor handles everything. It's very advanced."

"Wow," she said.

"I know that sounds strange," he said. "But you'll understand. Once you hear the whole story."

After a moment, she said, "So what's the whole story?"

He sighed. "You know I'm starting this new foundation. Don't you wonder why?"

"Because you care about civil liberties?"

"But why?"

She said nothing.

"It's because in the future, where I come from, there are no civil liberties. None."

"Oh," she said.

"I had never been disloyal," he said softly. "You can't be, where

I come from. Our thoughts are monitored. I'd been identified early as a promising scientist, and had risen through the ranks to head of my research division. We'd developed a high-energy device that possessed some unusual properties—like, it could project a man-sized object into the past, creating a branching timeline. Theoretically, at least. Completely useless, as far as our leaders were concerned, but interesting. Then one day the thought popped into my head: I could escape."

He stopped and stared out over the water. "Once I'd had the thought, I knew it was only a matter of time before I'd be picked up for 'neural re-education.' So I had to act fast. The problem was, even if I succeeded in traveling into the past, my voyage would create a temporal wake large enough for them to send someone after me."

He met her eyes. "I don't mean to scare you, Mira, but where I come from there are...secret police. Unlike anything you can imagine. Cyborgs. Shapeshifters. I'd have no chance against one of them. Unless..." He showed the hint of a smile. "In the same lab was something else we'd been working on. This armor." He raised his gauntleted hands. "Wearing this, I'd be impervious to anything. So I could escape, but at a cost—I must never take off the armor, not for an instant. Because if I did, the agent sent to punish me would surely strike."

She glanced around at the trees, the shadows. She shivered.

"And that's the story," he said. "So, do you still want to grab dinner sometime? I'll understand if you say no."

"I...I'll have to think about it," she said. "This is a lot to take in."

"I know," he said. After a moment, he added, "I should probably be getting back."

"All right."

As they retraced their route, she thought: He never takes off the armor. Never. Not for an instant, he said.

That was going to make it very hard, she thought, to kill him.

* * *

He took her to one of the finest restaurants in Washington, and it made quite a sight to see him sitting there in his armor, with a napkin in his lap, suctioning up his entree through the straw in his finger. In spite of that it was a pleasant meal. That is, until the middle of dessert, when he suddenly said, "I have to ask you something."

"Yes?" she said.

"About your bosses."

"At the museum?" she said sweetly.

"No." He smiled back. "In the government, I mean."

"All right. Yes. What?"

"Do they know what you are?" he said, suddenly serious.

"What do you mean?"

"Do they know," he said calmly, "that you were sent from the future to kill me?"

"What?" She laughed.

He waited.

"You think I'm—?"

"Yes," he said.

She put down her fork. Finally she said, "Yes, they know."

They watched each other.

"They want your armor very badly," she said. "They've made repeated overtures, and have concluded that you'll never cooperate."

"They're right," he said.

She shrugged. "So...they want the armor, I want you. We have an understanding."

"I see."

"When did you know?" she said.

"When I first saw you," he said. "From across the yard."

She laughed. "Bullshit. Why didn't you say anything?"

"I was having a nice time. I didn't want to spoil the mood."

"I think you're lying," she said. "I think you figured it out just now."

He shrugged.

"So I guess that's that," she said, tossing her napkin out on the table and reaching for her purse.

"Wait," he said. "I want to say something."

She paused.

"We find ourselves," he said, "in a branching timeline. We can't return to our own time, and no one else can follow us here. So they'll never know whether you succeeded or not."

"You're suggesting," she said coldly, "that I abandon my mission."

"I'm suggesting you do what's right," he said. "What's best for both of us."

She stood. "I am not a traitor. You are. And the punishment for that is death, as you well know. I was assigned this mission, and the faith of my superiors was not misplaced. Your armor is a clever gadget, I'll grant you, but no defenses can hold forever, and no matter how long it takes, no matter how safe you think you are, before this is over I will watch you drown in blood."

People at nearby tables were staring.

"Thanks for dinner," she said, and strode away.

* * *

He called her the next day.

"I had a really nice time last night," he said.

She stared at the phone. "Are you out of your mind?"

"No," he said. "Do you want to come over some time?"

She hesitated. "Is this some sort of trick?" she said. "Some trap?"

"No," he said. "I mean, what are you? A class eight?"

"Class nine," she said.

"We're in the twenty-first century," he said. "You could probably fight off a tank platoon. I don't even have a gun. I just want to talk."

"About what?" she said. "Treason?"

"No. No treason. I promise."

"What then?"

"Old books, shows, people. We're the only ones who remember the future."

"You're not afraid?"

"No. The armor will protect me."

"How can you be sure?"

"I designed it," he said.

"And what if I find a weakness?"

"You won't."

After a moment, she sighed. "All right. Fine."

"Swing by around eight," he said. "I'll cook dinner."

* * *

She drove over to his mansion, and he cooked her dinner, and they had a very nice time talking about old books and shows and people that were now known only to the two of them.

Finally she stretched and yawned. "Well, it's late."

"You're welcome to stay," he said. "I have a spare bedroom. Eight, actually."

"I don't think so," she said.

"Why not? It makes perfect sense."

"Does it?"

"I mean, what's your plan?" he said. "To disappear, change into someone else, and try to catch me off guard? It won't work. I never take off the armor, not for you or anyone. Your only hope is to find a weakness in the armor, and you won't get a better chance to study it than by staying right here with me." He added, "Besides, I like the way you look now."

She chuckled. "So what's in it for you?"

"The pleasure of your company. Plus I'll know where you are, and I won't have to go around wondering if everyone I meet is a secret assassin."

"That's it? Sounds like the risks outweigh the benefits."

"Let me worry about that," he said. "Anyway, I think you're underestimating the pleasure of your company."

"Ha."

"Also, if you get to know me better, you might decide you don't really want to kill me."

"I doubt that," she said. "Actually, I'm getting the opposite vibe."

He laughed.

"...and you said no treason. You promised."

"You're right. Sorry."

Finally she said, "All right, I'll think about it. Let's see the room."

He gave her a tour of the mansion, and when she saw the guest room she said, "Hey, this is really nice." She sat on the mattress and bounced a few times, testing it. "All right, I'll stay. For a bit."

"Great," he said.

She sprawled on the comforter, grinning. "You want to slip into something more comfortable?"

He laughed. "Goodnight, Mira. I'll see you in the morning."

* * *

She stayed with him for weeks, and they talked and talked, until they knew practically everything about each other. They went out to dinner, and to movies and plays, and they went on long, long walks. (Much longer than any normal person could walk, thanks to his armor and her cybernetics.) Many nights they simply lounged about doing nothing at all.

One night they played chess.

The first game ended with his king pinned in one corner. She put him in check with her queen, and he moved to an adjacent square. She moved her queen to put him in check again, and he moved back to the first square. This was repeated several times. The game was declared a draw.

The second game ended the same way. And the third.

"I suppose you think this is terribly funny?" she said.

He shrugged.

She swept the pieces onto the floor, and stood.

As she strode away, he called, "I'm sorry. Mira..." She ignored him. But when she was out in the hallway, she smiled. Her anger and frustration were feigned. Actually, things were going quite well.

She'd discovered a weakness in his armor.

* * *

They took vacations together—to London, New York, Tokyo. In Paris, at the top of the Eiffel Tower, as they stood looking out over the rivers and rooftops, she said, "Well, you were right, dammit. As always. I've grown awfully fond of you, Blair, and now the future seems like such a long time ago. So I guess you're safe."

"I'm glad to hear it," he said. "Though you'll forgive me if I don't strip off the armor just this second."

She laughed. "Of course."

Six months later though, it was starting to become an issue.

One night at dinner she said to him, "We need to talk."

"Yes?"

"Are you ever going to take off that armor?" she said.

He set down his utensils and studied her. He said, "When I fled into the past, I swore I would never take off this armor. Not for an instant."

"Because of me," she said. "Because I'd be sent after you. But that's all changed now."

"I knew there would come a time," he said, "when I'd start feeling safe, start letting my guard down. That's why I made the resolution then, when my sense of the danger was at its most acute."

After a moment, she said, "You still don't trust me."

He said nothing.

"Look at me," she said. "Can't you just look at me with your super-genius gaze and see that I'm telling the truth?"

"No," he said.

"Then I guess you're not as smart as you think you are," she said. "As you pretend to be."

"Do you remember what you said, Mira? When we first met? 'No matter how long it takes, no matter how safe you think you are—'"

"I know what I said. Look, I'm sorry, all right? I was a different person then. It was a stupid thing to say. I wish I could take it back, but I can't."

There was a long silence.

Finally she said, "What are we doing here? If you're never going to trust me, what's even the point of this?"

"Enjoying each other's company? That was the point, I thought."

"And in five years?" she said. "Ten? Will we still just be sitting across a table from each other, with you in a suit of armor?"

"I don't take off the armor," he said. "You knew that from the start."

"So there's nothing I can do? To prove myself?"

"There's one thing," he said, very serious. "You can hold my life in your hands and choose to spare me."

"But how can that ever happen?" she said. "If you won't take off the armor?"

"I don't know," he said.

* * *

When he woke the next morning, she was gone. He paced the empty rooms, seeking her. "Mira?" he called, his voice echoing.

He tried her phone, but got no response. He left message after message. Finally she answered. "Please stop calling me," she said.

"Where are you?"

"Away," she said. "Away from that house, away from you. There are other men, you know? Who aren't afraid."

"Please come back," he said.

"Will you take off the armor?" she said. "Ever?"

"You know I can't."

She hung up.

Six weeks passed without a word. Then one night his doorbell rang, and he opened the door to find her standing there.

"I'm sorry," she said.

He made her tea, and she sat in the kitchen and said, "Look, I understand why you wear the armor. It's all tied up with who you are and why we're here together, and I accept that. I hope someday I can prove myself to you, but even if you never take it off I don't care. We understand each other in a way that no one else ever will."

"Let's fly to Paris," he said. "Tonight. We had good times there."

"Yes," she said. "All right."

They hopped a private jet, and by the next morning they were in Paris. They revisited all their old haunts. On their third night there, they ate dinner at the hotel, then took a midnight walk down a cobbled street beside the Seine.

Suddenly Mira said, "We're being followed."

A hundred yards behind them lurked three men dressed in black. One carried a briefcase.

"Are they from the future?" she said.

"No," Blair said. "Impossible."

"Then what threat could they be to us?"

"I don't know," he said. "Let's not find out. Come on."

He began to hurry. Suddenly he halted. "Uh-oh."

"What?" she said.

"I can't move."

She glanced about as more men appeared from the shadows.

"They're special forces," she said. "Black ops."

"How do you know?"

She smiled. "Because they're with me."

Eight men surrounded Blair. Several carried boxes.

"I told you you weren't the only man in my life," she said.

One of the men stepped forward. He had a heavy jaw and short gray hair and cold, hard eyes.

"Captain." Mira nodded.

The man set his briefcase on the ground and bent to open it.

"How are you doing this?" Blair said.

She knelt over the briefcase. "We introduced a virus through the suit's communications array."

"That's impossible," Blair said. "Equipment to interface with the suit won't even exist for—"

"What, you mean like this?" she said, rising, gadget in hand.

Blair studied it, his face pale.

"All right, I'm impressed," he said. "Cramming that much R&D into so short a time. But it won't matter. In a few minutes—"

"You don't have a few minutes," she said.

The men opened boxes, yanked out equipment. Blair's eyes darted about.

"Laser cutters?" he said. "Diamond-tipped saws? You can't honestly believe those will even scratch this armor?"

"No," Mira said, nodding at the men. "But they did." She added, "What can I say? They're not geniuses."

The captain frowned. Then Mira backhanded him across the face, and his head flew a hundred feet through the air and splashed into the river.

The men screamed and drew weapons. Two ran. Of course it did them no good. A minute later Mira was piling their bodies on the ground at Blair's feet.

"I admit I'm a bit nervous now," he said.

She grinned. "Told you I'd make you drown in blood."

She fiddled with her gadget, and the armor knelt stiffly, and its right hand reached out and plunged its straw deep into the chest of the nearest corpse. Blair grimaced and turned his head aside as blood bubbled from the tube inside his helmet.

"Wow," he said. "Paris is definitely not as much fun as I remember."

"Keep laughing," she said. "While you can."

The straw drained corpse after corpse. Soon the blood rose above Blair's lips and threatened to engulf his nose.

"Any last words?" she said.

"Mmmm-mmmm-mmmm-mmmm," he said.

She came and stood inches from his visor. "Sorry, I didn't catch that?"

He watched her, his eyes wide.

"Do we agree," she said, "that there's absolutely nothing stopping me from killing you?"

"Mmmm-hmmm," he said.

"Good." She smiled. "Then take off that stupid armor and kiss me."

She flipped a switch, and suddenly Blair could move again. He tore off his helmet and hurled it to the ground, then swept her up in his arms, pressing his lips to hers.

* * *

Later, as they lay naked on a hotel bed, he murmured, "I knew about your device."

She stirred and said drowsily, "Hmm?"

"I could have stopped the blood," he said. "I was never in any danger."

"I know," she said. "The armor is flawless." After a moment, she added, "It only ever had one weakness."

"Me," he said, rolling onto his side, studying her. "We understand each other perfectly, don't we?"

"Yes," she said. "I think so."

"You still haven't decided whether or not to kill me. Have you?"

"No," she said.

"But either way you wanted me out of the armor."

"Yes," she said. "And you took it off, even knowing the danger."

"I love you, Mira," he said. "I couldn't stand being separated from you another moment."

"Sounds like the risks outweigh the rewards," she said.

"I think you're underestimating the rewards," he said, and she chuckled.

He added, "If your mission is that important to you, then go ahead and kill me. You might as well, if you don't love me."

"I think that's the sweetest thing anyone's ever said to me," she said.

And for a long time after that they lay curled together, drifting in and out of sleep. And if they dreamed, it was of the future—not the distant future from which they'd come, a cold and sterile place of surveillance and mind control, but the immediate future, of the breakfast croissants they'd soon enjoy, and the stroll they'd take through the fresh morning air, hand in hand. And the armor stood in a nearby corner like some exotic decoration, like some improbable furniture, watching over them with its transparent visor, a silent presence, waiting there, sleek, black, polished, empty.

Author's note: Power Armor: A Love Story

For such a light, breezy story, this one sure took a long time to write. In 2011 John Joseph Adams told me he was editing an anthology of power armor stories called *Armored*, and invited me to submit something. I've loved the idea of power armor ever since I first encountered it in Robert Heinlein's *Starship Troopers*, and I used to spend hours perusing the power armor designs in the *Rifts* tabletop role-playing game. I was sure I could come up with something great.

As a teenager I'd read a short story about a guy in power armor who walks into a town and declares himself king, because nobody can fight back against him. I liked that idea and wanted to take it a step further. I imagined that someone from the future might travel back in time and declare himself dictator of a medium-sized country, and no one would be able to stop him, because his power armor was more formidable than that country's entire military. At the end of the story a female assassin—possibly also from the future—would fill his suit with the blood of his bodyguards, drowning him.

Then I got stuck for weeks. I had a scenario and a climax, but no character or conflict. Who were these people? Why should anyone care if this guy got killed or not?

Finally I got the idea to make it a love story, and then things started to fall into place. I ditched the idea of the guy being a dictator. Instead of a hero, my female assassin was now the villain. (Or at least more of a villain.) Gradually I pieced together the backstory and the rules of this world.

The problem was the ending. If Blair plays it safe and never takes off his armor, the story feels unresolved. So there are basically two possibilities: He takes off his armor and Mira kills him, or he takes off his armor and Mira spares him. I went back and forth on which way the story should go. There were times when I felt that she definitely had to kill him.

For a long time the ending was going to be that Mira fills Blair's suit with blood, proving she can kill him, then spares him. He takes off his armor and they live happily ever after. But when I got to that point in the story, I felt like it didn't work. There's no way, I thought. He didn't see this coming? I don't buy it.

Sometimes a good ending needs to employ what we call "the third

284

alternative." There are two obvious ways the story could go, and the reader is trying to guess which one it will be, but the whole time the author is setting up a third alternative that the reader didn't expect. Finally I came up with an ending that I hoped was enough of a third alternative that readers wouldn't see it coming: Blair takes off his armor as a show of trust, even though he knows that Mira hasn't made up her mind about killing him. That also seemed to fit with the theme of the story, which is that romantic relationships are inherently dangerous, and entering into one means accepting a certain degree of risk.

By this point *Geek's Guide to the Galaxy* was getting pretty popular, and I thought it would be a nice gesture if I named a few characters after some of our biggest fans. (In the science fiction world this is called "Tuckerization," and there's a long history of it. For example there's a character called Lieutenant Dante Kirtley, named after me, in the Halo novel *The Cole Protocol* by Tobias Buckell.) One of our biggest fans at the time was a young woman in Romania, so I sent her the story and asked if she wanted me to use her last name for Mira. She was ecstatic, but there was a catch. "Mira is my aunt's name," she said. "She's a horrible person and doesn't deserve to have a character named after her. Can you change the first name to something else?" Geez, I thought, what are the odds?

I really didn't want to change Mira's name. I'd been working on the story for months, and her name was firmly fixed in my mind. Also it would alter the sound and cadence of practically every sentence in the story if I changed her name to something else. Sheepishly I told this young woman that I was just going to use a different last name for the character, and I would work her last name into my next story. Unfortunately "Power Armor: A Love Story" ended up being the last short story I wrote, so I still haven't had a chance to do that, but hopefully that'll change someday.

Charles Vess

Three Deaths

This is a tale of Mars, which the Martians call Barsoom—a dying planet that clings to life only through the striving of its most civilized inhabitants, the Red Men, who maintain its grand canals and atmosphere plant.

This is a tale of the wild Green Men of Mars, four-armed giants who roam in great hordes across the dead sea bottoms and who dwell amidst the ruins of ancient cities.

This is a tale of three deaths.

Our story begins on the day that a small band of Warhoon scouts crossed paths with John Carter of Virginia, and Ghar Han, one of the greatest warriors of the Green Men, challenged the Earthman to single combat. By all the laws of Mars such a challenge may not be refused, and the man so challenged must choose a weapon that is no better than that wielded by his adversary.

Ghar Han held swords in each of his four hands, and the skulls of half a dozen great warriors rattled upon his harness, for he had won many battles, and added the names of many a vanquished foe to his own. He towered over his opponent, and gazed with contempt upon the Earthman, who held but a single blade, and who seemed small and freakish with his strange pale flesh and black hair. Around them stood a ring of Green Men, including two young warriors, the arrogant Harkan Thul and the sly Sutarat. Nearby, the mounts of the Green Men, the eight-legged reptilian thoats, grazed upon the yellow grass that stretched away in all directions.

Ghar Han attacked, now stabbing with his upper right hand, now slashing with his lower left, his four blades a whirlwind of steel, glinting in the sun. John Carter backed away, ducking from side to side, parrying strike after strike. When the Earthman had been backed against the spectators and had no more room to retreat, Ghar Han employed his favorite attack, a devastating overhand chop with his upper right sword, a move which had cleft many an opponent nearly in two.

His sword buried itself in the sand as John Carter spun away and came around with a double-handed blow aimed at Ghar Han's exposed right shoulder. The Green Man raised his lower right sword to block it, but the Earthman's blade knocked the weapon aside and sank deep into Ghar Han's flesh.

Ghar Han stumbled back, feeling a terrible wrenching as the Earthman's blade was ripped free. Ghar Han's upper right sword fell from his nerveless fingers, and his upper right arm now hung from his shoulder like a pennon. That arm, his strongest, would never fully heal, he knew.

John Carter pressed the attack, and Ghar Han reeled, dazed. The Earthman's blade was everywhere, and Ghar Han hurled up sword after sword to deflect the blows, but three swords were not enough. He needed a fourth sword, a fifth, a sixth, to fend off the relentless attacks.

A crushing stroke swept the upper left sword from his grasp and sent it spinning away into the crowd, and then the tip of John Carter's blade lanced through Ghar Han's lower right forearm, causing him to drop that sword as well. Blood streaked the Green Man's side. Dizzy, half-blind with pain and fear, he sank to one knee, feebly holding up his last remaining sword.

John Carter kicked him in the chest, and Ghar Han sprawled, sliding backward through the sand.

He lifted his head. The sun was in his eyes, and all he could see was a dark form wreathed in blinding light. The shadow raised its sword and brought it down.

Ghar Han, one of the greatest warriors of the Green Men, felt his lower left arm part, and fall away.

* * *

He awoke, which surprised him, since duels among the Green Men are fought to the death. He was in his tent, lying on a mat, and it was night. He went to rub his eyes with his upper right hand, but nothing happened.

He glanced at his shoulder, and saw bandages there soaked in blood. More bandages bound his abdomen.

"We were forced to remove the upper right arm," came a woman's voice. "And the lower left was—"

"Where is John Carter?" said Ghar Han.

"Gone. The others brought you here."

"Get out."

"I—"

"Get out!" he said, sitting up. The woman fled.

Ghar Han fell back, writhing. Phantom pains lanced up and down his missing limbs. He cursed the cruelty of the Earthman, for not striking a killing blow. He cursed the potent medicine of the Green women. He was a freak now, a cripple. Two arms only remained to him—two, like any of the lesser races of men.

For days he did not leave his tent. He drifted in and out of sleep, haunted by strange, vivid dreams. In one he was running and fighting, stabbing and slashing, and he realized that he had four arms again, and felt elation. It was only a dream, he thought, only a dream that I had lost them. Then he woke in the tent again and moaned, despairing.

In another dream he'd lost all his limbs, even his legs, and he lay helpless on his back like a worm, staring up at the stars, at the twin moons, and Earth. From the darkness around him came the growls of circling banths, and somewhere above him echoed the cruel laughter of John Carter. It was a dream he would have many more times.

When he was awake, he replayed the duel over and over in his mind.

How was it possible, he thought, that he should have been defeated by such a small and wretched man? Not through skill, that was certain. No, rather this John Carter had come from another world, a world whose heavy gravity had given him muscles unmatched on Barsoom. It was treacherous, thought Ghar Han, to use Earthly muscles here. The more he thought about it, the greater grew his sense of outrage. John Carter did not belong here. John Carter had caught him off guard. John Carter had cheated!

We will meet again, Earthman, he thought. And next time I'll be ready.

Finally he strapped on four swords—one at each hip and two crossed across his back—and strode out into the harsh light of day. As he moved through the camp, the Warhoon regarded him with disdain. Harkan Thul and Sutarat emerged from behind a tent and stopped to stare. Normally they would never have the nerve to mock Ghar Han to his face, but now that he'd been shamed and crippled they jeered.

"Look!" cried Harkan Thul. "An intruder in our camp! What manner of creature is it, Sutarat?"

"I know not," said Sutarat, with a grin. "It almost seems to be one of us, but of course we have four arms, and this strange creature has only two."

"Perhaps it is the Earthman John Carter," said Harkan Thul. "And he has smeared himself with green paint in order to infiltrate our ranks."

Sutarat laughed.

Ghar Han scowled and walked on past. He sought out the tent of Xan Malus, jeddak of the Warhoon, and was shown into the presence of the great lord, a cold, imperious man who clutched a spiked scepter and sat upon a jeweled throne.

"Kaor, Ghar Han," said Xan Malus. "It pleases us to see that you are up and useful to us once more."

"Kaor, Excellency," said Ghar Han, crossing his two arms and bowing his head. "Thank you."

"Now tell us," said the jeddak, "why have you come?"

"Excellency," said Ghar Han, "if it please you, I should like to pursue the Earthman John Carter and challenge him once again to—"

"No, no," said Xan Malus impatiently. "It does not please us. John Carter's death is nothing to me, and in any event you would not succeed. I relinquish no asset, however small. I will not sacrifice one of my warriors, even a cripple, to no end."

"Excellency, I—"

"I know, I know," said the jeddak, with a wave. "You would prefer an honorable death to your present humiliation. But what care I for your honor, Ghar Han? I am jeddak, and you are mine, and so long as I breathe you shall be deployed to my ends, not yours. Tomorrow we strike camp and journey to retrieve the eggs of our offspring, and I desire that every able warrior be on hand to guard them. You know our wishes. Go."

Ghar Han bowed again, and departed.

He was not accustomed to being treated with such contempt, but in the days that followed he became quite practiced at it. Many of the younger warriors seemed never to tire of mocking him for his missing arms, and Harkan Thul and Sutarat remained the worst of his tormentors. Once, he would have simply challenged the two of them to duels, but without the use of his strongest arm he was no longer confident of victory, and besides, spilling their blood would not erase his shame. Only the death of John Carter could do that. Ghar Han's only hope now was that fate would deliver John Carter to him once again. In his dreams he slew the Earthman a hundred times.

As the months passed, he found that his feelings about his people had begun to change. From his lofty vantage as a fearsome warrior, the ways of the Warhoon had always seemed fair to him. Harsh, yes, for Barsoom was a harsh world that required a harsh people. But fair. Now though, he was not so sure. More and more the ways of the Warhoon seemed to him pointlessly cruel. Why should he, who had suffered a misfortune that might befall anyone, be so scorned? Did such ruthlessness make them stronger as a tribe, or weaker?

One day he was walking through camp and turned a corner into a shaded area between two tents, and came upon Harkan Thul and Sutarat and some of the others. They'd surrounded a young woman, who'd been knocked to her knees, and they were taunting her and laughing.

Without thinking, Ghar Han stepped forward. "Leave her alone."

Harkan Thul turned to regard him with contempt. "Oh leave us be, two-arm. You're not wanted here."

"Don't call me that," warned Ghar Han, and the others laughed.

For an instant he considered walking away. Then he took a deep breath, collected himself, and said calmly, "I said leave her alone."

Sutarat exchanged glances with some of the others, and they moved away from the girl and slowly closed in on Ghar Han, their faces dark.

Harkan Thul sighed. "Oh, what has become of you, Ghar Han? Not only do you *look* like one of the lesser races, now it seems you have one of their soft hearts as well. You don't belong here. You are not one of us. Go."

Ghar Han didn't move.

Harkan Thul reached for his swords. "Do you lust for suffering, Ghar Han? This will go worse for you than the day you faced John Carter."

"And how would you know?" Ghar Han said sharply.

Harkan Thul paused, caught off guard.

"How would *you* know what it's like to face John Carter? You never have. Only I have." Ghar Han's voice rose, his fury pouring out of him. "The Earthman was here among us. I fought him, and then he departed, and none of you raised a hand to stop him. Because you were afraid!"

Harkan Thul drew his swords. "Call me a coward? I will kill you."

"Oh, so brave!" cried Ghar Han. "To fight a cripple. But where were you when John Carter was among us?" He pounded his fist against his chest. "Only Ghar Han had the courage to face him then."

Harkan Thul was silent. Finally he sheathed his swords.

"It's true," he said. "Spilling your blood would be too easy. Bring me a real challenge. Bring any man of this world or another and I will face him. I am not afraid."

"We'll see," said Ghar Han. "Someday the Earthman will cross our paths again, and then we'll see who's not afraid."

Harkan Thul sneered and turned away. "Come on," he said to the others. "Let's go."

When they were gone, Ghar Han offered his hand to the girl.

"Here," he said, "let me—"

"Do not touch me, cripple," she said, furious, climbing to her feet.

* * *

Years passed, and Ghar Han grew ever more isolated and withdrawn, watching grimly as Harkan Thul and Sutarat amassed power and status. Harkan Thul attained the rank of jed and became leader of their scouting party, with Sutarat as his second-in-command.

One day the scouting party rode up over the crest of a hill and looked out on the valley below. Before them lay an ancient ghost town, a lonely place of stairways and minarets and white marble. Then the Green Men noticed, off in the distance, a lone figure trudging across the sand toward the village.

Sutarat said, "Who is that, who dares invade our territory?"

"Let's find out," said Harkan Thul, urging his thoat to a gallop.

As the beasts thundered down the hill, the stranger broke into a run, racing toward the village. Then, as the Green Men watched, astonished, he took a great flying leap, hurtling through the air. In two bounds he'd reached the outlying buildings, and then he sprang to a third-story window and disappeared.

Ghar Han's heart beat faster. John Carter! It must be, for only the unnatural muscles of an Earthman could propel such wondrous leaps. After all these years they would meet again. Here at last was his chance for redemption, or perhaps an honorable death.

When the Green Men reached the city gates, Harkan Thul wheeled his mount and cried, "Circle the village, all of you! Make sure he doesn't sneak off! I will enter and challenge him to a duel. Sutarat will be my second. Come."

"No!" said Ghar Han, riding forward. "John Carter is mine!"

Harkan Thul glared. "I am jed here, not you, and I say—"

"No!" yelled one of the warriors. "Ghar Han should face John Carter. If he dares."

"Yes," said another. "He was crippled and shamed by the Earthman. Let him fight."

Others muttered agreement, and Harkan Thul saw that he risked mutiny if he refused.

"All right," he said at last. "Ghar Han will have his chance. But if he fails, I will not. Come on."

As the others fanned out around the village, Ghar Han, Harkan Thul, and Sutarat rode through the gates. They tied their thoats to a hitching post, then proceeded on foot through the narrow streets, swords in hand.

Ghar Han heard footfalls on a nearby rooftop, and glanced up just as a dark form catapulted across the sky, leaping from building to building. An instant later it was gone, but not before Ghar Han had seen that this Earthman had yellow hair.

Yellow, not black like John Carter.

"Come on!" said Harkan Thul. "After him!"

They pursued the figure, and Ghar Han's mind raced. What if this was not John Carter?

If not, then Ghar Han would not be able to exact vengeance upon the man who'd shamed him, but he found that this thought no longer moved him the way it once had. What disturbed him more was the idea of more than one Earthman on Barsoom. Bad enough that John Carter had found his way here, through some arcane means, but now it seemed there might be two. And if two then why not three, or four, or ten? Any one of them a match for even the strongest native warrior. And suddenly Ghar Han imagined the Earthmen building great fleets, imagined those ships soaring across the void and landing here, disgorging armies.

As the Green Men burst into a courtyard, Harkan Thul cried "There!" and pointed.

Ghar Han wheeled, and regarded the shadowed third story window of a palatial manse.

Harkan Thul shouted to Sutarat, "Go! Down the alley! Make sure he doesn't slip out the back." Sutarat took off running.

Harkan Thul turned to Ghar Han. "I'll watch this side. Now enter, find the Earthman, and slay him. And do not forget the favor I've done you this day, and do not dishonor us."

Ghar Han nodded. He leapt through the open doors, then passed through an antechamber and made his way up a spiral stair. He glanced into the room where the Earthman had been, but it was empty.

"Earthman!" he cried. "Show yourself! I am Ghar Han. I dare you to face me."

He explored room after room, all of them empty. He moved cautiously, holding his swords before him, picturing the Earthman crouched in some shadowed nook, just waiting to fall upon him. Finally he grew exhausted. It seemed he'd explored every corner, and still there was no sign of the Earthman.

He glanced out a window into the courtyard. Harkan Thul was nowhere in sight. "Harkan Thul!" he shouted. "Sutarat!"

Silence.

He felt a chill. Could they have fallen to the Earthman? Or had the Earthman fled, and they'd gone chasing after him? But surely Ghar Han would have heard the commotion.

Then he knew.

It was a trick. The Earthman had never been here at all.

Ghar Han dashed out into the courtyard, cursing himself. He strained to hear, but heard nothing, so he picked a direction at random and began to run.

It was near sundown, and shadows filled the streets and alleys. In the empty silence of that dead city, he could almost imagine that he was the only living thing on all of Barsoom. Everywhere the black windows seemed to watch him like the eyes of skulls. He hurried down block after block, certain that he would miss whatever was about to happen.

But luck was with him. As he passed an ancient fountain, he heard a voice upon the air, and pursued it. He peeked around a corner.

In the center of a broad avenue stood Harkan Thul, facing one of the dwellings that lined the street. "This is your last chance, Earthman!" he called. "I know you're in there! My warriors have this village surrounded, and I have come, alone, to challenge you. If you defeat me, you will be permitted to depart in peace."

More lies, thought Ghar Han. The others would not allow the Earthman to escape. And where was Sutarat?

There. Down the street a ways, crouched at the base of a statue. And in his hand he held a radium pistol.

No! thought Ghar Han. Surely not. For to challenge a man to duel with swords and then ambush him with a pistol was the most heinous crime that could be dreamt of on Barsoom.

The Earthman appeared in the doorway.

A woman.

She was tall, for her kind, long-limbed and stern, her pale hair cut short, and she held a sword. She regarded Harkan Thul coldly as she emerged from the building. "All right," she said. "All right."

Sutarat leaned out from behind the statue and took aim at her back.

"Look out!" Ghar Han yelled.

The woman spun, and spotted Sutarat, who opened fire. Harkan Thul leapt to the ground as the woman fled, shots bursting all around her. She dove into an alley and disappeared.

As Ghar Han strode forward, Harkan Thul stood and screamed, "What are you doing?"

"What are *you* doing?" said Ghar Han. "This is shameful! Are you afraid to face the Earthman fairly?"

"No fight with an Earthman is fair," said Harkan Thul. "They *cheat* by coming here, from a world with such heavy gravity."

I once thought as he does, Ghar Han realized. And now he saw how petulant and contemptible he'd been.

"Listen, Harkan Thul," he said. "The Earthmen are stronger than us. That's a hard truth, but one we must face. With honor."

Sutarat approached, and leveled his pistol at Ghar Han's chest.

"So," said Ghar Han, "now you fear a fair fight with *me* as well?"

"Yes, put it away," said Harkan Thul. "Save it for the Earthman."

Sutarat tucked the pistol in his belt and drew four swords.

Harkan Thul raised his own swords as well. "Long have we despised you, Ghar Han, but it pleased us to mock you, so we suffered you to live. But no longer."

The two of them advanced, their eyes full of hate. Ghar Han backed away, drawing his own weapons, knowing he stood no chance against both of them.

"I challenge Sutarat to single combat," he said.

"No, you'll fight us both," said Harkan Thul, grinning. "Two opponents, one for each of your arms. It seems fitting."

Sutarat laughed.

Then suddenly the Earth woman was back, rushing Harkan Thul, slashing at him.

He spun, cursing, just barely in time to bring his sword around to block hers. As the two of them fought, Harkan Thul shouted, "Get him! I'll deal with her."

Sutarat leapt at Ghar Han, striking with sword after sword, and Ghar Han fell back before the onslaught, ducking and parrying as the blows fell. For an instant he despaired that his two arms could possibly prevail against Sutarat's four.

Then he remembered the day he'd faced John Carter, the way the Earthman had cut him to pieces. It was a battle Ghar Han had replayed in his mind a thousand times.

The next time Sutarat attacked with an overhand chop, Ghar Han spun aside and hacked at the man's shoulder, causing him to drop a sword, and then Ghar Han battered another of the man's blades, knocking it from his hand. Then it was two swords against two.

Ghar Han smiled. What came next felt almost inevitable.

When Sutarat attacked again, Ghar Han skewered him through the forearm, then kicked him in the chest, knocking him onto his back.

Sutarat groaned, fumbling at his belt, grasping the radium pistol, raising it. Ghar Han brought his sword screaming down. Both pistol and hand fell away, and the blade plunged deep into Sutarat's chest, killing him.

Panting, Ghar Han glanced back over his shoulder.

Harkan Thul was standing over the woman. She lay in the street, reaching for her blade, which had fallen just out of reach.

As Harkan Thul raised his swords to deliver a killing blow, Ghar Han snatched up the radium pistol and shot him in the back.

* * *

On the streets of a ghost town, beneath the twin moons, a Green Man knelt, staring at the pistol in his hand. Two corpses lay nearby.

The Earth woman came and stood beside him. "Hello."

He was silent.

"Who are you?" she said.

His voice was soft. "I don't know."

After a moment, he added, "We take the names of those we slay in battle. I am no longer worthy of those names. I have broken every law…"

"You did what you had to," she said. "You had no choice."

"I had a choice," he said, and fell silent again.

A bit later, the woman said, "My name is Suzanne. Suzanne Meyers. Of Earth."

"Earth," he echoed. "Tell me, Suzanne, how did you come to Barsoom?"

"I don't know," she said. "I just…woke up, and I was here."

"Do you know John Carter? Of Virginia?"

"No," she said. "I'm from New York. Who's John Carter?"

"Someone I met once," said the Green Man. "Long ago."

They were silent for a time.

The woman said, "Thank you for saving my life. I owe you. I mean, if there's any way I can help you…"

The Green Man said, "If you would do me one favor, it is this: I foresee a time when Earthmen will come to this world, not one by one, but by the thousands. Do what you can to ensure that, when that day comes, my people will not be utterly wiped away."

"You have my word," she said. "For what it's worth."

"Who are you, on your world?" he asked. "A great warlord? A princess?"

"No," she said. "I...I'm nobody, really."

"I understand," said the Green Man. "I am also nobody."

"Two nobodies," she said.

After a moment, she added, "Maybe we should stick together then. It would be fitting."

He raised his head and looked at her.

And why not? he thought. He could never return to his own people. Not now.

"Come on," she said, offering him her hand.

They stole through the quiet streets, to the place where the thoats were tied, and took two of them, and galloped away through the gates. Under cover of darkness they slipped the cordon of Warhoon scouts, though the warriors heard them, and pursued them.

When the two of them reached the hills, the Earth woman said, "Follow me. I came this way before." And she urged her mount up a narrow trail, near-invisible in the dark, and the Green Man followed.

Hours later, as dawn broke, they saw that they'd escaped. Then they paused atop a ridge and looked out toward the horizon, knowing that all the weird and wondrous landscapes of Barsoom lay spread before them.

"Where shall we go?" she said.

"Wherever we want," he replied.

"And what shall I call you?" she asked.

He reflected on this. Finally he said, "Call me Var Dalan. It means 'two-arm.'"

* * *

And that concludes our story, a story of three deaths.

The first death was that of the sly Sutarat, killed in single combat.

The second death was that of the arrogant Harkan Thul, shot in the back with a radium pistol.

And the third death was that of the fierce and terrible warrior Ghar Han, reborn now as he gallops his thoat across the yellow hills beneath a purple sky, a two-armed man who rides with a two-armed woman at his side. For the man that he was, who served the cruel whims of the jeddak, and who longed for the approbation of his people, and who was ashamed of the wounds he bore, and who lived for nothing but to take vengeance on John Carter, that man is dead now, dead as the dead sea bottoms of Mars.

Author's note: Three Deaths

In 2011 John Joseph Adams was putting together an anthology of Barsoom stories called *Under the Moons of Mars*, set to coincide with the release of the big-budget Disney movie *John Carter*. One day John emailed me and asked if I'd like to submit a story for the book. Several authors had backed out at the last minute, and he needed a few more stories to fill out the anthology. I was excited by the opportunity, but there were just two problems: The deadline was only three weeks away, and I had never read any of the Barsoom books. Still, by this point I was getting to be an old hand at writing stories to fit a theme. I said sure.

I hurriedly read *A Princess of Mars* by Edgar Rice Burroughs, the first Barsoom book. I had heard a lot of people trashing it over the years, and I wasn't expecting much, but actually I loved it. There was something about all those trackless deserts and abandoned cities that really spoke to me. It was also clear to me that Burroughs had had a massive influence on two of my favorite writers, Roger Zelazny and Gene Wolfe, in ways I had never appreciated. So while I wasn't the world's biggest Barsoom expert, I felt an instant affinity for the material.

The most striking aspect of that world to me were the Green Martians, the giant four-armed natives. I definitely wanted to do something with them, and it would have to revolve around the fact that they had four arms, since that was their most distinctive feature. What would it be like, I wondered, to be a two-armed person in a society of four-armed people?

I really liked that idea. One of the things I love about science fiction is how it can take something that seems completely normal to us, like having two arms, and show how someone from another culture could find it intolerable.

For three weeks I spent every waking moment thinking about this story. When I wasn't writing it, I was rapidly reading my way through *The Gods of Mars* and *The Warlord of Mars*, the second and third Barsoom books, hoping desperately that nothing I came across would contradict anything in my story. Fortunately nothing did.

I was really proud of this story, and John loved it. "This is great!" he said. "You should write more Barsoom stories." Unfortunately it was not to be. We had high hopes for *Under the Moons of Mars*, a beautiful hardcover book written and illustrated by some of the top names in the field, but Disney's *John Carter* movie flopped hard at the box office, and any interest it might have generated in the anthology quickly dried up.

Allen Koszowski

The Disciple

Professor Carlton Brose was evil, and I adored him as only a freshman can. I spent the first miserable semester at college watching him, studying the way he would flick away a cigarette butt, or how he would arch his eyebrow when he made a point. I mimicked these small things privately, compulsively, I don't know why. Because it wasn't the small things that drew me to him at all. It was the big things, the stories people told as far away as dear old Carolina.

You heard the name Brose if you ran with any cults, and I ran with a few. Society rejected us, so we rejected them. The more things you give up, the less there is to bind your will. There was power there, we were sure of it, but it was damned elusive.

I used to shop at an occult bookstore in Raleigh. A friend of mine worked there, and one day as he was shelving books he told me, "These guys you hang with, them I'm not so sure about. But Brose, he's the real deal."

"You believe that?" I said.

He stopped and got a slightly crazed look in his eyes. "I've seen it, man, personally seen it. Flies buzz up out of the rot and swirl in formation around him. He can make your eyes bleed, just from looking at him. The guy's tapped into something huge."

I was skeptical. "And he teaches a class?"

"Not just a class, all right? It's this special program. Only a dozen or so are admitted, and they get power. I've seen that too. Then they go away. Every spring."

"Go where?"

He shook his head. "Damned if I know. Places not of this world. That's what some people say."

"I don't buy it," I said. "If he's got so much going for him, why's he working a job at all? And what kind of school would let him teach it?"

My friend shrugged. "I don't know about that. All I know is that Brose is for real."

"Then why aren't you in his class?"

He scowled and went back to shelving. "Brose wouldn't take me. Said I had no talent, no potential. It hurt like hell, but that's another reason you know he's legit—what kind of fraud would turn people away like that?"

I had no answer, and I'd known a lot of frauds.

I traveled to Massachusetts, to the university where Brose taught. I sought out his office in a secluded corner of the Anthropology building, then sat on a bench in the hallway, pretending to read.

Finally the office door opened and Brose emerged. I glanced up, as if accidentally, as if his movement had caught my eye.

He stared back at me with eyes the color of a tombstone, and smiled knowingly. The shadows seemed to lengthen and darken as he passed. I shuddered, because I was sure just from that look that it was all true. Brose practically radiated power. On that day my initial skepticism transformed into the most helpless adoration. I enrolled in the school.

In the winter, I met with Brose for the first time. The inside of his office was like some terrible jungle. Loose papers drooped from the shelves. A filth-choked and apparently unused fish tank cast a pallid green light. From my seat, I could look out the window and see the lonely stretch of grey-green woods that was called the Arboretum.

Brose sat behind his desk, in those shadows of his own making, and said, "So you want to join the program?"

"Yes," I whispered.

"Why should I accept you?"

"I'll do anything," I said. "No hesitation. No regret."

His lips curled into that now familiar smile. "And what will you be bringing to the program?"

I knew he meant power. "Nothing. Not yet. But you can—"

He shook his head. "If nothing's what you have, then nothing's what you get from me. Go back to literature. It's really—"

"No!" I broke in. "I don't have much, that's true. I've lost things in my life, so many things, but I've gained something too—this rotting emptiness inside me, and I can use it. I swear I can use it. All the loss, it can't have been for nothing." I added softly, "I won't let it be."

He watched me for a long time. Finally he nodded. "All right, you'll do. I'll get the form."

I leaned back in my chair and let out a long sigh of relief as he disappeared into a back room.

Something on the shelf caught my eye. A black statue. Like Brose, it seemed wrapped in strange shadows. I rose from my seat.

The statue was a foot tall and depicted a creature resembling the head of a man, but with a beard of tentacles. Its eyes were utterly empty. It had no body, only more tentacles.

I went to pick it up and study it closer, but when I lifted it I gasped. The thing was unearthly heavy—heavier than anything that size could possibly be, heavier than I could hold in one hand. It tore itself from my fingers and lunged for the floor, where it thudded and lay still.

From behind me came Brose's voice. "Don't touch that." I started.

He placed a shoebox on his desk, then lifted the statue with two hands and returned it to its place on the shelf.

"I'm sorry," I said. "I…"

My voice died in my throat as Brose reached into the shoebox and lifted out a small white mouse, which squirmed and flailed and sniffed.

"What's that?" I said.

"The form. The application form." Brose paced over to that gruesomely overgrown fish tank and removed the lid. He offered me the mouse. I took it.

He nodded at the tank. "Fill out your application."

I stepped forward. The mouse nibbled gently at my fingers as I held it over the foul water.

This was a test. Of what? My willingness? My resolve? I let go. The mouse plunged into the water, then thrashed and screamed, clawing at the sides of the tank. Water soaked its fur and garbled its cries. Then it died, floating there, spinning slowly, its four pink legs hanging down, its tail trailing after.

"Congratulations," Brose said. "Your application's been accepted."

* * *

Our class met in a sprawling old house on the edge of campus, down in the dim cement cellar. The room had no windows, and its walls and floor bore eerie dark stains. There were thirteen students, mostly male. All had sallow flesh and haunted eyes.

Brose crucified a cat, right on his desk in front of us. The animal howled and squirmed, but the nails driven through its limbs held it fast. Blood trickled from its paws. Brose stanched the flow with a cloth.

He said, "The most important thing you must learn is to bind your will to that of another. Pain is conspicuous, it'll point the way, but don't depend on it. There are greater things than cats you must connect to, greater things than you, and they have never felt pain."

He turned to me. "Make it bleed again."

I was filled with the most aching desire to prove myself. I wanted him to think I was his most talented, most dedicated, most favored student. I would have done anything, endured anything, to make him adore me, the way I adored him.

I whispered desperately, "I don't know how."

He turned to another student, a tall young guy with dark, scornful eyes, and said, "Make it bleed."

The guy never even glanced at the cat, but instantly its paws began to bubble and ooze and spurt.

"Good." Brose nodded. "Very good."

At the end of class, he admonished us, "Tell no one what you learn here."

The next day I moved into the house. My room was a small square chamber with hardwood floors and peeling white paint. When my new roommate entered, I recognized him instantly. "Oh," I said. "You're—"

"Adrian," he replied.

"—the one who can make the cat bleed," I said.

"Yeah," he said, turning away, setting down his bags. "I can do a lot of things."

He began to unpack, saying nothing.

I said, "Maybe sometime you can—"

"Look," he said over his shoulder. "Let's get something straight. I'm not here to make friends. I'm here to learn. No distractions. So just stay out of my way, and we'll get along just fine."

I was silent.

"Nothing personal," he said. "But I'm here to excel. To be the best."

I felt a stab of jealous rage. I couldn't believe it was an accident, the way his words seemed calculated to tear at my greatest longing: to be favored, to be adored.

I said, "That's why we're all here."

"Yeah," he said. "Sure."

"There's more to this than just cats," I added.

He said coldly, "You think I should try something bigger?"

Then I felt a wetness on my lip. Turning to the mirror, I saw blood leaking from my nose, streaking down my chin. I grabbed a towel and pressed it to my face, leaning my head back.

"Don't lean back," Adrian said. "Keep pressure on your nose. The bleeding will stop."

* * *

I tried so hard, but it was useless. With each passing week I lagged further behind Adrian in absorbing the macabre lessons we received. Adrian was right. He was the best. Adored by the class. Brose's favorite.

If I could not be favored by Brose, I would have preferred to be disfavored, to be his enemy. In truth he was indifferent to me. I was not important enough for him even to despise.

As I walked the shaded pathways of the campus, I pondered the strange role that Brose played here. It was obvious that the other faculty suspected the dark nature of our program. They kept their distance, and shot us looks full of fear and hostility, but they made no effort to disrupt us. Were they simply afraid of Brose? I couldn't decide.

As the semester wore on, Brose grew more and more agitated, his lectures increasingly frenzied and mad. He raved of nothing but the binding.

"You must learn faster!" He pounded on his desk. "The hour is near. It has all led up to this." He took a deep breath. "You must bind yourselves to the impossible mind of the Traveler on Oceans of Night, the Stepper Across the Stars. If you ingratiate yourselves, you will earn a place as His favored disciples, and journey with him forever to those places only He can make by his dreaming."

I glanced at Adrian, but he kept his eyes fixed straight ahead. So now we knew our fate. We would gain the ultimate power we sought by pledging ourselves to this ultimate being.

Brose reached into his briefcase and pulled out the black statue, darker than any earthly object could ever be—the tentacled man-thing with its empty eyes. Then I saw something I'd never noticed before. Among its many limbs clung tiny human figures. That almost made me dizzy, for it meant that the creature must tower to unimaginable heights.

The Traveler on Oceans of Night. The Stepper Across the Stars.

It was Him.

That week I dreamed murky dreams of upside down cities built from granite and slime. One night I awoke to find Adrian lying on the floor and whimpering. He stared up in terror, as if something horrid hung from the ceiling.

"What?" I said. "What is it?"

"Oh god," he wailed. His usual swagger had disintegrated. "Can't you feel it? Are you blind and deaf and numb to everything? His boundlessness reaches across the void to poison our dreams."

Then I knew he wasn't staring at the ceiling, but at the sky and the stars and the dark emptiness beyond.

"The Traveler on Oceans of Night," Adrian whispered. "He's coming."

I had failed to win the adoration of Brose, but who was Brose, compared to all this? Compared to this great Traveler? Brose was nothing. He was a small man who lived a small life, pointing others along an exalted path that he himself dared not follow. I had found an object far more worthy of veneration. To be a disciple to such power, to be favored by the Traveler!

I would not fail this time.

* * *

The night of the binding arrived. The Traveler was near, his imminence palpable. The air crackled with magic. I looked out over the forest, and the trees themselves seemed to tremble.

My classmates and I donned black robes, and Brose led us into the Arboretum. We passed beneath withered branches and trod faint trails that wound between mossy boulders. Brose held the dark statue before him, and we didn't need light to see, because the statue seemed to suck the shadows from beneath our feet and pull them into itself.

In the deepest corner of the woods, within a grotto of gray stone, sprawled an ancient shrine overgrown with black ferns. Brose set the statue on the ground, and we seated ourselves in a circle around it.

I don't know how many hours we sat there. Then a breeze came, snatching up damp leaves and flinging them about, raising them into columns in the sky. The wind blew faster and louder, until it seemed to shriek in pain.

I was struck by a maddening sense of dislocation, a nightmare cacophony of unbearable sensations. Then the shadows leapt from beneath the trees to block out the stars and wrap themselves around our throats and sink behind our eyes.

The Traveler on Oceans of Night was there, his form stretching upward to infinity. All of him was far away yet somehow pressing close all around us. He was so enormous, so horrible, and so magnificent that we collapsed and wept helplessly and without shame to behold Him.

Through the confusion came the voice of Brose screaming, "Bind yourselves! Do it now!"

Adrian was first. He rose off the ground, arms outstretched, robe whipping about him, face full of ecstasy. One by one my classmates lifted from the earth until they circled around that great being. They were like the flies, I realized suddenly. Like the flies rising from the rot to swirl around Professor Carlton Brose.

I looked at him, and his expression was one I had come to know too well—indifference. Something was horribly wrong. I imagined I saw that same indifference mirrored on the incomprehensible otherworldly face of the Traveler.

I would not bind to Him. I crawled until I found a rock to hide behind, then I screamed to my whirling classmates, "We're the flies! Oh god, we're like the flies."

The Traveler made one ponderous motion with a million of His slimy tentacles, and He stepped away toward another star, another dimension, another world He had dreamed. Then the night was silent and empty.

Brose strode toward me. He said darkly, "You failed the binding."

I lunged at him, startling him. I grabbed his throat and forced him down against a stone.

"You lied," I said. "You said you'd make us His disciples."

"The Traveler on Oceans of Night is a great vessel," he whispered. "I would put you aboard."

"As what?" I said. "A rat in the hold? Or rather, a flea on a rat."

I imagined I saw the dozen bodies of my classmates, sucked away into the bitter black void between worlds, their frozen forms twirling slowly in an endless dance among the stars.

Then Brose seized my temples with his muddy fingers and made me look down into his cold, tombstone eyes. My own eyes began to bleed, spattering his face. I screamed, unable to turn my head, unable to look away.

As I flailed, my fingers fell upon the statue. I lifted it with two angry arms and brought it down on Brose's forehead. The statue sank without resistance until it reached the ground.

When I pulled it away there was nothing but a gaping hole where the face of Professor Carlton Brose had been.

The empty eyes of the Traveler could see things that humans never dreamt of, but He was blind to the pain of this sad world.

* * *

You were the best, Adrian, better than me. Better at a lie. Are you proud?

Today a student came to beg admission to my special program. He stood at the fish tank and clenched a mouse in his fist. Then he held it underwater until it drowned.

"Congratulations," I said. "You've been accepted."

He smiled.

I do this initiation—as I'm sure Brose did—to ease my conscience, to reassure myself that my students are cruel, and deserve their fate.

The college hates the program, but they know it's necessary, and after Brose died I was the only one who could replace him. New England has some dangerous people lurking about—ones who've latched onto darkness, or might—and they need to be dealt with. The harmless ones I turn away.

I've learned the truth that Brose knew: it's best to be a big fish in a small pond. Fish can't live outside the pond, and being a fish isn't so bad. Every spring, before I send them off to die, a new class studies with me. They are enthralled by my meager powers. They long for my briefest attention.

They adore me.

Author's note: The Disciple

One day at the Clarion writers workshop in 1999, I saw a student wearing a T-shirt that displayed an octopus-headed monster beneath the words "Miskatonic University." I asked him about Miskatonic University, and he explained that it was a fictional college invented by the horror writer H. P. Lovecraft. At the time I knew nothing about Lovecraft, other than once reading a review of the *Call of Cthulhu* tabletop role-playing game in *Dragon* magazine. But something about that combination of college and monsters really intrigued me.

When I returned to Colby College that fall, I read Lovecraft's collection *The Call of Cthulhu and Other Weird Stories*, and absolutely loved it. I loved the secret cults, the forbidden tomes, the evil gods from outer space. I learned that before Lovecraft, horror fiction had been mostly about the fear of eternal damnation, but Lovecraft's work was about something much scarier: the idea that the universe is bigger and stranger than you can possibly imagine, and that nothing out there cares about you or your soul.

I read a few more collections of Lovecraft's stories, as well as Lovecraftian fiction written by other authors. The book *Tales of the Cthulhu Mythos* featured a story by Philip José Farmer called "The Freshman," about a college student encountering black magic at Miskatonic University. I loved that idea, and definitely wanted to try something similar.

The summer after I graduated from Colby, I saw that a Lovecraftian anthology was open for submissions, and I decided to submit something. Unfortunately I didn't finish "The Disciple" until just before the deadline. The story was quickly rejected, and I suspect that no one actually read it. Undeterred, I mailed it off to *Weird Tales* magazine, which I had recently started reading, and which published a lot of Lovecraftian fiction.

Five months passed with no response. Finally I sent a follow-up letter asking about my story, and was told that they never received it, and to send it again. By that point another Lovecraftian anthology called *Dead But Dreaming* had opened to submissions. If I sent the story to *Weird Tales*, I would miss the submission window for *Dead But Dreaming*, so I submitted "The Disciple" to *Dead But Dreaming*. After waiting almost eight months, I finally received an acceptance letter.

Three months later, shortly before *Dead But Dreaming* was due to be published, I got a letter from *Weird Tales* accepting the story. I guess they got it after all.

Dead But Dreaming seemed like a cool anthology, but I really wanted to be in *Weird Tales*. *Weird Tales* was the magazine that had published Lovecraft's story "The Call of Cthulhu" back in 1928. I wanted to be part of that tradition. I wrote to *Weird Tales* explaining the situation, and they were like, "Oh huh. I guess we screwed up. Well, send us your next one."

I was crestfallen. I had no idea if I'd ever be able to sell another story to *Weird Tales*. (In point of fact I never did.) I mean, I had waited over a year just to get a response on *this* story. I wasn't about to let this sale slip away so easily. I wrote to the editors of *Dead But Dreaming* explaining the situation, and they said they would be willing to relinquish rights to the story so I could sell it to *Weird Tales*. I thanked them profusely.

I wrote back to *Weird Tales* with the good news. They responded by saying, "Well, we feel bad about leaving the *Dead But Dreaming* guys in the lurch, so here's what we'll do. We'll put 'The Disciple' in our next issue, and hopefully it'll come out before the anthology. If not we'll pretend not to notice." (As a fiction magazine they wanted all-new material. For an anthology like *Dead But Dreaming*, it didn't matter so much if the story had already appeared elsewhere.)

So the whole thing worked out really well. "The Disciple" appeared in the next issue of *Weird Tales* (otherwise it might have taken another year for it to appear), and was also published around the same time in *Dead But Dreaming*. *Dead But Dreaming* quickly gained a reputation as a minor classic of Lovecraftian fiction, and for a time it was highly sought after by collectors, with copies selling for hundreds of dollars.

In 2011 "The Disciple" was reprinted in Paula Guran's anthology *New Cthulhu*, a collection of the best Lovecraftian fiction of the decade. It was a huge honor to see my story listed alongside authors such as Neil Gaiman and China Miéville. And I owe it all to a Miskatonic University T-shirt.

The Skull-Faced Boy

It was past midnight, and Jack and Dustin were driving along a twisted path through the woods. Jack was at the wheel. He was arguing with Dustin over Ashley.

Jack had always thought she had a pretty face—thin, arching eyebrows, a slightly upturned nose, a delicate chin. She'd dated Dustin in college for six months, until he got possessive and she got restless. Now, Jack thought, maybe she was interested in him.

But Dustin insisted, "She'll give me another chance. Someday."

"Not according to her," Jack said, with a pointed look.

He turned his eyes back to the road, and in the light of the high beams he saw a man stumble into the path of the car. Without thinking, Jack swerved.

The car bounced violently, and then its left front side smashed into a tree. The steering column surged forward, like an ocean wave, and crushed Jack's stomach. Dustin wasn't wearing a seatbelt. He flew face-first through the windshield, rolled across the hood, and tumbled off onto the ground.

* * *

Jack awoke, disoriented.

A man was pounding on the driver's side window, which was cracked and foggy and opaque. Jack pushed at the door, which creaked open just enough for him to make out the man's face. The man stared at Jack, then turned and started to walk off.

Jack shouted, "Call for help."

But the man didn't respond. He wandered toward the woods.

"Hey!" Jack screamed. He brushed aside a blanket of shattered glass and released his seatbelt. He pushed his seat backward, slowly extricating his bleeding stomach from the steering column, then dragged himself out the door and onto the ground. He crawled after the man, who continued to walk away.

Finally Jack found the strength to stand. He lurched to his feet, grabbed the man by the shirtfront, shoved him back against a tree, and demanded, "What's wrong with you? Get help."

Jack glanced about desperately and added, "I have to find my friend."

The man gave a long, low moan. He was very pale, with disheveled hair. His face was encrusted with dirt, and his teeth were twisted and rotten. His eyes were...oozing.

Suddenly Dustin's voice burst out, "He's dead."

Jack turned. Dustin stood there, his nose and cheeks torn away. Two giant white eyeballs filled the sockets of his freakishly visible skull. Scraps of flesh hung from his jaw. Jack screamed.

Dustin stumbled over to the car, to where one of its side-view mirrors hung loosely. He tore off the mirror and stared into it. For a long time he neither moved nor spoke.

Finally he called out, "That man has come back from the dead. Look at him, Jack. He's dead, and so am I."

Jack shuddered and backed away from the man.

Dustin's eyeballs fixed on Jack's stomach.

Apprehensive, Jack looked down. He lifted his blood-drenched shirt to expose the mangled mess beneath.

"And so are you," Dustin said.

* * *

Jack and Dustin set out on foot. They climbed to the top of a high bluff and watched the bodies of dead men stumble through the grassy fields below. Dustin stood with his back turned, so that his ruined face was lost in shadows. He said, "It's everyone. Everyone who dies will come back."

The man who had caused the accident was following them. He stumbled from the trees and regarded Jack vacantly.

315

Jack approached him and said, "Can you talk?"

The man paused a moment, as if trying to focus, then gave another inarticulate groan. He wandered away.

Jack said to Dustin, "Why is he like that, and we aren't?"

Dustin said, "He dug himself out of the ground. He's been dead a long time—rotted flesh, rotted brains."

"Are there others like us?" Jack said.

"I don't know." Dustin leapt to his feet and called out to the valley below, "Hey! Can you hear me? Can you understand what I'm saying?"

The warm and fetid air carried back only wails. Dustin shrugged.

They followed the road until they came to a small house with its lights on. Jack said, "We can call for help."

"What help?" Dustin said. "We're past that."

But he followed Jack toward the house, whose front door was open wide. They paused on the porch. They could see into the kitchen, where a woman stood clenching a baseball bat. A dead boy had backed her into a corner. He shambled toward her, dry dirt tumbling from his sleeves, falling in a winding trail behind him.

He spoke, in a faint and quavering way: "Mom...help me."

"Stay back," she warned, her voice cracking. "Stay away from me. You're dead. I know you're dead."

Jack started forward, but Dustin held out an arm to stop him.

"Mom," the boy said. "What's wrong? Don't hurt me..."

"Stop it!" the woman shrieked, but her arms trembled and she collapsed, sobbing. The boy fell upon her, clawing at her hair, tearing at her scalp with his teeth.

Jack cringed and turned away. The woman screamed, then gurgled, then was silent. When Jack looked again, he saw that Dustin was regarding the gruesome scene with fascination.

Jack growled, "What's wrong with you? We could've stopped it."

"We're dead now," Dustin said. "We help the dead, not them." He gestured at the woman.

"You're crazy," Jack said.

Dustin ignored him. "I want to see this."

"You—" Jack stopped as the woman rose, her head a cracked and bloody mess. She stepped clumsily forward.

She moaned.

"You'd be like her," Dustin whispered. "Mindless...hungry. If that first one had gotten into the car, gotten its teeth into you, before you rose."

Jack strode into the kitchen, eased around the woman, the boy, and the blood-splattered floor, and stepped toward the phone.

"I'm calling home," Jack said, lifting the receiver. "I have to call my dad. Tell him I'm——"

"What?" Dustin said darkly. "All right?"

Jack hesitated.

Dustin said, "Jack, you're dead. You're lost to him. He'll never take you in."

Jack paused a moment, then began to dial. Dustin turned and stepped out into the night. The phone rang once, and instantly someone answered.

"Jack?" It was his father's voice.

"I'm coming home," Jack said. "I...can't stay on the line." He hung up.

He snatched some keys off the counter and slipped from the house. He spotted Dustin, who had walked out into the fields among the great crowds of the dead and was shouting to them, "Can you understand me? If you can hear me, step forward. If you understand just that much."

Jack circled the house, to where a car was parked. He took the car, and drove north for an hour, along Interstate 95, toward Waterville. He stared at his reflection in the rearview mirror. His face was jaundiced, discolored and sickly, but if he covered his gaping stomach he thought he might pass for living.

He pulled up in front of his house and got out of the car. In the front yard lay a body with a bullet hole through its forehead. Jack shuddered, and circled around back. The old wood steps creaked as he stepped onto the back porch and knocked. He hung back in the shadows. A curtain was drawn aside, and faces peered out.

From inside the house someone called, "Jack! It's Jack."

The door opened, and Jack's father stood there, clutching a rifle. He stared, then gasped and dropped back, raising the gun.

Jack cowered and said quickly, "Dad, listen! Please. I'm not like the others." The rifle was now aimed straight at his head. He stared into the depths of its barrel.

Then the barrel slowly sank, as his father lowered the gun.

Finally his father said, "Come inside, son."

Jack stepped into the house.

* * *

His father chained him to a rusty pipe that ran out of the side of the garage and into the ground. "I'm sorry," his father said. "It's only for the night. It's the only way they'll let you stay here." Nine people were holed up in the house—Jack's father had taken in some vacationers.

Jack said sadly, "I understand."

His father went back inside.

The moon was bright, and the garage cast a thick black shadow over Jack. All across the neighborhood, dogs were barking. The night seemed to go on forever, and Jack never slept. He supposed that he would never sleep again.

Days passed.

Several large groups arrived. Jack stayed out of sight, and most of the visitors departed, headed south. Those who stayed would sometimes let Jack inside, but they kept their distance from him, and always had weapons ready.

During the day the men went out, scavenging for food and ammunition, and at night they told stories of the dead men they'd destroyed. Then they would glance at Jack and fall silent.

He was chained up each night, weeks of that.

One night at dusk, Jack was sitting on a sofa in the living room when gunshots crackled outside. The residents brandished their weapons and took up positions by the windows.

Someone pounded on the front door. A gruff voice outside hollered, "Let us in! For god's sake, let us in. They're coming."

Jack's father, rifle at the ready, leapt forward and threw open the door. Two men in hunting gear rushed into the house, each of them carrying several guns. Jack's father slammed the door behind them.

One of the newcomers gasped, "We heard about this house. They said you'd take us in. We've got almost no bullets left."

Jack's father said, "It's my house, and you're—"

Then the newcomer spotted Jack and lurched wildly, falling back against the front door, violently cocking his shotgun. "They're in the house!" he screamed, raising his weapon.

Jack's father leapt in front of him and yelled, "Don't shoot! That's my son. He won't hurt you."

The gun's barrel wove in tight circles as the newcomer sought a clear shot. Jack called out, "Please! It's all right."

The newcomer glanced at his companion, who was now hunched in the corner and moaning, "Oh shit. Oh shit, it's in here with us."

Jack's father said firmly, "You can leave if you want."

There was a long, tense silence. Finally the newcomer lowered his gun and said, "All right. We'll let it alone." He glared at Jack, and added, "But you stay the hell away from me."

* * *

The newcomer was named Sam, and his companion was Todd. Sam was bigger and louder, and seemed to be the leader of the two.

After things had settled down, Todd explained, "We joined up with a militia to hold Portland. But the dead, they..." He stopped and stared at the floor.

Sam said flatly, "It's not good down there. Not good at all."

Jack's father said, "Where did you hear about this house?"

"In Freeport," Todd said. "Some people had stayed here. There was a girl too. She had a note for your son." Todd fished an envelope from his vest pocket. He glanced uneasily at Jack and said, "I guess that's him."

Sam grumbled, "Maybe that's not such a good idea."

Jack's father scowled and said, "Let him have it."

Todd shrugged and tossed the note out onto the table. Jack scooped it up and opened it.

It was from Ashley, letting him know that she was all right and that he should join her if he wasn't safe. She gave the address where she was. Jack stuck the note into his pocket.

Sam's voice was shaky. "South of here there's this dead kid with no face. People call him the skull-faced boy. He's smart, he can talk, like that one there." He nodded at Jack.

Jack murmured, "Dustin."

Todd said sharply, "What?"

Jack said, "He hurt his face like that. I saw it."

Sam stared, horrified. "You *know* him?"

Jack realized that he'd said something wrong.

"Dustin was a friend from school," Jack's father explained. "He was with Jack the night this...all started."

Todd's voice was almost hysterical. "Sam! This is crazy. He's one of them. One of the skull-faced boy's—"

"Shut up!" Sam growled. "Just shut up."

There was a long silence.

Jack's father said, "Come on, son. Let's go outside."

Jack was chained up again. Then he crouched there in the shadow of the garage, listening to the voices that drifted out through the bright cracks in the boarded-up windows.

First came Jack's father's voice: "What's this all about?"

Todd replied anxiously, "We lost Portland because of the skull-faced boy. He's organized the dead down there into some sort of army."

Sam broke in, "He's trained them. They go after people they know—family, friends. They act like they still have feelings. People hesitate, won't fight, then it's too late."

Jack's father said, "What's that got to do with us?"

"Don't you get it?" It was Todd again. "Jack is part of this. He's friends with the skull-faced boy. He's pretending to be nice, just waiting for his chance to strike."

"He's dangerous," Sam added. "He knows about this house, and now the one in Freeport too. What else does he know? He's got to be destroyed."

"No," Jack's father said.

Todd pressed him. "He's not your son anymore. Your son is dead and gone. Now it's just a thing, a thing in your son's body. Using your own love against you."

Sam added, "People have a right to protect themselves. If one of these folks here went out one night and shot that thing you keep in the backyard, I wouldn't blame them."

One of the other residents hissed, "Keep your voice down. He might hear."

After that the voices fell to a low, incomprehensible murmur.

Jack waited for hours. Then he watched as the back door swung open. A shadowy figure with a gun crept across the yard toward him.

Was it Sam? Or Todd? Or one of the others? In the darkness, Jack couldn't tell.

It was his father, who stepped from the shadows. He bent to unlock the chains and said, "It's not safe for you here anymore. I'm sorry."

"I'm sorry too," Jack whispered, rising to his feet. He hugged his father, then escaped into the night.

* * *

Jack found Dustin's army standing in a great field north of Portland. The thousands of dead milled about in loose formations, watching Jack with their empty eyes. Their groans filled the night.

Jack moved among them, shouting, "Dustin! I'm looking for Dustin. Dustin, can you hear me?"

Finally a voice responded, "Hey! Hey you. What do you want?"

Jack stopped and turned. A balding dead man in olive fatigues was approaching.

Jack said, "I'm looking for the skull-faced boy."

"The Commander, you mean," the man replied. "He'll want to see you too. We can use someone like you."

The man led Jack through the crowds, up to a low hill where a small crowd of dead men conversed in hushed tones. Dustin stood at the peak of the hill, his back turned. Standing like that he seemed normal, familiar.

Jack called out, "Dustin."

Dustin glanced backward, so that one white eye showed in his eerie skeletal profile. He wore a ratty army jacket. He said, "You've come back." Then he turned away, so that again all that was visible was the back of his head. "Where have you been?"

"Up north," Jack said.

Dustin asked, "Did you encounter any of the living? Any armed groups?"

"No," Jack said quickly.

"We'll be headed that way," Dustin continued. "North. Along 95, toward Waterville…your hometown." He waited for a reaction.

Jack said nothing.

Finally Dustin added, "Anyway, it's time for training." He walked out to the edge of the hill and regarded the hordes below. He shouted, "Don't shoot!"

They moaned back, "Don't…shoot…"

"It's me!" Dustin yelled. "You know me!"

The voices of the dead drifted up toward the sky. "It's me…you know me…"

"Please help me," Dustin shouted.

"Please…help me…" they wailed.

Dustin nodded with satisfaction, then turned away from the crowds. "That's our strategy, Jack. My soldiers possess determination, but not much else. A resemblance to loved ones is one of our few assets."

Jack said, "What are you doing? What do you think you're going to accomplish?"

"Peace," Dustin said, then added, "The living want to destroy us. All of us. Our only chance is to convert them, to make them like us."

Jack stared at the lines of moaning dead. They stretched away as far as he could see.

Dustin added, "And we're winning, thanks to my plan. I got the idea from that boy, who converted his mother, that first night. You remember."

"To hell with your plan," Jack said angrily. "I lost my home because of your plan."

Instantly Dustin turned to face him. "So you *did* go home." That menacing skull-face leaned in close. "Are people hiding there?"

Jack turned away.

"At your house?" Dustin pressed. "Is that where they are? My army's fragile, Jack. They're slow and clumsy and stupid. A nest of armed resistance, even a small one, can wreak havoc. I have to know about it."

Jack said, "Leave them alone. Leave my father alone."

"We're headed north, Jack," Dustin said. "The plan is already in motion."

"Don't," Jack insisted, then added, "Just for now. They won't bother you. Push east. Toward Freeport."

"Freeport?" Dustin was dismissive. "What's there?"

Jack reached into his pocket and pulled out the note. He answered in a low voice, "Ashley."

* * *

Later that night, Dustin said, "She'll have to be converted. It's the only way."

Jack said, "Killed, you mean."

"I want her with us," Dustin said. "She's in danger now. As long as she's alive, the dead will never stop coming for her. Eventually one of them will get to her, damage her mind—destroy what makes her special. She'll be safer this way."

Jack stared at Ashley's note. Why had he done it? Why betray her? To protect his father, yes, but...the truth? He wanted to see her again. Would she accept him, he wondered, if they were the same? If she were dead too?

He said, "It won't be easy."

"No," Dustin agreed. "That's why I need you with me. My soldiers follow orders, mostly. I tell them where to march, who to attack, what to say. But I can't stop them from feeding, Jack, which means that most of my new recruits arrive as damaged goods. There's not much officer material around here."

Jack was skeptical. "You want to make me an officer?"

Dustin answered, "I can't use regular troops for this. There's too much risk to Ashley. I have to use officers—men I can trust not to damage her—and I've got few enough of those."

Some of the dumb, moaning ones wandered past. Jack imagined them ripping at Ashley's soft forehead with their teeth.

"I'll go," he said then. "For Ashley. To make sure nothing happens to her."

"For Ashley," Dustin agreed.

* * *

Dustin called a meeting of his officers. He held up a photograph that showed him and Ashley standing by a campfire, embracing. "This is her," he said. "Make sure she's not damaged."

The army marched east, thousands of groaning dead shambling along the interstate. Dustin moved among them, shouting orders. "When we reach the town, seek out places you know, people you know. Remember what to say: 'Don't shoot! You know me! Help me!'"

The mumbled replies echoed through the trees: "Don't shoot...you know me...help me..."

Dustin had a dozen officers—dead men armed with rifles and pistols—who stayed close by his side. Dustin carried a shotgun, and kept a combat knife tucked in his boot. Jack followed along behind them, holding his rifle limply, staring down at the damp pine needles that passed beneath his feet. He was full of foreboding.

Dustin said, "They've probably never encountered dead men like us before—fast, smart, armed. That surprise will be our biggest advantage."

One of the officers grumbled, "They've spent weeks boarding up this house. How are we going to get in?"

Jack called out, "I can get us in."

Dustin turned and studied him, then nodded.

The house was a sprawling Victorian that sat in the middle of a grove of white cedars. Dustin led his squad forward. They crouched low and scurried across the lawn in a tight column, their weapons held ready. Jack and Dustin hurried up the front steps while the others ducked behind the porch or dropped into the long grass.

Jack hammered on the door and shouted, "Let us in! It's Sam! For god's sake, let us in, they're coming!"

After a few moments, he heard the bolt snap out of place. The door opened a crack. Dustin rammed his shotgun into the opening and pulled the trigger. Blood exploded through the gap, splattering crimson across the porch.

Dustin kicked open the door. The officers sprang up, firearms bristling, and charged into the house. Gunfire rang out all around. Jack was swept along into the foyer, which was littered with bodies. A staircase led up to the second floor.

"Cover the stairs," Dustin told him. "Make sure no one comes down."

Jack aimed his gun up toward the second floor landing as the other officers poured off into the side rooms. Sounds of violence shook the house.

Suddenly a doorway under the stairs flew open. Jack swung his rifle to cover it, but then a muzzle flashed and a bullet caught him in the chest. He stumbled back against a table, knocking over a lamp, which shattered on the floor.

Dustin shouted, "The basement! They're in the basement."

Three of the officers stormed down the basement steps. The floorboards rattled, and horrible screams filtered up from below. Jack stuck a finger into his chest and rooted out the bullet.

Another officer jogged up to stand at Dustin's side. "Sir, we've got your girl. She's in the study. Bleeding."

Dustin nodded. "I want to be with her when she rises. Finish this."

"Yes, sir." The officer walked to the open front door and called out, "Come here. Come on. Now."

Jack watched, horrified, as crowds of the moaning dead stumbled in through the door and began to gorge on the newly fallen corpses.

He grabbed Dustin's arm and said, "What are you doing? We can use these people."

Dustin said, "They'll try to shoot us as soon as they rise. It's better this way."

Jack cast one last grim look at the feeding dead, then followed Dustin through several doorways to the study.

Ashley lay in an overstuffed chair, flanked by officers. Her pretty face was still. A trickle of blood flowed from a single bullet hole in the center of her chest.

One of the officers said, "She's not breathing. It won't be long."

Dustin ordered, "I want to be alone with her."

The officers herded Jack from the room. He paced down a long, lonely hallway, then out the front door and into the yard. He sat there, leaning against a tall white cedar, waiting for Ashley to appear.

Finally she did, framed in the light of the doorway. Her figure was slender, her hair long and lustrous. But her beautiful face had been carved away, until there was nothing left but eyeballs and bone.

Dustin came and stood beside her, and their twin skull faces regarded each other.

* * *

Later that night, as Jack and Dustin stood together in the yard, Jack said bitterly, "I can't believe you did that. She was beautiful."

To which Dustin replied, "Ashley will always be beautiful. To me. You loved her face. I love *her*. Who deserves her more?"

"I want to talk to her," Jack said.

"No, you'll stay away." Dustin's voice held a nasty edge. "Or I'll tell her that you led us here. That you betrayed her."

Jack flinched, and Dustin strode away, calling over his shoulder, "I'm the only one who understands her now, understands what she's going through."

For hours Jack wandered aimlessly among the dead, among the masses of rotting flesh. Their awfulness, their stupidity, was overwhelming, and made him want to gag.

Then, through the clusters of corpses, he caught a glimpse of bone-white skull. He walked away.

He wound a path through the dead, and sneaked an occasional backward glance. The skull was there. It gained on him.

Finally, it caught him.

Ashley said, "Jack. It is you." She leaned her horrible skull-face toward him. Her exposed eyeballs studied him. She said, "Dustin didn't tell me you were here. Say something. Do you recognize me, Jack? Do you understand?"

He didn't answer.

Then she was suspicious. "Did you have anything to do with this? Did you help him do this?

Jack turned away and stumbled off into the hordes. In that moment he envied them—their lack of thought, of remorse. He couldn't bear to confront Ashley. Now there was only one thing he could do, that might deceive her, that might make her leave him alone.

"Don't hurt me..." he groaned loudly, desperately. "Please...help me..."

Author's note: The Skull-Faced Boy

When I was a kid I read a story called "The Patchwork Monkey" by Beverly Butler, and it scared me so much that I pretty much avoided horror for the next 10 years. I never watched *Friday the 13th* or *A Nightmare on Elm Street*, which was probably for the best, since I had nightmares just from hearing about them. I suppose there were a few exceptions. I did read Stephen King's collection *Skeleton Crew*, and I did watch *Aliens*. But that was about it.

In my early twenties I decided to learn more about horror. I read a lot of Stephen King, Brian Lumley, and F. Paul Wilson. I watched *Poltergeist* and *The Exorcist*.

One day I saw a listing for a zombie anthology called *The Book of All Flesh* that was looking for submissions. The guidelines helpfully included a list of some of the best zombie books and movies. I decided to immerse myself in all things zombie-related and write my own zombie story.

The first zombie movie I watched was Tom Savini's 1990 remake of *Night of the Living Dead*. I thought it was great. I watched *Dawn of the Dead* and *Day of the Dead*. I watched the whole *Return of the Living Dead* trilogy. I read Skipp and Spector's *Book of the Dead*. I really got into it. I was old enough now that horror didn't really scare me. Now I just thought it was cool.

I wrote "The Skull-Faced Boy" and submitted it to *The Book of All Flesh*. They said nice things about the story but passed on it. Fortunately I was able to sell it to *Gothic.net*.

Six years later John Joseph Adams was editing a zombie anthology called *The Living Dead*, and he asked to see my story. He ended up taking it for the book, though he made me remove all references to the zombies moaning, "Brains..."

The Living Dead was a massive hit, and "The Skull-Faced Boy" received far more attention than any of my other stories, before or since. Many people sent me fan art for the story, which had never happened to me before.

John and I went around to all sorts of bookstores and conventions and fan clubs talking about *The Living Dead*. Suddenly zombies were everywhere, and everyone wanted to talk about them. One night John and

I appeared on *Hour of the Wolf*, a science fiction radio show that ran from 2 A.M. to 4 A.M. on WBAI in New York. The host, Jim Freund, has a tendency to go off on tangents, and even after two hours on the air we'd barely mentioned the anthology.

After the show John and I stumbled out onto the sidewalk. The sun was just starting to peek up over the horizon. "I wish we'd gotten to talk more about the book," John said. By that point I'd become a passionate advocate for an exciting new form of media that most people had never heard of. It was called "podcasting." "You know," I said, "if we had our own podcast, we could talk about it as much as we want."

That's how *Geek's Guide to the Galaxy* was born.

Two years later, John edited another zombie anthology called *The Living Dead 2*, and asked me to write a sequel to "The Skull-Faced Boy." That's how I came to write "The Skull-Faced City," the final story in this book.

The Skull-Faced City

Park watched from his car as a pickup screeched to a halt in front of the supermarket. He'd known they would come. The armies of the living were on the march, and the living needed food.

The pickup's doors flew open and two figures leapt out—a black man and a blond woman. The man, who was older, maybe forty, carried a shotgun. He sprinted toward the store and the woman ran close behind him, her hands wrapped tight around a large silver pistol. The man threw open the front door and vanished into the darkness while the woman waited outside, keeping watch. Smart. But it would not save them.

Park slipped from his car, his scoped rifle clutched to his chest. He crept forward, using abandoned cars as cover. Finally he lay down on the asphalt and leveled his rifle at the pickup.

A dead man in a green apron wandered around the side of the building. He spotted the woman, groaned exultantly, and stumbled toward her, his arms outstretched. The woman took aim at his forehead.

Park pulled the trigger at the same moment she did. The report of her pistol drowned out the soft pinging that his round made as it drilled a neat hole through the pickup's gas tank. The dead man's skull smacked against the pavement, and the woman lowered her gun. She didn't notice the gas pooling beneath her truck.

Park sneaked back to his car and got in. He waited, watching as the woman took down several more of the moaning dead who strayed too close. Later her companion emerged, pushing a loaded shopping cart. The woman hurriedly tossed its contents into the bed of the truck while the man dashed to the store again. This was repeated several times. The commotion attracted an ever-growing audience of moaners, which the woman eyed nervously.

Finally the man and woman leapt into the pickup and peeled out. The truck careened across the parking lot, and the dead men who staggered into its path were hurled aside or crushed beneath its tires.

Park donned his black ski mask, pulled his goggles down over his eyes, and started his car. He tailed the pickup along the highway, keeping his distance. When the truck rolled to a stop, he pulled over too and got out.

The man and woman fled from the truck into a nearby field, which was crawling with the dead. Park followed them through the grass and into the woods. He watched through his scope as they expended the last of their ammo and tossed away their guns. Then they stood back to back and drew machetes against the clusters of moaners who continued to stumble from the trees all around.

Park approached, using his rifle to pick off the nearby dead men. One shot to each head, cleanly destroying each brain—what was left of them.

He pointed his rifle at the man and shouted, "Drop it."

The man shouted back, "Who are you? What do you want?"

Park shifted his aim to the woman and said, "Now. I only need one of you alive."

"Wait!" the man said. "Damn it." He tossed his machete into the brush. "There. Okay?"

"And you," Park told the woman. She hesitated, then flung her weapon away as well.

Park said, "Turn around. Kneel. Hands on your heads."

They complied. Park strode forward and handcuffed them both. "Up," he said. "Move."

The pair stood, and marched. The woman glanced back at Park.

"Eyes front," he ordered.

She gasped. "Oh my god." To the man she hissed frantically, "He's one of them! The ones that can talk."

The man turned to stare too, his face full of terror.

"Eyes front!" Park shouted.

The man and woman looked away. After a minute, the woman said quietly, "Are you going to eat us?"

"I don't intend to," Park said.

"So why do you want us?" she asked.

"It's not me that wants you," Park answered.

"Who does then?" the man demanded.

For a long moment Park said nothing. Then he removed his goggles, exposing dark sockets and two huge eyeballs threaded with veins. He yanked off his ski mask, revealing a gaping nose cavity, bone-white forehead and cheeks—a horrific skull-visage.

"You'll see," he said.

* * *

As dusk fell Park drove down a long straight road that passed between rows of corn. In the fields, dead men with skull faces wielded scythes against the stalks.

"Crops," said the man in the back seat. "Those are crops."

Beside him the woman said, "What do the dead need with food?"

"To feed the living," Park answered.

For the first time her voice held a trace of hope. "So we'll be kept alive?"

"It's possible," Park said.

And Mei? he wondered. He just didn't know.

In front of his car loomed the necropolis, its walls clumsy constructions of stone, twenty feet high. Crews of skull-faced men listlessly piled on more rocks.

The woman watched this, her jaw slack. She murmured, "What happened to your faces?"

Park glanced at her in the rearview mirror. The car bounced over a pothole, and the mirror trembled as he answered. "Faces are vanity. The dead are beyond such things."

He pulled to a stop before an opening in the stone wall. The dirty yellow side of a school bus blocked his way. He rolled down his window.

From the shadows emerged one of the dead, a guard. This one did have a face—nose and cheeks and forehead—though the flesh was green and mottled. A rifle hung from his shoulder. He shined a flashlight at Park, then at the captives.

"For the Commander," Park said.

The guard waved at someone in the bus, and the vehicle rumbled forward out of the way. Park drove on through.

The woman said, "That one had a face."

"That one is weak," Park snapped. "Still enamored with the trappings of life. And so here he is, far from the Commander's favor."

He drove down a narrow causeway bordered by chain-link fences. Every few minutes they passed a tall steel pole upon which was mounted a loudspeaker. Beyond the fences, scores of moaners wandered aimlessly in the light of the setting sun. The man and woman lapsed again into silence. Plainly they could see that this army of corpses presented a formidable obstacle to either escape or rescue.

Park remembered the first time he'd come here, almost three months ago, pursuing a trail of clues. Upon beholding the necropolis his first thought had been: The city that never sleeps.

He passed through another gate and into a large courtyard. "End of the line," he said, as he opened the door and got out.

A group of uniformed dead men with rifles and skull-faces ambled toward him. Their sergeant said, "You again. Park, isn't it? What've you got?"

"Two," Park replied. "Man and woman."

The sergeant nodded to his soldiers, who yanked open the car doors and seized the prisoners. As the pair was led away, the sergeant said, "All right. Come on."

Park was escorted across the yard. From a loudspeaker mounted on a nearby pole came the recorded voice of the Commander:

"Once you were lost," said the voice, "but now you've found peace. Once you were afflicted by the ills of the flesh. The hot sun made you sweat, and the icy wind made you shiver. You sickened and fell and were buried in muck. You were slaves to the most vile lusts, and you gorged yourselves on sugar and grease. But now, now you are strong, and the only hunger you feel is the hunger for victory, the hunger to destroy our enemies, to bend them to the true path by the power of your righteous hands and teeth. Once you were vain, preoccupied by the shape of your nose, the shape of your cheeks. You gazed into the mirror and felt shame. Shame is for the living. Let them keep their shame. We are beyond them, above them. Your face is a symbol of bondage to a fallen world, a reminder of all that you once were and now rightfully despise. Take up your knife now and carve away your face. Embrace the future. Embrace death."

Park was taken to a nearby building and led to a room piled high with small arms and clips of ammo—the currency of the dead. He filled a duffel. As he made his way back to the car, another skull-faced man came hurrying over and called out, "Hey. Hey you."

Park looked up.

The man gestured for him to follow. "The Commander wants to meet you."

This is what Park had been waiting for. He dumped his duffel in the trunk of his car, then followed the man to an armored truck. They drove together toward the palace. It had been a prison once, but now hordes of dead laborers had transformed it into a crude and sinister fortress.

They parked in a dim alley. Park got out and was led inside. He surrendered his handcuffs to an armed guard, walked through a metal detector, then retrieved them.

He was shown to an auditorium with two wooden thrones resting on the stage. A skull-faced man sat in one throne, a skull-faced girl in the other. The man wore a military uniform and held an automatic rifle across his lap. The skull-faced girl had auburn hair and wore an elegant white gown. A dozen skull-faced men, also in uniform, stood nearby.

Park stepped into the center of the room.

"Welcome," said the man in the chair. "I am the Commander. This is my wife." He gestured to the girl beside him. "And my generals." He waved at the assembled dead. "And you are Park."

"Sir," Park said.

"You're quickly becoming our favorite supplier."

Park was silent.

The Commander leaned forward and regarded him. "Tell me, Park. How did you die?"

Park hesitated a moment, then said, "Friendly fire. When my base was overrun."

And he'd been damn lucky in that. Those who died after being bitten by the dead always came back as moaners, as the rest of his company had.

The Commander said, "You were a soldier?"

"Scout sniper, sir."

The Commander nodded. "Good." He added wryly, "I like the look of you, Park. You remind me of myself."

"Thank you, sir."

"But tell me," the Commander went on. "Why do you keep bringing us the living? I'm grateful, but you can't still need the reward. You must have plenty of guns by now."

"I want to do more," Park said. "Help you. Convert the living. End the war."

The Commander settled back in his chair. "Yes," he said thoughtfully. "Perhaps you can help us. We'll discuss it after dinner."

Dinner. The word filled Park with dread. Fortunately he had no face to give him away.

* * *

She reminded him of his grandmother. A woman in her seventies, naked, gagged, tied to a steel platter. When she was placed on the table, and saw a dozen skull-faces staring down at her, she began to bray into her gag and thrash against her bonds.

The Commander, who now wore his rifle strapped to his shoulder, said to Park, "Guests first."

Park leaned over the woman, who whimpered and tried to squirm away. He wanted to tell her: I'm sorry. I have no choice.

He bit into her arm, tore. The woman screamed. Park straightened and began to chew. No flavor at all. The dead couldn't taste, though he did feel a diminishment of the perpetual hunger that the dead bore for the living.

The Commander turned to the skull-faced girl and said, "Now you, my dear." She began to feed. Soon the others joined in.

When it was over, Park looked up and noticed that the prisoners he'd brought in were now present. The man and woman. They stood in the corner, naked and trembling, held up by dead men who clutched them by the arms.

What now? Park wondered.

The old woman was moving again, moaning. The Commander ordered her released. He murmured, "We eat of this flesh, and proclaim death." To the woman he added, "Rise now in glory. Go."

There wasn't much left of her, really—a crimson skeleton festooned with gobbets. The thing that had once been a woman dragged itself off the table and lurched as best it could toward the exit.

"Now," the Commander said. "We have a bit of after-dinner entertainment. Some fresh material." He waved at Park. "Thanks to our friend here."

Park followed as the captives were dragged out the door, down a long corridor, and into another chamber. This room was smaller, with chairs lined up along one wall, all of them facing a king-sized bed. The man and woman were brought to the bed and dumped upon it, where they sat dazed. The chairs filled with spectators. The skull-faced girl sat beside the Commander, who seated himself in the centermost chair.

The Commander pointed at the man and said, "You. Take her. Now." The generals watched, silent but rapt.

The man stood, made a fist. "Fuck you, freak." Behind him the woman sat pale and stricken.

The Commander shrugged. "Maybe you're not in the mood. We have something for that." He turned to the door and called, "The aphrodisiac, please."

For almost a minute nothing happened. Then from the corridor came a terrible groaning. The sound grew louder, closer. The woman on the bed wrinkled her nose and whispered, "No." A dark form appeared in the doorway.

It was one of the ones who'd been buried in the ground before coming back. They always returned as moaners too, and had always rotted terribly.

The man and woman scrambled away, onto the floor.

The moaner wore a steel collar around its neck, which was attached to a chain held by a skull-faced guard. The moaner shrieked and slavered and swiped at the air with clawlike fingers. It lunged at the living, and its handler, just barely able to keep it under control, was half-dragged along behind it. With each charge, the creature came closer to the man and woman, who cowered on the floor in the corner, the man kicking feebly in the direction of the monster.

When the thing was just a few feet away the man shrieked, "All right! All right! Get it off me!"

The Commander lifted a hand, and the moaner was hauled back.

The man and woman trooped grimly to the bed. The woman was young, maybe twenty. Mei's age, Park thought. Had Mei gone through this? No. Don't think about it.

The woman lay down on the bed and the man climbed awkwardly on top of her. The Commander reached over, took the hand of the skull-faced girl, and held it. For a long time the man nuzzled the woman, pawed her, rubbed against her, but he was too frightened, and couldn't become aroused.

Finally the Commander called out, "Enough!"

The figures on the bed froze.

The Commander stood. "This grows tedious. Another night, perhaps?" The man and woman pulled away from each other and watched anxiously. The Commander said to them, "Don't worry. There'll be other chances. Next time will be better." To the generals he instructed, "Take them away. Put them with the rest."

The rest? Park thought.

"Park," said the Commander. "Walk with me."

Park followed him through several doorways, then up a few flights of stairs. They emerged onto what must have once been a simple rooftop, but which had been augmented through the exertions of the dead into a sort of parapet.

The Commander said, "So how did you enjoy that?"

"I...it was..."

The Commander said sharply, "Don't dissemble. I don't like that." All of a sudden there was real anger in his voice, and Park was afraid, but just as suddenly the man's eerie calm returned. He went on, "You were uneasy."

Park thought fast. "I just...you always say lust of the flesh is—"

"For the masses," the Commander cut in. "Black and white. Right and wrong. But men like you and I must take a more nuanced view. Besides, it's for a greater purpose. You'll see."

"I'm sorry. I didn't mean—"

"And don't apologize," the Commander said. "Now...there's something you want to discuss?"

"Yes." Park collected his thoughts. Then: "How does one become an officer in your army?"

The Commander studied him. "Tell me why you want to join."

"I hate the living," Park said. "Always have. Even when I was one of them. Especially then. But I never saw any alternative. Until now."

"I understand," the Commander told him. "You seem a useful sort, Park, and I'm always damned short of good men. I think I'm going to be glad I met you."

The Commander turned away and gazed out over the battlements, to admire his city, his domain. There in the darkness, with the man's back turned and no one else around, Park allowed himself one fleeting instant to glare at the Commander with pure, undisguised hatred.

No, Park thought. You won't be glad. Not at all.

* * *

So Park was promoted to "lieutenant," and given a room in a far corner of the palace. He was often called on to perform routine tasks, mostly drilling the other officers in marksmanship. The Commander's voice was a constant presence, as the loudspeakers blared forth an endless mix of propaganda and instructions for the maintenance of the city. Sometimes pairs of prisoners were brought out to perform for the Commander and his wife, but Mei was never among them.

Most information was still restricted from Park, and most areas of the palace were still off-limits. A few times he heard men refer to the top floor of the east wing as the "petting zoo." Was that where the living were kept? The palace was severely undermanned, but even so trying to slip in where he wasn't wanted would be chancy at best. Patience, he told himself. Wait and watch. This is who you are. This is what you do. And when you strike, you strike hard, and they never see it coming.

One day Park returned to his room to find someone waiting in the hall. It was Greavey, a stocky man with a scattering of red hairs whose jowls hung slack below his skeletal face.

Park nodded to him. "General."

"Park," said Greavey. "Can I ask you a favor? A private lesson?"

"Of course," Park said.

He retrieved a pair of rifles from his car, then took Greavey to a muddy yard nearby. Park lined up empty cans on a wooden table, then walked with Greavey to the far end of the field.

Greavey took aim and fired. His shot went wide. He growled, and said, "I was a soldier too, in life. Like you. Never was a terrific shot though."

Park fired and knocked over the first can. "It's easier now. Your body is more still."

Greavey raised his rifle again. As he sighted, he said casually, "You may have fooled him, but you don't fool me." He fired. A can went flying.

Park didn't answer. He took another shot, took down another can.

Greavey's voice was gruff. "You don't buy all his bullshit. His little cult. And neither do I." He fired again. Missed. "Damn."

Park had been expecting something like this. He took aim again. "And what if I don't?" He fired. Another hit.

"Listen," Greavey told him. "You're new around here. You don't know what he's like. We're losing this war, losing bad, because of him. We don't have enough officers, and every time one of us shows a little promise...well, he doesn't like rivals much. So watch yourself. It's only a matter of time before he turns on you too."

"So what's the alternative?" Park said. "The moaners are loyal to him. They've been listening to his voice every day and night now for how long? What's going to happen if he's gone? You think they'll obey you? You think you can control them?"

"Man, they'll listen to anyone"—Greavey waved at a loudspeaker— "who gets on that PA."

Park raised his rifle to his shoulder and sighted downrange. "It's too much of a risk."

"That's not what you'll be saying when the living storm in here and blow our brains out."

Park fired. Another can. "Who then? If not him?"

Greavey said, "You know he never did shit before all this? He likes to play soldier—all of them do—but he's just some college kid. Now, he's smart, I'll give him that, but not as smart as he thinks he is. We need someone in charge who knows this army and who's got real military training."

"You then?" Park said.

Greavey shrugged. "Seems sensible."

"I've got training," Park said. Another shot. Another can.

"Look," Greavey said. "You shoot real good, but come on. You just got here. Back me up and I promise I'll—"

"No."

Greavey was silent a while. He raised his rifle, hesitated, lowered it. Finally: "What do you want?"

"Half," Park said.

"Half what?"

"Half everything. The guns, trucks, troops—"

"No way."

Park raised his rifle again. "Maybe I should see what *he* thinks about all this."

Greavey stared as Park took down another can, then said, "Fine. If that's the way it's got to be. You and me. Full partners. All right?"

"All right." Park glanced toward the palace. "Except...no one but him's allowed to bring weapons in there. He's always armed, obviously he never sleeps—"

"He comes out sometimes," Greavey said. "To supervise things personally, or lead his army in the field. And like I said, you shoot real good."

At this, Park nodded slowly. "I see," he said, as he took down the final can.

Later, as Park strode through the palace, he thought: A good try. Convincing. Much of it likely true. Greavey plotting a coup? A lie. But the Commander too reliant on his army of moaners? Eliminating clever officers who might become rivals? Probably yes. Also true: The Commander not as smart as he thinks he is.

Park turned a corner toward the Commander's private suite. Two skull-faced men stood guard.

"I have to see the Commander," Park said.

The men eyed him. One of them said, "Wait here," and disappeared around a corner. A short time later he returned and said, "All right. Come on."

They walked down the hall to an office, where the Commander sat at a desk, his rifle resting nearby. He held a combat knife, which he fiddled with absently as he said, "Talk."

Park said, "Sir, Greavey is plotting against you."

The Commander leaned forward in his chair. "Give me details. Everything."

So Park relayed the conversation, leaving out nothing.

Afterward, the Commander stood and began to pace. "This is good to know."

Park said, "Sir, let me handle Greavey. I'll—"

"Greavey's fine."

"Sir?"

The Commander pointed his knife at Park and said, "Listen to me carefully. Nothing happens in this city without my knowledge, without my order. Do you understand?"

Park feigned bafflement. "You mean it was...a test?"

"An exercise," the Commander said. "I apologize, but it's necessary. I've been betrayed before. I have to make sure."

* * *

A few weeks later, just after dawn, Park heard a rumble from outside, as of distant thunder. He hurried to his window and looked out. A giant plume of black smoke was rising from the southern end of the city.

A short time later the Commander's recorded speech cut out abruptly. Then the Commander came on the PA and announced, "The city is under attack. The south wall has been breached. Muster at the south wall. I repeat, the south wall." The message continued in this vein, until the moaners got the idea and began to march to the city's defense.

Park lay low, hoping to be missed in the confusion. He waited until he saw a column of trucks go speeding away to the south. Eight trucks—enough to carry most of the officers who lurked about the palace. Park knew he might never get a better chance to scout out the "petting zoo."

He raced through the halls, but saw no one. The east wing seemed deserted. If anyone caught him—

No. They would not catch him. He'd make sure of that.

One time he heard footfalls approaching. He slipped into a shadowed alcove, and a guard passed by, heedless. Another time, as Park climbed a staircase, he imagined he heard wailing, but when he stopped to listen, there was nothing.

He reached the top floor and moved quickly down a long hallway lined with windows. To his right was a door, open just a crack. He crept up to it and peeked inside.

On a nearby couch sat the woman with auburn hair. She was bent over something in her lap, murmuring, "Hey. Hey, it's okay. Mommy's here."

Park shifted slightly and scanned the room. The walls were painted yellow. He saw cribs, toys…

Children.

Living children, six of them, none more than a year old.

The petting zoo. It was a goddamn…nursery. But…why?

No, he told himself. Ponder later. Get out now. Mei's not here.

The woman on the couch raised her head, and Park caught just a glimpse of her skeletal profile as he eased away from the door.

He heard voices then, back the way he'd come. He hurried in the other direction. He slipped through a door and onto a balcony. At its far end was another door.

The wall to his left was crenellated, and as he hurried along he could see down into the yard below, where a handful of dead men wandered, moaning, "The south wall…" Apparently they were attempting to join the battle but were too witless to find their way there.

A voice at his side said, "Oh. Hey."

Park leapt back, almost stumbling.

A decapitated human head was impaled on an iron spike between two battlements. The head was that of a young man, blond, who even in this grisly state retained a look of gentle innocence. "Sorry," said the head. "I didn't mean to startle you."

"It's all right," Park said, turning away.

"Wait," the head called. "Who are you? I've never seen you before. I'm Jack."

Damn it. Park said, "Look, I really have to——"

The head narrowed its eyes. "You're not supposed to be here, are you?"

Shit. Park eyed the head. It could report him to the others. Should he destroy it?

"Don't," the head warned, anticipating him. "He'll know something's up. Listen, you can trust me. I'm not on his side. I mean, he's the one who put me here."

Park was at a loss.

"I can help you," the head added. "I know things. What are you doing here?"

Park hesitated. Did he dare trust it? But what choice did he have? He said, "I'm looking for my sister. She was captured. I don't—"

"How old is she?" said the head.

"Twenty."

"Good." The head gave him an encouraging look. "Then she was probably kept alive to breed. The prisoners are in the south wing, down in the basement. But you'll need keys to the cells. Dustin's got a set, and Greavey's got the other."

"Dustin?" said Park.

"The Commander," the head explained. It added, "I knew him before all this. We were friends."

Park whispered, "Why did he do this to you?"

The head gave a sad, wry smile. "I tried to free the prisoners," it said.

* * *

Park made it back to his room without being noticed. Hours later one of the trucks returned. Park lurked in the corridor, watching as the Commander and Greavey strode back into the palace. The two men conferred, then the Commander headed off in the direction of his suite. Park tailed Greavey down the hallway.

After a minute, Greavey turned. "Oh, it's you."

Park sidled up. "What's the situation?"

Greavey was grim. "The living are inside the walls. They'll be here by nightfall. Tough bastards. Militia types, called the Sons of Perdition."

Park knew of them. They had a ghastly reputation.

Greavey said, "The Commander's gone to issue new orders. Where the hell have you been?"

Park nodded at some metal piping that ran along the wall from floor to ceiling. "Over there." Greavey turned to look.

Park grabbed the man and ran him into the pipes. Greavey's skull-face rebounded with a crack, and he went down. Park knelt and handcuffed Greavey to the pipes, then dug through the man's pockets.

A keyring. Park hoped the head on the wall—Jack—had been telling the truth.

As Park made his way to the south wing, the Commander's voice came over the loudspeakers: "Fall back to the palace. Defend the palace at all costs. I repeat, defend the palace."

Park spent maddening minutes navigating the unfamiliar corridors. Finally he clambered down a set of metal steps and emerged into a dim hallway lined with cells. He donned his mask and goggles, then moved from door to door. "Mei?" he called out. "Mei? Are you here?" Vague figures huddled in the darkness.

Then, from a cell he'd just passed, a weak voice: "Hello?"

She was there, her slender fingers wrapped around the bars. He ran to her. "I'm getting you out," he said, as he tried a key in the lock. It didn't fit.

"Park?" she said, unbelieving. "I thought—"

She stiffened then, as she watched him. In a near-whisper she said, "Take off your mask."

He tried another key.

"Park," she said, insistent.

He stopped. For a moment he just stood there. Then he carefully removed his mask and goggles, revealing his terrible skull-face for all to see.

Mei recoiled. "But...you're one of them, one of his—"

"It was the only way," Park said. He tried another key.

Beside her in the cell, a skinny white guy with curly black hair said, "I know you. You're the one who captured me, who brought me here."

Mei said, "Is that...true?"

"Yes," Park said. He couldn't meet her gaze. He tried another key, which turned with a click, and the door slid open.

The skinny guy tried to rush out, but Park stiff-armed him back and said, "Only her."

"No," Mei said. "We can't—"

"Mei, come here," he told her.

She shook her head, pulling away. Park looked down and saw that she was pregnant. She asked, "What's happened to you? You're—"

"I'm what I have to be!" he shouted. "To save you. Now come on!"

For a moment he thought he had her. She took a tentative step forward.

Then he heard clanging footsteps on the stairs behind him, and knew it was over.

The Commander strode into the hall, his rifle raised. Behind him came the skull-faced girl and Greavey. Handcuffs dangled from Greavey's right wrist. His left thumb was gone—he'd chewed it off to get free.

The Commander stared at Park with baleful eyes. There was a long silence. Then the Commander barked, "Get away from there!"

Park took a few steps back.

"Keep going! Move!" The Commander advanced. When he was even with the cell, he glanced at its occupants. "You brought us so many," he said to himself. "Why the change of heart?"

Park glared back, said nothing.

"No," the Commander declared then, with sudden triumph. "You're not the compassionate sort. You only care about...one." He swung his rifle around so that it was aimed at the skinny man in the cell. "Who's he here for?"

The man shrank back, holding up his hands. "Her! The girl! Please."

Park inched forward, but instantly the gun was back on him. The Commander said to Greavey, "Get her."

Greavey strode into the cell. With his good hand he snatched Mei by her long dark hair and dragged her stumbling into the corridor. He pushed her into the middle of the hallway, then stepped aside. She trembled.

Behind the Commander, the skull-faced girl said softly, "Dustin, she's pregnant."

"Not for long." He leveled his rifle at Mei's belly.

Park stared at Mei, his sister, as she stood there right in front of him after so long. He knew that there was nothing he could do to save her.

Then the skull-faced girl shoved the Commander as hard as she could.

His rifle fired, spraying rounds into the cement as he sprawled. The gun flew from his grasp and slid across the floor toward Mei. She spun and kicked it to Park, but not hard enough. The rifle slid to a stop near Greavey, who fell to his knees, grasping for it.

Park leapt forward, tackling him, and they went down together. Park wrapped both arms around Greavey's meaty right bicep, pinning it. The man's mutilated left hand brushed over the rifle's stock, but couldn't get a grip on it. The Commander scrambled to his feet.

Park pushed against the floor with his heels, pivoting him and Greavey. He kept hold of Greavey's bicep with one arm while with the other he reached out and snatched the rifle. He shoved its muzzle up under Greavey's chin and held down the trigger. Chunks of the man's fleshy jowls spattered across the floor. His body went limp.

Park rolled off him and came up in a crouch with the rifle aimed at the Commander, who slid to a halt just a few feet away. "Back!" Park said, and the Commander slowly retreated, holding up his hands.

Park said, "Mei! Come here."

She staggered toward him. "Park...we can't—"

He held out the keys to her and said, "Get these goddamn cells open. Now."

The skull-faced girl approached him. The prisoners watched her with a mix of fear and wonder. She said quietly, "And the children. Please."

Park considered this. "All right," he told her. "And the children."

* * *

An hour later Park returned to the cell block with a duffel slung over his shoulder. The prisoners were free now, around twenty of them, and were armed with weapons from the trunk of his car. The skull-faced girl had fetched the children, each of whom was being carried by an adult. The guards had fled. Park had taken care of the Commander.

Park said to the crowd, "You know the city's under attack by an army of the living. They're called the Sons of Perdition. You all know who they are?"

The crowd was somber.

"Anyone want to join them?" Park said. "Now's your chance."

No one moved.

"All right," he said. "Then let's get the hell out of here."

They formed a convoy of vehicles and set out north, away from the fighting. Park drove his car, and the others followed. The duffel rested on the seat beside him. In the back seat sat Mei and the skull-faced girl, each of them holding a child. At first Park was forced to barrel through clusters of moaners, but once he got away from the palace the streets were mostly deserted.

The skull-faced girl stared out the window. One time she spoke faintly, "I said I wanted children. I was just...I didn't think...He wanted to—when they got older—make them like us. He—"

"It's okay," Park said. "It's over."

The girl fell silent.

"What's your name?" Mei asked her.

"Ashley," she said.

They passed through the north gate without encountering any of the invaders. Park was faintly hopeful about slipping away unnoticed, but as he followed a two-lane road toward a cluster of wooded hills, a small fleet of pickups came racing out of the west, throwing up great clouds of dust.

"Shit," Park said. He hoped he could at least make it to the treeline before being overtaken.

He did. Barely.

"Get out," he told Mei and Ashley then. "Move to another vehicle." He passed the duffel to Ashley and said, "Take this. It's Jack. Look after him."

"I will," she promised.

Mei lingered. "How will we meet up after—?"

"Go, Mei," he said.

She insisted, "I don't want—"

"I said go!" he screamed.

She gave him one last worried look, then fled.

Park turned his car so that it blocked the road. Then he got out, fetched his scoped rifle, put on his mask and goggles, and crouched behind the car. Behind him, the rest of the convoy sped away.

The pursuers drew near, seven trucks. Park lay his rifle across the hood of his car, then put a round through the windshield of the lead vehicle. The truck slid to a halt, and the other pickups pulled up alongside it. Men with rifles poured out. Thirty guns, maybe more.

The driver of the lead vehicle, a giant man with a blond beard, shouted, "You shot my truck."

Park didn't respond.

The man yelled, "You have any idea who you're fucking with?"

Again, Park said nothing.

"Listen," the man called. "This is real simple. We saw you all coming out. We know you've got women. We need them, your guns, and your vehicles. And you're all drafted."

They didn't seem to realize that Park was one of the dead. Good. He shouted back, "We don't want anything to do with your army."

"Drafted means you got no choice," said the man.

Park crept into the underbrush and took up a position behind a tree.

"Hey," the man called. "What's your plan, huh? Just how do you think this is going to end?"

For you? Park thought. Like this.

He fired. The man's body toppled against the truck, then slumped to the pavement.

Park crawled away as the other men started shooting, their rounds shredding the leaves all around him.

* * *

By dusk Park was down to his last bullet. It didn't matter. He'd won. Thirty men had come charging up the hill after him, and he'd kept ahead of them, taking them out one by one. He'd dropped nine already, and there were moaners in these woods too who'd disposed of maybe two or three more. Mei and Ashley and the others were well away.

Park had been hit twice in the chest, and many more times in the arms and legs, but those scarcely troubled him. By now his pursuers must know that he was one of the dead, and they would be going only for headshots.

One of the men emerged from behind a boulder and crept closer, scanning the bushes. Make the last shot count, Park thought, as he eased his rifle into place and peered through the scope.

He was shocked. My face, he thought. My old face.

No, he decided then, studying the man. But close. We could be brothers.

Park's finger twitched, tapping the trigger. He could easily put a bullet through that face, but he hesitated. It had been such a long time since he'd looked in a mirror. Since he'd recognized himself.

Any moment now he'd be spotted. Take the shot, his mind urged. Do it. But what difference did it make? Mei was safe. Park continued to stare. He didn't want to see that face destroyed.

No. Not *that* face.

He remembered the eyes of all the people he'd delivered into the horrors of the necropolis. He thought of the old woman screaming as his teeth tore into her. He heard Mei's voice crying, "What's happened to you?" and his own replying, "I'm what I have to be. To save you."

Slowly he reached up and grasped a handful of fabric.

There. The man had seen him, was taking aim. For an instant the two of them stared at each other through their scopes.

Park removed his mask.

* * *

Dustin watched from the wall of his palace as an army of the living battled through the city toward him, but he was powerless to do anything.

In the yard below, one of his followers came into view.

"Hey!" Dustin shouted. "You! Up here!"

The man stopped and looked at him.

"Listen to me very carefully," Dustin said. "This is your Commander speaking. You are to walk around this palace to the main entrance. Once inside, turn right, and keep going until you reach the stairs. Take them to the top floor and continue on the way you were. You'll come to a door leading out onto this balcony. Then remove me from this fucking spike! Do you understand?"

The man stared back with vacant eyes. "Walk around the palace..." it moaned.

"Yes," Dustin said. "And the rest of it. Turn right—"

"Walk around the palace..." The creature took a step toward him, then away. "Walk around the palace..." it repeated, as it wandered, back and forth.

Author's note: The Skull-Faced City

In 2008 John Joseph Adams asked me to write a sequel to "The Skull-Faced Boy" for his anthology *The Living Dead 2*. I was thrilled to be in the book, but I had no idea how to continue the story of "The Skull-Faced Boy." I felt that the story of Jack, Dustin, and Ashley had reached its logical endpoint. What would happen next? Probably Dustin would continue to abuse Jack and Ashley. Maybe Jack and Ashley would try to stand up to him, but then Dustin would probably just crush them. Any story I could think of seemed to be a rehash of "The Skull-Faced Boy," and I didn't just want to repeat myself.

Finally I realized that I needed a new protagonist, someone even more dangerous than Dustin, who could introduce a new dynamic to the situation.

It had been almost 10 years since I'd written "The Skull-Faced Boy," and many things about the zombie genre now struck me as implausible. How could a decapitated zombie head talk without lungs? I guess it's just magic. A smart, healthy person can't dig themselves out of a grave, so how could a stupid, shambling zombie? I have no idea.

I was glad I was able to give Dustin his comeuppance. "The Skull-Faced City" has a fairly happy ending, for a zombie story.

After *The Living Dead 2* came out, John told me he was working on *The Living Dead 3*. Could I write a sequel to "The Skull-Faced City" and make it a trilogy?

That presented a serious problem. The story *really* seemed finished now. Park is permanently deceased, and Jack and Dustin are both just decapitated heads, which was going to make it hard to give them active roles in the third story.

I actually spent a few months working on it. Maybe Dustin could have a zombie minion who carries him around on a platter? Or maybe there could be a really big, strong zombie, and Dustin could ride around on his shoulders?

It's possible that something like that could work, but I was afraid the series would get too silly and overstay its welcome. In any event *The Living Dead 3* never happened, so I abandoned the idea. (John's publisher was afraid the zombie bubble was about to burst.) Maybe it's for the best. I'm pretty happy with the two stories the way they are.

How This Book Came About

In May of 2021 my friend Tom Gerencer, who I met at the Clarion writers workshop in 1999, released a short story collection called *Intergalactic Refrigerator Repairmen Seldom Carry Cash*. It was a self-published book that collected 19 of Tom's stories, most of which had previously appeared in some of the same books and magazines as mine, such as *Realms of Fantasy* and *New Voices in Science Fiction*.

Tom appeared in Episode 473 of *Geek's Guide to the Galaxy* to discuss the collection. At the time he had done nothing to publicize it, and it was only selling an occasional copy here or there.

Within 24 hours of the interview, Tom had sold over 200 copies of the book. We watched in amazement as that number climbed to 400 over the next two weeks. Tom has now sold over 600 copies, and even five months out from the interview, he's still selling one or two a day. Presumably those sales are almost all to *Geek's Guide to the Galaxy* listeners, since the book isn't sold in bookstores and has received no other promotion.

If you had asked me how many copies of a book an author could expect to sell by appearing on *Geek's Guide to the Galaxy*, I would have had no idea. Most authors I interview don't share their sales figures with me, and even if they did, any author whose books are widely distributed would have no way of knowing whether a given sale was due to the podcast or not. But I would have guessed the number was maybe 25 copies, and it wouldn't have surprised me if it was much less. The idea that an author can sell hundreds of books by appearing on the show is really exciting and surprising.

600 copies might not sound like much, but that's a big deal in

the world of short fiction. Large publishers rarely consider short story collections worth their time, and usually only publish them as a favor to their more popular authors. Single author collections are the domain of the small press, and science fiction authors can generally expect to make $1000 from publishing one, if that. Tom has already made much more than that.

When I saw those sales figures, my first thought was: Wow, *Geek's Guide to the Galaxy* is more popular than I thought. My second thought was: I should publish a collection!

It's possible that Tom's experience was a fluke, and this book won't be as lucky. Maybe people just really like Tom.

But if this book does well too, then there could be a bright future ahead for Geek's Guide Press. There are a lot of great fantasy & science fiction authors out there with work that could be published in book form. Many of them are friends of mine, people who have been known to appear from time to time on *Geek's Guide to the Galaxy*.

If that's something you'd like to see, please help spread the word about this book.

Afterword

I hope you've enjoyed reading *Save Me Plz and Other Stories*. You can learn more about me and my writing over at davidbarrkirtley.com.

If you haven't checked out *Geek's Guide to the Galaxy*, I hope you'll give it a look, as it represents my main creative output over the past eleven years. We've recorded 500 episodes of the show, so there's a pretty good chance that we've interviewed your favorite author or reviewed your favorite movie or TV show. Past guests have included Neil Gaiman, George R. R. Martin, Richard Dawkins, Wil Wheaton, Bill Nye, Margaret Atwood, Neil deGrasse Tyson, and Ursula K. Le Guin, among others.

If you'd like to read more short stories, your best bet is to check out the work of John Joseph Adams. He's the editor of *Lightspeed* magazine, the publisher of *Nightmare* magazine, and the series editor of *The Best American Science Fiction & Fantasy*. He's also edited many other anthologies, including the recent Dystopia Triptych (*Ignorance is Strength*, *Burn the Ashes*, and *Or Else the Light*).

A few single author short story collections that I've enjoyed recently are *The End of the End of Everything* by Dale Bailey, *We Are Where the Nightmares Go and Other Stories* by C. Robert Cargill, *An Agent of Utopia* by Andy Duncan, *Songs for the Unraveling of the World* by Brian Evenson, *Unpossible and Other Stories* by Daryl Gregory, *You Have Never Been Here* by Mary Rickert, *Across the Event Horizon* by Mercurio D. Rivera, *Ambiguity Machines and Other Stories* by Vandana Singh, and *Beyond the Rift* by Peter Watts. You can find interviews with all of those authors in the archives of *Geek's Guide to the Galaxy*.

I have a dozen published stories and several dozen unpublished ones that didn't make it into this book. Possibly they'll appear in a future volume. I have many stories about my adventures as a teenage writer that I'd still like to tell.

I want to give a huge thank you to the editors who published these stories, to the writers who critiqued them at various workshops, and to the artists who illustrated them. Big thanks as well to anyone who's ever come to one of my readings, written me an encouraging note, or left a positive review for one of my stories or podcasts.

The biggest thank you of all goes to my parents, John R. Kirtley and Kathryn Barr Kirtley, to my best friend John Joseph Adams, and to my girlfriend Steph Grossman. Most of my success is due to their constant support and encouragement.

About the Author

David Barr Kirtley is the host of the *Geek's Guide to the Galaxy* podcast on *Wired.com*, for which he's interviewed over 400 guests, including Neil Gaiman, George R. R. Martin, Margaret Atwood, Richard Dawkins, Wil Wheaton, Bill Nye, Joyce Carol Oates, Neil deGrasse Tyson, and Ursula K. Le Guin. His short fiction appears in magazines such as *Realms of Fantasy*, *Weird Tales*, and *Lightspeed*, and in books such as *New Voices in Science Fiction*, *The Living Dead*, and *New Cthulhu*. He majored in Government at Colby College and holds a degree in fiction and screenwriting from the University of Southern California. He lives in Austin with his cat Oryx and his girlfriend Steph Grossman. *Save Me Plʒ and Other Stories* is his first book.

Printed in Great Britain
by Amazon

78156539R00208